The Price of Fame

By
Lynn Ames

THE PRICE OF FAME

© 2010 BY LYNN AMES
COMPLETELY REVISED 2ND EDITION

ISBN: 978-0-9840521-4-1

This trade paperback original is published by

PHOENIX RISING PRESS
PHOENIX, ARIZONA
www.phoenixrisingpress.com

FIRST EDITION
© 2004 BY LYNN AMES
ISBN: 978-1-933113-04-9

CREDITS

EXECUTIVE EDITOR: LINDA LORENZO
COVER PHOTOS: PAM LAMBROS
AUTHOR PHOTO: JUDY FRANCESCONI
COVER DESIGN BY PAM LAMBROS,
WWW.HANDSONGRAPHICDESIGN.COM

Dedication

For Survivors of Childhood Sexual Abuse Everywhere:
In Survival There Is Strength, Courage, and Resilience
In Finding Your Voice You Can Make a Difference

Acknowledgments

The Price of Fame was not the book I had intended to write, but that is a long story.

In many ways, this book wrote itself; the characters, whom I love dearly, spent countless hours whispering in my ear. The result: plot twists that surprised even me.

I have always maintained that the best fiction contains elements of truth; as a reader, it's that believability that keeps you turning the pages. In that sense I owe a debt of gratitude to all those who provided me with such rich life experiences; you have fed me enough material to write an infinite number of novels.

Many thanks to Kathy Smith, for doing an outstanding job producing this book. Kathy gave me my first break in publishing with the first edition of *The Price of Fame*, and her belief and faith in me amaze me still.

Writing a book like this is made much easier when the author can rely on real-life experts to ensure accuracy. To Marcia Neville and Clair Bee, my eternal thanks for being so good at what you do and for your willingness to share that knowledge with me.

My undying gratitude to editor extraordinaire Linda Lorenzo for her patience and fortitude. Working on a second edition is difficult enough, but when that book is part of a series, it is nearly impossible. I'm a lucky author.

Other Books by Lynn Ames

Outsiders

What happens when you take five beloved, powerhouse authors, each with a unique voice and style, give them one word to work with, and put them between the sheets together, no holds barred?

Magic!!

Brisk Press presents Lynn Ames, Georgia Beers, JD Glass, Susan X. Meagher and Susan Smith, all together under the same cover with the aim to satisfy your every literary taste. This incredible combination offers something for everyone — a smorgasbord of fiction unlike anything you'll find anywhere else.

A Native American raised on the Reservation ventures outside the comfort and familiarity of her own world to help a lost soul embrace the gifts that set her apart.

A reluctantly wealthy woman uses all of her resources anonymously to help those who cannot help themselves.

Three individuals, three aspects of the self, combine to create balance and harmony at last for a popular trio of characters.

Two nomadic women from very different walks of life discover common ground — and a lot more — during a blackout in New York City.

A traditional, old school butch must confront her community and her own belief system when she falls for a much younger transman.

Five authors — five novellas. Outsiders — one remarkable book.

Heartsong

After three years spent mourning the death of her partner in a tragic climbing accident, Danica Warren has re-emerged in the public eye. With a best-selling memoir, a blockbuster movie about her heroic efforts to save three other climbers, and a successful career on the motivational speaking circuit, Danica has convinced herself that her life can be full without love.

When Chase Crosley walks into Danica's field of vision everything changes. Danica is suddenly faced with questions she's never pondered.

Is there really one love that transcends all concepts of space and time? One great love that joins two hearts so that they beat as one? One moment of recognition when twin flames join and burn together?

Will Danica and Chase be able to overcome the barriers standing between them and find forever? And can that love be sustained, even in the face of cruel circumstances and fate?

One – Love (formerly The Flip Side of Desire)

Trystan Lightfoot allowed herself to love once in her life; the experience broke her heart and strengthened her resolve never to fall in love again. At forty, however, she still longs for the comfort of a woman's arms. She finds temporary solace in meaningless, albeit adventuresome encounters, burying her pain and her emotions deep inside where no one can reach. No one, that is, until she meets C.J. Winslow.

C.J. Winslow is the model-pretty-but-aging professional tennis star the Women's Tennis Federation is counting on to dispel the image that all great female tennis players are lesbians. And her lesbianism isn't the only secret she's hiding. A traumatic event from her childhood is taking its toll both on and off the court.

Together Trystan and C.J. must find a way beyond their pasts to discover lasting love.

Other Books in the Kate and Jay Trilogy

The Cost of Commitment

Kate and Jay want nothing more than to focus on their love. But as Kate settles into a new profession, she and Jay are caught in the middle of a deadly scheme and find themselves pawns in a larger game in which the stakes are nothing less than control of the country.

In her novel of corruption, greed, romance, and danger, Lynn Ames takes us on an unforgettable journey of harrowing conspiracy—and establishes herself as a mistress of suspense.

The Cost of Commitment—it could be everything...

The Value of Valor

Katherine Kyle is the press secretary to the president of the United States. Her lover, Jamison Parker, is a respected writer for *Time* magazine. Separated by unthinkable tragedy, the two must struggle to survive against impossible odds...

A powerful, shadowy organization wants to advance its own global agenda. To succeed, the president must be eliminated. Only one person knows the truth and can put a stop to the scheme.

It will take every ounce of courage and strength Kate possesses to stay alive long enough to expose the plot. Meanwhile, Jay must cheat death and race across continents to be by her lover's side...

This hair-raising thriller will grip you from the start and won't let you go until the ride is over.

The Value of Valor—it's priceless.

CHAPTER ONE

Phil, do you have that last page?"
"It's right here, Kate."
"You're a prince."
"Have I ever let you down?"
"Do you really want me to answer that?"
"Hey, Roger, nice work on those shots from the train derailment—you really captured the feel of the scene."
The cameraman blushed. "Thanks, Kate."
"Okay, people, two minutes."
Bodies were in motion everywhere, and in the middle of all the chaos, the anchorwoman strode unhurriedly onto the set and sat in her chair. She clipped the lapel microphone to her silk suit jacket, inserted her earpiece, placed her copy on the desk, and ran her fingers through her hair one last time to settle it in place.
Katherine Ann Kyle was singular. It wasn't just the fact that she was classically beautiful, it was more the unconscious way that she carried herself—strong, assured, and completely unaware of her attractiveness. She had an intangible quality that made her appear at once captivating and unattainable.
"Kate, we're going to start with camera two and then shift to camera one after we roll the first piece of tape."
She didn't answer the director's disembodied voice in her ear, but he knew she'd heard him just the same; she was a pro.
"And, three, two, one, cue the music. Music fade, and...go."
Kate smiled up at the camera. "Good evening. This is the WCAP evening news for Wednesday, April twenty-ninth, nineteen eighty-seven. I'm Katherine Kyle..."

≈≋≈

Jamison Parker, Jay to her friends, shouldered her way through the hotel room door, trying to balance her briefcase and her garment bag at the same time. She dumped the briefcase as soon as she cleared the threshold and the door clicked closed behind her. Then she hung the garment bag in the closet and proceeded into the room, kicking off her shoes as she went and rushing to answer the already-ringing phone.

"Yeah, Trish, I agree with you...No, no. His press secretary and his scheduler both told me the governor would see me tomorrow at four...Yes, that's four p.m., ya goofball."

The petite, green-eyed blonde cocked her head and listened to her editor ramble on about how important this piece was going to be for the magazine, since this governor was being touted as a rising star and possible presidential material. She wandered over to the bed, flopped down on it with a grunt, and flipped on the television with the remote she'd found on the nightstand. She glanced at her watch—great, just in time to catch the local news and maybe get some idea of the regional issues before her interview tomorrow.

"Trish, you don't need to offer me your firstborn in exchange for a great story. Hell, I've met your son, you can keep him!" She said it with a smile in her voice, and Trish laughed and continued to prattle on. Jay's eyes drifted to the screen as the music came on signaling the start of the newscast. She rolled her eyes at something her editor said and was about to reply when she locked eyes on the news anchor.

"Oh my God, I can't believe it, it's *her*!" Jay didn't even bother to say goodbye before disconnecting the call.

She sat there, mesmerized, afraid to blink lest the image disappear. For five years this woman dominated her dreams and fueled her imagination. Now, there she was...Jay ignored the ringing of the phone again, knowing it was Trish calling back. *Katherine Kyle. Now I have a name to go with that unforgettable face and voice.*

CHAPTER TWO

A t precisely 2:30 p.m. the next day, Kate strolled through the door to the newsroom. She was impeccably dressed in a crème-colored, button-down, silk blouse and a rich blue silk pantsuit that complemented her deep blue eyes. She poked her head into an edit bay and greeted Gene, one of her favorite cameramen, who was laying down pictures to go with a report on dredging PCBs from the river. Then she continued on to her desk, fired up her word processor, and scanned the national headlines on the AP wire.

The newsroom was quiet at that hour. The day-shift reporters were all out covering stories, and the evening anchors and reporters weren't due in for another hour. Kate always liked to get in early, though; unlike some of her on-air colleagues, she refused to be just a talking head. She was a journalist first, and an anchor second in her mind. As the primary anchor or star, she was very rarely required to go out on the street to cover a story these days, but unlike her male co-anchor, she still insisted on writing her own news copy and took the time to research the day's happenings instead of simply reading somebody else's words in front of a camera. This fact earned her a great deal of respect among most of her peers, who appreciated her work ethic and intelligence.

As for her co-anchor, well, as she once told him when he complained that she was making him look bad, "You don't need my help for that, Gerry. You do a great job all by yourself." The entire newsroom erupted in laughter, and Gerry stalked from the room to spend his usual two hours in makeup reading the comics.

As Kate ran through the day's headlines, she listened with half an ear to the sounds of the newsroom that had become background noise to her over the years—the assignment editor barking into the phone at a field producer, the cameramen complaining about the reporters they were assigned to work with, the tapping of fingers on word processors, the police scanners, and the three television monitors that were tuned to each of WCAP's competitors.

Then her sharp ears picked up something unusual. She moved quickly to the nearest police scanner just as Phil, the producer, reached it. She turned it up.

"...(unintelligible) ...explosion at the capitol... (unintelligible)... eagle is flying..."

"Holy shit," he exclaimed. "Holy shit. The governor was in the damn building."

"Who've we got in the area?" Kate asked urgently.

"No one. Everybody's on something else or not in yet."

"Gene," she yelled. "Get your gear. Make sure you bring an extra camera, two extra battery packs, extra tape, and a couple of mics, including the wireless lavaliere. I'll get the satellite truck and meet you out back. Phil, get me a field producer ASAP."

"Kate," Phil started to say, but she was already out of earshot.

The scene on State Street was pure pandemonium. Kate and Gene weaved their way through the crowd of panicked people running in the opposite direction. It had been seven minutes since they left the station, which was located just on the outskirts of the city. Kate clipped on a wireless lavaliere microphone that would pick up her voice and transmit it back to the satellite truck for direct feed to the television newsroom. Next she inserted an earpiece that would keep her in contact with the newsroom, her cameraman, and the field producer, when one arrived on scene. She also carried a wireless microphone in her hand. She looked up at the building that was the centerpiece of the city and gaped at the hole that had been blown right through the area that housed the senate chamber.

She and the cameraman were standing some twenty feet from the building. "Get a picture of that, Gene. I'm going to find some eyewitnesses and try to get a handle on this thing. And Gene, tell the station we're gonna go live with the coverage beginning when I come back here. Get the feed up and running." With that, Kate disappeared from sight, swallowed up by the fleeing crowd.

Within seconds, she located several members of the state legislature, including the senate majority leader, whose suit jacket was torn and whose hair, for the first time Kate could ever remember, actually was disheveled. He had a small gash over his left eye, and his boyishly handsome face was covered in ash. Never one to miss an opportunity to be seen by his constituents, he quickly consented to be interviewed.

Of course, it didn't hurt that he had tried many times to pick Kate up when she first became a reporter in the area. Deferring to the fact that he was very married, among other reasons, she always politely declined his advances. Clearly he held no grudge against her.

She steered him over to where Gene was waiting so that she had the dramatic footage of the hole in the side of the capitol behind her. "Good afternoon," Kate said, looking directly at the camera. "This is Katherine Kyle reporting live from the scene of a tremendous explosion here at the state capitol building in Albany, New York. With me is State Senate Majority Leader Clyde Hicksdale. Senator, can you describe to us what happened?"

"I was in a meeting with the governor and the assembly speaker in the governor's office on the second floor. We were discussing the state budget. All of a sudden there was a thunderous boom, the lights flickered, and everything went dark. The governor's state police detail ran in, yelled that there had been an explosion, and they physically grabbed the governor and whisked him out of the building through a back entrance."

"Senator, can you confirm that the governor and assembly speaker are both safe and out of harm's way?"

"Yes, Kate, I can say that with certainty, since I just got off the phone with the governor several minutes ago. He is running a command post out of the governor's mansion, which, as you know, is several blocks from here."

Privately, Kate couldn't believe the man could be so stupid as to reveal the location of the governor publicly without knowing whether or not he had been the target of the explosion. But, as a journalist, she knew it just didn't get any better than this.

"Senator, I understand that the epicenter of the blast was the senate chamber on the third floor, is that correct?"

"Yes, Kate, that is what I was told by the state police bomb experts. Thank heaven the senate wasn't due to go into session for another forty-five minutes."

"You said you spoke with the state police bomb experts, Senator. Did they give you any indication what might have caused the explosion?" *God, could he really be foolish enough to tell me what I'm sure the police would wait weeks to reveal?*

13

"Kate, they believe it was a high-powered explosive planted somewhere in the senate gallery."

"That would be the area reserved for spectators?" At the senator's nod, she continued, "Senator, are all of your members accounted for? Have you been informed of any casualties?"

"My people are still getting in touch with everyone, but so far, I think most of the senators have been accounted for. We're still trying to reach a few."

"Senate Majority Leader Hicksdale, thank you for your time."

"My pleasure, Kate."

"To recap then," the anchorwoman said as she faced the camera fully and Gene zoomed in for a close-up, "an explosion rocked the state capitol building here in Albany at two forty-eight p.m. The blast apparently was centered in the senate chamber, and detonated some forty-five minutes before the senate was due to go into session. Senate Majority Leader Clyde Hicksdale, who was in a meeting one floor below the senate chamber with the governor and the leader of the state assembly, indicates to WCAP-TV that the governor has been escorted safely from the building and is monitoring the situation from his private office in the governor's mansion several blocks from the capitol. Although we have not had any confirmation from the state police as of yet, Senator Hicksdale informs us that he has been told by the state police's elite bomb squad that the explosion was the result of a high-powered incendiary device. We will try to get independent corroboration of that fact for you as soon as possible."

Kate knew most of her colleagues would have simply reported the news that the explosion was caused by a bomb as fact, but she wasn't any reporter, and she wasn't just going to take Hicksdale's word for the cause. In her mind that would have been journalistically irresponsible. It was one thing to attribute the supposition to her interviewee, and quite another for her to report it as absolute gospel truth.

Kate continued her report. "At this moment, it is unclear how many, if any, casualties there have been. As you can see over my shoulder"—she gestured as Gene panned the camera back and scanned the panicked crowd behind her—"there is much confusion here on State Street. In recent weeks there have been heated debates raging between the governor and the two houses of the legislature regarding—"

BOOM.

A second explosion rocked the building. Kate felt a white-hot surge of air from behind as she was lifted off her feet and thrown to the ground. She looked up to see Gene getting back to his feet. Ever the professional, he still had his camera running and he gave her the hand signal letting her know his equipment was still intact, that he had gotten the footage of the second blast, as well as of her going down, and that he was getting the images behind her of the new horror.

Kate rose to her feet and turned to face the spot where the entrance to the capitol used to be. She watched in mute terror as members of the legislature, staff, tourists, and children ran screaming into the street. There was blood and glass everywhere. Through the now-open space where the covered and columned entryway had been, she could see that the first-floor ceiling was starting to give way. She looked up briefly at the window that marked the governor's office. Catching Gene's attention, she began talking again.

"As you can see, a second explosion has just rocked the capitol." Kate raised her eyebrow, a silent question to Gene as to whether or not her microphone was working. Gene gave her a thumbs-up. "That window there," she pointed to the corner spot on the second floor, as Gene zoomed in on her, "is the governor's office."

Even as she continued talking to the viewers, she heard Phil say in her ear from the newsroom, "Kate, you're the only game in town. The scene got cordoned off before any of the other stations could get their people down there. CNN and all three major networks are carrying you live. No pressure here, girl, this is great stuff."

She could hear the excitement in his voice.

Gene followed her hand and zoomed in on the dramatic picture of the tattered curtains in the governor's office blowing out the hole where the window once had been. "As we have been informed by the senate majority leader, who was meeting with the governor at the time in that room right there"—she gestured again to the hole at the corner of the building—"the governor was taken to safety just after the first explosion."

Kate turned sideways to take in the scene behind her. What she saw touched her deeply as a human being—there were too many people still in harm's way. She knew her first responsibility as a journalist was to get the story, but as a person, and one who had extensive first aid training, she felt she had a more important obligation to help. Maybe, just maybe, she could accomplish both objectives.

She continued talking as she began running toward the building. "As you can see, there are a number of people hurt or trapped awaiting assistance. Rescue personnel are swarming over the scene, but the number of emergency workers is simply inadequate to deal with the number of casualties."

In her ear, Phil was screaming. "Katherine Ann Kyle, don't you dare put yourself in danger." Kate heard him but ignored him. "Kate, please," he pleaded. "Don't." The last was whispered quietly. "Stay safe," he murmured.

Gene moved to follow Kate, all the while training the camera on her as she dodged debris on her way to aid the injured. She motioned below camera level that he could get the general pictures of the scene and still pick up her audio without putting himself in jeopardy. She knew that he appreciated her gesture of concern, but was determined to stay with her as long as he could without losing transmission.

As she moved into the first-floor lobby, she kept up a running monologue for the sake of the viewers. "The ceiling has caved in here, as you can see, trapping a number of people." Kate spied a young blonde girl whose leg was pinned under a fallen a pillar of the side portico. The girl's watery green eyes and tear-stained face bespoke her terror and pain. Kate went immediately to the girl's side. "It's okay, sweetheart, we're going to get you out of here."

The camera zoomed in on the child. Kate first took the time to comfort the girl and then began leveraging her weight to try to move the pillar off her. With a monumental effort, she was able to shift the marble just enough to slide the youngster's body out from underneath. She hugged the girl to her briefly and called for a nearby fireman to come and carry the child to safety.

It wasn't until Kate moved on to the next victim that she allowed herself to acknowledge how much the little girl reminded her of another green-eyed blonde and another traumatic rescue.

It was a mid-winter day in 1982 and Kate was working as a member of the ski patrol at the college snow bowl.

As she paused to rest in the middle of a trail, a blur of movement caught her eye over on the far left side of the trail about 100 yards ahead. A big mountain of a man was barreling down the slope, completely out of control. Kate quickly scanned the area, already calculating the distance between him and anyone below him. "Shit!"

Kate already was in motion, knowing that she was going to be too late. She watched helplessly as the out-of-control goon slammed full speed into a much smaller female skier who had the misfortune to be in his path. The pair disappeared in a cloud of snow, arms and legs flying through the air in a tumble of bodies. Kate arrived before the plume of snow settled, releasing her skis and planting them to mark the accident even before she came to a complete stop. The petite blonde was lying motionless, her right arm and left leg at odd, unnatural angles. The behemoth was shaking his head. "Wow, man, that was really something," he remarked.

Kate didn't spare him so much as a look. "Are you hurt?" she asked him coldly, kneeling next to the woman.

"Naw, I'm tougher'n that."

"Grand, then just sit there until I can deal with you. If you so much as move a muscle, so help me I'll ram my ski so far up your ass it will come out your mouth. Got me?"

The big man's eyes opened as wide as saucers, and he just nodded mutely.

Kate was busy assessing the woman's injuries and checking to see if she was breathing okay. Pulling out her two-way radio, she called to the base patrol hut and radioed her location, calmly asking for a stretcher and leg immobilizer and instructing them to have an ambulance standing by. "And Ken, send up Robbie to deal with the jerkball who caused this thing; I don't ever want to see him on this mountain again."

"Roger that, Kate. It's going to take us a few to get to you— you're in a tough spot. Hard to reach."

"Do the best you can, Ken, she needs help now. Out."

Kate put the radio back in her fanny pack and looked down at the injured woman, who just now was coming around. Gently, she removed her charge's goggles, which were cracked but miraculously remained on her face.

"Did you get the license plate number of the t-truck that hit me?"

Kate laughed in spite of the seriousness of the situation. "Hey," she said softly, lowering herself so that the woman could see her without moving her head. "You're gonna be all right, but I need you to stay very still for now, okay?"

"Yes. I hurt so much."

"I know. I've got a team on the way so that we can move you safely. Hang in there."

"M-my shoulder."

17

"Mmm." Kate said. "It's dislocated from the looks of it. I can try to put it back in if you want. It will be less painful if I do."

"Ok-k-kay, but this is going to mess up my lacrosse season, isn't it?"

"'Fraid so."

Kate dug her foot into the snow and tried to get leverage. God, she didn't want to cause this poor woman any more pain, but she knew that the discomfort would be temporary, and that the end result would leave her feeling better. She braced herself and grasped the dangling shoulder, being careful to jar her as little as possible. Then, using direct pressure at the correct angle, she gave a quick push and felt the bone slide back into place. The woman gave a short yell.

"Okay?"

The blonde looked up at Kate and gave her a weak smile. Her lips started to quiver and her body shook from the shock of the accident and the cold. Without thought, Kate unzipped her own jacket, then slid carefully behind the injured skier, zipped the jacket with both her and the woman inside, and effectively used her own body heat to try to warm her. Feeling the young co-ed shiver uncontrollably against her, she wrapped her arms carefully around the slim waist and pulled her closer still.

Kate's lips were almost directly behind her ear. Murmuring soothing words, she tried to comfort her, wishing with her whole heart that she could take this woman's pain away. To distract her, she began to ask questions.

"What's your name?"

"J-jam-mison P-p-p-p-parker."

"Is that five p's or six?"

"V-very funny," Jay said, rolling her eyes. But she smiled just the same, a fact that warmed Kate's heart.

"That's a pretty name."

"M-my f-friends call me Jay."

"Ooh. Are you including me in that number?"

"S-sure."

"Boy, you're easy."

"D-don't let it g-get around."

"Hey, your secret's safe with me. You're a student, right?"

"Y-yes, a sophomore."

Kate looked around impatiently. Where the hell was the team? As brave as Jay was being, she was in shock and hurting, her leg was clearly broken, and it was vital to get her off the mountain and taken care of. She took out her radio once again and asked what the holdup was.

"Almost there, Kate. We're doing the best we can."

At that moment, Robbie skied up. "Whatcha got, Kate?"

She jerked her head in the direction of the big gorilla and explained to Robbie, who actually made the guy look small, what happened. "Get him out of my sight," she hissed.

Kate turned her attention back to her patient, whose lips were starting to turn blue, and whose skin was very pale.

"Is my leg broken? It h-hurts s-so much."

"I think so. No dancing at the Winter Carnival Ball for you, I'm afraid."

"D-darn. And I was s-so counting on b-bringing F-fred Astaire as my d-date."

"Um, isn't he dead, Jay?"

"Is he? See, there's another r-r-reason I c-can't g-go."

Kate was utterly charmed.

Just then a snowmobile came over the rise, instantly heading for the crossed skis in the snow. Behind it was a litter with all manner of medical equipment and four more members of the ski patrol. As soon as they pulled up, Kate apprised them of the skier's condition, noting possible frostbite, exposure, shock, a likely broken leg and dislocated shoulder. As they worked to get her leg stabilized and her arm immobilized, Kate swathed her in blankets and grasped her good hand, leaning over so that Jay could see her face.

Softly she asked, "Is there anyone you want me to call for you? Your parents?"

Jay hesitated and her face took on a faraway look. For a second, Kate wondered if she had heard her. Quietly, she said, "N-no, there's no one."

Something about the way she said it made Kate want to ask more questions, but she didn't want to push her just then. Instead she said, "How about a friend? Someone to meet you at the hospital?"

"Thanks. I'll c-call my friend S-sarah when I get there—she's got a c-car. Thanks for taking c-care of me. You m-make a great t-toaster oven."

Kate smiled at her, gave her fingers one last squeeze, and assured her that she was in great hands just before the sled started moving down the mountain.

Sighing, Kate zipped up her jacket, put on her sunglasses and gloves, and stepped into her skis. For the rest of her shift, which was

19

another five hours, she couldn't stop thinking of Jay. Finally, when she couldn't stand it anymore, she made her way to the base patrol hut, signed herself out, and drove to the hospital.

In the emergency room, she asked the nurse on duty about Jay's condition. She was told that the patient was released only half an hour earlier and left with a friend. *Satisfied that Jay had been well cared for, Kate headed back to her dorm for a hot shower.*

❦

At 2:45 p.m. Jay walked back into her hotel room after her run. She grabbed the remote and turned the TV to CNN as she peeled off her sweaty running clothes on her way to the shower. She had a little over an hour before her interview with the governor, and her run, as always, helped her to focus on the questions she wanted to ask and the ground she wanted to cover in the piece. She turned the shower on, adjusted the temperature, and stepped in, sighing with pleasure when the hot spray hit her sore muscles.

A half hour later, she emerged from the bathroom wearing a hotel bathrobe and toweling her hair. She froze in mid step on her way to the closet when she heard the familiar voice. Jay checked the logo in the corner of the screen; yep, it was CNN. What was Katherine doing on CNN? Then her mind registered the words.

"To recap, then..." the anchorwoman was saying. Jay sat down heavily at the foot of the bed, her eyes riveted to the TV. The scene unfolding on the screen was bedlam. She watched in horror as the camera shook violently but somehow remained focused on Kate, who was being tossed in the air like a mannequin. Jay gasped out loud and clutched a pillow to her chest.

At that moment, her hotel room phone rang. "Hello," she said numbly.

"Ms. Parker, this is Ms. Winston from the governor's office. Unfortunately, something has come up and the governor is going to be unable to keep his appointment with you this afternoon."

Jay marveled at the woman's power for understatement as she watched the images of the capitol on her TV screen.

"We will be in touch with either you or your editor later today or tonight to reschedule. We are very sorry for the inconvenience."

Inconvenience. That's what you call it when the capitol is destroyed by a bomb?

"That's quite all right, Ms. Winston, though I would like to reschedule as soon as possible."

"Of course, we'll be in touch sometime later today. Thank you for your patience."

Jay was already refocusing on CNN. When Kate came back into view following the explosion, she seemed unfazed, despite the fact that half the building behind her was now missing. When she turned and ran toward the building, Jay jumped up from the bed, screaming at her to get back. "No, Katherine. No!" Jay buried her head in her hands. This was like some bad suspense thriller; it couldn't be real. But it was.

Jay's first reaction was to go to her, but as she started to throw off her robe and pull on jeans, she realized the impossibility of the task. There was no way, with all that chaos, that she was going to be able to get anywhere near where Katherine was at the moment. She growled in frustration and began pacing the room while she watched.

The CNN anchor was voicing-over the footage of Kate running into the capitol. "You're watching dramatic live video of reporter Katherine Kyle of WCAP-TV in Albany, New York, where two explosions have just rocked the capitol building. Let's listen in..."

The audio switched back to Kate just as she reached the little girl. Jay smiled wistfully at Kate's efforts to comfort the child. She well remembered the soothing tone of that mellifluous voice and those caring, concerned eyes.

Jay sighed, turning her attention back to the coverage. CNN stayed with Kate live as she rescued the child Then they began interspersing images and audio of the reporter assisting other victims with the footage shot earlier of her interviewing the senate majority leader, anchoring a newscast, background information about her, commentary about the capitol, and speculation about how many people might have been in the building at the time of the explosions. They interviewed experts about the type of incendiary device that might have been used, other experts about the hot issues in New York state politics at the moment, still more experts about what person or groups might have been behind the attack, and everything else CNN could think of to round out the dramatic story that was unfolding less than ten miles from Jay's hotel room.

When she tired of CNN's experts, Jay flipped the channel to WCAP. There was Kate, crawling on her stomach in what appeared to be a very unstable area of the capitol, trying to reach a middle-aged man who was partially buried under a piece of the ceiling. Although the image was dark, Jay could see that Kate's once immaculate suit was shredded and covered in blood, her face and hands streaked with ash and small cuts. She sounded tired and strained as she talked to the man and began digging at the rubble. The sight made Jay's guts clench. "Oh, Katherine," she sighed sadly.

At 11:45 p.m., when Jay couldn't stand it anymore and it looked as though the station was about to end its coverage, she called the front desk and hailed a cab to take her downtown in the vicinity of the capitol. The closest the cabbie could get her was two blocks away.

Kate emerged from the wreckage that was once the capitol. Knowing she was off air, she spoke into the microphone to Phil, thanking him for hanging with her and assuring him that she was fine. He scolded her affectionately for ignoring his orders, then told her she'd done a fantastic job and to take the rest of the night off. She laughed as she unclipped the microphone, effectively severing their audio connection. She gave Gene a huge bear hug and a kiss on the cheek; his blush was visible even in the moonlight. She thanked him for his dedication and professionalism, and for his friendship. Then, handing him her earpiece and microphone, she told him to take the satellite truck and head home.

Kate walked off alone toward a marble bench in front of the fountain on the Empire State Plaza just across the street from the capitol. She sat down heavily and put her head in her hands.

From some thirty yards away, Jay watched as the reporter hugged her cameraman and then walked off by herself. Part of her resisted going further, not wanting to intrude on this heroic woman when she seemed to want to be alone. Jay could plainly see that Kate was exhausted both physically and emotionally. But a bigger part of her was desperate to offer comfort, so she followed her heart.

As Jay got closer, she began questioning what she was doing; she couldn't believe how nervous she was. *What if she doesn't remember me? Or what if she does remember me, but she doesn't want to see me? Heck, the last time she saw me I was pretty much catatonic.*

❧❧

Vaguely, Kate was aware of footsteps echoing on the marble walkway. She looked up slowly, trying to focus her tired eyes. *Wow, you must be more tired than you know—you're hallucinating.* For five years she tried hard not to dwell too much on the memory of the one woman who made her think that love at first sight might be more than a cliché. Now, for the second time that day, Kate found herself thinking about Jay. Not only that, this time she was seeing her as if she were really here, in Albany. Kate smiled until, unbidden, thoughts intruded about the last time she and Jay crossed paths, four months after the incident on the ski slope.

Kate was walking down the hill from the college radio station on her way to meet friends downtown following the eleven p.m. newscast, when she heard what sounded like a struggle.

She looked around, aware as she did that there had been a series of sexual assaults on campus in the previous two months. She spotted a small movement in the bushes just off the path some twenty feet ahead. She broke into a run, dropped the sweatshirt she was carrying, and yanked the bushes aside with her hand as she reached the noise. What she saw enraged her. A beefy man, his face covered with a nylon stocking, was straddling a young woman. He was in the process of pulling her pants down. She also saw the glint of steel in the moonlight.

Heedless of the danger, she coiled her body and launched herself at the man, careful to get under his arm so that the blade would be aimed upward, away from his victim. She knocked him sideways and off the woman, her momentum sending both the assailant and her careening into a nearby oak tree. The man caught his balance first, slashing at Kate with the knife he still held in his hand. She tried to roll away, but he managed to slice her right shoulder. Blood immediately poured from the wound but, furious, she ignored it. Pushing to her feet Kate smashed him in the stomach with one of her long legs, following that with a knee to his groin. He howled in agony, and she used that opportunity to kick the knife from his hand. As he recovered and reached for it on the ground, she stomped on his wrist so hard that she could hear the bones snap. Just as she was about to take a shot at his head with her foot, a local policeman came running up, his gun drawn, warning the man to move away from the

23

weapon and lie face down on the dirt. He cuffed him and looked up into Kate's eyes.

"Are you all right?"

"Yeah," Kate sighed. "But there's a woman over that way a little," she pointed over her shoulder, "who may not be."

"I'll radio for an ambulance right away, backup should be here shortly."

"You worry about him, I'll see what I can do for her." And with that, Kate already was streaking back toward the path.

She looked around for a moment, trying to locate the woman, before she spied the reflective tape on the back of a pair of running sneakers. And then she realized why she had such trouble spotting her—the victim was curled into a tiny ball, lying huddled near where Kate first encountered her and her assailant. She was in the fetal position, with her arms wrapped tightly around her knees, which were pulled up to her chest. The sight broke Kate's heart.

She moved quickly, but carefully, trying not to traumatize the woman any further. Bending down, she began speaking softly to her.

"It's okay. You're safe now." When she got no response, she tried again. "Can I just get a look at you, see where you're hurt?" Again, nothing. Kate didn't want to add to the woman's misery, but she knew she had to get a better handle on exactly how far the scumbag got and whether or not he cut her with the knife. In the position the victim was in currently, she couldn't even see her face.

"Hey, I only want to help you. He can't hurt you anymore, I promise. Please." It was a plea. The woman began to rock back and forth as if in mute comfort. Kate decided she had to make a move; she simply couldn't chance waiting any longer. Reaching out tentatively, she touched the woman on the back. The traumatized victim lifted her chin inches from its position tight against her knees as if noting someone else's presence for the first time. Kate gasped.

"Jay," she cried. "Jay, is that you?" All the while her mind was praying that it wasn't the young woman whose face had been visiting her in her dreams for months. Oh, God, not her. Tears sprang to Kate's eyes. She gently wrapped an arm around Jay, who flinched involuntarily at the contact.

Although she was stung by the reaction, Kate refused to pull back. "Jay, honey, are you hurt? I need to see. Can you straighten out your arms and legs so that I can see where you're hurt?"

Seeing a flicker of a response, Kate continued her coaxing. "I just need a peek, Jay, then I won't bother you anymore, okay?"

With tremendous effort, but without looking up, Jay loosened her death grip and dropped her arms to her sides. Kate moved forward instantly and, as gently as she could, examined Jay to determine her condition. Bile rose to her throat as she noted the ripped blouse, the cut bra, the half-opened jeans and the scrapes and bruises that liberally covered her chest and abdomen. She could see the swelling on Jay's jaw and the beginnings of a bruise there, as well as her split lip. Kate noted the bruising around Jay's nipple, too. God, she wanted to kill him.

She didn't want to ask the next question, but she knew she had to. Softly, circling Jay with her good arm and stroking her blonde hair, she asked, "He didn't penetrate you, did he, honey?" Kate closed her eyes against the answer, knowing that if it was in the affirmative, she might well take matters into her own hands and strangle the bastard.

Jay couldn't seem to find her voice. Instead, she shook her head no.

Kate squeezed her eyes shut as the tears of relief leaked out of the corners; thank God for small favors.

At that moment she heard doors slamming and the sirens of additional police cars. She looked down and was suddenly aware of how painfully exposed and vulnerable Jay looked. Kate remembered that she had dropped her sweatshirt just a few feet away and she moved to retrieve it.

"No, don't leave me."

Kate moved back to her instantly. "It's okay, Jay, I'm not going anywhere. I just want to get something for you to put on. Watch me, you'll see, I'm right here." She inched away slowly, making sure that Jay could still see her. She picked up her sweatshirt quickly and returned to her side. "Here, let me help you put this on, okay?"

Jay nodded her head numbly.

Not wanting to startle or frighten her, Kate described what she was going to do next. "Jay, I'm just going to help you get your jeans zipped up, okay?" Getting no reaction, she reached down slowly and put her hands on the waistband. Jay didn't pull away, so she grasped the zipper, pulled it up, and refastened the button. "There you go, that's better, huh?"

Kate was alarmed that Jay seemed to be so far away, unreachable, really, with the exception of that one exclamation when she let go of her. So far, that was the only verbal indication that Jay even knew Kate was there.

Two police officers approached, one male and one female, both looking at Kate with a question in their eyes.

"She's okay. I don't think he accomplished his goal—she doesn't appear to have been penetrated, but they should probably check just to be certain. She's got significant bruising and scrapes and he tore most of her clothes off." She was amazed at how calm her own voice sounded. In actuality, she was deeply shaken.

The officers appeared to note the oversized sweatshirt that covered Jay's upper body and pooled around her on the ground where she was half sitting. Following their eyes, Kate added, "That's mine. I just thought she should be covered up."

"Okay," said the male officer. "You need to come with me so that I can ask you some questions. Officer Dale will stay with her and question her." Kate didn't like his attitude, thinking him far less compassionate in his tone than she thought he should have been.

She sized up Officer Dale and addressed her instead. "I don't think she's in any shape to be questioned right now, you'll only traumatize her further. I can tell you everything I saw and what happened." Kate didn't want Jay to have to relive the attack over again so soon. "She needs medical attention."

"So do you," Officer Dale stated flatly, nodding in the direction of her right arm, which was dripping blood.

"I'm fine. We need to take care of her."

"Come with me, ma'am," the male officer said, tugging on Kate's good arm to get her going.

She reluctantly started to stand, but Jay grabbed her hand like a vise before she was halfway off the ground. "Don't go," she whispered. "Please don't leave me."

"I won't," Kate said, dropping back down next to her and staring up at the officers defiantly. To them she said with finality, "I'll answer your questions at the hospital after she's been taken care of. Don't worry, I'm not likely to forget anything I saw or did."

"Ma'am," the male officer started, "it's important to get your recollections while they're freshest. Hers too." He jabbed his chin in Jay's direction.

Kate just stared daggers at the man. "I assure you you'll get everything you need. Now where the hell is the ambulance?" She was starting to get light-headed from the loss of blood and she was worried beyond words about Jay's emotional state.

Fortuitously, two paramedics hustled up at that moment wheeling a stretcher. "Somebody rang for us?"

Kate looked up at the sound of the bright voice. "Jen, is that you?"

"Hey, beautiful. What's a nice girl like you doing in a dump like this?"

Kate was never so glad to see a friendly face in her life. Jen was a fellow member of the ski patrol. She was also a volunteer EMT. "Jen, this is Jamison Parker. She needs your help."

"So do you, from the looks of it, missy. Let me take a peek."

"Later, Jen, I promise. Jay first. Please?"

Jen looked intently at Kate. "Right." Addressing Jay the EMT said, "Hi, I'm Jen. I'm here to help you. Where does it hurt?"

Jay didn't respond, but her grip on the hand she was holding tightened imperceptibly. Kate leaned over and cooed softly in her ear, "It's all right, Jay, Jen's a friend of mine. You can trust her."

Jen squatted down in front of Jay and reached out slowly. "I'm just going to pull your sweatshirt up and have a little look see, okay?" This she said even as she already had her hands in the material and was tugging gently upward. She took the stethoscope from around her neck and the blood pressure cuff and began listening to her patient's chest and taking her pulse and blood pressure readings.

Kate waited expectantly. After completing her preliminary examination, Jen said, "Her heart rate's a little elevated, which you'd expect, and her pressure's up a bit too. Her pupils are non-responsive, which is indicative of deep shock. Do I need to use a kit?" She didn't need to be more specific. Kate knew Jen was asking if the asshole had raped Jay and if they needed forensic evidence that a rape kit could yield.

Kate swallowed hard, willing back the tears that the very thought of that monster defiling Jay evoked. In a voice choked with emotion, she answered, "I don't think so, but I'd prefer it if you went through the motions just in case. I want to make sure we nail the bastard good."

"Okay," Jen said to Jay, "we're going to move you to a stretcher now so that we can take you to the hospital and check you over properly, all right? Can you stand?"

Jay didn't move. Kate tugged on her hand gently, started to stand herself and pulled the traumatized woman up along with her, never letting go of her hand. Jen moved in and guided Jay to the stretcher, putting subtle pressure on her shoulder when the stretcher was maneuvered into position for her to sit. Kate recognized the panic in Jay's expression and stepped in as Jen laid her down on the gurney. "Don't worry, Jay, I'm coming with you." Kate swept Jay's disheveled blonde bangs off her forehead with gentle fingers and entwined their fingers once again as she walked alongside the stretcher.

Kate looked up when Jen bumped her with an elbow.

"You've lost a lot of blood, girlfriend. We need to do something about that."

"I'm fin—"

"Don't you dare tell me it can wait. Frankly, your color sucks."

"Thanks for the compliment. As soon as we're on the road, I promise."

Once in the ambulance, Kate allowed Jen to peel back the tattered sleeve of her t-shirt.

"Jesus. That's gonna need a couple of layers of stitches and a tetanus shot, to be sure, if you haven't had one lately." Kate barely noticed as Jen cleaned the wound and applied a pressure bandage as a stopgap measure until she could get stitched.

Kate wasn't interested in her own condition. She kept her gaze focused on Jay's face and made gentle circles on the back of Jay's hand.

Once at the hospital, Kate remained by a clearly panicked Jay's side as she was wheeled into a private area of the emergency room where a rape counselor was waiting along with an all-female medical team. Kate filled the clinicians in as best she could as to the events of the evening. After examining Jay briefly, the doctor told Kate, "I'm going to give her a sedative to help her relax a bit, and then we'll take samples for the lab."

Kate looked to the rape counselor beseechingly.

"She'll be all right." The counselor smiled kindly at her. "It's going to take time and a good support network."

Kate wondered if Jay had one, thinking back to the accident on the ski slope and her reaction to having her parents contacted. Then a name popped into her head: Sarah. She had mentioned a friend named Sarah. Kate asked Jay what dorm she lived in, but got no answer.

When the sedative began to take effect and Jay's eyes began to slide shut, Kate tried a different tack on a hunch.

"Jay, what's your roommate's name?"

"Sarah Alexander," she slurred.

Kate waited for Jay to fall asleep, then reluctantly disentangled their hands. She went in search of a college directory, looked up Sarah Alexander, and headed for the phone.

After making the phone call, Kate sought treatment for her wound. A dozen stitches to the underlayers of skin and another dozen sutures in the top layer later, Kate sported a stark white bandage wrapped around her shoulder, which was bare thanks to the fashion-ignorant doctor who had unceremoniously cut off her sleeve.

She spotted a harried-looking young woman come running in through the emergency room door and approached her. "Are you Sarah Alexander?"

"Yes, yes I am."

"Jay's in there." Kate motioned in the direction of the room just down the hall to the right. "She's asleep right now but she could sure use a friend." Irrationally, Kate was envious—she wished that friend could be her. "The counselor will fill you in, she's in the room with her."

Kate continued out into the emergency room waiting area, where she recounted for the officers from the scene everything she knew. Afterward, they gave her a ride back to campus.

Kate thought about checking back in on Jay, but decided that Jay didn't need her. She was in good hands with Sarah, who no doubt knew her well enough to know how to comfort her. *For some reason, that thought both heartened and saddened her.*

The footsteps stopped just in front of where Kate sat facing the remains of the capitol. She opened her mouth to speak, but nothing came out. *My God, it's been five years and you are even more beautiful than I remember.*

"Hi," Jay said shyly.

Kate motioned her to sit down. "Hello, Jay," she said warmly.

"You cut off your hair."

"You don't like it?" Jay half questioned. She reached up and patted her head.

Her resistance weakened, Kate reacted without restraint. She reached out and ran her long fingers through Jay's hair. "No, it's gorgeous," she said sincerely. "It suits you." Her palm briefly brushed Jay's cheek.

Jay grasped the hand that caressed her face in her own soft hands and turned it over to examine the palm. It was raw and bleeding.

Kate knew the rest of her didn't look much better.

"You need to go to the hospital, Katherine. You're hurt." Jay began to pull on Kate's good hand to get her to stand.

"No, Jay, the hospitals all have their hands full with the seriously wounded. I'm fine."

"No, you're not...you're bleeding, you're cut, and you need to be seen," Jay prodded stubbornly.

Trying to change the subject, Kate said, "My friends call me Kate."

"Oh, are you including me in that number?"

"Sure."

"Boy, you're easy."

"Don't let it get around," Kate replied, smiling tiredly at the repeat of their very first conversation.

"Your secret's safe with me," Jay winked. "And now that we've got that settled, let's get you to the hospital."

Seeing that she was going to have to do something to placate Jay, Kate decided to take a different approach. "I don't want to spend hours sitting in an emergency room—my doctor can handle my injuries."

"At this hour?"

"She's a friend of mine."

"Okay, then call her, because I'm taking you there right now."

"That's really not necessary."

"Let's go find a pay phone," Jay said determinedly.

"All right, all right already, I know when I've been outmaneuvered." Kate sighed and led her companion to the pay phone outside the entrance of the nearby convention center.

"Um, I took a cab here," Jay said sheepishly. "You do have a car, right?"

Kate laughed for the first time in many hours. "C'mon, one of my co-workers dropped my car off nearby hours ago." She led Jay across the plaza away from the capitol.

CHAPTER THREE

Although she put up token resistance, Kate secretly was glad that Jay wanted to drive. She didn't think she could keep her eyes open long enough to watch the road, and Jay seemed only too happy to slip behind the wheel of her sporty little BMW convertible anyway.

Kate sank into the leather of the passenger seat with relief and, after listening delightedly to Jay mutter under her breath about how far up she had to move the driver's seat in order to reach the pedals, Kate directed her through the city and into the suburbs beyond.

Kate just about drifted off when a thought occurred to her. "Jay?"

"Hmm?"

"What in the world are you doing here in Albany and how did you find me?"

Jay laughed. "Well, the 'how did I find you' was simple. Anyone with access to a television set today could have found you, Kate. As for what I'm doing here, I'm doing an in-depth profile on the governor for *Time* magazine. I'm based in New York City and I was hoping to interview him there, but the only way they could fit me into his schedule was to do it up here. It's going to be next week's cover story—they consider him a real future contender for the presidency."

"Mmm, they're right about that. Wow, that's fantastic, congratulations."

"Thanks. I was supposed to meet with him this aftern—I mean yesterday afternoon now, I guess, but the disaster changed all that."

"What time was your meeting set for?"

"Four o'clock. I was just getting showered and changed when I saw you on CNN and then someone from the governor's office called to postpone."

"Mmm, I'm glad you hadn't left yet." Kate couldn't imagine what her reaction would have been to find that Jay had been caught in that explosion.

కు

At 12:15 a.m. they pulled up to a brick office building where they were greeted by a wiry, bespectacled woman in her midforties.

"Kate, come on inside and let's get you looked at."

"Dr. Barbara Jones, please meet Ms. Jamison Parker. Jay, this is Dr. Jones."

"Barbara, please. It's nice to meet you," the doctor said as she reached out to grasp Jay's hand in a firm handshake.

"Likewise," Jay answered.

Once inside, the doctor led the way back to one of the examination rooms. "Feel free to come along for the ride, Jay, our Kate here could use a distraction."

Jay hesitated. She was embarrassed by the doctor's assumption that Kate would welcome her presence and she wanted to give Kate her privacy.

"It's fine, Jay," Kate said. "It'll be a heck of a lot more entertaining than what's in Barbara's waiting room. There isn't a magazine out there that's less than a year old."

Since Kate appeared to be taking it all in stride, Jay decided to shove aside her discomfort. Everything was fine until Kate started disrobing. Suddenly Jay found the diplomas on the wall fascinating.

Jay was grateful when Barbara returned with several suture kits, some fresh bandages, and cleansing solution.

"Geez, Kate, you look like hell."

"Thanks for the compliment, I feel better already."

From her vantage point in the corner Jay smiled at the easy camaraderie between the two women.

Jay watched as Barbara examined Kate from head to foot, stitched two major gashes on her hand and forearm, and applied burn ointment to her hands and salve to the cuts on her face and arms.

"Do try to stay out of trouble now, will you?"

"You know it's the trouble that always finds me, Barbara," Kate joked hoarsely. "Not the other way around."

"Yeah, right. Now get out of here so I can get some sleep."

❧❧

Just as the three women were headed to the exit, the phone rang.

"Now who would that be at this hour?" Barbara wondered aloud.

"Well," she sighed, "if they tracked me down here, it's a sure bet I should answer it."

After a moment, she handed the phone to Kate, shaking her head. "It's for you," she said, her eyebrows hiking into her salt-and-pepper hair.

"Hello, this is Katherine Kyle." Now she was all business, all trace of exhaustion gone.

"Hiya, Kate," her producer greeted her.

Kate sighed in exasperation. "First of all, how in the world did you track me down and what could you possibly want now, Phil?" she said with a mixture of wonder and respect. "And secondly, I thought you told me to take the rest of the night off."

"Number one, I have many skills," he said proudly. "Number two, I did, and now it's tomorrow morning."

Kate groaned. "Okay, what is it?"

"Great news. You're a star and you're in demand. All three networks want you on their morning shows tomor—er...today. First appearance at seven oh five a.m. You have to be in makeup at six at the NBC *Today Show* studios."

Kate was dead silent.

"Kate, did you hear me?"

A heavy sigh. "Yeah, I heard you."

"Terrific, a limo will be outside your house at three thirty a.m. That's...two and a half hours from now. Better get your beauty rest, not that you need any."

"Gee, thanks. I'll fly back and be here in time for the six p.m. 'cast, get me some reservations, will you? And Phil, I'm going to call you at six thirty a.m. sharp, and I want an update on everything we know to this point. See ya." She hung up before he had a chance to respond.

When she put the phone down, both Jay and Barbara looked at her with inquiring eyes.

"I'm the catch of the day, apparently. All three networks want me on their morning shows...six hours from now."

"Oh Kate," both women groaned together.

"Kate, you're in no shape to travel to New York right now, that's insane!" Jay said.

"That's okay, they're sending a limo to drive me."

"Oh, well, that makes it all better then."

"Come on, Jay, let me get you back to your hotel. Thanks for taking such good care of me, Barbara, as always."

✷

The ride to the hotel was companionably silent. Once there, Kate insisted on walking Jay to her room. Before they could get beyond the lobby, the desk clerk called out, "Excuse me, are you Ms. Parker?"

"Yes, I am," Jay answered.

"Thank God," the clerk exclaimed, apparently relieved. "I've got a message for you. This woman has been calling every half hour."

Jay smiled and shook her head. "Ah, that would be Trish." To Kate she said, "My editor."

Jay accepted the piece of paper from the clerk and read the note, groaning.

"What is it?"

"The governor has rescheduled the interview for...two thirty p.m. today...in his New York City office. It seems he doesn't want to appear to be cowed or deterred by terrorists."

Kate thought for a minute. She really didn't want to say goodbye to Jay again so soon. "I've got an idea." At Jay's raised eyebrow, she continued before she could lose her nerve. "How about if we get you checked out right now? You can come to my house with me. We can shower there, get changed and ready, and then you can ride with me in the limo back to the city." When Jay didn't respond right away, Kate rushed on, "That is, if you don't mind traveling at that ungodly hour, and I would love it if you would accompany me on the rounds to the shows. If you want to, I mean. I think you'd have plenty of time before your interview with the governor." She could never remember being so nervous and anxious about an answer before. It had never mattered like this.

"That sounds great...are you sure?"

Kate nodded.

"I'll just go get my stuff and be down in a minute."

CHAPTER FOUR

After throwing her few things together, Jay placed a quick call to her editor.

"Sure," Trish practically yelled at her in her heavy New York accent. "You, the most responsible person I know...first you hang up on me, and then, if that isn't bad enough, you go flying off somewhere and don't even bother to get in touch with me when the whole world is exploding up there. Jesus, Jay, I thought something really bad happened to you."

"I'm sorry, Trish, I guess I didn't think about it that way. Don't worry, everything's fine. I don't have time right now, but I promise to explain it all to you the next time we talk, okay?"

"Yeah. Okay this time, but no more heart attacks, all right? I'm too young to die."

"Cross my heart. Listen, I've already got a lift back to the city, and I'll be there in plenty of time for the interview."

"Jay, there's an awful lot riding on this interview now given what happened. Make me proud."

"Have I ever disappointed you?"

"Nope, and don't let this be the first time, either."

"Bye, Trish."

"See ya, kid."

The ride to Kate's house took a little over twenty minutes, with Kate driving this time, since it was easier than giving directions. When they pulled into the driveway, Jay was amazed at how beautiful and big the house was. "Wow, this is impressive."

Kate shrugged. "It's home."

The house was set back from the road on a cul-de-sac. The driveway, shaded by large old oak trees and extending perhaps three hundred feet, ended in a circular drive to the front door with a continuation to a three-car attached garage. From the front door, Jay couldn't even see the lights of the neighboring houses.

Once inside, Jay was stunned by the elegance of the interior—it was airy and open, with skylights in the high cathedral ceiling of the sunken living room. And yet it also had a cozy feeling that was most likely a result of the post-and-beam construction and the choice of furnishings.

Before Jay could make any more observations, Kate called out, "Hi, honey, I'm home! Fred, are you here, I brought somebody home to meet you."

Jay wasn't sure she could stay standing. She felt the air rush out of her lungs as Kate's words slammed her in the gut like a two-by-four. There was a sharp pain in her chest, and it was hard to breathe. How could she have missed something as major as a husband? Good Lord! Kate didn't have any rings on her fingers, but then that didn't necessarily mean anything. How could she have been so stupid? Of course someone as special as Kate would be taken.

Just as Jay was trying to figure out how she could extricate herself gently from the situation without making too much of an idiot of herself, a beautiful golden retriever came bounding around the corner from another part of the house. The dog had a stuffed parrot in his mouth and what looked like a big smile on his face.

"There you are," Kate said. "Now be a gentleman and introduce yourself." The dog sat obediently and stuck out his right paw for Jay to shake, his tail wagging furiously and his whole body shaking in excitement. "Jay, this is Fred. Fred, meet Jay."

The feeling of profound relief that flooded through her left Jay feeling light-headed. She reached out to take Fred's extended paw.

"Oh, and Fred," Kate said in a stage whisper, "no kissing on the first date." She winked at Jay, who stood there with a lopsided grin on her face. Now that she was pretty sure her heart was going to recover, she was absolutely smitten with Fred.

"How old is he?" Jay asked as she scratched him on the chest.

"Two years," his mother replied. "His parents are both breed champions."

"He's charming and handsome."

"Yeah," Kate agreed with obvious pride and affection. "But don't tell him that, it'll go right to his head."

Kate showed Jay to the living room and invited her to sit on the couch. "Can I get you something to drink?"

"No thanks, I'm fine."

"I'd light the fireplace, but I don't think we have enough time to enjoy it."

"That's okay, Kate, you don't need to worry about me. You must be exhausted."

After a short silence, Jay decided to take advantage of the moment. "By the way, I've always wanted to thank you for all that you did for me in college," she started conversationally. Kate made a dismissive motion as if to say, "it was nothing."

"No, really," Jay persisted. "You were always taking your clothes off for me," she said earnestly, referring to the sweatshirt and Kate's using her ski jacket to warm her on the ski slope.

As soon as the words were out of her mouth and Jay got a good look at how Kate's eyebrows were hiked all the way up into her hairline, she realized what she had said. She scrubbed furiously at her face, which turned beet red.

"Uh-oh. Damn, I didn't mean that the way it sounded. I mean, I did mean it but," she stammered. "Oh, never mind," she finished miserably.

Kate tipped her head back and gave a hearty laugh.

Jay thought it was the most wonderful sound she'd ever heard. "Let's just rewind the conversation, okay?"

"You're welcome. I was glad to be in the right place at the right time. Listen, I need to take a shower in the worst way."

"Me too," Jay agreed.

"Well, come with me, I'll give you the nickel tour so you can find your way around, and I'll show you to the guest suite."

Fred led the way out of the living room and into a fully stocked library, complete with built-in, floor-to-ceiling bookshelves. Jay made a mental note to come back and check the titles in Kate's collection. Some of them clearly looked like first editions. On the wall opposite the bookshelves was an apparently well-used fireplace.

"This is my favorite room in the house," Kate said. "Fred and I spend a lot of time in here reading by the fire."

Jay made note of the fluffy dog bed sitting next to a comfortable-looking recliner that sat at an angle to the fireplace. *Boy, I could get lost in here for days.*

Although Jay already knew the library would be her favorite room in the house, she found herself suitably impressed by Kate's well-used office, the high-tech family room, the pristine state-of-the-art kitchen and the picture-perfect dining room.

When they'd been through the entire downstairs, Kate said, "C'mon, let's go upstairs."

Kate showed Jay the three bedrooms upstairs, including the guest suite, which included its own large bathroom with a sunken tub. Finally, she stopped at the threshold to her own bedroom suite. With a gesture of her bandaged hand, she motioned Jay to precede her.

The room was large and airy, like the rest of the house, but with an intimacy about it that took Jay's breath away. The colors were warm and inviting, the furnishings tasteful and understated; the ceiling featured a huge fan, recessed lighting, and a skylight through which she could see the moon and stars shining above.

"It's fantastic... The whole house is."

"Thanks, I designed it myself."

"You designed the house?"

"Um, yeah."

"Wow." Jay looked at her with a mixture of awe and respect.

Kate kicked her shoes off and sighed. She began to shrug out of her suit jacket, although with her hands stitched and bandaged, it was obviously a challenge.

Seeing the flicker of pain cross Kate's features, Jay stepped forward. "I can help you with that."

"No, it's okay, I've got it." Kate winced again.

"For all the times you helped me, it's the least I can do, please." Jay pleaded.

Kate nodded her surrender.

Jay moved forward further, brushed Kate's hands aside gently, undid the two buttons on the ruined suit jacket and eased it from broad shoulders, then reached for the buttons on the silk blouse. She swallowed hard and her fingers shook slightly as she carefully opened each button, revealing more and more beautiful skin. She could see clearly the line where the ash and dirt ended and the flesh that had been protected by the blouse and jacket began.

As she exposed more skin, Jay looked up into Kate's eyes. The expression she saw there precipitated a flush of heat that began in her stomach and radiated downward. Trying hard to maintain her composure, she lowered her hands and unhooked the button on Kate's slacks and pulled the zipper down. Finally, reaching behind Kate's back, Jay released the catch on her bra and stepped back as if a snake had bitten her. She didn't trust herself to refrain from reaching out and touching that amazing body so close by. She turned away quickly and began studying the artwork on the walls.

Kate hastily excused herself to grab a silk robe off the back of the adjoining bathroom door. She returned to the bedroom wearing only the robe and her underwear.

"Um, why don't you go take a shower first, Jay, you can use the guest suite down the hall. I think I'll just rest for a minute before I shower."

Glad for a bit of normal conversation, and beyond relieved that she had a moment alone to compose herself, Jay readily agreed.

When she returned to Kate's room to let her know she was ready, Jay found her fast asleep curled up in the middle of the bed. Jay took a moment to study the sleeping form, acknowledging that Kate, even with her eyes closed, was by far the most beautiful woman she had ever seen. Knowing that Kate was exhausted, she was loath to wake her, though she knew she must—in only another hour the limousine would arrive. But Kate looked so peaceful.

Jay decided to delay the inevitable, and went instead to the kitchen to throw together something for them to eat. She was certain that Kate hadn't eaten in at least twelve hours, and she was hungry too. *Not that that was any great news flash.* She chuckled to herself. When she opened the refrigerator, it quickly became clear that Kate's kitchen not only was immaculate, but also largely unused. Aside from a carton of skim milk, a stick of butter, a dozen eggs, a slab of bacon, some cocktail sauce, half a dozen cans of soda, fresh oranges, some salad dressing, and a jar of pasta sauce, the refrigerator was a wasteland. "Well, Fred, she's got eggs, bacon, and"—she spied a bag of English muffins on the counter—"it'll have to do, my friend."

Fred sat on Jay's feet, apparently waiting for something to drop. Jay laughed at his antics. "Fred, you are one beautiful specimen, but your mama, buddy, now *she* is sensational." Jay noted that he didn't seem to be too crushed at the prospect of coming in second best.

Jay put the food in the seldom-used oven to keep it warm and went back upstairs to wake Kate. When she arrived at the bedroom door, she knew immediately that something wasn't right. Kate was thrashing around wildly on the bed, clearly in the throes of a nightmare. Jay ran the rest of the way to the bed as she called, "Kate, wake up, it's just a dream." When Jay got no response, she leaned one

39

knee on the bed and tried talking to Kate again. The sleeping woman's discomfort was increasing by the second. Her eyes moved rapidly under her lids and she screamed out in terror. Jay reached out and gently grasped Kate under the shoulders, careful not to jar her injuries. She slipped in behind Kate, holding her and restraining her at the same time, fearful that her thrashing would worsen her wounds. As Jay gently rocked Kate, she whispered nonsense words of comfort.

Kate awakened with a start, clearly disoriented. Jay watched as Kate slowly registered the fact that she was lying on her own bed, and that Jay was holding her.

Seemingly embarrassed, Kate sat bolt upright, apologized, and moved away. "I need to shower. The limo will be here soon."

Jay let her go and padded downstairs to the library, where she tried to focus on the books on the shelves. In reality, all she could think about was the way it felt to hold Kate in her arms, to feel that power and strength. She sensed that Kate was neither used to, nor comfortable with, anyone's seeing her vulnerabilities. She wished desperately for Kate to trust her enough to let her in anyway.

Kate spent a long time under the spray. She badly wanted to wash away the nightmare of the little boy's face, his staring dead eyes, his small crushed body. She wondered if she would ever get past some of the horror she had seen in the previous twenty-four hours. But she didn't need to burden Jay with that.

Kate threw on some worn jeans and a t-shirt and packed a garment bag with the outfit she would wear on the networks later that morning. She exited the bedroom and sniffed the air. *Something smells great.* The thought that Jay cooked something for her after the way she'd dismissed her earlier made Kate feel awful.

When she didn't find Jay in the kitchen, Kate poked her head into the library. Jay was standing in front of one of the bookshelves with Fred lying at her feet. Kate took a moment to admire her while she was unaware of the scrutiny. Looking gorgeous in an off-white pantsuit, she seemed lost in thought and a little sad. That made Kate feel even worse about the way she had just treated her.

"Hey," Kate said as cheerfully as she could, "I smell something mouth-watering."

"Yeah." Turning, Jay smiled at her. "I thought you might be hungry, and I always am, so I whipped up a little something. I hope you don't mind."

"Mind? Are you kidding, I'm starving."

Kate and Jay made their way into the kitchen, where they sat at the table in companionable silence and ate the meal Jay prepared.

"Thanks for cooking. You didn't have to do that, but it was fantastic."

"Judging from your refrigerator, I'd say it's safe to assume that if I didn't do the cooking, it wasn't going to get done."

"Ayeah, that would be too true," Kate said sheepishly.

At that moment, the limo pulled up outside; it was exactly 3:30 a.m.

"Showtime, I guess."

"You're going on network television looking like that?"

"What, you don't like my favorite jeans and t-shirt?"

Kate squirmed as Jay seemed to relish the opportunity to stare frankly at her.

"Oh no, they look great on you. I'm just not sure it's the image you're looking to project."

"Ooh, good save, Jay, well done. You have a future in the BS business to be sure." Her eyes twinkled. It felt good to get back on safe ground after the nightmare fiasco. "Actually, I brought my clothes with me so that I wouldn't wrinkle them before America got to see them."

"Oh great, so you'll look beautiful and I'll look like a shar-pei," Jay complained as she bent over to say goodbye to Fred, who was presently wrapped around his mother's knees.

"First of all, I think you look fabulous, and, second, the entire country is not going to be watching you. Now come on, our chariot awaits." With a hug and kiss for Fred and a gallant bow, Kate followed Jay out the front door.

"What happens to Fred while you're gone?"

"Oh, you needn't worry about the king. His minions take care of him and treat him like the royalty he believes himself to be." At Jay's perplexed look, Kate clarified, "The kids next door and their parents are gaga over Fred. They come in and feed him whenever I get hung up. You couldn't see it in the dark, but the entire backyard is fenced in with a doggie door into the garage and the mudroom. They'll let Fred out so that he can play and wander to his heart's content. In fact, most likely the kids will spend most of the afternoon throwing the ball for that pleasure hound. By the time I get home, that boy will be blissfully exhausted, well fed and well cared for."

CHAPTER FIVE

When the two women emerged from Kate's house, the driver was standing at attention outside the limo's back door. His instructions said that there was only one passenger, but it was all the same to him, especially when both of his charges were as absolutely stunning as these two were. They were like yin and yang—the one tall, dark and intense, with the bluest eyes he'd ever seen; the other about seven inches shorter, blonde and approachable, with sparkling eyes the color of emeralds. She lacked the overt power of her companion, but she was slender and graceful like an athlete and clearly in great shape. *Yeah, it's a tough job, but somebody's gotta do it.*

Jay smiled at the uniformed driver as Kate stepped aside to allow her to get in first. Just as she was about to slide in, Kate pulled her back. "Oh no you don't. I refuse to be responsible for you looking like a shar-pei." She winked. "Off with the suit jacket." Jay shook her head good-naturedly and complied. Underneath, she wore a simple sleeveless black shell; the top clung to her breasts and accentuated her slim waist, and the lack of sleeves showed off her muscular arms to good advantage. Kate was inordinately grateful that she could occupy herself hanging up the jacket. She was sure she must have been drooling. *Kyle, you've got to get a grip here.*

When they were settled in the car and the driver had raised the privacy glass, Kate turned to Jay. "I'm really glad you're here. I still can't believe you found me."

"You could've knocked me over with a feather when I turned on my TV set and saw you. I hung up on my editor in mid-sentence. Of course, she's always in mid-sentence."

43

After a while, Kate noticed Jay's eyelids growing heavy. Eventually, sleep claimed her. Smiling, Kate regarded her affectionately. "You look a bit uncomfortable to me, Jay." Her smile turned to a full-fledged grin. "I think I can fix that." Scooting back into the corner of the seat, she gently pulled Jay with her. She settled Jay's head against her chest, rested her cheek on her soft hair, enfolded Jay in her arms, and joined her in peaceful slumber.

Jay was having the nicest dream. In it she was resting in Kate's arms, listening to the steady beat of her heart. It was the safest, most content she'd ever felt. And then it dawned on her that dreams usually didn't involve the sense of smell. She inhaled again the delicious scent of Shalimar perfume that she identified so strongly with Kate. Hesitantly she cracked open one eye and her heart rate soared as she took in her position nestled against Kate.

She wasn't quite sure how she got to where she was, but she sure wasn't sorry. Feeling Kate's rhythmic breath ruffling her hair and the thump, thump of her heartbeat against her ear, Jay thought that she probably should move. The problem was, her body didn't want to go anywhere at the moment. So, with a blissful sigh, she closed her eyes again and drifted back to sleep.

The world intruded gradually on Kate's all-too brief nap. Her wounds were making themselves felt and her eyes were gritty. As she took stock of her location, she noted that Jay was still tucked tightly against her body where she was when she fell asleep. Kate's arms were wrapped securely around her, and Jay's arms were resting on top of her stitched and bandaged ones. The pressure accounted for some of Kate's pain, but she had no desire to let go.

It occurred to Kate that Jay would soon awaken. *Better move before Sleeping Beauty awakes, Kyle.* She considered her options and frowned. She either would have to prop Jay against the seat or let her fall to the floor. Kate shook her head. *Not gonna happen.* She settled for owing Jay an explanation when she regained consciousness, which, as it turned out, didn't take long.

Feeling Jay stir, Kate lifted her cheek off Jay's head. "Hi," she began. Jay made no effort to move. "Um, I hope you don't mind. Uh, you fell asleep in an awkward position and I didn't want you to be stiff and sore when you woke up. I figured I would be a decent pillow, and..." Kate stopped and released a breath. She was babbling uncharacteristically and she knew it. "Anyway," she finished weakly, not knowing what else to say.

"That's okay, you make a great pillow and that's the best rest I've had in a long time. Thanks."

Kate let out a relieved breath and released her grasp. Her eyes followed Jay's as they alighted on the position of their arms.

"Oh my God, Kate, did I hurt you?" Jay sat up and looked into Kate's face.

"Nope. Everything's fine." Kate schooled her face to hide her discomfort. Actually, her arms were throbbing.

At that moment, the limousine pulled to a stop. Kate looked out the window at the lightening sky and the NBC peacock logo, then back at Jay. "First stop. Are you ready for the circus?"

The door swung open on the curbside and the driver helped Jay from the car. Kate followed behind with Jay's jacket and her own garment bag.

"Are you going to wait for us?"

"Yes, ma'am, my instructions are to take you to each network, and then anywhere else you have to go today until I drop you at the airport. By the way, I was told to tell you that you are booked on a two thirty p.m. commuter out of LaGuardia."

"Okay, thank you. See you in a bit then." Kate helped Jay into her suit jacket, grasped her gently by the elbow, and escorted her into the Rockefeller Center studios of NBC's *Today Show*.

They were met at the reception desk by a harried-looking producer. Barely glancing at Jay, the woman gave Kate's outfit a disgusted look and grabbed at her arm to hustle her away. Kate didn't move. The woman looked up at her impatiently.

"I'm Katherine Kyle," Kate said with a barely disguised sneer. Already she didn't like the producer. "And this is Ms. Jamison Parker."

"I know who ya are, lady, that's why I'm hea."

Kate ignored both the woman's interruption and her grating accent. "Ms. Parker is with me. Would you please make sure that she is made comfortable and given something to eat and some coffee while I'm getting ready?" It was more a command than a request.

"Yea, yea, I'll take care a' it, okay, now let's go. They're waitin' on ya in makeup." Kate still didn't budge. Finally, the woman sighed in exasperation and turned to Jay with a plastic smile. "Um, would you please come wit' me, too, Ms. Pawka?"

Jay returned the expression in kind. "Why, of course, thank you for asking," she said in her sweetest voice.

Kate smirked behind the producer's back.

Satisfied that Jay was being well cared for in the green room, Kate relaxed into the makeup chair. "Good morning," she said to the man who smiled at her in the mirror.

"Hey there, sweetie," he enthused. "Oh, this is gonna be fun. Any last requests before I get started?"

Kate couldn't help but smile at the man's upbeat attitude. She knew she looked like hell. The small cuts and abrasions on her left cheek were going to be hard to hide completely, and her normally vibrant eyes looked tired. "Sorry for the major reclamation project," she said, "but you should see the other guy."

Her makeup stylist laughed delightedly. "Honey, it's gonna be a pleasure working with that gorgeous face and hair, believe me. Last week I had to make up Phyllis Diller. Don't even ask."

Half an hour later, Kate emerged from the chair and stopped the nearest official-looking person. "I need a phone," she said.

"There's one in the green room."

"Okay, let me go change my clothes, and then could someone point me in the right direction?"

"No problem. I'll wait outside the dressing room for you."

Kate took the garment bag with her and disappeared behind the indicated door. She emerged ten minutes later and followed her escort to the green room where guests sat until it was time for them to be on the air.

Jay was sitting in the green room in a comfortable-looking leather armchair with her eyes closed and a cup of coffee close at hand. Kate snuck into the room and gazed down at the adorable blonde head. A lock of hair had fallen into her eye, and Kate eased it off her face. "Jay," she whispered. "Jay, honey, it's time to get up."

Jay mumbled something unintelligible, then her eyes snapped open and she stared open-mouthed. "Holy mother..."

Self-deprecatingly, Kate looked down at herself in her "business" attire and smirked as Jay stammered.

"You look amazing," Jay gushed.

Kate gave her a brilliant smile. "Thanks. Coming from you that means a lot." In truth, Kate was surprised to realize just how much Jay's opinion mattered.

"I just need to make a phone call and then it will be time to go, okay?"

Jay nodded.

"How's the coffee, any good?"

Jay nodded again.

"Are you always this talkative in the morning?" Kate kidded.

"I'm not really a morning person," Jay confessed sheepishly.

Kate moved to the phone on the side table and dialed a number from memory. "Hi, it's Kate. What's the latest?" She listened intently for a few minutes. "Okay, I'm going to call one of my contacts over at SPD and see if I can't get anything more solid on the incendiary device. I doubt he'll give me anything, but you never know." A few more seconds of listening and then she hung up. She turned to Jay and said apologetically, "I'm sorry, I just need to make one more call. I want to make sure I've got everything there is to get on this story before someone asks me a question I can't answer."

"No problem," Jay smiled at her encouragingly. "You just do what you need to do."

Kate dialed another number from memory. "Good morning, Peter. I didn't wake you, did I?" She knew perfectly well that Peter Enright had been up all night helping the state police department sort through the rubble of the capitol to determine exactly what kind of explosive was used, how much, and by what method it had been smuggled in and detonated. This type of case was his bread and butter. He was an expert in explosives and security and was the man governments turned to when they needed answers and help. Very few people knew about Peter, but Kate made his acquaintance when she was working as a street reporter on a story on security at the governor's mansion several years ago, before she became the evening news anchor. She and Peter were now good friends.

"Hi, gorgeous. Have I told you lately how great you look while crawling on all fours through piles of rubble?"

"Very funny, Peter. Now give."

He gave a mock sigh. "I wish I had something for you. The best I can tell you is whoever did this really knew what they were doing. They used a sophisticated remote detonator and enough material to take down the whole building. The fact that they set off two devices tells me that they weren't leaving anything to chance. The problem is, it doesn't look like anything local—it has an international flavor to it, and that doesn't make any sense to me."

"Hmm. No prior intelligence, no warning?"

47

"Not that I can find...yet."

Kate knew that Peter wouldn't rest until he had every answer he could get.

"Oh, and Kate?"

"Yeah," she sighed, knowing what was coming next.

"You know you can't use any of that on the air, right?"

"Why do I like you again?"

"It's my charm and boyish good looks," he shot back.

"Oh yeah, remind me of that the next time I see you."

"Oh, don't worry, I will."

"No doubt. And Peter, let me know as soon as you've got anything I can actually say?"

"You got it, sweet thing."

"Bye, Peter, be careful out there."

CHAPTER SIX

A knock at the door signaled it was time for Kate's appearance. She reached out a hand to Jay, who remained sitting. "Come with me? You can stand behind the camera and make faces at me if you want. I imagine that kind of torture might appeal to you."

"Why, Ms. Kyle, whatever made you think I was that kind of girl?" Jay smiled wickedly.

The two women accompanied a program assistant to the set and stood silently just beyond the fake living room and out of sight of the cameras until the next commercial break. As the red light on the television camera switched off, a woman rose from the couch on the set and walked towards them. She extended her hand as she reached them. "Ms. Kyle, I'm Wanda Nelson. I'm guest hosting today."

As if she needed an introduction, Jay thought. *She's only one of the hottest actresses in Hollywood,* and *she has a fabulous mind.*

"It's a pleasure to meet you, Ms. Nelson," Kate responded. "This is a very dear friend of mine, Ms. Jamison Parker. I hope you don't mind her standing in the wings?"

"No, that's just fine. It's nice to meet you Ms. Parker. Haven't I read your byline in *Time* magazine? My husband Ted and I love your writing."

Jay was floored. Wanda Nelson and Ted Graham, the famous presidential biographer, read her stories? "I'm flattered, Ms. Nelson. Thank you. It's nice to meet you."

A disembodied voice called out, "Thirty seconds, people." Wanda did not appear even to have heard, though Jay knew she must have.

❧

"Clint," she called to an assistant, "please get Ms. Parker a cup of fresh coffee and show her where to stand to get the best view, will you?" To Kate she said, "Won't you come with me?" As Kate followed alongside her, Wanda said, "That was fantastic work you did yesterday. Very courageous."

"Thank you, Ms. Nelson."

"Please, call me Wanda."

They sat down and yet another assistant attached a lavaliere microphone to the inside of Kate's jacket lapel. The disembodied voice called out, "Five, four, three, two, one, and cue the music." The *Today Show* theme played and the camera panned in on Wanda.

"Good morning, and welcome back to *Today* on NBC. With us this morning is journalist Katherine Kyle of NBC affiliate WCAP-TV in Albany, New York. Welcome, Kate."

"It's great to be here."

Many of you will recognize Ms. Kyle's face if you were paying any attention whatsoever to the news yesterday..." Wanda recapped Kate's role in the incident at the capitol punctuated with taped footage of Kate's first report and images of her running back into the building after the second explosion as she helped to rescue and comfort the wounded.

When the studio camera went live again, the shot had been widened to include both the show's co-host and her guest—a classic two shot. Wanda asked Kate, "What was going through your mind when you turned around and ran toward the capitol building after the second explosion? Everyone else was running in the opposite direction."

Kate looked at her interviewer, even as she faced directly into the camera. "I was thinking that there was human suffering." She leaned forward slightly. "I believe strongly that there's a time when it's more vital to be a human being than it is to be a journalist." Kate's eyes conveyed her earnestness.

"Weren't you concerned about compromising your objectivity?"

"It was important first of all to be a human being. Second, I would hope that viewers didn't feel that they were cheated, that they didn't get the story they should have gotten. To me the real story here was that in a world where such cruel and senseless violence exists, there is also compassion and the triumph of the human spirit over terror. I tried very hard to capture that essence in my coverage. And if I helped a few people and eased a little suffering along the way, so much the better." Kate smiled an ironic smile at Wanda. "Did I break the rules of professional distance? Perhaps. I would hope the viewers didn't mind too much." She winked.

Several more minutes of gentle questions ensued, then the segment was over. Kate and Wanda stood and shook hands. "Thank you for what you did yesterday, Kate. In my opinion you gave all journalists a good name."

"Thank you. I just followed my heart and my guts. In the end, I have to be able to live with my choices. For me it wasn't about some television executive reading 'Q' numbers on a sheet of paper."

"It might surprise you to know that I've already seen yesterday's numbers. You outscored the president of the United States and me and my husband combined, Kate." Wanda smiled. "Congratulations and good luck."

"Thanks," Kate answered.

When she and Jay were settled in the limousine once again, Kate asked, "How did I do?"

"First of all, the camera and you are clearly having a love affair."

Kate blushed.

"Secondly, today you made me exceedingly proud to wear the title of journalist. You were phenomenal."

"Thanks, Jay."

❧

The interviews by the other two networks were equally smooth. As they walked down the corridor at ABC's *Good Morning America* headquarters near Lincoln Center, Kate reached in her pocket for her watch. She was unable to wear it because of the stitches and the bandages, but she hated to be without one. It was not even 8:30 in the morning.

She looked over at Jay, who appeared to be fairly wide awake. "I can't tell you what it's meant to me to have you here with me through all of this, Jay. You've really been a trouper."

"I would hardly classify the past eight hours as a hardship, Kate. I've loved every minute of it. I'm so glad I found you."

"You must be exhausted. I'd love to take you out to breakfast, but I don't want to monopolize your time or keep you from a well-deserved nap."

"Kate, I've never turned down a good meal in my life." Jay laughed lightly. "And I'm not about to start now, especially with such enjoyable company," she added shyly. "I'd love to have breakfast with you. I know a great place in midtown that makes the most amazing waffles."

"Is it a casual place? I'm dying to get out of this suit and back into my jeans."

"You bet."

"I'll just change here then. I won't be a sec."

❧

Finally spending time together without any distractions, Kate and Jay sat across from each other in a corner booth. At the same time, they both began to speak.

"So, tell me..."

They laughed. Kate gestured to Jay. "You go first."

"Okay. Where do you come from? What was your major when we were at school? How did you end up in Albany as a news anchor? How many kids are there in your family? What's your favorite pastime? And who's your favorite author?"

Kate, whose eyes had gone round, laughed. "Is that all you want to know?"

"Nope, but I figure it's a good place to start," Jay answered playfully.

"Okay, let's see. One—I come from a suburb about twenty-five miles north of where we're sitting right now."

"This is your hometown!"

"Close enough, and I thought I was going to answer all of your questions just the way you asked them—in rapid succession."

Jay covered her mouth. "I'm sorry. But you don't have an accent."

"Thank God." Kate rolled her eyes. "Can I keep going now?"

Afraid to open her mouth again, Jay just nodded.

"Two—I was an American history major with a psychology minor. Three—like most great things in life, it was an accident. Four—"

Jay started to ask exactly what that meant, but her jaw clicked shut at Kate's raised eyebrow.

"Four," Kate continued with a smirk, "I'm an only child. Five—that's a tough one. There are many things I enjoy doing, depending on my mood or the weather or the amount of time I have. Let's see...sitting in front of the fireplace in my library on a snowy night with a great book and Fred by my side. Hiking in the mountains with Fred on a beautiful, clear day. Playing tennis against a quality player.

Exercise. Traveling to explore new places or to visit favorite ones. Sitting quietly by the ocean or a peaceful lake. And six—Charles Dickens and Edith Wharton. Sorry, that one's a toss-up."

Jay was soaking in all of the information. She was amazed at how much they had in common.

"Now you know everything there is to know about me."

"Hardly," Jay blurted without thought. She was fascinated by Kate and doubted that she could ever know enough.

"Your turn." Kate sat up a little straighter and rubbed her hands together. "Only I'm going to ask my questions one at a time and reserve the right to follow up."

Jay rolled her eyes. "Were you a lawyer in your last life or something?"

"Ahem," Kate continued, clearly undeterred. "Where are you from originally? I know you're not from around here."

"What makes you so sure?" Jay's eyes narrowed.

Kate just gave her a look that said, "What, do you think I'm stupid?"

"Okay, okay," Jay relented. "I'm from Phoenix. Scottsdale, really."

"Hmm, I love that part of the country, Sedona in particular, but I've climbed Camelback Mountain in Scottsdale many times and had more than my share of ice cream at the Sugar Bowl."

Jay was surprised that Kate knew the area so well.

"Does your family still live there?"

Jay's shoulders tensed. She did not meet Kate's eyes, although she knew Kate was looking at her. "No. They moved a little further south to Tucson a few years back."

"Do you have any siblings?"

"I had a younger sister, but she was killed in a car crash when I was eight."

"I'm sorry, Jay." Kate reached out and touched the back of her hand.

"It's okay. It happened a very long time ago."

Kate changed the subject. "I know that you wrote for the college newspaper, and that you played lacrosse..."

Jay's head jerked up in surprise. "You do?"

"Yes. Geez, what kind of reporter would I be if I couldn't at least find out the basics?"

Well, she has a point there. Unless you were Jay and you *wanted* to keep someone a mystery. She knew she could have found out

Kate's name in college if she wanted to, but she didn't figure she would ever really get a chance to know her; the mysterious stranger was so far out of her league, and she preferred to use her imagination to fill in her heroine's life story. Now there Jay was, sitting across from Kate, completely entranced and finding the truth far more interesting than anything she imagined. She never would have thought this moment possible.

Kate's voice startled her out of her reverie. "What was your major?"

"Uh, American literature with a minor in political science."

"What did you think you wanted to do with your life?"

Jay didn't hesitate. "I wanted to be an author."

"What kind of books did you want to write and do you write now? Other than magazine articles, I mean."

"I wanted to chronicle the human condition. You know, write the next great American novel." Jay shook her head self-deprecatingly. "And yes, I still write for pleasure from time to time. I haven't had anything published yet, though."

"You will."

It was said with such confidence, Jay wondered how she could know that. The question must have shown in her face, because Kate went on, "I have a really good feeling about that. And besides, I've read all of your articles." She looked down at the table, apparently embarrassed by her admission.

Jay's face turned beet red. "You have? You didn't say anything."

"I didn't want you to think I was some sort of deranged fan or something. Your work is really excellent. I love your writing style, the humanity just shines through."

Jay was at a complete loss. She didn't know what to say and didn't trust her voice just then, anyway. She took a moment to compose herself, then said, "I think that writing is a product of one's own life experience." She surprised herself with the admission. She hadn't meant to reveal that much.

"Jamison is an interesting name. Where did it come from?"

Squirming in her seat, Jay began picking at a napkin and watching the shredding process with seeming fascination. "My father wanted a boy. He got me." When Kate didn't say anything, Jay grudgingly added, "Just one of many disappointments, I guess. We don't keep in touch much."

Kate was shrewd. Jay could see that she wanted to ask more about her parents, but was holding back. Jay was inordinately grateful for the reprieve.

"You know, Jay," Kate started softly, "I really wanted to come and see you after that incident on campus. I was terribly worried about you." She grasped Jay's hand. "But I wasn't sure that seeing me would have been such a great idea for you. I was afraid I would just be a reminder of what happened, and I didn't want to make things worse for you. I hope you never thought I didn't care, because I did. Very much." She let go Jay's hand.

Jay could hear the self-recrimination in her companion's voice and was surprised to look up and see unshed tears in her eyes. Jay bit her lip. "Can we take a walk?" she asked suddenly.

"Sure. We're not far from Central Park. How about if we walk there?" Kate threw some bills on the table and led the way out of the restaurant. Jay waited as Kate told the limo driver that they would be a while and arranged to have him wait for them near the Plaza Hotel where he would pick them up at noon.

The two women walked side by side in silence for several blocks, entered the park, and took the footpath that skirted the reservoir. Jay chewed on a non-existent cuticle and kicked at a few stones on the path. She looked up at the amazing woman walking next to her and thought about Kate's compassion and genuine caring, first on the ski slope and then during the attack on campus. She had been so gentle, yet so protective at the same time. She remembered how Kate covered her body with her sweatshirt and held her hand, never letting it go until she fell asleep in the hospital. And she thought about all the many times after that night when she longed to feel the comfort and safety of Kate's arms around her again to chase away the demons.

There really was no decision to make.

"Um, I'm not really sure where to begin." Jay's voice quivered a little.

"Tell me about your parents," Kate said softly. "Did he hurt you?"

Jay's head snapped up. "I..." She swallowed hard. She wanted to bolt.

Kate must've realized that, because she put a gentle hand on Jay's arm.

"I've never told anyone," Jay faltered, "except for the therapist I saw for a year after the attack on campus. I guess that night brought back a lot of bad memories for me."

They stopped walking, and Kate took Jay's hands in hers. Jay saw nothing but a mixture of fierce protectiveness and heartbreaking compassion in Kate's eyes.

"It's okay, Jay. He can't hurt you now."

At that, Jay began to cry great, gulping sobs. She relented as Kate took her into her arms and held her close until all of her tears were shed. Kate rocked her and rubbed her back and soothed her, seeming to will away all that hurt and misplaced shame.

Jay finally backed away and wiped her eyes. "It started when I was four. When my sister died four years later, I wished it had been me instead." Her voice broke. "I thought she was the lucky one."

"Oh, Jay," Kate whispered, "I'm so glad it wasn't." And Jay knew she meant it. It warmed her to her very core.

"Um, he told me if I told anyone about what he was doing to me, he would kill my mother and the family dog. I...I believed him." Jay looked up at Kate with tears on her lashes, and shrugged. "I look back on it now and I'm pretty sure they were just idle threats, but then, I didn't know that." She took a ragged breath. "He would come into my room in the middle of the night. I would be lying there and I'd see the doorknob turning, and I'd pray to anyone who would listen that it would be my mother checking on me and not him...but it never was."

Kate stroked the backs of Jay's hands in mute comfort.

"He...he would rape me and tell me how lucky I was to have him...that nobody else would ever care about me or want me."

"He was so wrong, Jay. So very, very wrong."

"Thanks. I always wanted to believe that. Anyway, it got so I wouldn't sleep at night because I was terrified of the middle-of-the-night visits. I know my mother knew on some level what was going on, but she just seemed incapable of action. I suppose she did the best she could. Who knows, maybe she had her own issues to deal with.

"So I tried to be invisible, just be the most perfect child, and then maybe no one would notice me and he'd leave me alone." She looked up again into Kate's eyes, which were filled with compassion. "He didn't. No matter what I did or didn't do. I started writing as a way to disappear. As he would be raping my body, my mind would be off somewhere creating the most wonderful stories with happy endings." Her tone turned wistful. "So I guess something good did come of it, finally. I learned to use my imagination and write fiction, because Heaven knows it sure beat the heck out of reality for me.

"Eventually, when I started getting my period, he left me alone." She glanced up, a somewhat chagrined expression on her tear-stained face. "So now you know."

Kate lifted Jay's chin gently with her fingers. "I'm so sorry for what happened to you. None of it was your fault, and it wasn't anything a child could prevent. I know it's hard to accept that, but it's the truth." She looked directly into Jay's eyes.

"You are an extraordinary woman, Jay, full of compassion, wonder, humor, and beauty. And you were an amazingly resourceful little girl who did what she needed to survive and become a lovely, talented, incredibly remarkable woman. I count myself blessed to know you, and I feel so privileged that you trust me enough to share your story. I want you to know that I will always be here for you. Always."

Jay knew somehow that she would.

They started walking again, and Kate kept hold of one of Jay's hands.

As they walked on, Kate decided they needed to lighten the mood. "I've got an idea. Will you humor me?" Her tone turned childishly pleading, but she didn't care. "Puh-lease? Please, please, please?"

"Oh, okay," Jay relented. "Boy, I can just imagine what you were like as a kid."

When Kate began to jog, Jay struggled to keep up. "Where are we going?"

"You'll see," Kate said mysteriously.

After several blocks, Kate pulled Jay out of the park and onto the street. Jay looked up and laughed.

"What?" Kate asked in an innocent tone.

"I might have guessed that you had a carefully hidden juvenile streak in you." Jay shook her head. They were standing on Fifth Avenue at Fifty-Eighth Street in front of FAO Schwarz, the world's largest toy store.

"So," Kate said, practically jumping up and down. "Can we go inside?"

"C'mon, ya goofball." Jay said.

Kate pulled her across the street by the hand.

They spent half an hour romping through the store, trying out the toys, playing with the train sets, jumping from key to key on the gigantic toy piano that took up a good portion of the floor, and generally being kids.

When they were both totally exhausted, Kate called a time-out. "As much as I can't believe I'm going to say this, we've got to go, Jay. The limo will be waiting, and I've got to get you back to your place so that you can get ready for your interview with the governor."

"Spoilsport," Jay joked. She stuck out her tongue.

Kate was glad she was able to help Jay have some fun after their serious conversation. She wished with all her heart that she could give her back the childhood she'd never had. She knew for sure that if she ever saw Jay's father, she would be hard-pressed not to put her hands around his neck.

Kate went off to place a quick phone call. When she returned, she and Jay made their way to the Plaza Hotel and the waiting limo. Jay gave the driver her address in Greenwich Village on Christopher Street.

Kate walked Jay to the door of her apartment.

"Can you come in?" Jay asked.

"I'd love to, but the limo is double-parked and your neighbors might not take too kindly to having their street blocked."

"Yeah." Jay sighed heavily. "I guess you're right."

Kate heard the note of dejection in Jay's voice. She didn't want their time together to end either, so she ventured, "Some other time?"

Jay smiled brightly. "You're on." She leaned forward and, on her tiptoes, gave Kate a sweet kiss on the cheek. "Thanks for everything. You sure know how to show a girl a good time." She stepped back and gazed up shyly into Kate's eyes.

Kate knew she couldn't just walk away this time. She gently pulled Jay to her and maintained eye contact as she inclined her head and softly touched her lips to Jay's. Then she straightened up again, stepped back, and smiled.

"I thought you said there was no kissing on the first date."

"Number one, those were Fred's rules...he's just a teenager, after all." Kate winked. "And number two, I wasn't aware that this counted as an official date. But, if that's the way you feel..."

"Me and my big mouth," Jay mumbled under her breath with an aggrieved expression.

Kate fought hard to keep the smile off her face. She pushed the door open a little wider and took a predatory step forward. Once inside the doorway, she slowly extended her arm and, staring hungrily at Jay's mouth, ran her thumb lightly across Jay's lips. "I happen to think you have a perfect mouth."

Jay swallowed hard. Her lips parted slightly as she leaned into the touch, her teeth just grazing Kate's thumb.

Kate thought she had never seen anything so sexy. She dragged her eyes away from Jay's mouth and up to her eyes, shut the door behind her with her foot, and bent her head in one smooth motion to capture Jay's mouth in a heart-stopping kiss.

Several long, languorous moments later, Kate pulled back slowly and smiled. "I," she began, but had to clear her throat before she could go on. "I hate to kiss and run, but I really do have to get going." The note of regret in her voice was unmistakable.

"Mmm," Jay hummed, her eyes still closed. "Oh." Her eyes flew open. "Yep. Right."

Kate turned to go and grasped the doorknob.

Jay put her hand on Kate's arm and squeezed. "Um, could...could I maybe call you tonight? You know," she went on in a rush, "just to make sure you got home all right?"

"Absolutely." Kate grinned.

When Jay didn't release her arm and began shifting uncomfortably from one foot to the other, Kate looked at her questioningly.

"Um, I don't know how to reach you," she said bashfully.

Kate grabbed a business card and a pen from her pocket and wrote her home number and address on the back in bold strokes. "Now you do," she said, as she handed over the card.

"Okay then, are you sure it's all right? I mean, I don't want to disturb you or anything."

"Jay," Kate laughed, "I've been disturbed for years." She opened the door, stepped into the hallway, and turned around to wink at Jay before she disappeared.

Once alone inside the limo, Kate leaned back into the leather interior and closed her eyes. A goofy grin split her face. "Oh no, Fred isn't getting to kiss you, Jay. You're already taken and I will not suffer the competition lightly."

CHAPTER SEVEN

J ay leaned her back against the apartment door and stared unseeing into her living room. She touched her fingertips to her lips, unable to process the wonder of what just happened, and not willing to trust that it really had. Her head was spinning. In less than forty-eight hours her entire existence was turned upside down. She had gone to Albany grudgingly because the governor could not see her at his New York City office. That one tiny scheduling snafu brought her face to face with a vital piece of her past and, she dared to hope, of her future as well.

From the first day Jay saw her, the mystery woman commanded her attention. For her last two and a half years in school, Jay used Kate as her muse, creating fiction around her dark, confident persona. It was Jay's jealously guarded and somewhat guilty secret. She smiled ironically. Nothing she had conjured or written came close to matching the reality she experienced the past twelve hours in Kate's presence.

Now there she was, standing in her own apartment, having just shared a mind-blowing kiss with the only woman who had the ability to touch her soul and make her fiction come to life. Jay was afraid she would awaken any second and find that it was all a dream. She fingered the business card Kate gave her just to be sure it wasn't.

For years she believed that the tall, dark stranger who owned her heart would never know it. Jay resolved to pour her energies into her work, making allowances for friendships and nothing more. She couldn't pretend to feelings for someone else when she knew the feelings belonged only to the statuesque, blue-eyed woman she barely knew. She laughed at herself more than once, noting it was like living some sort of Greek tragedy. But she could no more change her heart than she could change the color of her eyes.

Now...now. She sighed. If she ever doubted what she knew in her soul, the past day had crystallized her feelings with remarkable clarity. *Well, Jamison, you've always believed that things happen for a reason. There's a reason circumstances brought you to Albany and a reason you turned on the television when you did. This may be your one chance. Don't let it pass you by.*

Now that she'd made the decision, Jay felt more settled and alive than she had in quite some time. She nodded to herself and moved to her bedroom to change clothes for her interview with the governor.

At exactly 2:30 p.m., Jay was escorted into the governor's office high up in the World Trade Center. The governor stepped from behind his desk and greeted her amiably. "Ms. Parker, it's a pleasure to meet you. I've read some of your work. It's quite good."

"Thank you, Governor Hyland. Coming from you, that's high praise indeed." Jay smiled easily.

Hyland was a good-looking man—six feet two inches tall, with strawberry blonde hair and freckles underlining his Irish heritage. At forty-eight years of age, he was in excellent physical shape and enjoyed playing weekly basketball games with his state police protectors and reporters. In the summer, he pitched for an executive branch softball team. During her research prior to the interview, Jay discovered that the governor was as competitive on a field of play as he was in the political arena—stories about his will to win were legendary.

He motioned her to a pair of wing chairs across the room. She noted that he did not seem to have suffered any injuries in the explosion. Had it only been the day before? Jay marveled at how time seemed to lose its relevance in Kate's presence. Then, just as quickly, she admonished herself for letting her mind wander when she needed to focus on what she was doing.

She fixed the governor with a concerned look. "Are you all right after what happened yesterday? You weren't injured?"

"No. Fortunately, I was able to escape without a scratch. I wasn't in the building when the second explosion occurred."

Jay leaned forward a bit in her chair. "Your wife must have been so worried."

"Oh, yes. You can bet I got an earful. She heard the first explosion from the mansion several blocks away and immediately called the front gate to find out what it was. It was all her security detail could do to keep her from coming over to the capitol. I had to go home just to prove to her that I was fine, she wouldn't believe anyone else." He shook his head.

"It must be hard, knowing that danger always exists for you. Do you think about it often?"

"No, but my wife certainly does."

"I can understand that," Jay agreed. "Does her concern change anything that you do or any decisions you make?"

"I try to be considerate and sensitive to her fears, but the truth of the matter is that I have a job to do, and I must do it without reservation. The people are counting on me."

"I bet your wife wasn't too happy about you coming to the office today."

"Oh, you're right about that. She threw a fit. In the end, though, the governor of the great state of New York can't appear to be cowed by an act of violence. To stay away today and do anything less than carry on the full duties of the office would have sent the message that terror works. And it would have been disrespectful to those individuals who lost their lives so tragically yesterday. Their deaths will not have been in vain. The good works of this administration will continue, even in the face of acts of cowardice."

"It is obvious, Governor Hyland, that you are a man of deep principles. In that sense this must be a very difficult time for you. I know that the legislature has been debating state funding for family planning services and abortions. I also imagine that yesterday's attack will ratchet up the talk that has been rather loud lately about reinstating the death penalty in New York. I have heard you say on many occasions that, as a deeply religious man, you are morally opposed to both abortion and to capital punishment. And yet, you have gone on record as supporting public funding for abortion, and you have said you would sign a capital punishment bill if one were put before you. It must be incredibly tough to reconcile your personal feelings and principles with your professional judgment. I can't imagine having to make those types of choices. Does that ever bother you? Does it make you worry that you might have to abandon your faith to fulfill your role as governor? Has it ever made you sorry you chose politics as a career?"

"I think, Ms. Parker, that there are moments in every politician's career when he or she wonders if this is the right path. The sacrifice can be enormous, as you have gleaned. And yes, there are times when the types of decisions you referred to keep me up at night. But the rewards far outweigh the price I have had to pay, or may yet have to pay. The amazing opportunity to improve the lives of so many is a great comfort. The professional judgments I make, if you will, are arrived at with the conviction that, when it is time for me to be judged, my steadfast desire to help humanity will count heavily in my favor and my individual actions will be weighed accordingly."

"Governor, I know that you are both a student and a scholar of the history of the presidency. It is a topic that has always fascinated me." Jay smiled at him and wrinkled her nose slightly. "I'd be a fool to pass up an opportunity to learn a little something here."

"If I can enlighten you in some way, Ms. Parker, it would be my pleasure."

"I had a history professor once who included as a final exam essay topic the thesis that, at least in the twentieth century, governors tend to make better presidents than those who have never served in that position. He claimed that history had borne him out and he cited as an example Franklin Roosevelt."

"Ooh, that must have been some tough final. How did you answer the question, Ms. Parker and how much time did you have to do it in?"

With an embarrassed shrug Jay answered, "I respectfully disagreed with the hypothesis, citing a list of governors turned presidents who I thought were less than stellar in the higher office and an equal number of non-governors who I thought had done excellent jobs as president. I backed up each choice with facts and events. And I did it in ten pages in twenty minutes." She looked across at him with something akin to defiance.

"Hmm. Sounds like you're still carrying some bitterness at the end result. What was your grade on the essay?"

"I got a B minus. It was the only time in that class that I'd gotten anything below an A. It wrecked my average."

The governor laughed. "I bet you were steamed."

"Yep, I sure was," Jay agreed. "So, do you think he was right?"

"Well, in theory he should have been, but in practice I tend to agree with you..."

"I knew it."

For the next half hour the governor of New York, a man thought by many to be a likely presidential candidate, explained at length why governors should be better presidents, but weren't always. It was great stuff. Jay knew that she got what she came for—the human being behind the politician, a deep thinker and philosopher with a pragmatic streak and a keen sense of history.

At 4:00 p.m. the governor's secretary buzzed him to tell him he would be late for his next appointment if he didn't get going. He appeared to be disappointed that the interview was at an end.

For her part, Jay couldn't believe that an hour and a half had passed. She thanked him for his time and started to excuse herself.

Governor Hyland said, "Ms. Parker, my wife and I would love it if you would join us as our guest for the Legislative Correspondents' Association Show in Albany. Have you ever been to one?"

"No," Jay answered, caught off guard by the invitation.

"Well, that settles it then. No individual's life is complete without the experience." There was a smile in his voice. "I'll have my secretary give you the details. My wife will be so pleased to meet you."

"Thank you, sir," Jay said. "I look forward to meeting Mrs. Hyland as well."

With that, the secretary ushered her out the door.

Kate checked her watch for the millionth time. She arrived home from the airport with just enough time to give Fred a good scratch, shower and change her clothes before heading to the station. Since arriving, she had been checking facts, following up on leads, and writing copy for the six o'clock broadcast. And thinking about Jay. That brought an unconscious smile to her face and her eyes back to her watch one more time. *Yep, right about now,* she thought. Then she sighed as yet another street reporter passed by her desk and pretended to be so engrossed in the piece of paper in front of him that he didn't even notice her.

Fame, however fleeting, was a funny thing. The station management, the photographers, and the producers all went out of their way to congratulate Kate on her performance on the "big three" that morning. Her co-anchor and the reporters who aspired to sit in her chair someday avoided her like the plague. Their jealousy was so obvious she was surprised they hadn't literally turned green. She just shook her head. She had done what she had to do, not in some quest for glory, but because it was her job, and it was the right thing to do. She didn't care what they thought, she had work to tend to, and a little less than an hour before she had to be on set.

❧

Jay opened the door to her apartment at 4:45 p.m. and smiled with relief. She loved her apartment. The location was great—in the heart of Greenwich Village in a beautifully restored brownstone with easy access to the subway. The space was somewhat cramped, but the cost of living in New York City was obscene and this was the best she could afford. Still, she had done wonders with the place, and she thought it was both comfortable and quaint.

Her bedroom was in a loft overlooking the living room, which, like the rest of the rooms, showcased Mission-style furniture. Off the living room underneath the loft was her office, and a bathroom, and to the right was a small dining area and a reasonably sized kitchen. Racks with well-worn pots and pans and wine and champagne glasses hung from the kitchen ceiling. The floors throughout were hardwood, and one wall of the living room featured floor-to-ceiling windows that looked out over a small park.

Jay changed into her comfortable clothes, then went into her office to work. She sat down with the intention of organizing her notes and revisiting background interviews she did with some of the governor's close associates and personal friends. Her mind kept straying, though, and her stomach was tied in knots. Telling Kate about her childhood triggered the fear that something terrible would happen now that she exploded the secret, just as her father had said it would so many times, so long ago.

At exactly five o'clock, someone buzzed Jay from the lobby. Not expecting anyone, she frowned. She pressed the intercom button and asked who it was—a delivery for her. Hmm. Jay was no New Yorker by nature, but she was cautious.

"Where is the package from?"

"I was told not to ruin the surprise, miss."

"Well, I have no intention of accepting an unidentified package that I was not expecting. So either you tell me where the package is from or who sent it, or you can just turn right around and take it back with you."

"Um, I was told that if you gave me a hard time, I was to tell you that it was from a close personal friend of Fred's?" The question at the end of his statement underscored that he didn't get it either.

"From Fred's friend, huh?" Jay smiled. "Okay, bring it up."

❧

Jay waited at the door to her apartment. Whereas she was wary at first, now she was just flat-out curious and excited. What could it be? When she caught sight of the package (she couldn't see the delivery boy behind it except for his legs), her eyes went wide as saucers. *What the...?* She accepted delivery and slid the huge box into her living room. It was bulky, but surprisingly light. There were no markings to indicate where it came from, or who sent it, though the hint the delivery boy gave her clarified that matter.

Jay grabbed a pair of scissors from her desk drawer and cut the tape binding on the box. Her stomach fluttered happily in anticipation, and her first reaction was to laugh after she pulled the top flaps back. Then her face took on a wistful expression. "Aww. That's just too cute for words, Ms. Tough Anchorwoman."

In the box was a massive cuddly teddy bear. Jay lifted it out of the box and stroked its soft fur; he had such a cute face and a little potbelly that protruded over his plaid shorts. Then she noticed that he had a card pinned to his adorable little vest. It was the same bold, flowing handwriting from the business card Kate gave her earlier in the day.

The card read, *"Jay, this guy looks as though he's got a lot of hugs to give, which is exactly what you deserve. Since I couldn't be there in person, I thought he made a pretty good substitute. Thank you again for the gift of your trust. You are a beautiful person and I enjoyed every minute we spent together. I hope we'll have many more. By the way, his name is Theodore E. Bear. Your friend, Kate."*

Jay wiped at the tears that leaked out of her eyes. It was as if, from a hundred fifty miles away, Kate saw inside her, answered her doubts and calmed her fears. In her entire life, no one had ever been so solicitous or so attuned to her emotions and thoughts. She knew intellectually that Kate could not have known how rattled she was feeling just then, but it felt as though she had.

Jay closed her eyes and nuzzled against his face. She hugged the stuffed animal to her, and her eyes popped wide open. She pulled back a fraction and sniffed at his fur, grinning delightedly. "Oh, Katherine, were you testing him out? You just got caught." Jay took another whiff of the traces of Shalimar that clung to her new companion, and she knew she would be giving Kate a hard time about it later. But for right now, she just wanted to enjoy Ted E. Bear's company and the delicious scent that had been bringing her such comfort for so many years. She decided that a nap was definitely in order and, carrying her buddy, she trundled off to the loft.

CHAPTER EIGHT

K ate was so tired she wasn't sure she could even make it up the stairs. Not counting the brief nap in the limousine and the even shorter shuteye she had when she and Jay came back to the house to shower, she had been up for nearly forty-eight hours straight. Phil practically had to prop her up to do the eleven o'clock newscast.

To be sure, it had been a long day but, she mused, there were some good points. Immediately, Jay's face loomed in her mind's eye, her smile like the sunshine on a brilliantly clear day. Kate wondered for the umpteenth time what Jay was doing right then, if she enjoyed her surprise, and if she was dead tired too.

As if she willed it to happen, the phone rang just as she reached her bedroom. Already knowing who it would be, Kate grinned broadly, flopped gracelessly onto the bed, and picked up the receiver. "Fred's Pizza Palace."

There was a second's hesitation on the line, and then a melodious laugh. "Yes, I'd like a thick crust with all the fixins. Oh, but could you hold the anchovies, the olives, the green peppers—they give me gas—the sausage, the meatballs, the onions, the mushrooms, the tomatoes, and the artichokes?"

"So, let's see, then. You want a plain cheese pizza with sauce, right?"

"You got it."

"Well, Fred could probably make that."

"I'm willing to bet that you can't."

"Hey, I resemble that remark!"

"Hi, Kate. How are you? Did you get home all right? How was your flight? Did you get a hero's welcome? How was the rest of your day?"

"I'm tired, but fine. Yes. Fine. Yes and no. Long."

"Ugh. I've got to learn to start asking you one question at a time."

"Uh-huh." Kate's amusement at Jay's mock frustration was obvious.

"You won't believe what happened to me today a few hours after you left. A mysterious package arrived, no identifying marks, no labels, no return address, no nothing. I try to be very careful about my safety...after all, this is New York City. The delivery guy tried to give me some cock and bull story about the sender not wanting the surprise to be ruined so he wouldn't tell me where the package came from," she scoffed.

Kate was dead silent for a few seconds. "Gee, how odd. Um, so, what did you do?" There was a note of panic in her voice although she tried for reserved nonchalance.

"Well, what do you think I did? I turned the guy away, made him take it back. What idiot would accept a big, unmarked box like that without knowing where it came from? Especially if she wasn't expecting anything. Can you imagine?"

Kate had a sinking feeling in the pit of her stomach. "Yeah, what idiot, indeed."

Jay laughed. "Hah. Gotcha good that time, girl! I love my Ted E. Bear. He's so cute and cuddly. In fact, we took a nap together this afternoon."

Kate felt an unexpected surge of jealousy. *Of a teddy bear, what is that, Katherine?* "You rat."

"Hey, I just want you to know that I can give as good as I get."

"Evidently." Kate had to smile at being taken in. Jay was pretty convincing.

"Seriously, I do love him and that was amazingly sweet of you. When did you do that? I was with you the whole time."

Kate thought about her trip upstairs to use the phone in FAO Schwarz. She saw the bear sitting in a huge rocking chair on her way to the back of the store. She was thinking about everything Jay had been through and how courageous she was, and how hard it must have been for her to tell Kate about it. She couldn't imagine what that felt like, and she knew she wanted to do something to comfort Jay. She hefted the bear experimentally, first checking to make sure she was quite alone. Then she hugged it to her chest and rubbed her cheek against his face. Yes, he would do quite nicely. She went to the store clerk nearby and explained what she wanted done. He looked at her strangely, but when she pulled an extra fifty-dollar bill out of her wallet, he gladly went along with her wishes.

"Jay?"

"Yes?"

"Let's just say I have many skills." She laughed.

"Um, there is one thing I don't understand about him, though," Jay said.

"What's that?"

"How come he smells like you, Ms. Tough Anchorwoman?"

Uh-oh. Kate knew she was busted. *She knows what I smell like?* She spluttered and hemmed and hawed, trying to come up with a plausible explanation. After a few seconds, she knew she had been caught. "Well, I couldn't very well entrust just anyone with such an important job, you know, I had to make sure he was up to the task. There was only one way to do that." She said it with as much dignity as she could muster under the circumstances.

"Careful, something like that will kill your image."

Suddenly serious, Kate said, "It will have been well worth it if it did. I'm so proud of you, Jay, for everything you've accomplished and the person you are. You're very special and words can't express how much it means to me that you shared such a vital part of yourself with me. I really do wish I could be the one there hugging you, but since I can't, I tried for the next best thing. I hope I succeeded."

The line was quiet for so long Kate wondered if Jay still was there.

"I'm so glad you're the one I shared it with, Kate." Jay's voice was choked with emotion. "No one has ever made me feel as safe or as understood as you do. I can't tell you what that means to me. And your gift came at just the right moment. I was just starting to freak out that now that I've exploded the secret, all my father's dire warnings about terrible things happening would come true. Ted E. and your note chased the demons away. Thank you from the bottom of my heart."

Kate's chest ached at the thought of Jay being alone in her apartment and afraid. "Nothing bad will happen, Jay, I promise you, especially since you're choosing not to carry the burden alone any longer. Your father told you those things to scare you into silence. When you're a helpless child, it's easy to believe such lies. But you're not that kid anymore, Jay, and he doesn't have that kind of power."

"You're right."

"Any time you need to talk or be comforted, or just not to be alone, I'll be there for you, Jay." More quietly, Kate added, "If you want me to be, that is."

"I'd love that."

"Are you going to be all right to sleep?"

"I will be now. And besides, I've got a big old teddy bear to keep me company."

"If you have any trouble, it doesn't matter what time it is, call me. I mean it, Jay."

"Thanks. Hey, it's Friday, well, actually, Saturday now that I look at the time. What are you doing for the weekend?"

Kate sighed. "I have a lot of leads to track down on the bombing story. It's sort of my baby now, and the news doesn't take the weekend off, as you know. So, while I won't have to anchor this weekend, I'm going to be putting together some new material that I can get through some of my contacts. I'm going to be pretty much flat out. What about you?"

"I have to have my story on my editor's desk by ten a.m. Monday, so I'll be spending my weekend writing. Aren't we just a couple of live wires?"

"Sounds like it. Can I call you tomorrow to see how you're doing, or will that disturb you?" Kate asked hesitantly.

"To quote a very dear friend of mine, 'I've been disturbed for years.'"

"Touché."

"I'd love it if you'd call, Kate."

"In that case, I'll need your number."

On Monday morning Jay caught the subway uptown to turn in her story. She worked throughout the weekend, taking breaks only to eat, go running, and talk to Kate. The very thought brought an unconscious smile to her face. True to her word, Kate called Saturday afternoon.

Jay was in her office, engrossed in some interesting personal stories about the governor she had collected from her interviews of his longtime friends. She was contemplating how many, if any, of the anecdotes to include in her piece when the phone rang, startling her.

"Hello?"

"Hey there, I'm looking for the next great American novelist."

Jay chuckled. "Sorry, you must have the wrong number."

"Oh, do you mean to say that Jamison Parker doesn't live there? You know, beautiful blonde, about five four with golden hair and eyes the color of the Caribbean?"

Jay blushed. *She thinks I'm beautiful?* "I don't recognize anyone by that description."

"Hi, Jay, how did you sleep?"

"Ted E. kept me great company, and I slept very well as a result, thank you."

"I'm glad." The warmth in Kate's voice soothed Jay.

"How about you? Did you catch up on some sleep?"

"I don't think you can ever recapture lost shuteye, but I logged in a good nine hours, and I feel much better for it. How's the story coming?"

"Pretty well, I think. I'm just trying to balance the man with the governor at the moment to make sure that the readers are left with a good, well-rounded sense of who he is."

"I have every confidence in you."

"Anything new on the bombing?"

"Unfortunately, just more victims dying, an ongoing search for survivors and bodies, and loved ones looking for those who are still unaccounted for. So far there's nothing more on who might have been responsible. The whole town is pretty subdued. Government is the big industry in this area, and almost everybody knew someone who was in the building at the time of the explosions."

"Doesn't sound like an uplifting way to spend a Saturday."

"It's not, but it's my job. Well, I didn't want to bug you, I just wanted to...um...let you know I was thinking about you and say hi."

"Thanks, Kate. I was thinking about you too." Jay hesitated, and then plowed ahead, "Same bat time, same bat channel tomorrow?"

"Don't tell me you were a Batman fan!"

"Yeah," she admitted sheepishly.

Kate laughed. "I loved the costumes for Batgirl and the Catwoman."

"You letch!"

"Oh, and you didn't?"

"I didn't say that, now did I?"

The Sunday conversation was equally easy, light and comfortable. Jay told Kate things about herself and Kate shared her life too. Jay found out Kate was partial to Wonder Woman, Aquaman, Captain America, and the Flash and Jay shared her affinity for the Green

Lantern. It felt great to get to know Kate better and Kate seemed to be enjoying her company too. The laughter and teasing were a good distraction.

Jay smiled as she recalled Kate's uncertain parting words. *Would it be all right if I called you tomorrow sometime?*

"I'd love that. I have to go into the office in the morning to file my story and I'll probably be there until late afternoon."

"I get a dinner break around six forty-five p.m. How about then?"

"Perfect."

"Until then, Jay. I'll see you around."

"Yeah, see you around."

The screeching of the subway wheels on the tracks brought Jay out of her reverie. She rushed up the steps and into the Manhattan morning with countless other commuters on their way to work. Trish was already there and on the phone when she arrived at the office, so she opened her briefcase, pulled out the sheaf of papers, and dropped them in the middle of Trish's cluttered desk. Trish rolled her eyes and indicated that she was going to be a while on the phone. Jay motioned back that she was going to her desk so Trish could find her there when she was ready.

❦

"Did I tell you, or did I tell you?"

"You told me." *Time's* managing news editor handed Jay's story back to Trish.

"And I was right, wasn't I?"

"Yes, Patricia, you were right. Parker certainly captured the essence of the man. It is a compelling piece."

"Ha! So you admit that just because she's young, doesn't mean she's green."

"Only three years on staff makes her green by definition, but you're right that she got a unique take from a guy who's been interviewed hundreds of times."

"She's a great writer."

"I'm not arguing with you, Patricia. Now get the hell out of here."

Trish couldn't wait to tell Jay.

"Hey, kiddo."

"Hi, Trish. Something I can do for you?"

"More like something I can do for you."

Jay's eyebrows shot up. "Come on, Trish, you're killing me here. What did you think? Was it okay?"

"Nope, it wasn't okay."

"It wasn't?" Clearly crestfallen, Jay spoke so softly Trish barely heard her.

"Nope. It wasn't okay. It was the best damn cover story I've had come across my desk in ages, and believe me, girlfriend, that's saying something." Trish grinned for all she was worth.

Jay's head shot up and she stared at Trish as if she'd sprouted wings. "Really?" Her face lit up like fireworks on the Fourth of July.

"Really," Trish nodded. "In fact, it was so good, I took it directly to Herb."

"You took my story to the managing news editor? Before you came back to me with suggested changes?" Jay's voice rose with each word. "B-b-but. Are you crazy?"

"Well," Trish scratched her ear, "lots of people tell me so. But I know a great piece when I see it." She regarded the young writer seriously. "Jamison Parker, that was fantastic work—truly first rate. In fact, it was so great that I want you to do a follow-up story for next week's issue. It may be a cover again, we'll have to wait and see what else develops during the week."

"You...you do?"

Trish nodded at Jay with pride as a thought occurred to her. "By the way, you owe me a story, as I recall. Where in the hell were you when I was trying to find you all over that measly little town up there?"

"Oh, that. Well, it's a long story."

Trish parked herself on the corner of Jay's desk, intrigued at the blush that crept up her neck. She folded her arms across her chest. "That's okay. I've got a few minutes."

Seeing that she wasn't going to get out of it that easily, Jay decided to give Trish the short, very tightly edited version. She could feel the heat in her face, and she wasn't ready just yet to share too much about Kate and their friendship with anyone. "When I got into my hotel room, I turned on the television. The news was on and the anchorwoman turned out to be a fellow alumna. I recognized her immediately, although I hadn't seen her in five years. She hadn't changed a bit." Jay worked hard to school her face not to break into a grin at that. "When the explosion happened, I was getting out of the shower, and I had the television tuned to the news. I saw that she was down at the scene, so I decided to track her down."

It was quiet for a few seconds. "That's it?" Trish's voice was a shrill shriek. "You saw some broad you knew in college and you walked into the middle of bedlam to say hello? Have you lost your mind, girl?"

Jay glanced up sheepishly. "Well, yeah, I figured if I didn't track her down then, I wouldn't be able to find her." Silently Jay was praying that Trish wouldn't think too hard and realize that there was only one reporter at the scene, and it was Kate.

Trish shrugged. Kids these days. "Speaking of the bombing and reporters, that's sort of what your next assignment is."

Jay looked at her editor expectantly.

"There was one reporter that captured the world's attention in this whole thing. She was local, but she's got big time written all over her. Her name is Katherine Kyle. Did you happen to catch any of her coverage?"

Trish didn't wait for an answer. She was looking at her notes, which was a good thing, since Jay practically passed out at the mention of Kate's name.

Trish continued, "We want a full spread on this chick. The angle is something like 'The New Breed of Journalist' or something similar. I think you can find her at WCAP-TV in Albany. She's a news anchor there. You can look up the number." Finally, Trish looked up at Jay. "Can you handle it, kid? 'Cause you're going to have to get started right away, like yesterday, even."

Jay paused before opening her mouth. She wasn't all that sure she was capable of speech at the moment. They wanted her to do a story on Kate? Maybe even a cover story? What she said was, "Of course, Trish, I'll get right on it. I think I know what you're looking for. I might want to shadow her for a few days, you know, see how she works, what impact this story has had on her, talk to her colleagues."

"Right, kiddo, sounds like just the ticket. We don't need too much of the personal stuff here. Probably won't have room for it. Focus on the career and the professional approach she takes to her work, her philosophy, you know."

"Yep. In fact, you're right, there's no time to waste. I'll try to get up there this evening if I can, start following her right away. Let me guess, you want it on your desk at ten next Monday morning, right?"

Trish just smiled as she walked away and winked at Jay over her shoulder.

As soon as she was out of sight, Jay looked around to make sure that she was alone. Assured that she was, she let out a little whoop and did a happy dance in her chair. This was too good to be true.

She noted that it was one o'clock. Kate wouldn't have left for the office yet. Jay took the much-thumbed business card from her wallet and dialed Kate's home number. The phone was picked up on the second ring.

"Hello."

Jay thought she sounded a little distracted. "Hi. Is this a bad time?"

"No, it's never a bad time for you, Jay. Are you okay? Is something wrong?" They weren't supposed to talk until later in the day, and Kate was the one who was supposed to make the call.

"No, no," Jay hastened to assure Kate. "Everything's fine. In fact, I think it's pretty great right now."

"Oh yeah? Why's that?"

"Well, for one thing, the editor and the managing news editor loved my story. Trish said it was the best piece she's seen in ages!"

"That's terrific, Jay, I told you your stuff was awesome. I'm glad to see that others have good taste as well." The note of pride and happiness was clear even over the phone. "Really, that's great news. We'll have to celebrate sometime. I'll buy you dinner."

Jay hesitated, suddenly unsure of herself. "Well, now that you mention it, there is a part two to this news."

"Hmm, what's that?" Kate sounded distracted again.

"Kate, are you sure this isn't a bad time?"

"Huh? Oh, no. It's just that I was on the floor wrestling around with Fred and I lost an earring. I'm on my hands and knees just trying to find it before he swallows it or I step on it."

Picturing the scene, Jay took a deep breath and plowed ahead. "They want me to do a related story for next week. It may be another cover… they're not sure yet."

"That's great."

"Yeah, I think so too. Especially since you're the subject of the story." There was a loud thump on the other end of the phone. "Kate, are you all right? Kate?"

"Oh yeah, I'm fine, just lost my balance for a second there…must have been the way I was kneeling." She paused for a moment. "Let me make sure I understand you correctly. Your bosses, the editors of

Time magazine, want you to write a story about me. Does that about sum it up?"

"Yep."

"You're not making this up to get one over on me, are you?"

Jay was charmed by Kate's befuddlement. "Nope."

"Are you going to give me more than one-word answers?"

Jay smiled mischievously. "You never do."

"That's different... Jamison, please tell me more details," Kate said in her most contrite voice.

"That's better." Jay gloated at the small victory and explained what she wanted to do. "So, I can be there in a few hours, get myself settled in the hotel, and then come over to the station."

"What?" Kate practically screamed into the receiver. "There's no way you're coming to my town and staying in a hotel. You can stay with Fred and me... In the guestroom," she added. "We have plenty of space, as you know, and it would be much easier for you to study your subject."

"I don't want to impose, Kate."

"It's no imposition at all, and I won't hear another word about it. How about if you catch the three fifteen p.m. Amtrak and I'll pick you up at the train station on my dinner break? The timing should be just about right and we can get a bite to eat, then I'll take you back to the station with me."

Jay didn't want to say no, so she didn't.

CHAPTER NINE

P hil beckoned to Kate as soon as she arrived at the station. "Hey. How are you feeling?" The producer was almost never serious, so his tone took her by surprise.

"I'm all right, Phil. You know me, tough as they come, a few cuts and stitches aren't going to stop me."

"Yeah, I know. But I have a right to worry too, okay?"

"There's nothing to worry about, friend."

"Good, 'cause the next few days aren't going to be easy."

"Why don't I like the sound of that?"

"The brass wants you to put together a one-hour special, 'Crisis at the Capitol.' They want you to talk to the families who lost loved ones, and people who were in the building at the time. They want it to be a gritty, moving piece. And they want it to air on Thursday." At the last, he couldn't even look her in the eye.

She let out a slow breath. "Geez, they don't ask for much, do they?" she asked rhetorically. Her wheels were already spinning. "I get to name my crew, including the cameraman, the editor, and the producer."

"Absolutely."

"Am I expected to anchor at the same time? I can't put together a quality program and do my regular job properly."

"They want you to stay visible, Kate. Heck, you're the hottest thing since Miss America lost her crown for posing for explicit lesbian photos!"

Kate glanced sharply at Phil, who, in his oblivion, was busy reviewing that night's storyboard. *Nah, he couldn't know.* It wasn't that Kate wasn't comfortable with who she was. It was more that being a woman in her business was difficult enough—as recognizable as she was, being an out lesbian simply was out of the question. She would have been fired in a heartbeat and blacklisted in the industry. That was one of the reasons she was so careful about whom she slept with. That and the fact that she couldn't find anyone who could keep her interest or capture her heart.

In college, she and Jen became lovers when they both served on the ski patrol. It was a mutually satisfying arrangement—good sex, and someone to have some fun with. But that all changed the night Jay was attacked. The arrangement with Jen simply lost all its appeal, but at the time, Kate didn't make the connection.

In the years since, Kate tried hard not to examine too closely why she kept tabs on Jay and why, whenever she heard something about Jay or read one of her articles, it made her stomach flip and brought a smile to her lips.

Well, there was no denying what Kate felt this time around. She knew it the second she looked up from that bench to see Jay standing in front of her. She was glad to be seated, because the jolt in her guts would have been enough to bring her to her knees. No one else had ever come close to making her feel that way before. It was terrifying and exciting at the same time, and Kate had no intention of running away.

Kate reluctantly returned her thoughts to the present. "Fine, Phil. Then at the very least I want to name the copywriter for the nightly news so that I don't end up looking like an idiot on the air."

"Done."

"Oh, and buddy"—Kate towered over him as he sat behind his cluttered desk—"I think you should know that *Time* magazine is doing a feature on me for next week's issue, sort of a 'New Breed of Journalist' type of thing. There's going to be some backlash, I'm sure, but I expect you to see to it that the writer who will be putting the piece together is given full access to anything she wants and is treated like royalty. Right?"

"Anything you want, Kate."

"Good." She walked away to begin planning the special.

Kate was surprised to find her desk papered with phone messages from family members of people lost in the blast and from people who had been in the building who wanted to talk to her.

As she returned the first few calls, the pattern became clear to her—the media were crawling all over these poor folks like vultures, leaving them feeling overwhelmed. They had seen Kate's coverage, had watched her run back into the ruins to help the injured. They wanted to talk only to her—the rest of the media be damned. Kate made appointments to visit one of the victims and one of the families that night, and more the next day. By the four o'clock story meeting, she had returned every phone call and made arrangements to see all of them. Those interviews would form the backbone of her special. The six o'clock newscast was a blur, as Kate had too many things swirling around in her mind. Although her performance was flawless, she hardly remembered a single story. As soon as the red light went out, Kate bolted from her chair and hustled down the corridor from the set to the newsroom, grabbed the keys off her desk, and flew out the door.

She made her way to the inbound platform just as the train from Grand Central Station pulled in, and she watched anxiously until she saw the familiar blonde head pop out of the business-class car. With three strides and without thought, she met Jay as her feet hit the platform, caught her up, and spun her around.

Jay's face turned beet red. She pulled back a little in the circle of Kate's arms. "Yikes, how am I supposed to stay professionally detached with a hello like that!"

There was a note of teasing in Jay's voice, but Kate also detected genuine concern. She dropped her arms to her sides and quickly took a step back, giving Jay some space. The rebuke stung a little, even as gentle as it was, but Kate understood what Jay was telling her—this was business.

"Of course. I'm sorry, Jay, I guess I got carried away."

"No, Kate. That was the best greeting I've ever gotten. I'm thrilled. I'm the one who should be sorry."

"Forget it." Kate shrugged. "I hope you're hungry, because I've got a great place picked out for dinner." Kate made sure to keep about three feet of distance between her and Jay.

"Sweetie, I'm always hungry," Jay said with a laugh.

Dinner was at Sam's, an out-of-the-way Italian restaurant on the outskirts of the city. The food was fabulous and Jay loved that everyone catered to Kate as if she were royalty. The chef came out to make sure that their meals were satisfactory, the owner came over to make sure the service was good, and the bartender, who obviously knew Kate was still working, sent over free sodas.

Jay kidded Kate gently about the special treatment, and Kate blushed an appealing shade of pink and mumbled something about this being one of her favorite restaurants.

81

From dinner, Kate drove them back to WCAP, where Gene and Phil were waiting with a station car. She made the introductions, explaining teasingly to Jay that she'd been given her pick of a crew, and motley as they were, this was it. Jay thought she might recognize the cameraman as the man Kate had hugged at the scene of the explosion that night, and she knew the name Phil from Kate's phone conversations with him. If Kate hand-selected them, she must have thought very highly of their work. Jay made a note to herself to get each of them aside and talk to them about Kate.

※

Kate did not miss the appreciative looks both Gene and Phil gave Jay when they thought no one was paying attention. While she admired their taste, she was surprised to find herself feeling both protective and a bit jealous. But this was no time for that. This was business, after all.

She already had filled Jay in on the parameters of her assignment and how she spent her afternoon. Jay asked if it would be okay to come along on the interviews. Kate agreed, as long as the families were comfortable with the arrangement.

The first visit was to a man who had a broken leg and burns to his hands and arms. Kate remembered him as one of the unfortunate folks who was trapped on the first floor under the rubble of the second blast. She had helped to free his leg. As soon as she walked into the room, his face lit up with a smile. Kate made Jay and the crew wait outside for a minute to make sure that he was okay with being taped and with Jay's presence. When he enthusiastically agreed, Kate motioned the three into the room.

While Gene set the camera up, the injured man gestured to Jay to approach the bed. In a conspiratorial stage whisper he told her, "Katherine saved my life, you know. She was amazing. I've never seen a woman that strong. She moved that hunk of marble like it was made of Styrofoam. I've thanked God for her every day since." His voice choked with emotion and tears leaked out of the corners of his eyes. "She's an angel."

Jay smiled at the man gently and patted his shoulder.

The interview didn't take very long. Kate managed to get her subject to take her through his actions up until the point of the explosion and his thoughts once he knew what had happened. It was poignant and emotional, and powerful—just what she was looking for.

The group thanked the injured man, and Kate lingered behind at his request for a more personal goodbye. His eyes moist, he hugged her and said, "I don't know what to say to you except you are the strongest, most courageous person I have ever met. I wouldn't be alive today if it weren't for you walking right into the face of danger like you did. You'll always be my angel, Katherine, always. And I'll keep you in my prayers. Thank you."

Kate leaned over and gave the man a hug. "I didn't do anything anyone else wouldn't have done in my place, but you're welcome. You just get well now, okay?" She winked at him on her way out the door.

When they gathered outside in the parking lot, Phil looked at his watch and then at Kate questioningly. It was nine o'clock. It was up to her how close she was willing to cut it to get back to the station and get ready for the eleven o'clock broadcast. She told him they could fit in one more interview.

Ten minutes later they were standing outside a tidy little home in a quaint residential section of the city. While the others hung back, Kate knocked on the door. She introduced herself, explained who was with her and asked if they might come in. The woman of the house ushered them all into a neat but well-used living room. She sat with her husband on the couch and motioned Kate and the others to be seated.

As soon Gene had the camera rolling, the couple began to cry. The man wiped his eyes after a few moments, looked up at Phil and Gene, and finally settled his gaze on Jay.

"You'll have to forgive my wife and me, you see, our Joey just died this morning. He was only eight years old."

There was a stunned silence in the room. Kate motioned to the cameraman to turn the camera off. She crossed the room and knelt before both of the grieving parents. There were tears in her eyes.

"I didn't know, I'm so sorry. He seemed so strong. I want you to know that he was very brave in there. He didn't cry at all, and even smiled. He told me how much he was looking forward to going to a baseball game with you. I don't know what to say."

"Ms. Kyle, we wanted to thank you from the bottom of our hearts."

They each held of one of Kate's hands, but it was the wife who spoke this time. "Joey was so excited that he got a chance to meet you, it was all he talked about. He told us how you told him stories and kept him from being afraid. You were a great comfort to him and for that we are more grateful than we can say." The woman turned to Jay. "We want to make sure you put in your story what an angel Ms. Kyle was. We want you to tell that story to the world so that everyone will know that she was a hero to our little boy."

"I will," Jay promised.

As they bid their farewells, Kate took down the information for the funeral. She wanted to be there.

Once they were back in the car, the producer complained, "Kate, we can't shut the camera down when it gets emotional like that or we won't have any material to work with. That was great stuff."

Jay watched as Kate's eyes flashed dangerously.

"It's my call, Phil, and there is no way in hell that I'm going to take advantage of pain like that just to get a story. It was too personal, too raw. For God's sake, the kid just died this morning. Gene and I are going to get some footage of the funeral on Wednesday, don't worry."

Phil wisely didn't answer and the remainder of the short ride to the station was made in silence. Once inside, Kate went directly to her desk to look over the copy for the eleven o'clock newscast. Jay took that opportunity to pull Gene aside and talk to him about her subject.

It quickly became quite clear to Jay that Gene was in love with Kate. It was written all over his face and in the way he spoke about her. Jay felt a rising surge of jealousy and fought hard to keep it from showing. Gene had been working with Kate since she first came to the station, and he shared many stories with Jay about some of the more interesting assignments they'd been on. Some of them were humorous, and some, like the explosion, were downright horrifying. When they were through talking, Jay felt she had a much better sense of Kate as a journalist.

At 10:56 p.m., Kate came over to where Jay was grilling one of her favorite editors. Leaning down menacingly toward the editor, Kate said, "No telling tales out of school or I'll have you back cutting commercials for toilet paper and tampons." The editor only laughed and winked at Jay. Kate turned to Jay. "If you want to see the magic of television, you'd better come with me now."

Obediently, Jay rose and followed Kate through the labyrinth of offices and corridors to the set. Kate showed her to a seat just out of camera range and gave her an earpiece so that she could hear what Kate heard. From that vantage point, Jay could watch the anchors, the director and producer in the booth off to the side, the cameras and the teleprompters. Jay watched the newscast unfold in wonder as each member of the team did his or her job, and the end result appeared seamless.

Although Jay knew that Kate was deeply shaken by the earlier visit with Joey's family, there was no sign of it in her performance. She marveled as Kate looked directly into one camera while reading without seeming to be, then shifted to another without losing the thread of her thought, the director relaying instructions into her ear all the while. Jay couldn't understand how she could keep track of it all.

On the breaks, new pieces of copy were handed to the anchors and instructions given as to where to insert the words and what to delete to keep the newscast on time. The anchors were also informed whether the newscast was running over or under time at any given point and whether they would have to speed things up, drop things, or fill time. Reporters came and went on the set, along with the meteorologist and the sportscaster. All in all, it was a whirlwind of activity.

When it was over, Jay flexed her shoulders. She didn't realize she'd been so tense. She watched as Kate joked around with some of the crew and then came to get her.

"Well, what did you think?" Kate asked as she took the earpiece out of her ear and collected Jay's as well.

"I think you're the most amazing person I've ever met." When Jay got no response except for a single raised eyebrow, she added, "Objectively speaking, of course."

"Of course," Kate laughed. "What do you say we call it a night? I'm beat, and Fred is so excited that you're coming, he broke out a new tennis ball."

Jay chortled. "Who could turn down an enticing prospect like Fred waiting with a nice, slimy ball?"

❧❧

True to form, Fred was waiting at the door for his mistress and her affectionate friend, tennis ball in mouth. As soon as his mother crossed the threshold, he began weaving in and out of her legs, his tail wagging, all the while making noises that sounded like Chewbacca, the Wookie from *Star Wars*.

Jay shook her head. "What is that racket?"

Kate looked at the seventy-three pounds of dog fur between her legs. "Fred, apparently your friend doesn't know talking when she hears it."

She paused while the beast continued his welcome home ritual. "What's that?" She bent her ear to him. "We should forgive her this time? You're too easy, buddy." She gave him a few more scratches in just the right places and sent him on to the next hapless victim.

Jay quickly got the idea that if she didn't make space between her legs for Fred, he was going to do it for her. "You are too much, my boy." To Kate she said, "So it's okay for him to get between my legs on the second date, but not to kiss me on the first date? What kind of manners are you teaching this teenager?"

Kate laughed and pushed Jay ahead of her into the kitchen, apparently choosing not to answer. "Are you hungry or thirsty?"

"Neither, just whipped."

"Mmm, me too, it's been a heck of a long day. May I show you to your quarters, m'lady?"

"Why, yes, madam, that would be lovely." Jay let Kate guide her by the elbow upstairs to the guest suite, where she deposited her suitcase.

"I hope you'll find the accommodations at this hotel more than satisfactory, miss. There is a customer service survey that you can fill out at the end of your stay so that we can work to improve our performance. Should you need anything, please feel free to call the front desk."

Jay smiled. "Has anyone ever told you you're a nut?"

"Yes," Kate deadpanned, "but no one who has lived to tell about it. Now, about the activities available to you at this resort...tomorrow morning—er, make that this morning," she said, glancing at her watch. "At eight a.m. sharp, the workout facility will be open in the basement. At exactly one minute after nine a.m., a run will commence from the front steps. Breakfast is served, should you choose to skip the continental breakfast, at approximately ten a.m. in the main kitchen. You may shower at your leisure."

"Wow. I guess this really is a full-service hotel."

"You have no idea," Kate grinned wickedly at her friend and winked.

No, but I'm dying to find out. "Is there a personal fitness trainer that goes with the workout and run?"

"Of course. What kind of second-rate dive do you think we're running here?"

"Well then, all of those activities appeal to me, so I guess that means I'll be at the gym doors when they open at eight."

"My able assistant and I look forward to your presence. Until then, please enjoy the hospitality and sleep well." Kate turned on her heel and summoned Fred, who had made himself quite comfortable on the floor at the side of the bed. Reluctantly, with a sidelong glance in his new friend's direction, he followed his human out of the room.

In her own room, Kate shed her clothes as she headed to the bathroom. She splashed her face with ice-cold water, hoping that would cure her of the fervent desire to kiss Jay senseless. She wasn't sure how she was going to make it through these next few days. Keeping professional distance from that gorgeous woman down the hall was proving to be damn near impossible for her.

Still, she was determined to play this by Jay's rules, and she had no intention of inviting any more rejections of her affectionate overtures. She was surprised, truthfully, at how much that gentle rebuke hurt. Kate shook her head to clear it and set the alarm for 5:15 a.m. It was already 12:25 a.m., and it was going to be a short night for her, but she had an appointment to keep at 6:00 a.m. and she couldn't be late.

Down the hall, Jay finished unpacking her clothes and toiletries. She bit her lip and fought hard the urge to sneak down the hall and crawl into bed with Kate. No, she didn't think that would qualify as professional detachment. Instead, she took a quick cold shower and put on her sleepwear, went to the bed and turned down the covers. What she found there made her laugh out loud in delighted surprise.

Sitting underneath the covers were three original-issue Green Lantern comic books and a flashlight. The note clipped to the first cover read: *"In case you have trouble sleeping, I thought you might enjoy these. Sweet dreams, princess. See you in the morning. K."*

87

That woman is just too much. Is there anything she doesn't think of? Jay scooped up the comics, turned on the flashlight, turned out the light and settled down to read *The Adventures of the Green Lantern.*

CHAPTER TEN

At precisely 7:58 a.m., a disheveled Jay appeared in the kitchen. She smiled when she caught sight of the coffee, tea, and choices of orange, tomato, and grape juice on the counter. A note there read: *"Good morning, sunshine, I wasn't sure which was your poison, so I thought I'd cover my bases. After all, this is a five-star resort. Follow the light to your right and open the door to a world of total fitness. K."*

Jay turned to the right and noticed an open door leading to a set of stairs. From above, she had a perfect view of a well-equipped gym and a magnificent body in a cropped t-shirt that revealed perfectly sculpted abdominal muscles glistening with sweat. A pair of short running shorts rounded out the outfit. *Wow.* Jay sighed. "You have a complete Nautilus circuit in your basement?"

"Well, what kind of five-star resort would this be without one?"

"You have a point there. Good morning, Kate, thanks for the coffee and juice, by the way."

"You're quite welcome. Did you sleep well?"

"I made it through one and a half comics before I couldn't keep my eyes open any longer. Where in the world did you find those, anyway?"

"I'd tell you, but then I'd have to kill you. And I hate to be violent so early in the morning. It interrupts my routine."

"You have lost your mind." Jay laughed. That was when she noticed that Kate's gaze was glued to a television strategically placed on a wall that could be seen from every machine. Reaching the bottom step, she guffawed. "You mean to tell me you're watching reruns of *Charlie's Angels*?"

"Naturally, what else would you work out to?"

"Is that why the workout is scheduled at precisely eight a.m. and the run at one after nine? I wondered about the timing."

"It might be."

"Okay, favorite angel."

"That's easy, Farrah Fawcett. Cheryl Ladd was a close second."

"No, no, you've got it all wrong. Jaclyn Smith had it all over those two."

"Hey, to each her own, missy. Most disappointing development?"

"Simple—losing Cheryl and Kate and adding Shelley Hack and Tanya Roberts."

"Can't disagree with you there, that's for sure."

Kate handed Jay a set of workout gloves and the two women set about their routines. It wasn't easy, since Kate had one eye on Jay and the second on the television where Farrah was chasing down one of the bad guys on a racetrack in her Mustang.

Kate had to work hard to keep from drooling at Jay, who was appealingly tousled and wore a form-fitting sleeveless workout top and a brief pair of nylon shorts. *Good Lord. As if I wasn't having enough trouble controlling my libido. Well, I could always blame it on Farrah if my drool starts to show.*

She helped Jay adjust the machines to fit her stature and tried to refrain from making too many short jokes in the process. For her part, Jay only called her "Stretch" once, so Kate considered that they were even. At 8:58 a.m. as the credits rolled, she turned off the television and gestured for Jay to precede her up the stairs. The two spent several minutes stretching side by side before heading to the front door.

Once on the street, Jay asked, "Just how far are we going, anyway?"

"I usually go five miles, but we can go shorter or longer as you like. What's your pleasure?"

"Five is fine."

Kate led them through tree-lined streets and onto a path that followed along the Mohawk River. Along the way, she pointed out spots of interest and explained a bit about the history of the area.

"It's beautiful, Kate, I can only imagine what it's like when the leaves are changing in the fall."

Before she could think about what it meant, Kate said, "Guess you'll just have to see for yourself, then."

"Yes, I guess I will," Jay smiled up at Kate.

As they looped around to head back toward the house, a man appeared out of the shadow of a large oak tree, brandishing a long butcher knife and waving it menacingly at Kate. His eyes glazed and spittle frothed at the corners of his mouth. He didn't seem to take any notice of Jay. In one easy move, Kate put herself between the man and Jay.

"I told you you were going to be mine, cunt, and I meant it. All those nights you been taunting me in my livin' room, begging me to take you. Well, here I am, are you ready?"

Kate was cognizant of Jay's palpable fear, and her mind flashed on the thought that being confronted by this man might set off Jay's memories of that night in college. That angered Kate more than having to deal with the lunatic. She needed to buy them some time and keep him as far away from them as she could. Kate addressed her assailant. "I got your letters, what is it that I've done to offend you?"

The man was shaking with obvious rage. He took a step closer. Kate reached behind her and put one hand on Jay's waist to make sure she knew precisely where she was and to let Jay know to stay behind her.

"I seen the way you look at that bastard. I ain't stupid, you know. I know what's going on between you two."

"You mean Gerry, my co-anchor? What is it you think is going on?"

He took another step, and Kate put subtle pressure on Jay's waist letting her know to back up a pace, which they both did. The foam was dripping from the deranged man's mouth. "Don't play with me, cunt," he roared, "I'm gonna put an end to it right here." He lurched forward and came at her, still seemingly unaware that there was another person present.

Out of the corner of her eye, Kate caught movement to her right from the direction of the street. As the maniac took one last lunge at her, she used the hand she had resting on Jay's waist to throw her to the side, out of harm's way. At the same time, she pivoted in the opposite direction, and her assailant stumbled past her. Within seconds, two uniformed police officers and a detective tackled the man and disarmed him.

Kate ran to where Jay lay several feet away on the grass, reached out her hand and pulled Jay to her feet and into a hug. "Are you okay?"

Jay nodded into the chest she was pressed against.

"It's over now, can you stay here by yourself for a second?"

Another nod.

Kate walked over to where the detective was speaking into a two-way radio. The uniformed men already had the suspect on his feet and were leading him to the street and the waiting squad car. "Hi, Bob, that was a little close for comfort."

"I'll say," the detective wheezed, clearly out of breath. "It took us a while to figure out where he was hiding. We saw him watch you leave the house, and then we lost him in the trees for a few minutes. That was some fancy footwork there, for a desk jockey, Ms. Kyle."

"Thanks...I think. You're sure this idiot was acting alone, right? Is it finally over now?"

"Yes, we're confident that we've got him and you'll be safe now."

"Good work, Bob, and thanks, I owe you," she smiled at him.

Bob blushed and looked down at his feet. "Just doing our jobs, Ms. Kyle. Thanks for your patience. We'll be in touch." With that, he too headed off in the direction of the street.

When Kate turned, she realized that Jay was close enough to have heard the entire exchange.

"This wasn't random...you knew he was stalking you."

"No, Jay, I knew he was threatening me," Kate corrected gently. "I had no idea he would take it to that level, or I never would have had you anywhere near me." She was cursing herself for not thinking of Jay's safety.

Jay's eyes flashed with anger. "Me. You're worried about me? Katherine Kyle, that man wanted to kill you!"

"He didn't know what he wanted...he wasn't rational, Jay."

"He could have killed you," Jay said softly, tears rolling down her cheeks.

"Hey." Kate lifted Jay's chin and gently wiped the tears away with her thumbs. When Jay finally looked up at her, Kate continued. "The point is that nobody got hurt, and he'll get the help he so desperately needs. I was well protected, as you can see."

"How did the police know to come here?"

Kate blew out an explosive breath. She wouldn't lie to Jay. "I've been getting letters from this guy for months now. Lately they've been getting more violent and more explicit. When the rhetoric escalated, I went to station management and the police were brought in." She shrugged her shoulders. "When you're in the public eye like I am, unfortunately sometimes things like this happen. Usually it isn't this serious."

"Thank God for small favors," Jay mumbled. With a hint of sarcasm, she added, "I feel much better now. You still didn't answer how the police knew to come to this spot."

"I'm pretty much a creature of habit, Jay. I follow the same routine almost every morning. The police have been watching my house and me for weeks now, just in case something like this happened. I knew they wouldn't be too far away."

Jay apparently still was not satisfied. "That was too close. He could have killed you before they had a chance to get here."

Kate looked into eyes that brimmed with more unshed tears and obvious concern. "He didn't, and he won't be hurting anyone now...I promise. Let's just go home, okay?"

"Yeah, I'd like that."

ॐ

When they arrived in the kitchen, Fred was waiting for them, tennis ball in mouth. Kate looked at Jay apologetically. "I usually spend a few minutes with the big guy playing ball in the back yard before breakfast. I know you must be starving." In truth, she thought a good, fun distraction might be just the thing to take Jay's mind off what just happened.

"Are you kidding me," Jay said. "Nothing like a good game of fetch to get your blood pumping in the morning when nothing else has."

"Uh-huh." Kate rolled her eyes at Jay's sarcasm. "In that case, smarty pants, you can be the one to play with him. I'll just come along for the entertainment."

Fred led the way to the atrium door that opened onto a two-tiered wooden deck. In front of the deck was an expanse of lawn that stretched nearly as far as a major league baseball park. The entire thing was fenced in with privacy fencing. "My God, Kate, I didn't notice this before. It's incredible...it's so big."

"Coming from someone who lives in the middle of the city where there are no lawns, and who grew up in the desert, I suppose I should take that with a grain of salt."

Jay bumped her with her hip. Fred, meanwhile, was impatiently pacing back and forth in front of the pair and eagerly pointing his nose to the spot where he dropped the ball at their feet. Kate made the first throw.

"Nice arm, there, ace. So, from this I take it she plays softball."

"Oh, brilliant deduction, my dear Watson," Kate intoned in an awful British accent. "The governor always tells me I'm the best left-handed shortstop he's ever seen. I always answer that I'm the *only* left-handed shortstop he's ever seen."

"You know the governor that well?"

"We've had some 'friendly' games of basketball in his driveway and we've played softball on opposite teams. And occasionally we have some fascinating conversations about politics and religion. He's a very bright guy, very interesting to debate."

By this time Jay's mouth was hanging open. "Kate, you knew I was writing an in-depth piece on him. Why didn't you tell me you knew him so well and share your insight?"

Kate shrugged sheepishly. "I didn't want to influence you in any way. Like I told you before, I love your work." At this she looked directly into Jay's eyes. "I thought your piece would be better if you had a chance to make your own judgments." More quietly, she finished, "You didn't need me to write a great story. I can't wait to read it."

Jay blushed an appealing shade of pink at the compliment. At that moment, seventy-three pounds of fur ball was headed directly for her at a dead run. Her eyes opened wide.

Kate laughed. "Um, Jay, you'd better spread your legs in a hurry."

That earned her a fully raised eyebrow, but Jay complied, which was a good thing, because right about then Fred, his tail wagging vigorously, flew into the space she made for him.

Kate instructed, "If you scratch his haunches, he'll march in place for you, it's his favorite thing to do." And sure enough, Fred was true to form.

"All we need now is a John Philip Sousa march," Jay muttered under her breath, and she laughed at the dog's antics. He finished going all the way through her legs then, and came back around, depositing the ball at her feet and staring at it. She reached down, grabbed the ball, and launched it almost as far as Kate had before her.

"Ah, a fellow ball player, I do believe."

"Mmm-hmm, I play in a league in Central Park in the summer."

"What position do you play? No, wait, let me guess." Kate pretended to size Jay up. "I'm fairly confident that it's not first base."

"Wise ass."

"So I'm told. Let's see," Kate scratched her chin. "You look quick enough to be an outfielder."

"Nope." Jay seemed to be enjoying the flustered look on Kate's face.

"No?"

"Right."

"Hmm, well, you've obviously got a good arm...third base?" Jay made a sound like a buzzer. "Oh for two there, Stretch."

"Okay, okay, you don't play the outfield and you don't play first or third." She looked at Jay sideways. "Are you sure?"

Jay's eyes sparkled with amusement. "Positive. You'll never get it, woman, so why don't you just give up?"

"No, no, one more shot, I still have one strike coming to me. You play shortstop too?"

"Ooh, I'm sorry, you lose!" But Jay didn't sound sorry at all.

"Well," Kate said exasperatedly, "aren't you going to tell me?"

"Oh, okay, since you can't seem to figure it out yourself...I'm a catcher." Jay looked up guilelessly.

"You've got to be kidding me. At your size?"

"Yes." Jay straightened up to appear as big as possible. "Size isn't everything, you know. You've never seen me block the plate!"

"That, I'd love to see."

"You're on, wise ass, this summer."

Kate smiled broadly at the assumption that they would have an ongoing relationship. "I can't wait."

As they made their way back into the house, Kate asked Jay whether she wanted to shower before or after breakfast.

"I'm famished, if you can stand the smell of me a little longer, I'd opt for food before cleanliness."

"You're on. What do you say to the house special—cinnamon French toast and a side of bacon."

"I'd say it sounds like heaven."

"Coming right up."

After a few minutes during which Kate concentrated on mixing up the batter and starting the bacon, Jay spoke. "Kate, I know it's none of my business, but I'm worried about your safety. And before you say anything, I'm willing to bet that he isn't the first nutcase to bother you."

Kate was about to give a glib reply when she snuck a peek at Jay's face. She seemed genuinely disturbed. For some reason, Kate didn't want to be the source of even the slightest worry for her. "I tell you what," she said at length. "I'll give my friend Peter a call right now. He's a security expert. He's been bugging me for a while to install a state-of-the-art security system here at the house. I'll let him come over today and go to town, if he has the time and the inclination. Okay?"

"Yeah." Jay brightened perceptibly.

In truth, her lack of security had been the cause of one of the only fights Kate and Peter ever had. He was appalled that she wouldn't take him up on his offer to put in a specially designed motion-sensitive detection system. As recognizable as she was, she was a sitting target for just about any fanatic with the will to find her. Not wanting to admit that she might be vulnerable, she had always rejected his offer.

After that morning it would be hard to argue that he hadn't been right. She had just been kidding herself. Still, Kate might not have given in except for the fact that she wanted to make sure that Jay would be safe in her house. That was enough to make her pick up the phone.

The two women were showered, dressed, and on their way to the station to pick up Gene, Phil, and the station car with the equipment. They had a bunch more interviews lined up for late that morning and early that afternoon before Kate had to be in the newsroom to get ready for the six o'clock broadcast.

Into the comfortable silence, Jay said, "I'm glad your friend agreed to come over to put in the system today. I don't want to have to worry about you. Not that installing security in your home will prevent everything, but at least it will cut down on the chances of something terrible happening."

"If you're happy, I'm happy."

Jay looked over to see if she was being tweaked, but Kate's eyes revealed only sincerity. She smiled in return.

"By the way, if it's okay with you, I told Peter that in return for doing the work today, we would take him out to dinner on my break tonight. I really want you to meet him. He's a neat guy and one of my best friends. I trust him with my life. If I were ever in trouble, he's the man I'd call."

"I can't wait to meet him." Jay had the distinct feeling that Kate didn't bestow her trust lightly. She was curious about the kind of man that could inspire that feeling in Kate.

❦

The day was flying by. Kate and her crew conducted six more interviews by the time three o'clock rolled around, and the still photographer for *Time* showed up in time to take some pictures of the last interview. At the moment they were all headed back to the station—Jay so that she could conduct some interviews of her subject's colleagues, and Kate so that she could prepare for the six o'clock newscast. She explained to Jay that the next day she would attend the funeral of the little boy who passed away Monday, and then spend the bulk of the day in the editing booth, putting together the special that would air Thursday night in prime time.

The news director agreed to allow the *Time* photographer to take pictures of Kate on the set during the early newscast, provided of course, that the shots included the station logo in the background. The photographer also snapped some film of Kate in an editing booth, as she pointed out to an editor some footage she wanted included in one of her stories.

As soon as Kate stepped off the set following "the six," as they called it, she collected Jay and pushed her out the side door to the parking lot. "C'mon, Scoop, or we'll be late for our dinner date."

"Scoop? Did you just call me Scoop? Nobody calls me Scoop," Jay hurried to catch up to Kate.

Since she was caught up in getting ready for the broadcast while Jay was busy digging up dirt on her, Kate didn't see Jay for hours. She was surprised to realize just how much she missed her in that short time. "Looks like I just did. Whatcha gonna do about it, Short Stuff?"

"Ooh, aren't we full of ourselves. Just don't forget, the pen is mightier than the sword, and this "Scoop" hasn't even put pen to paper about you yet. You'd do well to keep that in mind and be nice to me." Jay smirked.

"Well, don't I just feel suitably threatened. Why, I do believe my hands are shaking." Kate held up her hand and wiggled it as though it were trembling in fear. In response, she got hip-checked into the car door.

"Hey, young lady, that was a little uncalled for."

"Hardly," Jay snorted as she settled herself in the passenger seat.

In ten minutes' time, they were sitting at a table in a tavern on the outskirts of town near the state university. The smell of beer and burgers was almost overwhelming and college kids were everywhere.

Jay looked around and laughed, "Wow, Stretch, you take him to the nicest joints, don't you?"

"I gave him his choice," Kate answered defensively, as a shadow fell over the table and she felt herself lifted into an embrace from behind.

"That's right, she did give me a choice...this place or McDonald's."

"Listen, if the two of you are going to gang up against me, you can just eat by yourselves."

At that, the man came around the table, grasped Jay by the elbow with a gleam in his eye, and said, "Shall we?"

Jay nodded and grinned. "I believe we should."

"Wait a minute," Kate interrupted, looking pointedly at Jay. "You haven't even been introduced to this letch yet and you'd just go off with him? You floozy!"

Peter and Jay looked at each other mischievously. They each stuck their hands out at the same time.

"Peter."

"Jay."

"You ready to go?"

"Yep."

"Just like that?" Kate exclaimed indignantly.

In unison, Jay and Peter said, "Yep!"

From there, dinner turned into a raucous affair. Peter regaled Jay with stories of his exploits with Kate, and Kate revealed some of Peter's more embarrassing moments.

When Kate excused herself to go to the restroom, Jay turned to Peter and asked urgently, "Will that security system that you installed today really keep her safe?"

Peter looked at her appraisingly. He had taken a shine to her right from the beginning, which was most unusual for him. And, observing her with Kate, it was as plain as day to him that there was some serious chemistry at work there. The thought made him happy. Heck, if he couldn't have Kate, Jay would do just nicely for her.

At first, Peter tried hard to get Kate to fall for him. Finally, as delicately as she could, Kate explained the facts of life to him. He reddened, chuckled, and said, simply, "Ah, I get it now." And that had been the end of it, except for the endless jokes, asides, and friendly contests to pick out the prettiest women everywhere they went. But deep down, Peter knew that Kate kept herself too far apart from the rest of the world. It broke his heart that she was lonely and didn't even know it. He could see, though, looking at Jay, that he wouldn't have to worry too much longer.

"As long as she's in the house and the alarm is set, she'll be as safe as a babe in her mother's arms."

"Good, because what happened this morning scared the living daylights out of me for her."

Peter looked at Jay oddly.

"She did tell you what happened, didn't she?"

"No."

"She was attacked this morning by a stalker. She didn't mention that?"

"No." Now he was angry.

Jay placed a gentle hand on Peter's arm. "She's fine, not even a scratch. The police caught him after his first pass at her. It must have slipped her mind."

"I'll just bet it did," he said ominously. "It's okay, Jay, she probably didn't tell me because she knew I'd go down there and beat the tar out of the jerk."

"That's right," a low, sexy voice rumbled from behind him.

"Geez, you sure know how to ruin a guy's good time."

"Yeah, I know, I feel so sorry for you. Listen, Technowiz, it's not that I'm not having a great time, because I am, but we've got to run. Some of us have a job to do." Kate winked at him. "Thanks again for taking care of the security system so quickly."

"No problem, Anchorbabe, I'll meet you at the house at midnight so I can set the system with your code. That's how you set and disable the alarm."

"Great, we'll see you there."

As she made to leave, Peter held her back just a little. In her ear he said, so that only she could hear him, "I can set it to recognize a different code for Jay, too, if you want her to be able to get in and out of your place."

Kate stiffened.

"I really, really like her, kiddo…she's special. And, whether you know it or not, you've got amazing vibes going on between you. I think it's fantastic. Now just don't mess it up."

"I'll try not to, thanks for the vote of confidence." Kate jogged a few steps to catch up to Jay, and they disappeared into the parking lot.

༄༅

True to his word, Peter met the two women in the driveway at midnight as they pulled into the garage. Peter explained the security system's features at length and then took them to the main control panel in Kate's office so that he could individualize the program. He quickly punched a sequence of numbers and symbols then told Kate to enter the four-digit code she wanted to use. Then he entered another string of numbers and the system beeped. Next he turned to Jay, who was watching the process with interest.

"Okay, Half-pint, your turn."

Jay didn't move. "Are you talking to me?"

"Are there any other vertically challenged individuals in this room?"

Jay looked from one of them to the other. Kate nodded at her and said, "Let the man do his job, Jamison." Her eyes sparkled.

"Y-you want me to be able to arm and disarm your security system?"

"Is there some reason I shouldn't trust you?"

"Well, no, of course not, but—"

"Then follow the man's instructions. After all, it's your fault I'm stuck with this damn thing now anyway." Kate hid her smile behind her hand at the look of befuddlement and wonder on Jay's face.

Within minutes, the programming was completed and tested. Remote consoles inside the front door, inside the garage door, and in Kate's bedroom would each allow the system to be activated and deactivated with the proper code sequence. Peter already had taken the time during the day to ensure that the laser beams on which the system functioned would not be set off every time Fred came bounding through the house.

The exhausted women bid Peter goodbye and headed into the living room.

"Peter seems like a great guy."

"Yeah, he's the closest thing to a brother I have. And he's pretty handy to have around, as you can see."

"I guess. Does he work for the police?"

"Technically, no. His main job is with the New York State Department of Correctional Services...in other words, the state prison system. He's their technology, tactical, and weapons expert. He knows more about explosives, weapons, electronic surveillance wizardry, and security than anyone else in the country. Which means he does a lot of freelance work on loan to other agencies and companies. He designed the security systems for the White House and the governor's mansion, for instance. And anytime there's a bombing anywhere in the country, it's Peter they call to come figure it out."

"He sounds like a good guy to know."

"Mmm, he can be your best friend, or your worst enemy. Let's just say I'm glad he's on my side...I'd sure never want to piss him off."

"I'll try to remember that."

Suddenly feeling nervous but wanting to ask Jay her plans for the rest of the week, Kate fidgeted for a minute. She couldn't believe how quickly Jay was becoming a part of her life. She was fun, companionable, intelligent, compassionate, and beautiful. Kate wasn't sure how much more material Jay would need in order to put together her story, but she didn't imagine it could be much. And that would mean that she didn't need to be there...with her.

Jay interpreted Kate's fidgeting in an entirely different way, wondering if perhaps she wasn't overstaying her welcome. In truth, she had more than enough material to write the story already, but she didn't want to leave. She could justify staying to experience her subject's reaction to the funeral of a boy she had rescued and the editing of the special, both of which would take place tomorrow, but beyond that...

Jay had never met anyone remotely like Kate. She enjoyed everything about her—her sense of humor, her passion for everything she did, her intellect, and her unconscious elegance and beauty. She had a toughness and strength about her that belied her thoughtful, caring, gentle, and compassionate nature. Jay wished she could find a way to prolong her assignment, and was desperately afraid that Kate might not want her to.

"Um, how's the story coming along, Jay?"

"Good, good, your co-workers have given me some interesting material to work with." At this Jay smiled mischeviously.

"You're not going to write anything embarrassing, are you?" Kate's voice rose an octave.

Jay let Kate sweat for a minute before she let out a hearty laugh. "This isn't the *National Enquirer*."

"Oh, right." Kate seemed to relax a bit.

"And some of the families and victims have helped me to see how much what you did that day meant to them. It puts a completely new perspective on what makes a good journalist and where the lines are between professional objectivity and inserting humanity into a story."

"Sounds like you've got most of what you need then, huh?"

"I guess so. I was going to stay for the funeral and the editing of the special tomorrow, and then I could get out of your way. I'm sure you'd like to have your life back." She couldn't even look up.

"Um, actually, I was planning on taking Thursday off, and I wanted to ask you if you could take the time too? I know you have to have the story in on Monday morning, but I would love it if you could spend a day off with me. If you needed to, you could even start writing here. I promise Fred and I won't bother you at all."

Jay couldn't believe her ears. Was Kate asking her to spend a day off with her, as in a date? She needed confirmation. "Are you asking me for a date?"

Kate wouldn't look her in the eye. "Yes," she answered so quietly Jay was barely sure she'd heard her.

"I can't think of anything I'd rather do." Jay's face split into a grin from ear to ear, a look that mirrored the one facing her. "I can go home and start writing on Friday, and finish on Saturday morning before I have to come back up here."

"You're coming back up here this weekend?" Kate didn't know what to make of that. *Has she met someone up here already, someone who beat me to it, and she's going on a date Saturday night? That was quick. One of my co-workers? Well, duh, Katherine. She's a knockout and everybody in the world wants to be around her, of course she's found someone.* But hadn't she just agreed to a date with her? Kate's heart dropped into her stomach.

"Didn't I tell you? The governor invited me to join him and his wife for something called the Legislative Correspondents' Association Show. It's this Saturday night."

"You're going to the LCA Show?" Kate tried to sound nonchalant as her heart found its way back up into her chest.

"Well, yeah, the governor invited me. Do you know anything about it?"

"Sure, sure. It's sort of a spoof of state government put on once a year by the journalists who cover the capitol beat. It's supposed to be pretty good. I'm sure you'll have a great time."

"Do you know what I'm supposed to wear? I have no idea."

"It's formal. Are you sitting at the governor's table?"

"Yes."

"Wow, that's amazing." Kate tried to kick start her brain. "You know, Jay, that show ends pretty late. You're not going to want to travel back to the city afterwards. Why don't you just plan to stay here Saturday night? You could go home Sunday morning, if you want."

"Oh, Kate, I don't want to be an imposition."

"Are you kidding me? Didn't we go through this once before? Fred and I would love to have you. I've got plans Saturday night, but I should be done right around the time you are, so it should work out fine. In fact, if you can catch a cab to the show, I could pick you up and take you home."

"I don't want you to have to cut short your plans just for me." Jay sounded inexplicably dejected to Kate.

"Trust me, Jay, the timing will work out perfectly. I'll pick you up outside the Convention Center when the show lets out, okay?"

"Okay."

"Well, now that that's settled, I'm beat." Kate's announcement was punctuated with a yawn. "The funeral's at eleven, so the activities schedule for tomorrow morning will be the same as today's...if you're interested. Or, you could sleep in."

"What, and miss an episode of *Charlie's Angels*? No way. I'll see you in the fitness center at eight sharp."

"Sleep well, Jay."

"You too, Kate. G'night, Fred."

CHAPTER ELEVEN

A t 7:15 a.m., Kate snuck back into the house. She sighed. Just one more day and she wouldn't have to be up before the sun anymore. She couldn't wait. This burning the candle at both ends stuff was for the birds. She scratched her faithful canine behind the ears and made her way quietly upstairs to change into her workout clothes, glad that her houseguest seemed to be a sound sleeper.

As she had the previous day, Jay found freshly brewed coffee and orange juice on the kitchen counter. She smiled at the notion that Kate had observed her choices of the day before—gone were the tea, the grape juice, and the tomato juice.

When she reached the bottom of the stairs in the basement/gym, Jay said, "Good morning. How did you know I wouldn't want something different to drink today?"

"That's easy," Kate said smugly. "You ordered coffee and orange juice when we had breakfast in the city, you accepted coffee gratefully at the *Today Show* interview, and you chose coffee and orange juice yesterday. Do I need to say anything more?"

I can't believe she was paying that close attention! "Humph. I guess I need to work at being less predictable."

"I don't know," Kate replied, "I think there's something to be said for being steady and reliable."

"What about boring and mundane?"

"Jamison Parker, those are two words I would never use to describe you. Now get your butt the rest of the way over here. Your girl Jaclyn is just about to lay out one of the bad guys."

The rest of the workout was spent in silence with the exception of occasional comments about the action on the television screen.

As the two women headed out the door for their run, Kate turned to Jay. "Do you want to take a different route today? Is it going to bother you?"

"No, I think it will be fine. It's such a pretty run, I don't want to let anything spoil that." But as they reached the spot of the previous day's incident, Jay tensed up.

Kate must have noticed, because she reached out, touching her on the arm. "It's okay, Jay," she said softly. "He's in a very secure place and he can't hurt me anymore. Please don't worry."

Jay smiled a half smile. "I know you're right, it's just..."

"We can't spend every minute worrying about what might be around the next corner, or we'll forget to live in the moment, right?"

"Right," Jay agreed.

After completing the rest of the run without any difficulty, they played ball with Fred, ate breakfast, and showered in preparation for the day.

Once they were in the car on their way to the funeral, Jay looked over at Kate. "This is going to be hard for you, isn't it?" She saw two nights ago how deeply affected Kate had been by the news of the little boy's death.

"It just seems so damn senseless. The kid goes on a field trip to learn about the history of his state, and he ends up crushed under the rubble of the capitol. Why? All because some nutcase somewhere has a beef with someone or something that has nothing to do with this poor little boy, who just happens to be in the wrong place at the wrong time."

Knowing there wasn't anything to say to that, Jay merely reached out and wrapped her fingers gently around Kate's arm in mute comfort. The contact lasted only for a few seconds, but Jay thought it made them both feel better.

✎✎

The church was packed. Kate stopped to give some instructions to Gene, who was already set up in an unobtrusive position with his camera. Then she and Jay made their way midway up the aisle and chose seats on the end of a row. They were barely seated before Joey's father approached them from the front of the church. "Ms. Kyle, I know it's short notice and a lot to ask, but we'd be greatly flattered if you would say a few words about our Joey. He was so taken with you and so excited to meet you. It was all he talked about the last two days of his life." Tears coursed down the man's cheeks.

Kate didn't know what to say, the request caught her so far off guard. Her eyes also welled up with tears. Quietly, she said, "I'd be honored. Thank you so much for asking me."

Seemingly pleased, the man went back to his seat, his head bent close to his wife's. She looked back at Kate and smiled. Kate smiled sadly in return.

As the service began, Kate's breathing changed. She was struggling with her emotions, a fact she knew wasn't lost on Jay. Her suspicions were confirmed when Jay reached out and took her hand. Kate squeezed Jay's hand in gratitude.

When it was her turn to speak, Kate straightened to her full height and made her way gracefully to the altar. A buzz of recognition went through the crowd of mourners, but Kate barely noticed. She had not known what she would say until the moment she looked out across the sea of faces.

"I look at you all today, united in your grief and sadness for the loss of a small boy who had his whole life in front of him, and I share your pain. I only got a chance to know Joey for a brief moment in his young life, and even in that short time, I knew there was something special about him. He had a light, a vibrant curiosity about the world around him. Lying there, trapped under the rubble, we spoke of baseball and his favorite teams. He showed no fear, just bravery and maturity well beyond his years. We here on earth may have been robbed of his presence, but I know that his spirit and courage will live on as an example for me for the rest of my life. I hope he has touched you all in a similar way. I know that I am a richer person for having had the opportunity to meet him. Good rest, Joey. Thank you."

As she made her way back down the aisle, Kate searched for Jay. What she found in Jay's expression was a haven of compassion and understanding in a world that made no sense. When she was seated again, Jay leaned close and whispered, "That was beautiful. I can't think of a better tribute to such a special young man. I'm sure you brought many people comfort with your words."

Kate could only nod a thank you, unable to speak around the lump in her throat and unwilling to lose her composure there. Jay must have sensed that, because she said nothing further.

They were almost to the car when Joey's parents stopped them. "We just wanted to thank you one more time," the mother said, tears blinding her vision. She grasped Kate in a hug. "What you said about our Joey was so true, and so beautiful. He will always live in our hearts."

"Mine too," Kate said as she pulled back a little. "I'm so sorry for your loss. I hope you find peace."

"God bless you, Ms. Kyle," the father said. "We'll never forget you." He put his arm around his wife and led her away.

Kate ducked quickly into the driver's seat before her emotions could get the best of her. She drove around the corner and down several side streets before pulling over in a small, deserted alleyway. "I'm sorry," she said to Jay, "I just need a minute." She would never have allowed herself to let down her guard in front of anyone else, but with the wonderful, gentle soul sitting beside her, it was different. She felt safe. Tears running down her cheeks, she bowed her head against the steering wheel.

Jay moved the center console and scooted closer to Kate. She ran a hand up and down Kate's back in a comforting motion. After a few minutes, Kate straightened up and gave Jay a watery smile. "Thanks, I needed that."

"Anytime, Kate. I'm glad I could be here for you."

"Me too." She started the car again and drove them to the station.

Kate settled herself in front of her word processor and began writing the introduction to her special. She explained to Jay apologetically that she would be tied up for several hours putting together the verbal part of the one-hour show. After that, Jay could join her, Gene, and one of the editors as they combed through the mountains of taped material that would yield the pictures to go with the words.

Jay requested that Kate set up an appointment for her with Gene to go through old footage of her stories and, although it made Kate uncomfortable, she could think of no real reason to say no.

By 2:30 p.m., satisfied with what she had written, Kate went in search of Jay. She found her holed up in one of the back editing rooms with Gene looking at a story she did four years ago about the discovery of toxic waste contamination at a local manufacturing plant. She groaned as she looked at herself on the screen.

"If you two are quite finished, can we get started on some real business here?" Kate smiled into Jay's somewhat bloodshot eyes.

"Ready when you are, boss," Gene said. Kate summoned the editor and the three of them moved down the hall to one of the new, spacious, state-of-the-art editing rooms.

Kate handed each of them a copy of the script so that they could get a sense of what she had in mind, and so that they could all be looking for the pictures that would tell the story as much, or more, than the words could. Gene, who shot all of the footage they would be using, proved to have a phenomenal memory when it came to finding specific shots and the interviews Kate indicated she wanted to use. Kate and Gene had a language all their own. Kate knew exactly what they had on tape, and Gene knew where to find it. Each piece of footage was clocked for time, so they would know if they had enough to cover the words in the script.

Once they had all the footage they thought they would need, Kate put on a set of headphones, sat down in front of the microphone that hung down from the ceiling, and laid down her voice on tape. In those spots where an interview was to be inserted, she paused, indicated the correct interview to be slotted, and counted down from five to one. She explained to Jay that the countdown was so that the editor would know where to insert the interview and wouldn't have to worry about running over or stepping on the words. The countdown would be deleted in the editing process.

When Kate was satisfied with her delivery and speed, the editor gave a listen and indicated that the quality was fine. Kate explained to Jay that her voice was recorded on audio channel one. The interviews and ambient sound would be laid down on audio channel two, and the two tapes would be melded together into one master audiotape, which would then be matched with the video images.

With Kate's initial part of the process complete, she left to deliver the six o'clock news. Jay was to stay with the cameraman and editor as they took the selected images and matched them to the words from the script to tell a compelling story.

By the time Kate returned from the set, the preliminary draft of the special was ready. She suggested that they order dinner in and watch while they ate. Everyone agreed, the pizza order was placed, and the viewing began. Every so often, she had the editor stop the tape and made a comment, or suggested a small change or the addition or deletion of a piece of video. Two hours and two large pizzas later, everyone was satisfied with the finished product.

The special included footage taken from home movies of Joey at his last birthday party and again at a little league game the previous summer. Then the scene shifted to the eight-year-old trapped under the rubble of the explosion and his parents at his funeral just that morning. Finally, an image of Joey's parents standing together, strong in their faith, delivered the message that their son would live on in their hearts and the hearts of many others as a beacon of courage and bravery. Similar segments with other victims and families drove home the theme of the triumph of the human spirit over terror.

When the last credit rolled and silence filled the room, Kate turned to Gene and the editor expectantly. "Well, what did you think?"

Gene weighed in first. "I think it was edgy and powerful. Fast in the places it needed to be, and slower and more subdued where it had to be. I like the pacing."

The editor agreed. "You know, everyone is expecting a rehash of what happened—the who, what, where, when, and how. Anybody could have done that. What you did here is far more potent. It gets past the mechanics and material issues and into the emotional stuff. I love that."

Kate merely listened to the comments, processing the information. Finally, she turned to the person whose opinion mattered most to her. "Jay, what about you?"

Jay seemed surprised to be asked. "Well, I can't speak to the technical aspects of the piece like these guys can. But as a viewer my gut reaction is that it's alternately the most depressing and uplifting story imaginable. Watching it, I felt the helplessness and hopelessness of the moment. And then, I was so moved and inspired by the ability of these victims and their families to bounce back and take something positive from the most devastating of horrors. In the end I was left with a warm, powerful feeling inside my heart about the strength of the human spirit. Wow."

Kate simply nodded when Jay was done talking, but a slight blush was creeping up her neck. She couldn't have asked for a better reaction. Turning to Gene and the editor, she said, "Great work, folks, thanks for making it so good. I think that's a wrap." Then she took the master dub and walked down the hall to hand it to the news director.

An hour and a half later, shortly before she was getting ready to go on the air, Kate's boss appeared at her desk. Without preamble he said, "Nice job, Kate, that showed great vision. I loved it."

Shocked by the compliment, which was rare at best coming from the news director, Kate mumbled her appreciation and thanked him again for giving her the next day off. Then he was gone, and she was off to the set.

❧

At midnight they were once again walking through the front door of the house. "I've got some ideas what we could do tomorrow," Kate said, "but I'm also flexible if you've got something else in mind."

"Try me," Jay said as she stripped off her suit jacket.

"Okay, I thought maybe we could skip the workout and run in the morning. You could sleep in a little longer, and then we could go hiking instead for part of the day. There are some beautiful trails in the Catskill Mountains that I'd love to show you. We could pack lunch and have a picnic, take our time, then come back here, shower, and relax a little before I take you out for a fabulous dinner at a wonderful place I know."

Jay sighed with pleasure. "That sounds fantastic. I can't think of anything I'd rather do. The only drawback is that I didn't think to bring my hiking boots with me."

"That's okay, the hike isn't too terribly difficult. You could do it in your sneakers, or we could stop and I could buy you a new pair of hiking boots if you'd be more comfortable."

"No, no," Jay replied, "my sneakers will be just fine."

"Great then, that's settled. There's no rush to get going in the morning, so whenever you wake up is perfect."

The two women walked up the stairs together.

"I'm glad you liked the documentary, Jay."

"I thought it was incredible, Kate. I was moved to tears. You did a magnificent job with it."

"Thanks." They reached the top of the landing. "I'll see you in the morning. Sleep well, Princess."

"You too, Stretch."

❧

Two hours later, Jay was sleeping soundly, dreaming of lying in Kate's arms. This was a recurring dream for her, one she'd been having off and on since their first encounter on the ski slope. It always brought a smile to her face.

So caught up in the dream was she that it took her several moments to register the sensation of her hand being tossed up into the air. At first, she thought it was part of the dream. Shortly, however, a whine made it clear something else was going on. Finally, as more of her senses awakened, she figured out that Fred was trying to get her

111

attention. The canine was pushing his nose under her hand and throwing it up into the air in an effort to wake her.

As her brain began to kick in, Jay registered the dog's agitation. He was poking his nose at her and tugging at her clothing. In the several nights she had spent in Kate's home, Fred had never left Kate's side at night. Jay sat up quickly.

"What is it, buddy, what's wrong?" As she talked to Fred, trying to calm him, she heard a noise. She was quiet for a few moments, and then she heard it again, this time more distinctly. It was Kate, and she was screaming.

Within seconds, Jay was down the hall and pushing Kate's door open further. The light in the hallway that spilled into the room combined with the bright moonlight filtering in through the skylight to allow her to see clearly. Kate was thrashing around, screaming and crying in her sleep.

Jay experienced a moment of uncertainty. Before when she tried to awaken her from a nightmare, Kate pushed her away, growing cold and distant. That was the last thing Jay wanted to have happen, but she couldn't stand by and watch Kate suffer.

She moved to the bed, gently grasped the struggling woman by the shoulder, and shook her. "Kate, please wake up. Kate, honey, you're having a bad dream. Please, sweetheart, wake up."

As Kate moved toward consciousness and her eyes began to flicker open, Jay backed away from the bed. She didn't want to risk the reaction she got the last time she was in this situation, so she started to move toward the door, apologizing as she went. "I'm sorry, Kate, Fred came to get me. You were having a nightmare...I just wanted to make sure you were okay."

"It's okay, Jay. Come here, please," she motioned for Jay to sit on the bed. More softly she added, "I could use a friend right now."

Jay joined Kate and sat on the side of the bed. Tentatively, she reached out and took Kate's hands. "What was it about...do you want to talk about it?"

Kate shrugged. "I just can't seem to get the images out of my head," she began. "It was the same thing I saw in my dreams last week, right after the bombing. Something I saw while I was in the building. I was crawling through the remains of the first floor, helping some of the kids who were in the lobby when the explosion happened. In fact, I had just finished freeing Joey, and moved maybe another ten feet or so when I stumbled across something. I looked down, and there was this young boy, he was probably a classmate of

Joey's. His eyes were fixed and staring unseeing at the ceiling, as if in a silent plea. Part of the first-floor roof had collapsed on him." Tears began to stream down her face. "I haven't been able to get his face out of my mind, and I wonder if I ever will."

"Shh. Oh, Kate, it's okay, sweetheart." Jay moved closer and took Kate into her arms. "It's going to be all right." She rocked and comforted Kate until all her tears were spent, then reached to the bedside table and handed Kate the box of tissues that was sitting there.

Jay pulled back a little and used her thumbs to wipe away Kate's tears. Impulsively, she leaned forward, replaced her thumbs with her lips, and placed light kisses on Kate's cheeks and eyelids. The combination of the feel of the silky smooth skin and the scent of Shalimar that had been etched in her memory for so long was almost too much for Jay.

Slowly, she pulled Kate to her, reached up, and ran her fingers through her hair. Their mouths met in a kiss that was at first gentle and undemanding. As their lips became better acquainted, it was Jay who deepened the contact, wanting to express with her kiss the feelings she had never spoken.

Kate moaned at the sensation of Jay's tongue mingling with hers, united in a dance of welcome and desire. She ran her hands up and down Jay's back, reveling in the delicious texture of the sheer satin nightgown as it brushed against her palms. When she felt the aroused state of Jay's nipples where they pressed against her, it was all she could do to hold herself back.

Breathing raggedly, she pulled away from the kiss. She looked into eyes darkened with passion and teased, "Aren't you afraid you'll compromise your professional objectivity?"

Jay groaned. "I don't care anymore, I'll make it work. Professional detachment is driving me crazy."

Kate laughed. "Glad to hear it's not just me, but you'd better be getting back to your room or I won't be responsible for my actions."

Jay agreed. "Are you sure you're all right?"

"I am now."

As she stood, Jay leaned over one last time and kissed Kate passionately. Then, with a small smirk and the raising of an eyebrow, she turned and made her way across the room to the door. "I'll see you in the morning."

"I can't wait," Kate replied huskily.

CHAPTER TWELVE

At 7:45 a.m., Kate quietly let herself into the house from the garage. As soon as she stepped into the kitchen and saw Jay, she froze. Jay wore a look of such abject fear and despair on her face that it broke Kate's heart. She barely had time to open her arms as Jay threw herself into them, burying her head in Kate's chest.

Not knowing what else to do, Kate held on and tightened her grip, rubbed Jay's back, and kissed the top of her head. She couldn't begin to fathom what prompted such a reaction. At length, she pulled back enough to see Jay's face. "What's wrong, are you okay? Did something happen while I was gone?"

Jay shook her head no, but her lower lip trembled. "I was worried about you after your nightmare, and I couldn't sleep, so I thought I would just check on you to make sure you were okay. That was at a little after six this morning, and when I didn't find you in bed, I began to wonder where you might have gone. I searched the whole house and then, when I realized you weren't here, my imagination started running away with me and I was afraid something bad had happened to you. It sounds so stupid now when I say it out loud," she finished meekly.

Kate smiled. "It doesn't sound silly to me at all, Jay. It sounds as if you care, which is a foreign concept to me. No one has ever worried about me that way before, and I'm deeply touched. I'm sorry I gave you such a fright, I didn't mean to. I just wasn't thinking...I should have left a note. Forgive me?"

Jay nodded.

"Now, can we start the day off properly?" Kate put her hands on either side of Jay's face and looked deeply into eyes that reminded her of a beautiful summer day. Just as she was about to lower her mouth to Jay's, she knew a moment of uncertainty. She asked, "May I?"

"Please."

The long, slow, thorough kiss that followed made Kate's pulse race. Every nerve in Kate's body begged for more, but she was in no rush. She would not push Jay too far, too fast. She wanted to be sure of Jay's feelings rather than make assumptions. Heaven knew Kate knew what she felt. She sighed. "Now that was the way a day like today should start."

"I'll say," Jay said dreamily.

Kate wanted to be as honest as she could be. "I stopped by to see Barbara before her day got too busy so she could take my stitches out. See?" She held out her hand and arm for Jay to examine. Indeed, the tiny rows of X's were gone, leaving only healing pink scars in their wake.

Jay ran her fingers over the thin lines that bisected Kate's palm and the other marks that marred her perfect forearms. She lifted one of the injured hands and kissed the palm gently.

Kate tried hard to contain the involuntary shiver of pleasure the contact evoked, knowing that if she were to pursue her impulses, they would never get out of the house that day. Still, her eyes revealed the desire that was building in her, and Jay's eyes sparkled with the knowledge.

Finally, the magic of the moment was broken when Fred pushed between them, unceremoniously depositing his ball at their feet. Both women laughed and shook their heads. Kate went to play with Fred while Jay took a shower. Within an hour, both women were clean, dressed, and sitting at the kitchen table over coffee and Raisin Bran.

"Ready to go?" Kate asked as she cleared the bowls and cups from the table. She was anxious to show Jay the beauty of the Catskill Mountains and it was the perfect day for it—sunny and seventy-two degrees with just a sprinkling of clouds.

"You bet. Where are we going, by the way? And what, pray tell, is in that huge backpack?"

"In keeping with your love of American literature, I thought I'd take you to one of the most oft-described vistas of the romantic era. Is it safe to assume you've read James Fenimore Cooper's *The Pioneers*?"

"Of course. Eighteen twenty-three. Natty Bumppo and all that. Why do you ask?"

"If you go back and look at the book, you'll find that Natty gives a wonderful description of the view from one of the spots we're going to hike to today."

"Really? Now I'm going to have to dig out my old copy and reread it."

"No need." Kate smiled indulgently. "I've taken the liberty of marking the passage and bringing along my copy, which is one of the things in that backpack." At Jay's raised eyebrow, she added, "Hey, I've got all the essentials. Lunch, water for humans and Fred, binoculars, and James Fenimore Cooper."

Jay laughed. "Who could ask for anything more?" She narrowed her eyes. "You read *The Pioneers*?"

Kate gave Jay one of her full-fledged, intimidating, arched-eyebrow looks. "Just because I'm a television news anchor doesn't mean I'm illiterate, ya know. You'd better be nice to me or I'll start spewing Shakespearean soliloquies from *Macbeth*."

"Ooh, we wouldn't want that, now would we, Fred?"

With the top down, it was virtually impossible to hear, so the drive was a relatively conversation-free affair. Fred happily occupied the back seat with the backpack and left the driving and navigating to the humans.

Almost an hour into the drive, Kate was startled out of her reverie by the feel of a warm hand covering hers where it rested on the gearshift. Tentatively, slowly, smaller fingers wrapped around her larger ones and she glanced over to see Jay looking at her, a question in her deep green eyes. Kate smiled broadly, picked up their joined hands, placed a delicate kiss on the back of the Jay's hand and brought them both to rest on her thigh. She sighed happily.

A little more than half an hour later, as they neared their destination, Jay released her hold on Kate's hand so that she could downshift and guide them to a stop. "Where exactly are we?"

"North Lake, to be specific. The hike we're going to take is a five-mile loop encompassing Kaaterskill Falls and the Cliff Walk. I really wanted to share this with you because it's one of the most scenic, peaceful, least populated trails around here, and a personal favorite of mine. I hope you'll like it as much as I do. The views are sensational, especially on a clear day like today."

Kate hoisted the heavy pack onto her back as if it weighed nothing, cinched the chest and waist straps, and shifted the weight until it was perfectly balanced. Fred, waiting impatiently for Kate to give him the signal that he could begin blazing the trail, leapt with glee when her hand gesture finally indicated that he was free to go. She checked her watch and turned to Jay. "How hungry are you?"

"Is that a trick question?"

Kate laughed. "No, in this case it's not. We can either hike to the falls first, in which case lunch will be in half an hour, or we can hike the Cliff Walk first, in which case lunch will be in two and a half or three hours. The choice is yours."

"Hmm, decisions, decisions. Do I want to eat first and then walk it off, or do I want to work up an appetite first and feel as if I've earned my meal? That's a tough call, Stretch."

"I have faith in your ability to figure it out and come up with the perfect solution, Scoop."

"Oh you do, do you? In that case, I say we go to the falls and eat first, since I want to make sure I have an appetite for dinner tonight."

"Wise choice, young lady, as dinner will be a spectacular affair. The falls it is. Right this way." She swept her hand in the correct direction, indicating that Jay should lead the way and set the pace.

A short time later the trail led through a stand of virgin hemlock trees, emerging at the lower basin of the falls. Jay stood at the bottom of the falls looking up, her mouth hanging open. The roar of the water crashing down was overwhelming and, even from a good distance away, the spray proved powerful enough to coat them with a light mist.

"My God, Kate, this is amazing. I've never seen anything like it." Jay seemed to regard the scene with a sort of childlike wonder, turning around in a circle to take in the entire view. "And there's nobody else here."

Kate smirked, knowing that she had picked that picnic spot for that very reason. She was fairly confident that, so early in the season on a weekday, the place would be relatively empty of tourists and day hikers. She was glad beyond words that she had been correct.

She led them farther down the trail, far enough away from the noise and spray, yet close enough that the view of the falls was still breathtaking. They were standing on the edge of Spruce Creek, which featured a number of huge stones.

"Come over here and give me your hand."

"Why?"

"Has anybody ever told you, you ask too many questions?"

Jay chuckled and moved closer, making a grand show of presenting her hand. Kate pulled Jay to her and scooped her up in one smooth motion.

"Wha— what are you doing?" Jay wrapped her arms around Kate's neck.

Kate smiled down at her mischievously. "Well, I assumed that you didn't want to get wet, and since our picnic spot is over there..." With her head, she gestured to a huge, flat rock in the center of the creek. "I thought this might be the best mode of transportation for you. Now, if you'd prefer..." She made as if to set Jay down in the water.

"No!"

"I didn't think so." Carrying Jay in her arms with little effort, Kate picked her way across the rocks that populated the creek and over to the designated dining area. Since the water wasn't particularly deep at that point and her hiking boots were waterproofed, unlike Jay's sneakers, she wasn't concerned about getting her feet wet. When she reached the giant boulder, she gently set Jay down on top of it. "How's that?"

"Mmm, great." Jay's arms were still around Kate's neck.

"Um, Jay? You can let go now."

"Oh, sorry."

"Glad you like it." Kate removed the pack from her back and spent several minutes looking around inside for the items she wanted. First, she pulled out a red-and-white checkered tablecloth, which the two of them spread out on the rock. Then she produced two paper plates, napkins, and silverware, which she arranged on the tablecloth. Next, she unloaded several sandwiches, bags of chips and pretzels, fruit, and carrot sticks. Finally, she removed two bottles of water from the pack and hoisted herself up onto the surface of the boulder.

"Wow, this is quite a spread."

"I wasn't sure what kind of sandwiches you liked, so I got a bunch of different ones for you to choose from. You get first pick. There's turkey with mayo, roast beef with Russian dressing, grilled chicken breast on a hard roll, and a lettuce, tomato, and cheese sandwich with mayo."

"Wow! You are amazingly thoughtful, you know that? I can't believe you went to all this trouble and carried all this stuff in that pack. It must weigh a ton!"

"Nah, it's not too bad, and besides, since I didn't work out today, this will substitute nicely."

Jay selected the turkey sandwich, some Fritos, a handful of carrot sticks, and an orange and arranged them on her plate. Kate handed her a bottle of water, took the roast beef sandwich, some of the remaining carrots, and the other orange, and the two women sat side by side watching the falls and laughing at Fred, who was hunting for rocks on the creek bed.

When they finished eating, Kate collected the plates, orange peels, chip bags, and silverware and placed them in a plastic bag before putting them back in the pack. Then they folded up the tablecloth and she stuffed that in as well. With everything cleaned up and put away, she leaned back against a shelf in the mammoth rock, motioning for Jay to lean against her. Jay complied, fitting herself in the space Kate made between her legs and resting her back against the convenient chest.

Kate wrapped her arms around Jay's waist and rested her cheek on the fair head. Jay, in turn, placed her arms on top of Kate's and turned her head slightly. "That was a fantastic lunch. Thank you for putting it all together. This is a beautiful spot."

"Mmm, almost as beautiful as you, but not quite." Kate smiled as a blush crept up Jay's neck and into her cheeks.

"Yeah, right." Jay shifted uncomfortably.

Kate put her fingers briefly to the lips below her and tightened her grip around Jay's waist, bringing them into even closer contact. "Don't, Jay. Don't do that. You are by far the most beautiful woman I have ever seen. Please don't dismiss or discount how incredible you are. I wish you could see yourself the way I see you."

Jay was quiet for a moment. "My father used to tell me that I was ugly and nobody but him would want me and that I was lucky to have him. I guess I believed him, and even though you'd think I should know better by now, part of me still believes him."

Once again, Kate was glad she'd never met the man, because she would have strangled him if she could have. "Your father was a sick man, Jay. The things he told you were designed to lower your self-esteem and keep you under his control. They weren't the truth." She let her words sink in for a few seconds before continuing. "Do you trust me, Jay?"

Jay clearly was surprised by the question. "More than I've ever trusted anyone in my life. Why?"

"Because I want you to know that you can always, always trust me to tell you the truth, and the truth is that you are gorgeous, and amazingly desirable, and that, right now, I'm having a really hard time keeping my hands to myself." Kate's eyes darkened with longing. The urge she felt to touch Jay was nearly overwhelming.

Shifting in the circle of Kate's arms, Jay buried her hands in the dark mane of hair and urgently drew Kate to her mouth. This kiss was filled with passion, promise, and desire, and ignited a fire deep inside Kate. She felt Jay dig her hands in deeper as she moaned deep in her throat. For several long minutes, the rest of the universe ceased to exist, until reality finally intruded in the form of the sound of hikers in the distance.

They both pulled back at the same time, breathing heavily, eyes locked on each other. Kate ran her finger along Jay's jaw line and across her lips, then gently disentangled herself. Without a word, she stood up, shouldered and settled the pack, and hopped down off the rock. Without breaking eye contact, she lifted Jay into her arms and carried her back across the creek to the trail where, reluctantly, she set her back on the ground.

"Shall we go on?" Kate asked huskily. "It's a magnificent hike from here along the Cliff Walk."

"I'm all yours," Jay said with a twinkle in her eyes.

"I can only hope," Kate said softly. "C'mon Fred, let's go." Fred bounded out of the water and back onto the trail, shaking himself off and managing to spray Kate in the process. "Gee, thanks, buddy, I guess you could tell I needed some cooling off."

Jay just laughed.

They moved along the trail at a comfortable pace, with Fred running ahead several hundred feet and doubling back to check on their progress every now and again. By the time the day was over, he would cover twice as much ground as Kate and Jay.

After a short time they came to a series of open overlooks atop steep outcroppings of rock. On two sides were clear vistas of mountains, and below was Kaaterskill Creek that led to the Hudson River. They stopped for a few minutes to enjoy the view and to allow Fred to rest and get a drink, since his tongue was hanging out the side of his mouth.

"Let's keep going," Kate said. "The view gets even better when we get to Sunset Rock and Inspiration Point." And, true to her word, as the pair approached those landmarks they came upon a riot of wildflowers lining the path, along with colorful butterflies and several varieties of birds.

"Oh, Kate, it's amazing."

"Yeah, this is my favorite time of year to hike the Catskills because all the wildflowers are in bloom. I sometimes spend hours up here just looking out at the mountains and flowers. It's a great place to get away from it all and just be. I've never brought anyone else with me before."

Jay reached out and took Kate's hand. "Thank you so much for sharing this with me. I feel so privileged that you wanted to show me this place."

Kate squeezed Jay's hand and held on. They began moving again. The trail was wide enough there to accommodate their walking side by side, and they continued on through forest until they came to a stop at a grassy knoll. Jay looked around. The only visible thing was a junction with another trail. At her inquiring look, Kate explained, "This was the site of the Kaaterskill Hotel. It was built in eighteen eighty-one and burned to the ground in a fire in nineteen twenty-four. At its peak, this area was *the* place to see and be seen by the rich and famous. Presidents, movie stars, and socialites all gathered here in the Catskills to play and vacation."

"I think you missed your calling, Stretch. You should have been a tour guide."

Kate rolled her eyes and tugged on Jay's hand as they resumed their hike. The trail led them through open fields with views of the surrounding mountains and through dense forest where the smell of pine trees was overwhelming. Twenty-five minutes later they emerged from the forest into a large open space.

"Let me guess," Jay said, "Another hotel site."

"Very good, Watson, but not just any hotel. This was the famous Catskill Mountain House."

"You've got to do something about that British accent, woman. Either do it right or give it up, because I gotta tell ya, ya just ain't got it."

"Everybody's a critic. Just for that, maybe I won't share this with you." She waved the copy of James Fenimore Cooper's book in front of Jay's face.

Jay did her best to look contrite. "Okay, okay, I'm sorry, I didn't mean it. I promise I'll try to behave."

"That's better." Kate turned Jay slowly in a full circle so that she could appreciate the view of the entire valley as it stretched below her, and then she began to read a passage from *The Pioneers*.

Jay closed her eyes and listened. "Wow. It still looks the way he described it a hundred and fifty years ago. That's incredible!"

"I thought you might appreciate that. Just think, someday one hundred years from now, people like us will be walking along on a hike, quoting from a classic great American novel by a giant of her time named Jamison Parker." At the incredulous look on Jay's face Kate added, "If you dream it, it can come true, Jay. Don't ever give up on your dreams...they're too important and you're too talented."

Jay seemed about to make light of the compliment, but said simply, "Thank you."

"Are you ready to go? We're almost at the end of the hike, and if we go now we'll have time once we get back to the house to relax for a bit and shower before dinner."

"Sounds great."

Once settled in the car and on the road, they held hands all the way home while Fred, having gotten his fill of exercise for one day, was sound asleep in the back seat.

As the women were putting the finishing touches on their outfits for the evening, the front doorbell rang. Kate called out, "Jay, could you get that, please? I'm not quite ready yet."

"Sure," Jay answered from downstairs.

Jay opened the door to reveal a deliverywoman carrying two long rectangular boxes. "Can I help you?"

"I'm looking for Jamison Parker."

The expression on Jay's face was one of shock. "I-I'm Jay Parker."

"Well then, I guess these are for you. Somebody must like you a whole lot, that's for sure. Well, have a great night."

Jay slowly untied the ribbon and opened the first box. "Oh, my, these are gorgeous." She put the bouquet of twelve blood red roses to her nose and gave an appreciative sniff. Then she reached inside the box and found the card that came with them.

"Thanks for a fantastic day. I'm so glad you could spend it with me. Love, K."

"Wow, you are something else, Ms. Kyle, aren't you?" Her curiosity piqued, she unwrapped the second box. Inside were a dozen perfect yellow roses and another card.

"I haven't had a chance to figure out your preferences yet, so I thought I'd take the coward's way out and hedge my bets. I hope I guessed right with at least one of these choices. May your life always be filled with the beauty and joy you've brought to mine these past few days. Love, K."

"Fred," Jay addressed the canine that was busily scouting out the new scents, "your mother is a closet romantic. The more I learn about her, the more I want to know."

"I hope so," Kate said as she strode into the room.

"These are so beautiful, I can't believe you did this." Tears sprang to Jay's eyes. "In my whole life, no one has ever treated me like this."

"Their mistake." Kate moved forward another step and enfolded Jay in her arms. "You look magnificent," she murmured into the strands of golden hair. Jay was wearing a rich, rust-colored silk pantsuit with a crème-colored button-down silk blouse that revealed just a hint of cleavage. "Now, are you going to tell me which color you prefer?"

"Are you kidding, when I could keep you guessing and continue to get double the flowers? What do I look like, a fool?"

"Jamison Parker, what makes you think you'll ever get more if you don't state a preference now?"

"Um, because I'm irresistible? Charming? Witty?"

"Full of it."

"Hey, I resemble that remark!"

"Yes, you certainly do, but I'll forgive you this time." Kate kissed Jay's head and released her.

"You look pretty sensational, yourself there, Stretch." Kate wore a jet-black linen pantsuit with a scooped-neck pale blue silk camisole underneath that Jay thought picked up the color of her eyes perfectly. "Are you going to tell me where we're going yet?"

"Thank you, and we're going out to dinner."

"Oh, that was helpful and informative."

"Well, excuse me, Miss I-won't-tell-you-what-color-roses-I-prefer, if I'm somewhat less than forthcoming, but two can play that game."

"Oh, you are such a brat!"

"Yep, that's just what my mother used to say. Now come on, or we're going to be late."

"Wait," Jay said as Kate began to push her out the door. "I want to put these in water first. Do you have a vase?"

Kate returned with two cut crystal vases, and Jay trimmed the stems on the yellow and red blooms. She arranged them to her satisfaction, leaned over one more time to take in their spicy fragrance, then allowed herself to be ushered out the door.

సించ

Within half an hour they pulled up to a well-lit mansion with a wraparound driveway. A valet parking attendant greeted each of them and helped them out of the car. Kate took Jay's hand, placed it in the crook of her arm, and escorted her up the front steps.

"We're eating at someone's house? You're taking me to dinner at someone's house?"

Kate chuckled. "Not exactly, but you're close. This was once the home of General Burgoyne during the Revolutionary War. It has been preserved in its original style. Have you ever heard of the Battle of Saratoga? It was one of the turning points of the war."

"You know, being around you is an education. I can see I'm going to have to read up on my history."

"Actually, no need, you can read the abbreviated version on the menu once we sit down."

"Ah, Ms. Kyle, it's so nice to see you this evening. Everything has been arranged for you as you requested. Ma'am." The tuxedoed man turned to Jay with a nod and a bow in polite greeting. "Please, come right this way."

Jay wondered what in the world Kate was up to. She followed along like a curious puppy as they were led through the stately foyer, past the great room, the library, and the sitting room and into a private dining room overlooking the river. There was a single antique mahogany table set for two, with two antique pewter candlesticks, white tapers burning in each. A single red rose sat in the center between the two candles. The cutlery was sterling silver and the plates fine china. Cut crystal glasses rounded out the table setting. A waiter pulled out Jay's chair and motioned for her to sit down with a bow. When she was seated, Kate sat as well.

The waiter handed each woman a heavy, leather-bound menu and asked Kate if she wanted him to open the bottle of champagne. "Jay, do you drink champagne? I didn't know if you did or not, so I had them chill a bottle just in case. Is there something else you'd prefer?"

"I'm not much of a drinker, but a nice glass of champagne would be great, thank you."

Kate motioned for the waiter to fill their glasses, which he did before discreetly disappearing. She held up her glass and proposed a heartfelt toast. "To a very special, very beautiful woman, thank you for the most fabulous day I've spent in a very long time."

A blush crept up Jay's neck and face as she touched glasses with Kate. "I should be the one thanking you. I feel like a princess in a fairy tale. This has been the most wonderful day I can ever remember, and believe me, I have a pretty good memory."

They opened the menus, concentrating for a few minutes on the choices. Jay settled on the seafood Newburgh and Kate opted for the salmon in an orange-sauce glaze. Jay spent a few extra minutes reading the description of the battle and the history of the mansion in which they were sitting.

When she finished, she looked up. "They've turned the general's house into a restaurant? What about historic preservation and all that?"

Kate shyly glanced at Jay. "It's not exactly open to the public. I pulled a few strings and called in a couple of favors. And the room you're sitting in was the general's own private dining room where, legend has it, he sat and watched the progression of the fight across the river."

They spent the remaining time while waiting for dinner to be served talking of favorite places they'd traveled, sights they'd still like to see, and the most significant influences in their formative years. As the food was served, they were still chatting.

When dessert was cleared and coffee served, Kate took Jay's hand and asked, "Have you enjoyed this evening so far? Is there anything more you want right now?"

Oh, yeah, there's definitely something more I want, but not here. She answered, "Let's see, you've called in favors from curators of historic landmarks and top-flight chefs in order to provide the ultimate romantic, private dining experience. Gee, I'm sure there must be something you've forgotten." She laughed. "What did I ever do to deserve you?"

Kate laughed too. "Um, got run over on a ski trail?"

"You had to remind me, didn't you? It took months for my leg to heal. Hell, I missed the entire lacrosse season that year." More seriously, Jay said, "But it was more than worth it to meet you." She debated whether to reveal her secret and, after a second's hesitation, decided that if she really wanted Kate, and God did she, then she needed to come clean. "In fact, I've always thought of that as one of my luckiest days—the day I found my muse."

Kate's eyebrow hiked into her hairline. "Me?"

Jay chuckled. "Oh yes, you." Sheepishly she admitted, "You were the cause of the only real fight my girlfriend at the time and I ever had." She was too embarrassed to hold Kate's gaze, so she lowered her head to take in their joined hands and began fidgeting. "Sarah read some of the, um, writings in my journal and accused me of having an affair with you in my heart, if not in fact."

"She did?" Kate's voice was full of wonder.

"Yep, and with good reason too. I got really mad at her for invading my privacy, but it should have occurred to her that I never argued whether or not the substance of her accusation was correct." Quietly, she added, "I couldn't argue that...she was right." Jay hazarded a look up into Kate's face.

"She was?"

"Mmm-hmm, she most definitely was. That was when I started to realize that what I had with Sarah wasn't the real thing. I felt more when you held me, innocently trying to warm me in your jacket on that ski trail, than I had ever felt while making love with her."

"You did?"

"You turned a switch on for me. It was as if, in you, I found something that I had been searching for my entire life, and I never even knew I'd been looking. But I figured I didn't stand a chance with someone like you, so I shrugged it off, except in my dreams and my journal. Sarah and I stayed together until graduation, but my heart wasn't in it. Since then I've sworn off relationships. I never again wanted to cause the kind of pain that I caused her."

"And now?" Kate asked hesitantly.

Looking up directly into those fathomless eyes, Jay knew that these might be the most important words she would utter in her lifetime. "And now we're here, and you're so much more than I ever imagined, and I know that I must be dreaming, but if I am I don't ever want to wake up again." She took a deep breath and decided to go for broke. "You may think I'm crazy, but I've known from the very first time you held me in your arms five years ago that you were the one for me. Being with anybody else would have been a sham. I don't know if you believe in soul mates, but I do, and I have been waiting for you forever, Katherine Kyle, and I'm so glad I've found you again."

Kate let out a shaky breath. "The night that you were attacked on campus, the EMT who helped you was my girlfriend. She broke up with me a short time after that. She said she'd been waiting two years for me to look at her the way I looked at you when I held you in my arms that night. At the time, I didn't understand what she meant. But the night of the explosion, when I looked up and saw you standing there, I finally got it. No one has ever made me feel the way you do just by looking at you, Jay, and she must have seen that mirrored in my face. I guess what I'm saying, sweetheart, is that I feel that connection between us too. I've always felt it." Kate picked up their joined hands and reverently kissed Jay's.

"I can't believe this is happening to me...it's too good to be true," Jay mumbled.

"Ms. Parker, may I take you home now, before I make a scene and ravish you right here in the middle of this historic establishment?"

A brief shadow of fear made Jay shudder once. "By all means, I can't have you ruining your reputation with such a public display of wanton lasciviousness, now can I?" *You know this is everything you've ever wanted, Jamison, so why are you scared all of a sudden?*

As they made their way out of the mansion and to the waiting car, Kate said, "You know you're safe with me, right, Jay? You know you don't ever have to be afraid that anything will happen that you don't want, right?"

"Of course." But Jay inwardly cursed that tiny, irrational part of her that was terrified for no logical reason.

CHAPTER THIRTEEN

C an I get you anything else to drink?" Kate asked as she led Jay into the family room.

"No, I'm fine, thanks."

Kate moved over to the fireplace and lit a match to the wood that she placed there before they left for dinner. Almost immediately, the fire began to cast a warm glow throughout the dimly lit room. She opened the French doors leading to the deck and stepped out, inviting Jay to join her. For a few moments they stood there, gazing up at the profusion of stars above and the full moon that hung overhead.

"It's a gorgeous night, isn't it?" Kate asked.

"Mmm, it most certainly is that. I can't remember when the last time was that I saw this many stars this clearly."

"That's the price you pay, living in a big city...you tend to lose the sky, don't you?"

"Yeah, I guess you do, although until now, I never gave it that much thought." Jay shivered slightly as a light breeze buffeted her.

"Are you cold?"

"Just a little."

"Come here." Kate opened her arms and surrounded Jay with her warmth. After a moment she asked, "Is that better?"

"Mmm, you're like a walking electric blanket. How do you do that?"

"Just warm-blooded, I guess. Would you like to go inside? We can leave the doors open to enjoy the night and take advantage of the fireplace to take the edge off the chill."

The two women walked back through the doors and into the family room.

"Do you like to dance?"

Jay smiled. "I love to dance, but I haven't had much chance lately."

Kate was at the stereo, selecting a homemade tape from her collection. "We can fix that." She held out her hand to Jay and moved them to the middle of the floor as the first notes to the Bee Gees' megahit *How Deep Is Your Love* began to flow out of the speakers. "Do you know how to swing?"

"I've seen it many times, and always wanted to try it, but I've never danced with anyone who knew how."

"Well, it's your lucky night. We can solve that too. Just follow my lead, okay?"

Jay just nodded her head and smiled. She would have followed this woman anywhere, and she knew it.

Kate took Jay into her arms and steered her expertly around the floor. She started with a series of simple moves and spins and then progressed to more difficult handholds and positions. "You're a natural, Scoop, you move very well. Just relax and let the music take you...that's it." Kate spun her partner one last time as the song was ending, brought her back into her body, and dipped her slightly as the last notes faded.

Jay laughed. "Where did you learn to dance like that, Stretch? That was so much fun! Will you teach me more moves?"

"Anytime you want, but probably not on a full stomach." Kate's eyes twinkled.

"Yeah, that's probably a wise decision." Jay patted the somewhat stuffed body part in question.

"So for tonight, how about if we keep it nice and slow?"

"Slow sounds lovely," Jay murmured, as the sounds of a Whitney Houston song began to fill the room.

Kate pulled Jay close and took the lead, moving them gently in a circle to the rhythm of the music. Jay rested her forehead against the side of Kate's neck and sighed happily as the now-familiar scent of Shalimar filled her nostrils. Smiling when she felt the brush of lips against her hair, she closed her eyes and concentrated on the music and the feel of the incredible woman who was holding her in her arms.

"Is this okay?"

"Oh, yes, it's wonderful...a perfect ending to the perfect day, in fact. A beautiful hike, lovely flowers, a truly special, romantic, private dining experience, topped off with dancing in a fire-lit room. You certainly know how to treat the ladies."

"Actually, I've never done this for anyone before. I've never wanted to."

"You haven't?" Jay asked.

"No, I've never had a woman in this house before. There was never anyone I wanted to bring into my home...until now. As I told you earlier, I've never taken anyone on that hike, nor have I ever bought flowers for a woman...only for you, Jay." She tipped Jay's chin up, and Jay could see the emotions behind the words in Kate's eyes. "Only for you."

As Whitney Houston transitioned into Lionel Richie and Diana Ross's *Endless Love*, Kate reached down and caressed Jay's face and neck, drawing her in for a passionate kiss. Jay's hands moved of their own accord. They slid under the back of Kate's jacket as she ran her palms over the softness of the pale blue camisole, and she could feel the heat of the skin beneath.

Kate moaned into the kiss and deepened the contact, matching the rhythm of the tongue that sought hers as she buried her long fingers in Jay's soft golden tresses.

Without ever breaking the kiss, Jay began to unbutton Kate's jacket, coaxing it from her broad shoulders. She needed to explore more of the delicious body before her.

Kate redirected her lips to taste Jay's neck and throat, as Jay tipped her head back to give her better access. Kate's hands made short work of the rust-colored jacket, tossing it on the nearby sofa without missing a beat. Through the thin material that still separated them, each woman was acutely aware of the feel of the other's firm breasts and taut nipples aching to be touched.

Jay groaned in pleasure as Kate took a sensitive earlobe into her mouth, and grazed it with her teeth while using her hands to trace Jay's rib cage through her blouse. Kate grasped the crème-colored material, and began tugging it free of the slacks, seeking the skin underneath. Jay immediately stiffened in her arms and Kate pulled back slightly to look into her eyes. Jay tried, but failed to hide the small dose of fear that she knew was mixed in with her desire.

Kate stilled her hands and rested them on Jay's waist. She gazed intently into Jay's eyes before she leaned forward and placed a nearly chaste soft kiss on Jay's lips. Then Kate pulled back again. "There's no rush, darling. I'd wait forever for you."

Jay studied Kate's expression. She expected to find pity or disgust. When she saw nothing there save love, passion, tenderness, and understanding, she began to cry and tremble. She shook her head, and cleared the tears from her eyes. "Oh, Kate, I don't want to wait. I want you, and this, more than I've ever wanted anything in my life, but I'm scared and I so don't want to be afraid."

In truth, Jay had never been in a situation where she hadn't been in complete control at all times. She had never given herself fully to anyone, always achieving a measure of detachment in her head and her heart, even in the midst of lovemaking. Now she was there, with the woman who had fueled her fantasies and dreams for what seemed like forever. Not only did she know with certainty that she couldn't maintain any distance from her, she didn't want to, and it frightened her to death.

Kate's eyes burned into her. "Tell me what you want, sweetheart, I'll do anything it takes to make you comfortable."

There was nothing to do but follow her heart. "Make love to me." Jay slid her arms around Kate's neck, and she pulled her down into a mind-numbing kiss that stoked the burning embers into hot flames.

Kate reached down and scooped Jay into her arms. They continued to kiss all the way up the stairs, never breaking the sweet contact until they arrived in the master bedroom, where Kate set Jay back on her feet.

✍✍

Kate's hands trembled as she raised them to unfasten the buttons on Jay's blouse. For Kate this was about so much more than sex—it was about freeing her heart and opening it to true love for the very first time. And then there was the beautiful, gentle soul before her against whom sex had been used as a weapon when she was a child. It was no wonder Jay was scared. Kate was determined to do everything possible to make their first time together perfect, and to leave no doubt in Jay's mind what was in her heart.

The shakiness of Kate's hands must not have been lost on Jay, since she placed her hands on top of Kate's and helped her to unbutton first her blouse, then her slacks. As Jay stepped out of the pants, Kate tried to memorize every inch of flesh revealed.

Her fingers were barely a whisper on Jay's skin as she swept the blouse from her shoulders. Her fingers and lips ran lightly over Jay's creamy flesh, as she caressed shoulders, neck, and throat. Kate stepped back, locked gazes with Jay, and slowly removed her own clothes.

Desire was written all over Jay's face as Kate stood naked, bathed in the moonlight that streaked in through the skylight.

Kate moved forward and skimmed her fingertips over Jay's perfect lips before leaning down to capture them once again with her mouth. She reached behind, unclasped Jay's satin lace bra, slid it down off her well-developed shoulders, and dropped it on the floor at their feet. Then she hooked her fingers in the matching lace underwear and supported Jay as she stepped out of them.

"You take my breath away," Kate murmured, wondering if her heart would start to beat again anytime soon. The woman before her was lithe and toned, flawlessly proportioned and balanced, and without question the most magnificent creature she had ever laid eyes on.

An appealing blush crept up Jay's neck to her cheeks. "That's okay, love, because if Michelangelo had had you to use as a model, he could've retired a wealthy man."

Kate smiled and ran her fingers along Jay's jaw line. She mapped out the eyebrows, the cute little nose, the well-shaped lips, and the rounded cheekbones before sliding her hand down to stroke Jay's neck and shoulders. Unhurriedly, she threaded her fingers into the golden strands of hair and initiated a soul-searing kiss while bringing their naked bodies into full contact for the first time.

As liquid fire spread through her veins, Kate backed Jay up, gently guided her down onto the bed, and came to rest beside her on one arm as she continued to kiss her. She touched and tasted the body beneath her with her mouth and her hands, finding and memorizing especially sensitive spots, taking her time and enjoying Jay's reactions to her attentions. She was completely focused on satisfying Jay, blocking out her own rising excitement, not wanting to be distracted even for a second. There would be time for that later. At that moment, it was all about Jay.

Kate brought Jay to the edge several times, but eased her back in each instance. She didn't want her first time making love to Jay to be over just yet. She wanted to imprint each taste, each touch, each look, smell, and sound, in her memory forever, because no one had ever made her feel the way Jay did. Finally, when she couldn't deny her any longer, Kate claimed Jay with her body, her heart, and her soul.

"Oh, God, Kate!"

"Shh, I'm right here, love. I've got you. Shh." Kate rolled over and pulled Jay on top of her. She held her close and soothed her with her hands and her voice. They stayed like that for several moments, catching their breath, until she felt the moisture on her shoulder where

Jay was resting her head. She brushed her thumb gently across Jay's cheek and it came away wet.

"Hey, hey, honey, what's the matter?" Kate began to panic, worry coloring her tone. She lifted Jay's chin with her fingers and tried to look into her eyes as her heart plummeted through her stomach. "Oh, love, I didn't hurt you, did I? Please, God, tell me I didn't do anything to hurt you."

Jay shook her head emphatically. "No, no, Kate…it's nothing like that. Quite the opposite, in fact. That was the most incredible feeling I've ever experienced. I'm just completely overwhelmed, that's all. I never, in my wildest fantasies, imagined it could be like that."

"It should never have been otherwise, sweetheart. I wish with all my heart I could change that for you."

"You already have," Jay said, wiping at her tears. "You didn't simply make love to my body, Kate…you nourished my soul. I don't know how else to explain it."

"So, you're telling me these are tears of joy, then?"

"Oh yes, that they most certainly are." Jay smiled a watery smile and planted a small kiss on Kate's forehead.

"Well, I guess that's okay, then."

"Okay? I'd say it's a whole lot more than okay, Stretch." Jay's eyes swept hungrily over her, and the look sent an involuntary shiver through Kate.

Jay placed feather-soft kisses on Kate's shoulders, neck, and collarbones. She ran her fingers slowly up Kate's sides until she was nothing but a mass of goose bumps. Then Jay shifted her focus to the finely chiseled abdominal muscles and Kate's navel, licking, tasting, and touching everywhere. She bit down lightly on a taut nipple, and Kate nearly launched into orbit.

For the next hour, Jay experimented, testing for sensitive spots, teasing, and generally driving Kate crazy. Finally, when Kate couldn't stand it anymore and begged for mercy, Jay drove her over the edge.

A short time later, uttering twin sighs of blissful contentment, the two women fell asleep.

CHAPTER FOURTEEN

Several hours later Jay awakened. It was still the middle of the night and she was snuggled securely in the arms of easily the sexiest woman in the world. She marveled at the feel of their bodies intertwined as if it had always been and would always be; they fit together perfectly.

A wave of warmth flowed over her as she conjured the memories of their lovemaking. Kate was alternately tender, gentle, and attentive, and passionate, exciting, and provocative. Jay surrendered to her body and soul, knowing intuitively that Kate would be able to breach all the barriers she had spent a lifetime erecting. She made a conscious decision to allow herself to be vulnerable, to let go of her fears, and to place her trust in the exceptional woman who touched her in ways she never imagined possible. Jay smiled. Her faith had been well placed. No one ever made her feel so well loved or so complete.

Jay gazed adoringly at the strong profile and nudged aside a stray lock of dark hair that had fallen onto that remarkable face. She felt no more fear, only desire and passion. She wanted to give everything to this woman, and to take everything in return. Her hands began to play over the silky skin as her lips danced along a strong shoulder, then across the swell of a high, firm breast. Her tongue flicked the tip of an awakening nipple and she took it into her mouth, groaning in delight at the taste and texture.

Another moan joined hers as Kate came awake, her body responding instantly to the stimulation. Their eyes met in a gaze that promised unrestrained passion. This time the lovemaking was not the slow, sweet, tantalizing seduction of earlier in the evening. This time it was more like the intensity of a sudden electrical storm, with sparks flying, igniting a fire that consumed everything in its path. Both women crested together, bodies straining and hearts pounding, lost in ecstasy.

Eventually, their breathing calmed and their bodies began to cool. Running her fingers over Jay's face, Kate leaned in to kiss her reverently on the mouth. "Do me a favor. If that was a dream and I'm still sleeping, please don't bother to wake me up, okay?"

"Mmm, I know what you mean." Jay sighed dreamily as she smoothed her palm over the softness of Kate's backside. "I'm sorry I woke you, I just couldn't seem to help myself."

"Honey, don't ever apologize for waking me like *that*." Kate chuckled. "You can do that anytime you like...believe me, you'll never get a complaint from me." As she kissed the tip of Jay's nose, her eyes began to close again involuntarily.

Within seconds, both women were sound asleep, smiling, sated and exhausted.

❧

The next time they opened their eyes, the moon had been replaced above them by blue sky. Rolling onto her back, Kate pulled Jay tight to her side. She reached over and smoothed the disheveled blonde hair. "How are you feeling?"

"Mmm, I've never felt better in my life. You?"

"That about sums it up." Kate's gaze turned serious. "Thank you, Jay, for trusting me. I know that can't have been easy for you, and I hope I didn't disappoint you."

"Disappoint me? Oh, sweetheart, believe me, let down is the last thing I feel." Jay propped herself up so that she could look directly into those baby blues. Running her fingers lovingly over the high cheekbones and tempting lips, she tried to let everything she felt show in her eyes and her touch. "Kate, I have been dreaming of a night with you like last night since we first met, and I have to tell you, nothing I envisioned came close to the reality of making love with you. It was everything I ever thought I wanted and so much more, love." There were tears in her eyes.

Kate raised up and kissed Jay's eyelids, which were wet with her tears. "I'm so glad, sweetheart. I feel the same way, you know. All these years I've been waiting for someone to make me feel anything close to what I experienced the first time I saw you. I never found anyone who could measure up to that, not even remotely, so I stopped trying a long time ago. I guess I knew there was only one person who could make me feel that way, and I didn't think I'd ever see her again."

"Me?"

"Yes, you, Jamison Parker. I told you last night, you're the only one for me...there is no doubt in my mind, or my heart." Softly she added, "I love you, Jay."

At that Jay did start crying, her tears spilling onto Kate's neck and chest. "I love you too, Kate, more than I ever thought possible. I've been in love with you from the very first, but I never imagined that I'd get the chance to say those words to you out loud, much less hear them from you. I'm at a complete loss here."

"Well, how about you kiss me and we take a shower together for starters. What time do you need to leave?"

Jay hated to contemplate the idea, but they both knew that she had to go back to the city to write. There was no sense even pretending that she could get the work done where she was.

Jay leaned down and captured the waiting lips below her, losing herself in the kiss for several precious minutes.

"It's five after six now, if I catch the seven twenty-five, I can be in the city by ten thirty. That should work."

"In that case, we'd better get going." Kate vaulted off the bed and pulled Jay with her.

They washed each other, both trying hard, with mixed success, to control their wandering hands and mouths long enough to get clean. When they were done, Kate steered Jay over to sit on the edge of the bed with the best of intentions as she began drying her off. Kneeling before Jay, carefully drying her breasts, she found the temptation was simply too great. The thought of a day and a half passing before she could see Jay again was making Kate crazy. Her eyes grew heavy lidded with arousal as she nestled between Jay's legs. She tasted the sweetness there and quickly brought Jay to a shattering climax while pushing herself to the edge as well.

When she recovered sufficiently, Jay rose from the bed without a word and took Kate by the hand, returning them to the shower. She turned on the spray and began to touch and taste Kate as she guided them into the stall. Jay positioned Kate so that her broad back blocked the spray, then Jay sat on the ledge facing her and pulled her close.

The combination of the warm water pulsing on her back and the exquisite pressure building between her legs made Kate's knees weak. She reached out and braced her arms against the shower wall. Both women moaned as Jay took Kate in her mouth and drove all thoughts of trains and schedules out of their minds.

Finally, they were clean, dressed, and on the road with less than twenty minutes to make it to the train station. Kate promised Jay that she would have her on that train without fail. "You'd better, Stretch, since it's all your fault that we're running late," Jay joked.

That earned her an arched eyebrow look. "Oh, right, you had nothing to do with it, Little Miss Innocent."

"Well, you started it..."

"That's true, but you sure didn't have any trouble finishing it, now did you?"

"Are you complaining?"

"Do I look like an idiot to you? Of course I'm not complaining! I'm merely setting the record straight, that's all."

Jay reached over and took hold of Kate's hand. "I'm going to miss you, Kate."

"I know, me too, sweetheart. I'll pick you up outside the Convention Center tomorrow night after the LCA Show though, and at least we'll have tomorrow night."

"Right."

"Well, here you go...two minutes to spare too. Let me get your bag and your briefcase, you just worry about getting to the platform. I'll be right behind you."

Moving before the car even come to a complete stop, Jay reached the conductor just as he was making the last call. Kate came up right behind her.

"Here you go," she said, handing Jay the bag and briefcase. "Travel safely. I'll see you tomorrow night." She didn't know if Jay understood sign language, but she made the sign for "I love you" anyway.

Jay leaned down quickly from the steps and brushed her lips against Kate's ear. "I love you too," she said, so quietly that only Kate could hear her. And with that, she was gone. Kate stood there for a minute and watched the train pull out of the station before she headed back to the illegally parked car and home.

She walked into the kitchen where Fred greeted her enthusiastically, weaving in and out of her legs as he always did. Everything should have felt comfortingly normal, and yet...the place seemed empty and lonely, and she knew why. In just a few short days, one single little blonde whirlwind had transformed Kate's house from a place to live into a home. God, she missed her already, and she'd barely left. Pathetic.

She scanned the cupboard since they hadn't had time for breakfast before leaving. Well, they hadn't had time for food, anyway. Kate smiled as she remembered their last bout of lovemaking—just thinking about it made her skin flush. Jay was the most talented, most enticing lover she had ever known. Somehow, Jay just seemed to know what she needed, and when. It was as if their bodies were speaking to each other in their own language, rendering words redundant. That had never happened to her before.

She sighed. What she felt for Jay went so far beyond physical compatibility. It wasn't just about the sex, although that was a most pleasant development. It was everything about her. It was the way she looked at the world, her sense of humor, her gentle nature and compassion. It was her intelligence and natural curiosity, her beauty and spirit. Kate was sure if she looked hard enough she could probably find something about Jay that she didn't like or love, but for the life of her, she didn't know what.

Spending twenty-four hours a day with Jay for nearly four days, she hadn't felt the least bit boxed in or smothered. For a woman as independent and solitary as Kate, that was extraordinary. "Now what, Fred? Back to the routine, I guess."

Kate went upstairs to the bedroom to change into her workout clothes. She found herself standing at the threshold to the guest suite instead, where she closed her eyes and extended her senses, detecting a trace of Jay's perfume in the air. She stepped into the room and moved to the bed to pick up Jay's pillow. *God, you've got it bad, Kyle.* As she reached for the pillow, a folded piece of white paper fluttered to the floor. She picked it up and opened it to reveal neat printing.

Guest Satisfaction Survey, it said in block letters across the top. Laughing, she said to Fred, who had followed her upstairs, "Well, I did tell her it was a five-star resort and she could rate her stay on the way out. I ought to be more careful what I say, shouldn't I, buddy?"

She began to read. *"Accommodations: Excellent, especially the last night. Service: Outstanding, loved the personal touch (pun intended), and the comic books were great. Facilities: Superb, particularly enjoyed working with the personal trainer and the rent-a-beast. The kitchen could stand some...well...use. Activities: Top-*

notch, do you really want me to go there? Overall Impressions of Resort: Mmm. Need I say more? Would You Recommend This Establishment to Others: Absolutely, but it better not be open to others."

By the time she finished reading, Kate was laughing so hard she was in tears. "You are too much, Jamison Parker. What am I going to do with you?" Stopping for a moment to think, she got serious. "The bigger question is—what am I going to do without you for a whole thirty-six hours? Yuck." As Kate pondered what was in store for the following night, a wicked smile crossed her face. The wait might be worth it, after all. She made her way down the hall to her room to change into her workout gear. It was going to be a long, busy, lonely day and a half, and she needed to get started.

෩

Trying to organize her thoughts in preparation for writing the article as the train carried her home, Jay had her notes from the past four days spread out on two service trays in front of her. Professional detachment, that was what she said she needed. "Well, so much for that," she chuckled to herself. Then she got serious. How was she going to separate the Kate that she knew from the anchorwoman and journalist that the rest of the world had seen? Was there a difference? Gazing out the window at the Hudson River as it sped by, Jay smiled as she thought about the last four days. Images of Kate swam before her eyes—her lover lost in rapture, her friend with eyes full of caring and concern, the woman she loved, vulnerable and uncertain. And her professional demeanor—resolute, powerful, intelligent, engaged, and compassionate. Oh, yeah, there was definitely a difference.

Jay began to review the impressions she put to paper on Monday, the day she had arrived and gone with Kate and her crew to interview Joey's parents and the man whom Kate rescued from the rubble. If she were going to be able to maintain any semblance of objectivity, it would be by focusing the article less on her own very personal knowledge and more on the opinions of people like these and Kate's co-workers.

Jay began to concentrate and get lost in her work. She had a lot to do to get the story ready before she got back on a train to return to Albany the next night, but she was determined to have it done before she saw Kate again. She didn't want anything to detract from the time they could spend together, and for that she needed her mind and her calendar to be clear on Sunday. She sighed. It was going to be a long, busy, lonely day and a half.

∻

It was Saturday night, it was almost time, and Kate was nervous—not for the obvious reason that most people standing where she was right then would have been, but because her conversation earlier in the day with Jay had left her unsettled.

"How do you know you'll be finished with whatever you're doing when the show lets out tonight?"
"Don't worry, I'll be there, love."
"How can you be so sure, Kate? Where are you going, anyway?"
"If I told you that, I'd have to kill you, and you know that violence at this hour of the day disrupts my schedule."

She had tried to keep her tone light, but Kate knew that Jay was upset with her for being less than forthcoming about her plans for the evening. She only hoped that Jay would forgive her when she understood why—and that, Kate mused, would happen soon enough.

She thought back to Jay's reaction Thursday to her not being in the house so early in the morning. It was clear to her that Jay was expecting the worst. *I guess that's what happens when that's what you've always gotten.* It only strengthened her resolve to make sure that she never gave Jay cause not to trust her. Kate knew, in the end, only time and consistency would prove to Jay that she needn't worry anymore, and those were two things Kate hoped they would have forever.

"Kate, it's time," a disembodied voice said from close by.
"Yes, it is." She smiled.

∻

An intense thirty-six hours after she left, Jay was back in the capital. She was tired, and a little grumpy, and just wanted it to be midnight already. Her conversation with Kate earlier in the day left her a bit out of sorts.

Now Jay was going to be stuck for the next three-plus hours trying to be cordial to a man who might one day be president of the United States, when all she really wanted to do was to see Kate and be reassured. Well, she was committed now, she might as well make the best of it.

A plainclothes state police officer met Jay at the door to the Convention Center and ushered her inside to the governor's table, directly in front of the stage. The governor, resplendent in a black tuxedo, stood as she approached. Jay looked positively elegant in a strapless, floor-length, black gown and matching heels. The dress hugged her slim form and highlighted her creamy skin and well-toned shoulders and arms. Her neck was adorned with a beautiful emerald and diamond choker that complemented the emerald teardrops in her ears and the emerald ring on her right hand. Every man within fifty feet sucked in his gut, straightened his bow tie, and stared at the extraordinary beauty. The governor was no exception. He offered her his hand and politely introduced her to his wife, the lieutenant governor and his wife, and the other members of his administration at the table.

Just then the lights flickered once in warning. Jay took the seat the governor held for her to his right, less than fifteen feet from the front of the stage. The huge room, which was filled to capacity with every manner of state official and journalist and their guests, went pitch black for a full minute. In the darkness, the orchestra began to play and a beautiful voice pierced the silence with the first notes of a song. Jay recognized the tune as the Carpenters' *We've Only Just Begun*, but the words had been changed.

And then the curtain rose to reveal the singer. Jay thought she might pass out right on the spot. All thoughts of being tired and grumpy disappeared. In fact, if she were old enough, she would have sworn she was having a hot flash. There was Kate in three-inch heels and a bright red, sequined, cocktail-length sheath with plunging neckline and spaghetti straps, leaning on a high stool perched in the very center of the stage and looking directly at her. Her hair was swept up in a French knot, revealing her long, slender neck. Smiling broadly, she arched her eyebrow a fraction, enough for Jay to know it was meant just for her, and winked at the governor as she parodied his penchant for trying to build consensus in a government where no one could agree on anything.

Jay's mind was reeling. *Busy tonight.* Kate had said she was "busy"! The rat fink. When she got over her initial shock and the guilt she felt for giving her sweetheart a hard time about where she was going to be that evening, Jay allowed herself the luxury of watching Kate and letting the timbre of her voice penetrate directly into her heart. *My God, she's got an amazing voice. I wonder what other little secrets she's been keeping?* She decided she would grill Kate later. Right then, she just wanted to listen and ogle, which was pretty much what everyone else in the room was doing.

Kate sang two more numbers during the course of the evening, one to the tune of Carole King's *It's Too Late* regarding the perennially late state budget, and another sending up the governor's ongoing negotiations with the senate Republicans over the death penalty to the Beatles' *We Can Work It Out*. The crowd ate it up, laughing uproariously at the new lyrics and applauding Kate's singing talent. And, Jay had to admit, the other performers and skits were very entertaining too. All in all, the night was a smashing success.

It was time for the finale. The capitol bureau chief for one of the major New York dailies walked onto the stage in a stodgy pinstriped business suit singing his own version of the first stanza of *You're the One that I Want*, from the musical *Grease*. He had a rich, deep singing voice and even looked a little like John Travolta. There was a dry-ice fog rolling in from the other side of the stage, and then the entire Convention Center rose to its feet as one, whistling and catcalling as Kate emerged from the fog singing the second half of the duet. Her hair cascading freely down her back, she was clad in tight black leather pants over leather boots and a sleeveless, ribbed knit, black v-neck sweater. Jay's eyes nearly popped out of her head.

Kate prowled to the middle of the stage where her singing partner was standing. As they continued singing their own hysterical lyrics to the song, she moved right up against him and seductively ran her fingers up his chest and ripped off his suit. Jay nearly growled in jealousy at the sight. She reminded herself that it was all part of the show, but boy, could Kate act. Underneath the suit, the newspaper reporter was wearing his own tight black pants and black muscle t-shirt. He ground his body against Kate's as they danced and sang in perfect harmony. Jay clenched her teeth, knowing every guy in the place was wishing he were on stage with her lover. Then, just as she was sure she was going to commit murder, Kate locked eyes with her and gave her a smile that was reserved for her alone. Jay melted and felt her own mouth respond with an answering grin.

The show ended with a thunderous standing ovation and several curtain calls for the performers. Kate got the biggest cheers of all. As the lights came up, the governor turned to his guest. "Did you enjoy the show, Ms. Parker?"

"Oh yes, it was fabulous. Who knew that journalists had such hidden talents?"

"Yes," the governor agreed, "they were rather amazing, weren't they? It's tradition for the governor to respond to the performance with one of his own. I promise to leave you in splendid company, though. Will you wait here for a moment?"

"Certainly."

He stepped away for a minute as Jay surveyed the crowd. Within a very short time he was back. "Ms. Parker?"

Hearing her name, she turned around to find the governor standing next to her once again. "I have someone I'd like to introduce you to." He smiled as a figure emerged from behind him. Jay's eyes went wide. "Ms. Jamison Parker, may I present one of the capital's true treasures, Ms. Katherine Kyle. Kate, Ms. Parker is a fine reporter for *Time* magazine. Perhaps you are familiar with her work?"

Kate didn't miss a beat. She took Jay's hand in a formal handshake, addressing the governor but focusing directly on Jay with a completely sincere look, "Yes, Governor, I am a great admirer of Ms. Parker's work. I have found it to be most stimulating."

Jay choked and spluttered. The governor patted her on the back and asked with concern, "Ms. Parker, are you all right?"

"Oh yes, I'm just fine," she rasped. Jay gave Kate a murderous glare behind the governor's back. "I'm a big fan of Ms. Kyle's, as well. Her work takes my breath away."

Apparently oblivious to the undercurrent between the two women, the governor offered a self-satisfied smile. "Good, then I can see I'll be leaving you in excellent hands while I tend to business." To the show's star he said, "Kate, please take my seat and keep Ms. Parker company while I pay you back for your impertinence."

Without taking her eyes from Jay, Kate responded, "It would be my pleasure." She held out the seat for Jay as the governor and his tablemates made their way backstage.

∽

When they were both seated, Kate turned to her companion and gave her a brilliant smile. "You look magnificent." Lowering her voice to its lowest, sexiest register, and fixing Jay with her most lustful stare, she added very quietly so that only Jay could hear her, "Good enough to eat."

Jay flushed. She leaned over and purred in Kate's ear, "Promises, promises." Then she straightened up once again. "And you look rather fabulous yourself, Ms. Kyle-who-was-going-to-be-busy-tonight." She raised one eyebrow in challenge.

Kate snickered. "I couldn't spoil the surprise," she said apologetically. "I did tell you that you were going to love the show, didn't I?"

"Yes. But you failed to mention that you were the star attraction."

"I was not." It was Kate's turn to blush.

"Yeah," Jay slapped her lightly. "Tell that to the five hundred people who were busy drooling over you, and especially tell it to the guy who was trying to get inside your pants on stage at the end. Thank God there was no room in there." There was an edge to Jay's voice.

"Aww. You're not jealous, are you?"

Jay hesitated a beat.

Kate couldn't believe it. Turning to face Jay fully, she stared at her intently with eyes gone dark. *Expect the worst, right? Oh, honey, we're going to have to work on this.* For Jay's ears only, she said with all of the feeling she could summon, "Ms. Jamison Parker, you are the only one for me, now and forever. Don't you ever doubt that. They can look all they want, but you are the one who lives in my heart and who owns my body and soul."

Jay's eyes began to tear just as the lights were dimmed once again. "Oh, sweetheart. What did I ever do to deserve you?"

Kate reached under the tablecloth and caressed Jay's hands where no one could see them. "I believe that's already been asked and answered before. Besides, I'm the one who should be asking that question, love, not you."

When the governor's rebuttal finished to laughter and applause and he returned to the table, Kate took her leave. Turning to Jay, she took her hand formally once again. "It was a pleasure to meet you,

145

Ms. Parker. I hope I'll get to see you again very soon." Her eyes twinkled.

"Yes, I would like that very much," Jay responded, smiling.

"I'm glad you two hit it off," the governor said. "I thought you'd like each other—two smart, beautiful, talented women. That's great." As his words trailed off, Kate was surrounded by well-wishers. Everyone wanted to compliment her on her performance. Over the heads of those encircling her, she watched Jay make her way to the exit. As if sensing eyes on her, Jay turned around. Kate gave her a look as if to say, "You're the only one I'm thinking about." Jay grinned and proceeded through the doors.

Five minutes later, Kate met her at the elevators to the parking garage, as they agreed before the governor returned to the table. "What's a gorgeous lady like you doing in a place like this? Can I interest you in a ride in my car, perhaps?" Kate waggled her eyebrows suggestively.

"Do you think I'm so easy that I would swoon over a little red convertible?"

Kate paused dramatically for a beat and then grinned. "Yep."

"Humph." Crossing her arms over her chest in mock indignation, Jay pretended to think. "Do you come with the car, or is that à la carte?"

"That depends."

"On what?"

"On who is asking," Kate said.

Jay dropped her voice an octave and moistened her lips, raking her eyes with exaggerated slowness over Kate's leather-clad form. "I'm asking," she said huskily.

Feeling a chill chase itself up and down her body, Kate swallowed convulsively. "Um, in that case, I definitely come with the wheels. Yep. Definitely."

"Good," Jay said triumphantly, hooking her arm through Kate's. "Then you've got a deal and a date."

CHAPTER FIFTEEN

They barely made it through the door of the house before Jay grabbed Kate by the arm and spun her around so that her back was against the wall. She stepped between Kate's leather-clad legs and reached up, tangled her fingers in the dark locks, and pulled her head down for an incendiary kiss.

When they finally broke apart, Jay said, "God, I missed you so much I thought I would lose my mind."

"Mmm, I know the feeling." Kate ran her hands up and down Jay's mostly bare back. "Have I told you how fabulously sexy you look tonight?"

Jay laughed. "Once or twice, but that's okay, I don't mind hearing it again."

"You look amazingly sexy tonight, Ms. Parker, and you made it incredibly difficult for me to concentrate on what I was supposed to be doing. All I could think about was how much I wanted to have my arms around you, and how quickly I could make it to your table if anyone tried to make a move on you."

"As if—" Jay began, but was stopped by the look in Kate's eyes.

"Jamison, there wasn't a guy within fifty feet of you who didn't have his tongue hanging down to his shoelaces…not that I blame them, I felt the same way."

"Sweetheart, you've got nothing to worry about. This body and this heart belong only to you. I think they probably always have, and I know they always will."

"Mmm. I like the sound of that. Jay, about our conversation today…"

"Oh, Kate, I'm so sorry I was such an idiot…I feel terrible about that. I shouldn't have pushed you and I shouldn't have doubted you. When I first saw you up there on stage, I just wanted to run up there, fall at your feet, apologize, and beg forgiveness."

"Well, that would have been quite a show." Kate gave a small smile. "I know that this is going to take some time for you to get used to, and I know that you've had reason in the past to expect the worst of people, but I promise you with all my heart, Jay, that you can trust me, and that I will never knowingly hurt you."

Tears sprang to Jay's eyes. "I know that, love, or at least a big part of me does. It really isn't even about you. It's just this little internal voice that says that I don't deserve happiness, and I don't deserve to be loved, especially not by someone as perfect as you. It's an expectation, I guess, that something will happen to take you away from me. I know it's not rational, and I try to fight the feeling, but sometimes I don't win," she finished dejectedly.

"Hey," Kate said, lifting her chin so that their eyes met again. "We'll get through this together, okay? Like I said, I know it's going to take time, and I hope we'll have all the time in the world, right?"

"You don't want to walk away because I'm an insecure fool?"

Kate pulled Jay close, then kissed her forehead and her temple. "Sweetheart, I don't want to walk away for any reason, let alone a false one. I love you, Jamison Parker, and nothing and no one is going to change that. You're stuck with me for good, okay? How about if we agree that when this kind of stuff comes up we'll talk through it together until there are no doubts, huh?"

"That sounds great," Jay agreed, awed and humbled once again by the depth of Kate's understanding and compassion.

"Now, if you don't mind," Kate said with a gleam in her eye, "I'd like to take a very beautiful woman to bed. I've been burning the candle at both ends for weeks now, and I'm just about at the end of my rope. Getting up to rehearse for the show every morning before dawn and working until midnight rots."

Realization dawned on Jay. "That's where you were Thursday morning when I was so worried? You were off singing your heart out?"

"No, actually my heart was at home pacing in my kitchen, as I recall." She grinned. "But yes, I was off practicing with the rest of the cast before I went to get my stitches out, just like I had been every morning for three weeks." She paused. "Oh, Jay, when you told me you were coming to the show, I just wanted it to be a wonderful surprise for you. I didn't mean for my evasions to make you worry. I'm so sorry. I should have just told you."

"No, it was a great surprise, fantastic really. It's not your fault that my imagination tends to work overtime."

"Well, how about if we redirect that energy and put your imagination to great use right now?" Kate waggled her eyebrows suggestively.

"Lead on, woman."

And with that, the two lovers retired to the bedroom and a night of blissful togetherness.

Running her fingers lightly over Jay's bare back, Kate sighed contentedly. They made love well into the night, first with the urgency of new passion, and then again more deliberately as each of them strived to express with her body what her heart was feeling. She had never known such happiness. For the first time in her life, her heart and soul felt full and the future looked bright.

The future—she never gave it much thought. She always chose to live one day at a time, tackling whatever challenges life presented her as they arose. But the day and a half she spent without Jay by her side made her pensive. She was miserable on her own, wondering how Jay was progressing with her story, what she was thinking, and whether or not Jay was missing her as much as she was missing Jay.

For five years, her career had been her only focus, the only driving force in her life. Not anymore, she realized with a start. Without giving it a second thought, she knew that this relationship was now the most important thing and she would put it above anything else.

"What are you thinking about, love?"

"I'm sorry." She smiled affectionately at Jay. "I didn't mean to wake you. Why don't you go back to sleep."

"Hmm. I'm not sure if that was a deliberate evasion or not, but I do know, even in my weakened state, that you didn't answer the question."

"What weakened state is that?"

"Well, someone, whose name shall remain anonymous but whose initials are Katherine Ann Kyle, managed to turn me into a bowl of Jell-O last night and I haven't fully recovered yet."

Kate chuckled. "In that case, we're even, so there's no advantage there. Good morning, by the way," Kate said, as she leaned in and kissed Jay.

"Mmm, good morning, but it's not working, Stretch. Out with it. I know that little brain of yours is chewing on something, and I want to know what it is before I have to torture it out of you."

"Ooh. That could be fun." At Jay's raised eyebrow, Kate relented. "I was just thinking about the future, that's all."

"Well, that's kind of a broad topic. Could you be a little more specific, perhaps?"

While they said many things to each other over the course of the past few days, Kate was still fearful of pushing Jay too far, too fast. She didn't want to scare her away, and she didn't want to pressure her before she was ready. *This is all happening so quickly!*

In less time than it took her to shop for running sneakers, she had gone from complete self-reliance and independence to not wanting to spend a single night without Jay. She had never felt that way before. With Jen, all she wanted was to maintain her own space and to keep it light, seeing Jen when it suited her. Now she couldn't imagine a day without Jay in it. Did Jay feel the same way?

Kate suddenly was afraid of the answer. What if she didn't? Even though Jay made it clear that she wanted to be with Kate, what if she didn't mean that kind of total commitment? She had a life of her own, with a successful career and dreams for the future. What if there wasn't room in her plans for a life lived together? What if she only wanted to be with Kate every once in a while when it was convenient? Did the hundred and fifty miles that separated their lives matter to her?

"Hello, Earth to Kate," Jay said as she tapped on Kate's chest with her forefinger. "Honey, your heart is beating a million miles a minute and you look as if your best friend just died. Please, tell me what's going on."

Kate chewed on her lip. She still didn't know what to say. "Um, Jay, how did you sleep Friday night?"

"How did I...fitfully. Why?"

"Well, I didn't sleep much, either."

When no more words were forthcoming, Jay said, "And that's why your heart is beating out of your chest now?"

"I slept poorly because you weren't here with me and I missed you," Kate blurted out in a rush.

"I missed you too, sweetheart." Jay seemed a bit at sea about the direction of the conversation.

God, this was so hard! Why was she thinking about this right now, anyway? She couldn't do this yet. She wasn't ready. After all, they'd only spent two full nights together, right?

Who was Kate kidding? She already knew that she wanted to make a life with Jay, to live together facing the future as one. That fact alone was enough to scare the living daylights out of her, but what if Jay didn't share the same vision, didn't want the same thing? Could she live with that? Was it too soon to ask her? Jay narrowed her eyes. "It's okay, love. Whatever it is can wait, I mean, geez, we haven't even had our morning coffee yet, right? We've got time, and I'm a *very* patient woman." She grinned evilly.

"Oh you think so, do you? I wouldn't call the way you were last night patient, Princess."

"Well, that was different, I was going through withdrawal at the time. That didn't count."

"I see." Kate was relieved at the banter. She felt much more at ease.

Jay adjusted her position and kissed Kate passionately.

"I thought you said you were Jell-O."

"I was, but I'm young, I bounce back quickly," Jay said as she began exploring the body below her with single-minded intent.

Coming up behind Jay and putting her arms around her, Kate asked, "What would you like to do today, love?" It was just before noon. They were finally dressed, showered and standing in the kitchen.

Jay tilted her head back and gazed up into Kate's eyes. "Truthfully, I've been on the go non-stop for the past few weeks, and I know that you have too. What do you say we just pick up the Sunday paper, sit in that wonderfully decadent swing on the deck, do the crossword puzzle together, and enjoy the day? Then, if you're nice to me, I'll cook you a fabulous dinner and we can watch an old movie on television."

"Mmm, my idea of a perfect, lazy Sunday afternoon." Kate squeezed Jay's waist and nuzzled her neck.

"But first, we're going shopping."

"What?"

"Well, Stretch, even I can't make a feast out of Raisin Bran and American cheese. You need some food in this house."

Kate groaned. "I hate to shop."

"That's because you haven't shopped with me."

"Mmm-hmm," Kate said dubiously. "I'll do it, but only if dessert is included with the meal." She gave Jay a lecherous look.

"I'll think about it." Jay smirked as she slipped out of Kate's grasp and bent down to scratch Fred behind the ears.

೭ುಞ

Two hours later they were comfortably ensconced in the two-person hammock swing on the second tier of the deck. Kate was semi-reclining with her back and head resting on a pillow, her legs stretched out the length of the swing. Jay was lying between her legs, using her as a backrest. Jay held the *New York Times* Sunday crossword puzzle in one hand and a pen in the other. Kate leaned her chin on Jay's shoulder as they studied the puzzle together.

"Tell me again why we're doing this in ink instead of using the more widely accepted and cautious pencil?"

"Because, Stretch, it shows that we have confidence in our answers. Only wusses use a pencil. But if you don't think you're up to playing with the big boys..." The blonde tresses were ruffled by a loud exhale. Jay nodded. "Just as I thought. We need a ten-letter word for 'strong in battle or possessing powerful weapons.' Any ideas?"

Kate looked at 22 Down, where Jay was pointing. "Yep."

"Care to share?"

"Armipotent."

"You're making it up."

"Am not, go look it up."

"Humph. I'll trust you, and besides, it works with the other answers."

"Of course it does."

Jay turned her head a little so she could look at Kate. "How did you know that?"

Kate shrugged. "Dunno, just did."

"You're so smart." Jay lifted herself up a bit and kissed Kate on the mouth.

"Nope, just full of useless trivia." Kate smiled down affectionately at her.

They worked on the puzzle for another hour or so, managing to fill in most of the answers. Jay yawned and stretched.

"I saw that, young lady. That's about the tenth time in the last five minutes that you've yawned. Ready for a nap, perhaps?"

"Only if I can take it right here, lying in your arms."

"I think that can be arranged." Scooting down further so that they were lying more prone, Kate used her leg to start the swing rocking gently. Jay turned so that she was lying on top of her, and the two of them promptly fell asleep.

It was several hours later when they awakened and the sun was just beginning its descent in the western sky. It had cooled down quite a bit and Jay shivered involuntarily.

"Cold, love?"

"Just a little."

"Wait here." Kate disentangled herself and disappeared into the house, returning several moments later with a quilt, which she laid over them after re-positioning herself. "Is that better?"

"Much. I feel like I'm in heaven here. I never want to leave."

"Fine by me." Kate smiled fondly at Jay.

Jay thought about what she just said. She really meant it, but did Kate mean what she said? Would she want her to live there with her? Was it too soon to talk about that? *How about if we start small, Parker, eh?*

"Kate?"

"Hmm?"

"Would it be all right if I stayed until tomorrow morning instead of going home tonight? I could catch the six o'clock train and be in the city by nine a.m., plenty of time to get to the office and turn in my story."

"Do you really want to?"

"Oh yeah." Jay's smile lit up her green eyes.

Kate pulled her up closer and hugged her tight, whispering in her ear, "I'm so glad. I've been wanting to ask you all day, but I was afraid you'd say no."

"Never," Jay said, and leaned in for an ardent kiss.

Jay was standing in front of the kitchen counter, chopping vegetables to sauté for the pasta primavera she was making. She had changed into jeans and a light sweater under which she wore nothing. She had already prepared the garlic bread and put it in the oven to bake and was just getting ready to toss the veggies into the pan.

Kate stood in the doorway for a moment, admiring the way Jay looked in her jeans. With a lascivious glint in her eyes she stole up behind Jay and began nibbling on her exposed neck, reaching under the sweater at the same time to cup Jay's high, firm breasts and brush her palms over responsive nipples. "God, you look so sexy," she said in between bites and licks.

"Hey...ooh...I was...ahh, trying to...mmm...cook here."

"Yeah, you're looking pretty hot to me." Kate dropped the pitch of her voice to a low, sexy register. She had already undone Jay's jeans.

Jay gave up on preparing dinner. "Agh, Kate, in a minute I won't be able to stand...ohh, baby..." She reached her arms back over her head, and grabbed Kate behind the neck in an effort to remain upright as her knees began to buckle.

"It's okay, love, I've got you." Kate wrapped one arm firmly around Jay's waist as Jay began to climax.

For several minutes worth of heartbeats, they stood suspended there, panting and struggling to regain their equilibrium. Finally Jay gave up the fight and sank slowly to the floor, pulling Kate with her.

"That was such an unfair sneak attack."

"Hey, life's unfair."

"I will get you back for this, you know."

"Oh, I'm counting on it."

Eventually dinner made it to the table, as did the two women, and they spent a leisurely time just talking quietly and enjoying the food. After the meal Kate insisted on doing the dishes and cleanup, telling Jay to go relax in the family room and pick a movie from her tape collection.

When Kate joined her, Jay was sitting on the couch with *Casablanca* in her hands, quietly looking at the fire she built in the fireplace. "Ah, excellent choice. Humphrey Bogart and Ingrid Bergman in one of the finest performances ever." Kate took the tape from Jay, placed it in the VCR, and sat down next to her, pulling a quilt over both of them. At critical moments in the movie, they both recited the lines along with the characters, and at the end they were both crying.

When it was over, Kate put her arm around Jay and they walked together upstairs to bed. "Jay," she said, "I think this is the beginning of a beau-ti-ful friendship." Jay bumped hips with her and smiled as they made their way up the rest of the stairs.

It was 2:30 a.m. and Jay hadn't slept a wink. She tried snuggling closer to Kate, which was difficult since she was practically on top of her already.

"What's the matter, love, can't get comfortable?"

"No," Jay smiled, "I'm more than comfortable, I just can't seem to fall asleep." In truth, she couldn't stop wondering when the next time was she would be able to see Kate, and it was bothering her. How were they going to make this work? Would they only see each other on weekends? Would they see each other every weekend? God, that would never be enough for her. But did Kate feel the same way? It was so clichéd to talk about moving in together less than two weeks after finding each other again, wasn't it?

"Something bothering you?"

What should she say? Two thirty in the morning, two and a half hours before she had to get up and catch a train, hardly seemed like the appropriate time to be having a conversation with such important implications. "Maybe if you sang to me I could fall asleep. Did I tell you how beautiful your voice is? What other little secrets are you hiding from me?"

"There are no secrets from you, love, just more things to discover about each other. Do you really want me to sing something?"

"Yes."

"Any requests?"

"Oh, you take requests?"

"Only from you." Kate kissed her on the nose.

"Anything you want to sing is fine by me, sweetheart."

Kate was quiet for a minute and then, with a deep breath in, she began to sing an old Anne Murray tune, *A Love Song*. "I want to sing you a love song, I want to rock you in my arms all night long..."

Jay closed her eyes and listened as the melody washed over her. Kate's voice was magnificent, and the song was perfect for the occasion. She let herself drift, feeling the vibration of Kate's diaphragm beneath her ear. By the time the last notes faded away, she had fallen peacefully asleep.

At five a.m. the alarm went off, startling both of them. A long arm snaked out and swiped at the insistent buzzer. "Argh."

A second groan was audible, and a disheveled blonde head poked out from underneath the covers. "That clock can't be right, it is not possible that it could be time to get up already. For Pete's sake, we just went to sleep."

"Come on, sunshine, we don't have a lot of time to spare this morning, got to get up and face the day."

"Don't want to."

"Have to."

"Don't have to like it."

"Nope, I'll give you that." Kate chuckled. "But you do have to get upright. Come on," she grunted as she pulled Jay up with her. "I'll get the coffee started, you get the shower going."

"Oh no, we're not going to have a repeat of Friday morning." Jay felt a tingle as she thought about their impromptu lovemaking session in and out of the shower.

"What, you didn't enjoy Friday morning?"

"Oh, I didn't say that." Jay grinned. "I just said we couldn't repeat it this morning. We don't have time."

"Aw, honey, where's your sense of adventure?"

"I think I lost it when we were doing ninety-five miles an hour on the interstate so that I wouldn't miss my train."

"Humph. And I thought you liked to live dangerously."

"Sweetheart," Jay said as she reached up and planted a kiss on Kate's cheek, "there's dangerously and then there's dead. One's okay, I'm not so crazy about the other."

Kate swatted her on the behind and headed for the kitchen, Fred following closely at her heels, his tail wagging vigorously.

They both managed, with much difficulty and not a little grumbling, to behave themselves and get showered, dressed, and ready to go without much delay. The ride to the train station was depressingly silent, both women clearly unhappy at having to separate. Jay clutched at Kate's fingers and Kate rubbed her thumb lightly over the back of Jay's hand.

"I don't want to go."

"I don't want you to. Unfortunately, you have to turn in your story and go to work, and so do I."

"You know what, Kate?" Jay asked, turning her face up to gaze at Kate.

"What, love?"

"Sometimes being a grown-up sucks."

Kate laughed. "You've got that right, sweetheart. I promise I'll call you later, okay?"

"I guess it will have to be, won't it?" Jay sighed unhappily.

"I guess so." Kate used the cover of darkness in the parking lot to capture Jay's lips in a sweet goodbye kiss. "I love you so much, Jay. I hope you know that."

"I do, love," Jay said as she nibbled at Kate's lower lip. "I love you too, you know."

"Yes, I do. Come on, we've got to get going before you miss your train and blame it on me."

Jay got out of the car and ran around to the driver's side, jumping into Kate's arms where she stood. "I'm going to miss you so much." There were tears in her eyes and she clung desperately to the strong body pressed against hers.

"Me too," Kate rasped. She stroked Jay's hair. "It will be all right. Hey, it's a big day for you—your second cover story in as many weeks. Pretty soon you're going to be too important to talk to the likes of me."

"Too important to talk to the woman who made the cover of *Time* magazine? Somehow I don't think so." She smiled and stepped back, a bit of her usual self-control evident once again. "Okay, let's go."

Together they made their way to the platform and the waiting train.

≪≫

As she had before, Jay selected a window seat with a view of the scenic Hudson River. For a little while she just enjoyed the sights as they flew past her—the sailboats catching the wind, a tug pulling a barge, and some ducks paddling around in the tall grasses near the shore. Focusing on nature helped to calm her a bit and to restore her normally good humor.

Leaving Kate was more difficult that morning. At least the last time they parted she knew that they would be seeing one another in two days. She was unsure when they could be together next, and it was making her nuts. She shook her head, trying to get a handle on her feelings.

This was so unlike her—she had spent years being completely work driven and single-minded of purpose to the point of walling off all other parts of her life. She had never noticed how lonely her existence was, or how solitary, until this incredible thing called love happened to her. Suddenly all she wanted was to be with the woman who owned her heart, and nothing else seemed to matter very much, including a coveted cover-story assignment. Were it not for the fact that it was Kate who was to be on the cover, she wouldn't have cared at all, and that scared her silly.

She thought about the piece she had written. Would Kate like it? Would she think it was accurate and fair? What if she doesn't? Jay pushed the thought from her mind. As a professional, she shouldn't be concerned with what her subjects think about her work as long as it stays true to the facts and the presentation is balanced and insightful. But this wasn't just any subject—this was the woman she had desired right from the first and the owner of the other half of her soul.

Kate hadn't asked her about the story even once—hadn't asked to read it, hadn't asked how it turned out, hadn't even inquired as to whether or not she would like the outcome. She seemed to understand intrinsically that Jay needed to keep some professional distance about the piece, and for that Jay was eternally grateful.

It actually was easier to stay objective than Jay thought it would be. The extensive interviews she did, the amount of time she spent just observing Kate at work and the reactions of those around her gave Jay a solid foundation from which to write. For that period of time that she was working on the story, Jay set aside her own thoughts and let the interviewees and Kate's performance speak for themselves. In the end, the question she asked herself was if the piece was something she would have written about a subject she had never met before and knew nothing about. She was confident that it was.

Kate sat at her desk, but she wasn't really there. Her heart was a hundred and fifty miles south and her head was busy contemplating when she could see Jay next. She closed her eyes and remembered the feel of Jay clinging to her in the parking lot. There was no question that Jay was as distraught as she was about parting. *What we really need is time. Yeah, a solid block of time without any distractions. Just the two of us together, getting to know each other, seeing if we're compatible and if we could live together in harmony.* She laughed at herself. *Oh, who are you kidding, Kyle, you've already made up your mind, you just want time to convince Jay.* Chuckling again she thought, *So, what's wrong with that?*

"Hey, you okay, Kate?"

She hadn't realized how long she'd been sitting there with her eyes shut, so deep in thought that she hadn't even heard Phil and Gene approaching. "Fine, just a little tired, I guess."

"Yeah," the producer said, "you've been working really hard lately, and then there was the LCA Show. When's the last time you took a vacation, kid?" He knew the answer—never.

Gene piped in, "I meant to tell you, Kate, you were fantastic in the show. Thanks again for the tickets. I tried to congratulate you Saturday night, but there was a huge crowd around you and I couldn't get close."

"Thanks, Gene, that's sweet." Smiling at him, she patted him on the arm, which made him blush.

"Hey," Phil exclaimed, "I just remembered, wasn't that Jay Parker I saw at the governor's table?"

Kate's heart rate sped up at the mere mention of Jay's name, but she answered casually, "Yeah, I guess he invited her to be his guest when she interviewed him for this week's cover of *Time*."

"Whoo boy," Gene shook his head. "She looked hot, and I mean hot with a capital H! Did you see that dress she had on? Wow! Do you think she's single, Kate?" Without waiting for an answer, he prattled on, completely oblivious to the change in Kate's demeanor. "If I had any balls I would've gone right up to her and—"

"If you had any balls you wouldn't know what to do with them," Phil interrupted, laughing.

"Gentlemen, and I use the term very loosely, if you'll excuse me, I've got some work to do." Kate stalked off.

"What got into her, you think?" Kate heard Gene say.

Kate gripped the sink in the bathroom so hard her knuckles were white. She knew if she stayed there even one moment longer she would have slugged Gene. It wouldn't do to haul off and deck a co-worker for encroaching on her girlfriend when he didn't even know he was doing it.

Once she was satisfied she was under control again she returned to her desk. An idea was forming in her head, sparked by her own thoughts and something Phil said. But first, she had to make a phone call.

After stopping at her apartment to drop off her suitcase and change her clothes, Jay arrived in the office a few minutes ahead of schedule.

Trish greeted her as she was passing by, stopping and leaning on the corner of Jay's desk. "Hey, you look like you got a little color this weekend. Do anything interesting?"

Oh yeah, I spent it with the love of my life, snuggled up doing nothing except crossword puzzles, napping outside in the sun, and making love. "I went up north to the Catskills and did a little hiking. It was beautiful and I guess I must have forgotten the sunblock." *Well, that was the truth, wasn't it?*

"Well, whatever you did, you look great, kind of like you're glowing or something." Trish paused for a second. "Okay, kid, come with me and let's see the goods."

Obediently, Jay got up. She brought the manila file folder with the story, her notes and background materials with her. She stood in front of Trish's desk, unsure whether she should just hand her the piece or sit down. Her dilemma was solved when Trish pointed to the chair and put her hand out for the story.

Jay chewed on her lower lip and handed it over. For the next twenty minutes, as Trish read, grunting occasionally, Jay's anxiety level increased. She couldn't read anything in Trish's expression as her eyes danced across the pages.

Finally, just when Jay was sure she would spontaneously combust, Trish looked up. "Jamison Parker, I have to tell you, you've outdone yourself again, girl. This," she pointed at the papers, "is the most three-dimensional piece I think I've ever seen, and believe me, I've seen plenty. I mean, really, Jay, it shows uncommon insight into the subject. Congrats. This chick must have given you unprecedented access. Geez, what'd she let you do, spend twenty-four hours a day with her or something?"

Jay almost choked. *You have no idea,* she thought, but the words that came out of her mouth were ones she knew would have made Kate laugh. "She was most accommodating."

"Well, you keep this up and you're going to be writing every cover from here on in. Now, why don't you go review the pics they took and help them decide which ones to use. Then maybe I'll give you some time off for good behavior."

"On my way, Trish, and thanks." Jay beamed. She was overjoyed at Trish's comments about the piece and, if that wasn't enough, she was going to get to spend her afternoon looking at proofs and eight-by-tens of the most gorgeous woman in the world.

"Don't mention it, kiddo," Trish said indulgently as she turned to the other piles of papers littering her desk.

When Jay stopped by her cubicle to drop off her folder on the way to the photo department, the phone was ringing.

"Hello, Jamison Parker."

"Hi, beautiful."

The warm, seductive quality of that voice cut through Jay's business demeanor like a hot knife through butter. "Hi yourself, Stretch."

"How was your trip down?"

"Uneventful. I even managed to get to the office a few minutes early."

"That's great. I'm not catching you at a bad time, am I?"

"Well, I was just about to go review pictures of the sexiest woman alive, but..."

"Oh yeah? Who might that be?" A note of indignation crept into Kate's voice. "I need to know who my competition is."

Jay chuckled and shook her head. "It's you, ya goofball. I was talking about you."

"Oh, well, I guess that's okay then. Everything all right?"

Jay smiled, understanding Kate's reluctance to ask directly about the story and appreciating the gesture. "Everything's more than okay. Trish loved the piece. She said, and I quote, 'It shows uncommon insight inta da subject...dis chick musta given ya unprecedented access...what'd she do, let ya spend twenty-four owas a day wit ha or somethin''?"

Kate's laugh was hearty. Finally, she croaked out, "That's a pretty mean Noo Yawk accent you've got there, Scoop. I can't wait to hear how you answered her question."

"I just told her the truth," Jay paused for effect, knowing that Kate must be dying on the other end of the phone.

"You told her...the truth."

"Yep," Jay answered smugly. "I told her you were very accommodating."

"Oh, you are such a brat. Hey, that was a pretty good one."

"Well, I told the truth, didn't I?"

"That you did, love, that you did. So, what's next for you?"

"I don't know yet, Trish said something about maybe giving me some time off for good behavior." Jay let the comment dangle there, hoping Kate would understand the implications.

"Oh, that's nice," Kate said, seemingly distracted all of a sudden. "Listen, love, I've got to run. Want me to call you when I'm done tonight, or are you going to be asleep?"

Jay tried to hide her disappointment. "Um, you don't have to call if you don't want to."

"Of course I want to, sweetheart." Softly, she added, "I love you, Jay. I miss you."

"Miss you too. Love you, bye."

᭬

Jay swatted at the alarm, but the incessant ringing didn't stop. Blearily, she opened one eye and peeked at the offending instrument. Nope, she'd been right, she hadn't set the damn thing by accident. So what could be making all the racket? Oh yeah, the telephone.

She grumbled and searched for the receiver by feel. She wasn't ready to open both eyes just yet, not having gotten much sleep after her brief midnight conversation with Kate. Jay hadn't had much to say. She was depressed because Kate didn't mention seeing each other again, even though she told her that she had the rest of the week off. It wasn't in her to invite herself to Albany. She resolutely told herself she would not beg, although that's exactly what her heart wanted her to do.

It was obvious Kate didn't want her there. If she did, she would have offered. After they hung up, Jay cried for a long time, finally tiring herself out and falling into a fitful sleep at around three a.m. Now it was nine a.m. on her first day off, she had nothing to do and nowhere to be, and the phone was ringing.

"Hello," she mumbled, her voice rough from crying and too little sleep.

"Hi. I'm waking you, aren't I?"

Jay cleared her throat. "It's okay. What's up?"

"Um, Fred misses you."

Still half asleep, Jay muttered, "Then how come he's not the one calling me?"

"He's a little shy and he doesn't want to appear to be needy."

"Hmm, I didn't realize he was that deep a thinker. Hold on, it's hard to hear, there's a fire engine going by outside." Jay paused for a moment, noticing as she came more awake that she was hearing the siren in stereo. "Kate?"

"Yes." The sound of the siren faded into the distance.

"Where are you, exactly?"

"At the pay phone outside your building. You can probably see me if you look outside your window."

"Are you kidding me?" Jay was fully awake now.

"Nope."

"Get up here, you goofball! I'm hanging up, go to the door so I can buzz you in."

Within seconds Kate was bounding up the stairs, arriving at the door just as it was being flung open. She stepped into the apartment and shut the door behind her with her foot as she had the very first time they kissed. She scooped Jay into her arms. This time, though, there was no limousine waiting downstairs and nothing on Kate's mind except how much she loved and wanted the wonderful woman in her arms.

She leaned down and reverently ran her hands over Jay's face, finally tangling her fingers in the sleep-tousled golden strands and pulling her into a heart-stopping kiss that didn't end until they were both desperate for air. "Which way is the bedroom?" Kate asked huskily, her eyes darkened with passion.

Without saying a word, Jay took her by the hand and tugged her toward the loft, where she quickly stripped them both, all the while backing Kate toward the bed with purpose.

"I missed you so much, sweetheart, I couldn't stand not having you in my bed last night. I never knew I could feel this way." Kate had to stop talking then, because Jay had inserted a thigh between her legs and the delicious pressure was driving her to distraction.

"Mmm, I think I like the sound of that. Is this what you were missing, baby?" Jay was hovering over her now, her breasts tantalizingly close, but just out of reach of Kate's mouth.

"Oh, yeah." Reaching up, Kate ran her thumbs over the aroused nipples, watching avidly as Jay's eyes closed in reaction and she leaned in to the contact. They were both so ready they knew they couldn't stand much more in the way of foreplay, but they continued to tease, taste and touch as long as they could before giving in and taking each other completely.

"Oh God, Kate!"
"Don't stop, Jay, please...don't stop..."
"I won't, love."

ও৬ঌ৯

Sometime later, when they both recovered and were lying peacefully entangled with one another, Jay asked, "Not that I'm complaining, because I'm not, but what are you doing here, love?"

"If I have to explain it to you..." Kate chuckled, indicating their entwined torsos.

"I don't mean that and you know it, wise guy. I mean, it's Tuesday morning, it's ten a.m., and you're a hundred and fifty miles south of where you're supposed to be four hours from now."

"Oh, that. Hand me my jeans, will you?"

Jay shook her head, once again baffled by a non sequitur. She leaned over the edge of the bed and found the jeans where they had been dropped in haste. "Here you go. Are you planning on running out right now or something?" Jay laughed nervously. "If so, then please disregard the question."

"No, love, of course not. I'm trying to answer you."

"And you need your pants for that?"

"Yes," Kate supplied as she dug around in the pockets. "Ah, here we go. Close your eyes."

"What?"

"Do you always have so much trouble following simple instructions? Close your eyes, woman."

Jay did as she was told.

"Now hold out your hand."

She did, and Kate placed a flat item in her palm, closing her fingers around it.

"Okay, you can open your eyes now."

Jay cracked one eyelid, peeking into her outstretched hand, where a brochure rested. She opened the other eye and studied the picture on the front. It showed an endless expanse of sun-drenched white sand and ocean, a beach chair, and the inviting caption, *This could be you.* She looked up at Kate questioningly.

Kate smiled broadly, making her blue eyes twinkle in the sunlight seeping into the loft. "I, um, thought you might enjoy a little time away." She pointed at the brochure. "That's St. John in the U.S. Virgin Islands."

"I don't understand, you're sending me away?"

"Oh, sweetheart." Kate shook her head and pulled Jay on top of her. "I'm sending *us* away, as in a vacation, as in just the two of us, as in quality time with no distractions, as in we have a plane to catch in," she looked at the bedside clock, "three and a half hours."

Jay leaned up on one elbow and stared hard into Kate's eyes. "You're serious."

"Oh, yes, I certainly am," Kate offered sincerely. "I love you, Jamison, and all I want to do is spend more time with you. Will you come away with me? Today? Now? I know I didn't give you any warning, or any choice about the destination, but..."

"Yes. Yes, love, I would follow you to the end of the earth...or at least to a beautiful beach in the Virgin Islands." She smiled and winked. "But how...when...how long..."

"I know there's a question in there just dying to get out, sweetheart. I didn't want to say anything last night until I was sure I had all the arrangements worked out and everything set. That didn't happen until very late, and then I had it in my head that I'd rather surprise you in person than tell you about it over the phone."

"How did you get the time off? Didn't you tell me this is sweeps month? And you're going to be the hottest property going once the magazine hits the newsstands."

"I asked. Yes, it is. And I agreed to be back on the air Monday night, the day the magazine comes out."

"Wow. I can't believe this." Jay's eye's shone with delight and anticipation. "A whole five days alone with you on a tropical island. Well, this will be tough to take. My God, I've got to pack!" She jumped off the bed and ran to her closet to retrieve her suitcase. Before she'd gotten five steps away, she turned around, ran back, and kissed Kate soundly on the mouth. "You're the best, you know that? God, I love you so much."

"I love you too, sweetheart. Now come here. We've still got time and I am nowhere near done with you yet." Kate pulled Jay back down onto the bed and pinned her in one smooth motion.

CHAPTER SIXTEEN

Two silhouetted figures strolled hand in hand on the deserted beach, their bare feet splashing softly in the surf, their bodies barely illuminated by the sliver of moonlight and the profusion of stars.

"Kate, this is the most breathtaking place I've ever seen. The sand is so soft and the water so warm." Jay smiled up at Kate, her eyes sparkling. "This feels like such a dream, being here with you. It's like magic."

"I'm glad you like it, sweetheart."

Their flight had gone without a hitch, and the resort was everything it promised to be. They had a secluded villa with a bedroom, living room, dining room, kitchen, and a balcony overlooking the water. Most importantly, they had each other and time to spend exclusively together without interruption in this island paradise.

"Can we go snorkeling tomorrow? And I want to try sailing too."

"Honey, we can do anything you want tomorrow, anytime you want to do it. As long as I'm with you, nothing else matters." Kate stopped for a moment, brushed her fingers along a rounded jawline and leaned down to kiss the waiting lips.

Jay felt the truth of Kate's statement and it made her heart soar. Could it have been just last night that she lay crying herself to sleep, unsure whether Kate wanted to spend time with her? She sighed, knowing that her past demons once again led her to expect the worst. So far, all she had gotten from the woman at her side was the very best, and she repaid her with doubts and insecurities. She scowled.

"Hey, beautiful, what's with the frown? Did I say something wrong?"

Jay's head jerked up. "No, no, of course not. Just beating myself up a little, that's all."

"Any particular reason?"

"It's nothing, really." She was dejected and it showed.

"Not good enough, Scoop. Come on, let's talk about it so we can get past whatever it is." When Jay didn't look up or respond, Kate added, "Please?"

"Okay, but I feel so stupid."

"Love, you are many things—gorgeous, talented, exceedingly bright, criminally good in bed, funny, compassionate, and caring, but one thing you most certainly are not is stupid." Kate squeezed the hand she still held.

"Well, sometimes I sure feel dumb." Jay took a deep breath. "When you didn't seem interested that I had the rest of the week off, I thought maybe you didn't want to spend the time with me, even though I desperately wanted to spend it with you. I guess I went down that road pretty far and managed to get myself into a state where I cried myself to sleep last night for three hours."

"Oh, sweetheart, believe me, I was plenty interested, but I didn't want to get your hopes up in case I couldn't get the time off or couldn't make the plan work. I'm sorry if I led you to think anything different. Nothing could have been further from the truth."

"You don't need to apologize to me, love, it wasn't you…it's just that disappointment has always been a fact of life for me. Reacting to you based on my past experiences isn't fair. I'm the one who owes you an apology. You deserve so much more credit than I've been giving you."

"Jay, look at me." Kate waited until Jay locked eyes with her. "I will never fault you for reactions that are second nature to you. All I ask is for the chance to re-train your mind until there are no doubts left to erase and no insecurities to overcome, until you can trust in me, trust in us. Can I have that? Can we have that?"

"You are so much more than I deserve. How can it be that of all the women in the world you could have, you want to be with me?"

"Because of all the women in the world, you are the one who owns me, body and soul and the only one I'll ever want or need. I love you, Jay, with all my heart."

"I love you too, Kate." Jay waited a beat, then bumped her companion with a hip. "Criminally good in bed, eh?"

"Oh yeah."

Wednesday dawned bright and clear, sunlight splashing across the bed where a sole occupant lay sprawled. Jay reached out, expecting to find Kate, but instead connecting with the soft cotton sheet. She frowned and picked her head up. No human teddy bear. Disappointed, she listened for sounds coming from the bathroom. Hearing none, she turned her attention to the kitchen, where she was rewarded with the smell of freshly brewing coffee. She followed her nose and discovered the caffeine, but still no sign of Kate.

A quick check of the entire villa confirmed that Kate was AWOL. Still naked, Jay walked to the sliding glass doors that opened onto the balcony and looked out at the beach. She strained her eyes and spied a single figure running gracefully along the surf, long strides eating up the vast expanse of sand, head up, hair flying in the breeze. She smiled. The sight of her lover, caught unaware as she was outlined against the rising sun, took her breath away.

Several minutes later, dressed in a pair of very short running shorts and a cut-off short-sleeved shirt, Jay stood with her toes in the sand at the water's edge, a bottle of water in hand. As she watched, the solitary runner came into view, her features resolving themselves as she got closer.

"Good morning, love." Kate swept Jay into her arms and kissed her lightly on the lips before setting her back on her feet.

"Hi."

"What are you doing out of bed?"

"I missed my snuggle partner."

"Sorry about that. I didn't want to wake you. You were sleeping so peacefully. I get restless sometimes in the morning and it was so beautiful out, I thought I'd come out and take a quick run. I didn't think you'd miss me."

"Honey," Jay chuckled, "I miss you when you go to the bathroom. And I always have a cure for morning restlessness." She waggled her eyebrows suggestively.

"Oh you do, do you? Well, I'll have to remember that, although I also seem to recall that you're not a morning person."

"For that, I'd make myself into a morning person." Jay slipped her arm through Kate's as they made their way up the beach to the villa. "I thought you might need this," she said, handing Kate the water bottle.

"Thanks, as a matter of fact, I could use some. Now all I need is a shower and I'll be good as new."

"Well you'd better be quick about it, because I have plans for you."

"Oh yeah?"

"Mmm-hmm." Jay proceeded to describe in great detail exactly what she had in mind. After all, they were on vacation.

They lay side by side on a beach blanket, soaking up the sun as it dried their salty skin. Snorkeling gear and fins sat dripping nearby, a testament to their first foray into the lush underwater world of the warm Caribbean waters. It was a lot of fun, swimming together along a nearby reef, pointing out to each other all of the colorful tropical fish as they bustled along their way. They spotted clownfish and angelfish, lobsters and kissing fish and some species whose names neither one of them knew.

Now they rested quietly on the peaceful stretch of beach they claimed for their own. Kate was remembering the earlier part of the morning. Given the proper motivation, she managed to get showered in record time and returned to the bedroom to find Jay impatiently waiting for her. Jay made good on everything she promised and more, and it was a wonder that Kate was able to move at all afterward. She smiled—having Jay as a lover would never be boring, that was for certain.

"What are you smiling about, Stretch?"

"Mmm, just thinking about making love with a very beautiful woman this morning. You're going to spoil me, you know. I'll be ruined for life."

"I'm counting on it," Jay responded. "Wait until you see what I have planned for dessert tonight."

Kate groaned, but her grin gave her away. "Still interested in going for a sail?"

"Yeah," Jay replied enthusiastically.

"Okay. How about we dry out a little more, then I'll go make the arrangements while you find the ingredients for a picnic lunch at sea."

"Ooh, that sounds great. You've got a deal."

The fifteen-foot Javelin skimmed along the water, Kate at the helm and Jay hanging backward over the side as the boat heeled almost halfway out of the water. "Prepare to come about," Kate yelled to be heard over the rush of the wind. She waited until Jay nodded before yelling, "Coming about!"

At the command, Jay ducked under the boom and came up on the other side of the boat, where she assumed the same position she had on the starboard side. It went on like this for nearly an hour until they came in sight of a tiny island off the port side. Kate maneuvered them into the wind, dropping the sails as Jay threw the anchor overboard. They were about twenty-five feet from shore and blocked from the bulk of the wind by the trees.

"Hungry?"

"Am I ever not hungry?" Jay asked, slapping Kate lightly in the stomach.

"I guess that was a stupid question. Let me rephrase it…are you ready to eat lunch? This seems like a nice spot."

"It's perfect, and I'm more than ready for food, as always." From under the hull, Jay dragged the mini-cooler with their supplies. She brought out a tablecloth, a hunk of cheese, some French bread, a couple of mangoes, and a half-split of champagne with plastic glasses, along with some water, then closed the cooler to double as their table. "Will this do?"

"Looks great to me. Want me to do the honors?" Kate asked as she pointed to the champagne.

"Please."

She popped the cork smoothly and poured two glasses, handing one to Jay. "To a fantastic vacation with the most extraordinary woman in the world."

"I'll drink to that," Jay agreed, interlocking arms with Kate as they drank from their glasses.

They settled side by side on a bench, sharing cheese on bread, licking each other's fingers to ensure that they hadn't left any crumbs behind. In between the bites of food, they traded kisses and nibbles.

"I didn't know you knew how to sail, Stretch. Yet another one of your many secret skills, I suppose."

Kate chuckled. "I told you, love, I have no secrets from you, only things we have yet to discover about each other. I grew up on the Atlantic Ocean…it was natural to learn to sail. I learned when I was about ten to skipper boats just like this one. It feels like coming home."

"Yes, I suppose it would. Who taught you to sail?"

"Friends of the family. They would take me out in all kinds of conditions just to make sure I knew how to handle myself out there in the elements. It was great training and good for my confidence. It taught me how to think quickly, be decisive, and react under pressure. All things that have served me well."

"Mmm." Jay wanted to ask more, wanted to know all about Kate's family, but as she never seemed inclined to talk about them, Jay was reluctant. She didn't need to know for the cover story since the focus was on Kate's career, and though she knew she could have asked in that context, she didn't want to satisfy her curiosity while hiding behind a professional pretext.

Wondering when another opportunity might present itself and fearing that it wouldn't, Jay decided to broach the subject delicately. "Your parents didn't sail?"

Kate's posture stiffened imperceptibly—imperceptibly, that is, to anyone who didn't know her body as Jay did. "No. They never went out with me."

"We've never really talked about your family. I'm sorry, if it's a sore subject, we can drop it."

"No, no, that's okay, love. Nothing is off limits to you. Ask away. I don't want there to be anything but honesty and full disclosure between us." Kate's eyes darkened. "My mother was a strong woman. She was an artist and an advocate for those less fortunate than we were. She volunteered in the court system for abused spouses and fought single-mindedly for the things she believed in...a great athlete too. She's the one who taught me how to play tennis." Kate smiled at the recollection. "She was tough, but very smart and passionate about social causes and the difference between right and wrong. There wasn't much gray with her, everything was black or it was white."

"It sounds like you loved and admired her very much." Jay reached out and touched the back of Kate's hand. "But you talk about her in the past tense."

"Yes." Tears sprang unexpectedly to Kate's eyes. "Both my parents were killed by a drunk driver when I was eighteen."

"Oh, sweetheart, I'm so, so sorry. I didn't know." Moving the few inches and wrapping her arms around Kate, Jay offered comfort for a pain that would never end.

"My father always wanted a Corvette. He finally found a mint condition '68, maroon with tan leather interior and a stick shift. He was in heaven...I called it his mid-life crisis car. He and my mother were driving home from a party late one night on the Hutchinson

River Parkway when a drunk slammed into them from behind, knocking them headfirst into a tree at eighty-five miles an hour. They didn't stand a chance."

"Love, I don't know what to say."

"It's okay, at least they didn't suffer. They were both pronounced dead at the scene. Their best friends, who were also lawyers and the executors of their estate, called me at school. It was December twenty-second, three days before Christmas my freshman year. They took care of the details of selling the house and all of that kind of stuff, and set up a trust for me. There was plenty of money for me to finish college and live comfortably afterward, but..."

"But you'd give it all back just to have them alive, wouldn't you?"

"Yeah, I would. I didn't have any brothers or sisters, so it's just been me ever since."

"Seems like we've both become orphans, in a way."

"There are two kinds of families, Jay. Those you are born into, and those you create. To me you are my family now, and nothing could make me happier."

"Me too, love. Me too."

They sat for a while, holding each other silently and enjoying the peaceful solitude of the water and the nearby uninhabited island. As the wind began to pick up a bit and the sun crawled across the sky, Kate roused them from their reveries and headed them back toward the resort.

The candles flickered in the breeze, creating interesting shadows across the faces of the lovers as they enjoyed a romantic dinner for two on the outdoor patio at a local restaurant on the water. They were so wrapped up in each other that they barely took notice of the other restaurant patrons around them, some of whom stared at them in open disgust.

"Can you believe they just sit there like that, holding hands as if it were normal? What is this world coming to, anyway? Somebody ought to do something about that sort of thing. Earl, go over and talk to them."

"I'm not goin' anywhere. I'm gonna sit here and eat my meal and mind my own business, and I suggest you do the same."

"Humph. Well, I tell you, they're ruining my appetite."

"Yeah, I can tell," Earl said uninterestedly, as he pointed to his wife's mostly empty plate.

Kate, whose hearing was extraordinary, caught the entire exchange, but chose to ignore it and concentrate instead on the beautiful woman sitting across from her.

"What are you smiling about, Stretch?"

"I'm just trying to remember what I did before I had you in my life. Right about now, if it wasn't a work night, Fred and I would be sitting in the library reading a good book and munching on stuffed animals." At the raised eyebrow, she clarified, "Of course, the book is for Fred and the stuffed animals are mine."

"Of course." Jay's eyes twinkled.

"You've brought so much into my life, Jay. I'm so thankful to have you."

"Right back at ya, sweetheart. Right about now I'd be sitting on the sofa with a magazine and a bag of popcorn, critiquing the competition's writing style. Shallow, but somehow satisfying."

Kate laughed. "Aren't we just a couple of live wires. Can I interest you in dessert, perhaps?"

Jay smiled evilly. "Only if you're on the menu."

"I dunno, have you read the menu? Do you know your choices?"

"I know that I would choose the same thing every time, I don't even need to see what's available."

"In that case, may I escort you home, princess?"

Unable to resist the temptation on the way out, Kate stopped at Earl's table. She pulled Jay to a halt with her and didn't let go of her hand. Kate put on her most charming smile, oozing charisma, and in her best southern accent drawled, "Excuse me, but we couldn't help but notice what a lovely couple you make. How long have y'all been married, if you don't mind my askin'?"

"Forty-two years," the wife replied, puffing herself up like a peacock.

"Well, I do declare. Jam'son, did y'all hear that? I just hope that someday we can be just like you...so in love after so many years. In't that right, sugah?"

"Why yes, honeybunch," Jay played along.

"By the way," Kate lowered her voice conspiratorially, snaring the old woman with her gaze and resting her free hand on her arm, "I just luuv your outfit. Liz Claiborne, if I'm not mistaken...one of my personal favorites. It looks just perfect on you, honey."

"Thank you very much."

"Well, we'd best be goin' now and leave these nice folks alone, right, Jam'son?"

"Right, peaches. It was so nice to meet y'all. Have a great night."

As Kate and Jay walked away, the old woman swatted Earl on the arm. "Well, wasn't that nice. I had no idea those kind of people had such good taste. They know a good marriage and proper clothing when they see it." Earl didn't answer. Kate could feel his eyes follow her and Jay as they disappeared from the restaurant.

Once outside, Jay turned to Kate, her eyes gleaming. "Okay, want to tell me what that was all about, sugah?"

"Just having a little fun, that's all," Kate smiled warmly.

"Because...why?"

"The old bat took exception to our public display of affection, and I thought I'd play with her a little. Thanks for going along with me...that was great sport."

"How did you know she was wearing Liz Claiborne, a lucky guess?"

"Nope. Her tag was hanging out in back."

"You are so bad."

"You're about to find out how bad," Kate purred in her sexiest register.

Jay whimpered.

CHAPTER SEVENTEEN

Kate brushed her fingers lightly over Jay's bare buttocks and back, reveling in the feel of silky soft skin and the scent that was so uniquely Jay. She was overwhelmed with a desire to show Jay exactly what she felt for her. She started with slow caresses and deep kisses, added some strategically placed nibbles and bites, and luxuriated in the thrill of Jay's rising excitement. She stilled Jay's wandering hands, wanting her instead to focus exclusively on her pleasure.

"Tell me what you want, sweetheart, all of it. I want to make everything you've ever fantasized about, everything you've ever dreamed, come true."

"You already have," Jay said.

"Is this what you want?" Kate ran her tongue up the inside of one thigh and lightly kissed the engorged tissues, briefly sucking her lover into her mouth and then letting her go.

"Argh. God, Kate, that feels so good."

"Or would you prefer this?" She smoothed long fingers over downy soft skin and into blonde curls, barely dipping into the wetness, swirling her fingers around once and retreating.

"Ahh. Oh, love."

"Tell me what you want, sweetheart, and it's all yours."

"Please, take me now, I need you so much. I want you so much. I can't stand it."

When Kate sensed that no further instruction was forthcoming, she made her own decision, entering Jay slowly with long, slender fingers, seeking the sensitive spots she knew so well, adding to the pressure with a thigh, setting the rhythm, following the rise and fall of her lover's hips. Then she lowered her head, took an aroused nipple into her mouth, swirled the tip, and bit down gently. Jay moaned, grasping Kate's hair and pulling her more firmly onto her breast. Kate

177

complied, biting down harder, as Jay cried out her name and exploded in orgasm.

Kate continued to stroke Jay lightly, allowing her breath to settle briefly before replacing fingers with tongue, taking first quick and then long, firm strokes until Jay was once again begging for release. Kate grasped Jay's buttocks and pulled her tighter against her mouth, increasing the pressure of her tongue against the already swollen tissues. Immediately she felt Jay shudder with pleasure and heard her gasp as she came again.

Kate moved up to lie alongside her exhausted lover, brushed stray blonde strands from her eyes and kissed her with as much feeling as she could convey. "I want you to know how incredibly good you taste, love. You are my life. I love you, Jay."

"I love you too, sweetheart, and I'd love to show you just how much. Unfortunately, someone has worn me out completely for the moment."

"That's all right, all I want right now is to hold you."

When she awoke just before dawn, Kate was as content as she'd ever been. She closed her eyes again and waited for Jay to wake.

Kate and Jay spent the remainder of the morning lying on the beach, taking an occasional swim, and snorkeling. In the afternoon, they sailed to the spot they discovered the day before. Once again, Kate took the helm, but this time, she explained to Jay as she went, teaching her what she knew. Halfway out, she motioned Jay to join her at the tiller, positioned her between her legs facing outward, and placed her hand on the tiller as well.

"Here, just pick a point over the bow and keep the tiller pointed at it. With your other hand, you hold the ropes that control the mainsail and jib. Pull tighter if you want to catch more wind, let them out a little if you want to slow down, okay? If you want to get stopped dead in your tracks, head directly into the wind."

"Sounds easy enough," Jay said.

Kate let them run along that way for a bit so that Jay could get the feel of it. "Ready to turn?"

"Just tell me what to do." And Kate did, letting Jay do some of the work, but never relinquishing full control. "How'd I do?"

"Not bad. Don't forget the tension on the sails, that's critical, and make sure you warn the crew when you're about to shift directions."

"Got it."

They practiced together all the way out to the island, with Jay getting more and more excited about her new skills as they went. Kate smiled at her enthusiasm, loving the sparkle in her eyes that matched the color of the water.

"Honey, I don't want to stop just yet. Can we sail around the island, and can I take the helm by myself?"

"You think you're ready for that?"

"Nothing to it," Jay replied.

Kate, who was a seasoned sailor, was a little leery of letting Jay handle the boat by herself. Then she remembered the first time she had gotten to solo—her mentor had taken her out to an island not that different from this one and let her loose, calmly correcting her when she made mistakes and giving her the freedom to learn. That trust had meant so much to her. "Okay, let me just get us around this corner, then it's all yours."

Kate moved out from behind Jay and positioned herself on the starboard side for the moment. "Okay, pick a point and follow it with the bow and the tiller."

Jay did.

"Good, now pull in the mainsail just a little bit and point the tiller a little to your left so that we catch a little more wind. Not too much, though."

"Aye, aye, Cap'n."

"Easy, there, matey, easy...that's too much, let it out a bit."

When Jay pulled the sail tight into a left turn, the wind filled the sail, and the boat picked up speed at what clearly was to Jay an alarming rate.

"It's okay, love," Kate shouted to be heard over the wind and the water rushing by. In an attempt to keep them from heeling all the way and capsizing, she leaned far out over the boat. She could see the panic building in Jay's eyes as they grew wide. "Don't worry. Just let the sail out a little, don't make any sudden shifts."

But even as she said the words, Jay lost her balance. As she fell, Jay yanked the tiller hard, and the boat yawed violently to the right. The mainsail line slipped through her fingers and the sail flapped wildly in the wind. The boom swung hard the other way with the sudden shift in direction. Before she had time to duck, it caught Kate in the side of the head. The force of the blow knocked her unconscious, and the momentum pitched her overboard and into the water.

Jay barely had time to blink in the space it had taken to lose Kate. Her scream died on the wind.

On the shore of the tiny island, some tourists who had disembarked from a nearby cruise ship witnessed the entire scene. The two crew members who had transported the passengers in a motorized dinghy saw the tragedy unfolding as well, and they were in their craft even before Kate hit the water and were speeding to the rescue.

"Hang on. We'll be right there," one of the men yelled.

As the men reached the sailboat and grabbed hold of the side, Jay dove into the water, desperate to find Kate. She surfaced to take a breath and dove back down, trying valiantly to see despite the tears that clouded her vision. Jay struggled to clear her mind and let her lifesaving-instructor training take over. She tried to gauge the current and figure how far the boat had moved past the spot where Kate went overboard. Jay ran out of air again and broke the surface one more time before she re-submerged. It had been two agonizing minutes, and every additional second decreased the chances of finding Kate alive.

There! Finally, she spotted the still figure, lying limp on the ocean floor, fifteen feet below the surface. Kicking hard, Jay propelled herself downward, reached out and grabbed an arm, then planted her feet on the bottom and pushed off with all her strength. Breaking the surface, Jay pulled Kate into a lifesaving carry and signaled to the circling dinghy. Within seconds, one of the men pulled alongside, grabbed the unresponsive woman under the armpits and hauled her into the dinghy. Then he reached over again and assisted Jay into the craft.

"Can you get us to the island? Please hurry." Jay turned her attention to Kate. She checked for a pulse and breathing. "She's not breathing, but she has a pulse." Jay's voice shook and her whole body trembled, but she put everything aside except the thought of saving the other half of her soul. Nothing else mattered.

She laid Kate out and rolled her onto her side, then cleared her mouth and compressed her abdomen to empty her stomach of water.

Jay checked again for breathing and pulse. The pulse was there, although weaker, and she still wasn't breathing.

"Miss, we're at the shore now." There was a hand on Jay's shoulder. "Let us help you get her onto the sand."

"Hurry, I have to save her. I have to."

"We'll do everything we can, miss."

Two passengers on the shore met them as they hit the sand. They grabbed the dinghy and beached it, then helped the crew member lift the unconscious woman out of the boat and onto the ground.

Jay dropped to her knees by Kate's head, checked one more time for a pulse and breathing, then tilted Kate's head back, pinched off her nose, and began mouth-to-mouth. This couldn't be real—it had to be a nightmare, that's all. The only sounds Jay could hear were the beat of her own heart hammering in her ears and the whoosh of the air she was breathing into Kate's lungs. In between breaths, she watched for the telltale rise and fall of the chest and listened for air escaping Kate's mouth. For an agonizing minute, nothing happened save the continued rhythm of the mouth-to-mouth breathing every five seconds.

Tears streamed down Jay's face as she leaned over one more time, breathing life into the woman without whom she was sure she would die. "Please, love," she pleaded, "please don't leave me now, I couldn't bear it. I need you so much. Please, please stay with me." She turned her head to the side, placing her ear near Kate's lips and watching her chest. Just as she was about to turn and give another breath, Kate coughed weakly and made a choking sound. Quickly, Jay inserted herself behind Kate's upper back, sitting her up a little to clear her airway. With Jay holding her tightly from behind, Kate coughed several more times and gasped for air.

"Jay..." It came out as a hoarse whisper.

"Shh. Don't talk now. You're okay, love, you're going to be okay." She rocked Kate back and forth in her arms, forgetting for a moment about her head injury, ignoring that there were other people present, blocking out everything except the feeling of life coursing through the body pressed against her chest.

After a moment, Kate leaned to the side and vomited, as Jay soothed her and rubbed her back.

"Miss, she really needs to be checked out. We have a doctor aboard the ship." The young crew member pointed in the direction of the cruise ship, which was now plainly visible from this side of the island. "We could take you on board and let him have a look. She took a nasty blow to the side of her head...it could be dangerous still."

"Thank you, you're right. Are you sure that would be okay?"

"Yes, ma'am," the other crew member smiled at her. "I'm sure Doc would be happy to help. He's always complaining about being lonely."

Looking around for the first time, Jay noted the crowd of people that had gathered. She also noticed that the sailboat had been towed safely onto the sand. She wiped her eyes self-consciously, never letting go of Kate, who was wheezing and semi-alert.

One of the male bystanders said, "We could lift her into the dinghy for you."

"That's very sweet, thank you."

"No problem, and don't worry, we'll be careful not to move her head. Okay guys, give me a hand."

Three other burly men stepped forward, gently lifting Kate into the dinghy. Jay never let go of Kate's hand and scooted in behind her in the boat as the men helped the crew members give it a shove off.

Within minutes they arrived at the side of the large cruise ship. Several more crew members met them and helped attach lines to the dinghy so it could be mechanically lifted to deck level, where a stretcher and the doctor were waiting. For the first time, Jay realized that the crew members must have been in contact with the ship by radio and transmitted news of the emergency so that everyone would be ready to assist. She was grateful beyond words.

"I don't know how to thank you two. You saved her life. I don't know what I would have done without you." Tears spilled down her cheeks.

"No, no, miss. You saved her life, we just lent a little bit of a helping hand."

There was no time for more talk just then because the mechanical lift ground to a halt. The crew members and doctor sprang into action. They transferred Kate to the stretcher and carried her to the infirmary.

"Hi, I'm Dr. Hanratty," the medic said.

"I..." Jay cleared her throat around the emotion that still threatened to choke her. "I'm Jamison Parker and this is Katherine Kyle."

"Nice to meet you both. Trust me, I promise to take good care of your friend." He smiled kindly at Jay. "Do you want to sit down for a minute?"

"No," she said too quickly. She didn't want to let go of Kate's hand, couldn't bear to lose contact with her.

"Okay. Well, let me tell you what I'm going to do. I'm going to take a quick look at her, then x-ray her head. I understand she took a nasty blow, is that right?"

Jay simply nodded, unable to answer around the lump in her throat, knowing it had been all her fault.

"Don't worry, young lady, I'm sure she's going to be just fine, and from what I hear, she owes that to you. You're quite a hero."

"I don't feel like a hero. If it hadn't been for me, she wouldn't have gotten knocked in the head in the first place."

"Excuse me," a voice said weakly from the stretcher. "Jamison." Kate motioned Jay to lower her head so that she could make eye contact with her. "This was not your fault...it was an accident. Stuff happens. I love you, and I'm here with you and that's all that matters, okay?"

"Okay."

"Look me in the eye and say that like you mean it, Scoop."

Jay smiled for the first time in what seemed like hours. "Okay, Stretch," she said more strongly, glad beyond measure just to be able to hear Kate's voice.

"That's better. Okay, Doc, let's get this over with, I've got a vacation to get back to."

"That's the spirit," the doctor said, and proceeded with his examination.

❧

Outside, the two crew members were talking.

"Man, that poor woman took a hell of a whack to the side of her head. That boom was really moving."

"No kidding, she sailed about five feet in the air before she landed. You could tell by the way she hit the water that she was already out cold. Sank like a stone."

"The cute blonde did all right, though, finding her so quickly. Must have had some training. She knew just what to do."

"Yep, handled everything by the book, just like they teach you. Come to think of it, that was pretty amazing, considering how shook up she was. Did you see the way her hands were trembling?"

"Wouldn't yours have been if it had been you? Jesus, her friend would've been dead, or at least brain damaged, in another minute or two."

"You think something's going on there?"

"You mean do I think they're more than friends? Hell, I wish my wife would look at me the way they looked at each other. Yeah, I think something's going on there."

"Too bad, they're both awesome looking. Nice bodies, too."

"Man, you need a girlfriend."

"You got that right. By the way, the captain says we can use the dinghy to take the two of them back to the main island if the tall one checks out okay. We can tow the sailboat behind. It should be alongside by now. They're bringing it with the other dinghy that went out to cover the passengers we left on the island."

"Good, I'd like to see it through, make sure they get back all right. I feel bad for the kid. You know she's got to be thinking it was all her fault. Bet she's gonna have trouble sleeping tonight."

"Yeah, can't say I envy her. I wouldn't want to live with that."

"If the wind hadn't picked up just then like it did, she would have been fine."

"Yeah, and with the direction it was blowing, we could hear the instructions, but she obviously couldn't. Her friend was telling her the right thing. If she could've heard her, she probably could've made the correction in time. Poor kid."

The ship's captain joined them.

"Hi, guys. Any word on our visiting patient?"

"She and her friend are in with Doc right now."

"Good, I think I'll take a peek." He opened the door to the infirmary.

◈◈

The doctor glanced up at the sound of the door opening. "Hi, Bert. How are you?"

"Fine, Jake, just fine. How's our guest doing?"

"Captain Bert Higgins, I'd like you to meet Ms. Jamison Parker and Ms. Katherine Kyle. Ladies, this is the man in charge of this tub."

"Hey, old man, watch how you talk about your home. Hello, ladies, it's a pleasure to meet you both, though I wish it were under better circumstances."

"Captain, we can't thank you enough for offering us your facilities and the assistance of your crew. The doctor and your crew members have been fantastic."

"You're quite welcome, Ms. Parker. We're all happy we could help. Do you have everything you need? We'll be docked here for another few hours, and I've instructed the boys to take you back to the main island when you're ready. We've got the Javelin too, and you can tow that behind. He looked at Jay, who was wet and shivering in her bikini. "If you'll excuse me for a minute, I'll be right back."

"Okay, Katherine." The doctor turned his attention back to his patient. "Here's the deal. You've got a pretty bad concussion and you're going to have a heck of a headache for a while. The bump should go down by tomorrow morning as long as you ice it every now and again. I don't see any skull fracture, which is a good thing. Your pupils are still a bit dilated and your vision isn't as clear as I'd like, but I think that will resolve itself by tomorrow. It seems as though your brain is working fine, and your hearing is clearly superior. As for your lungs, you took in quite a bit of water and that's got to clear your system. You and your friend here managed to get rid of most of it, but there may be some hiding in there. I'm going to give you some antibiotics just in case—can't have you developing pneumonia on your vacation, after all. I'd rather you didn't lie flat tonight and I don't want you sleeping for too long with that concussion. Jamison, your job is to wake her up every two hours or so to make sure she's all right. No heavy exertion for the next couple of days, and you should probably stay out of the sun tomorrow. Otherwise, you're going to be just fine. You're young and strong and you obviously have a hard head."

"Hey, I think I should resent that!"

"Who are you kidding, Stretch, you know he's right."

"Whose side are you on, anyway?"

Captain Higgins returned at that moment carrying something in his hand. "Not that you two don't do those bathing suits justice, mind you, but you looked a little cold. I thought you could use these." He held out two brand-new sweatshirts bearing the ship's logo and likeness.

"You didn't have to do that, sir, but thank you." Jay took the offered clothing. She kept the medium for herself and gave the large to Kate.

"Bert, I think these lovely ladies are ready for transport anytime you're ready. That is, unless you have any questions, ladies?"

"Doctor, we can't thank you enough." Jay threw her arms around him and hugged him briefly, which made him blush.

"If all my patients were like you two, I might actually enjoy my work." He winked as he and the captain helped Kate off the examining table.

Kate walked slowly toward the door. She shook hands with the doctor and thanked him on her way out.

"Jamison, can you wait a second?" He motioned to the captain to walk Kate out.

She looked at him expectantly.

"Listen, you've been through quite a trauma yourself. Watching your friend go overboard and nearly drown, saving her, doing mouth-to-mouth—that takes a lot out of you, especially when it's someone as important to you as Katherine clearly is." He looked at her kindly. "I want you to know that what you did was extraordinary. You saved her life. She wouldn't be here if it hadn't been for your quick thinking and good reactions. You did better than most professionally trained personnel under a heap of pressure. I'm very proud of you."

Jay still hung her head. "None of that would have been necessary if I hadn't screwed up in the first place. And enough hours with Resusci-Annie ought to prepare anyone for mouth-to-mouth. I've never been so glad to be a certified lifesaving instructor in my life, believe me. At the time I took the course and started teaching it was just a way to earn extra money lifeguarding at the college pool."

"Well, the training certainly paid off. And, young lady," he added, lifting her chin with his fingers, "to hear Katherine tell it, you were doing just fine out there. Sometimes circumstances have a way of wreaking havoc with us, and there's not much we can do about it. She doesn't blame you. In fact, she's more worried about you than she is about herself. When you stop to breathe, this is all going to hit you pretty hard. When it does, remember how lucky you are to have each other and count your blessings, not your faults. Now go on, she's waiting for you."

"Thanks, Doctor"—Jay reached up on her tiptoes and kissed him on the cheek—"for everything."

CHAPTER EIGHTEEN

By the time they returned to the villa and settled in, it was late afternoon, and it was the first time they were alone together since the accident. Jay moved around the room. She put away their things, opened and closed the drapes, and generally kept herself busy doing anything and everything except look at Kate.

"Sweetheart, come here."

Jay stopped mid-motion. "Um, are you hungry? Gosh, you must be. Let me go get you something to eat." She started out of the bedroom.

"Jamison, please, come here." Kate held out her hand, beckoning to her.

Jay perched on the far edge of the bed, where she picked at her shorts with nervous fingers.

"Not good enough, Scoop. I want you right here." Kate patted the bed next to her.

Still without making eye contact, Jay moved gingerly next to her.

"Look at me, love."

Jay didn't.

"Jay, please, don't do this. I'm sitting right next to you and I miss you desperately. Look at me."

The eyes that met hers were filled with so much pain, so much agony, that it made Kate bleed inside. "I love you so much, sweetheart," she said as she took Jay's hand in hers and kissed it. It was freezing.

The physical contact was all it took for the dam to break. Jay threw herself into Kate's arms, great heaving sobs wracking her body. "I could've killed you. I nearly did. It was all my fault, I..." She couldn't go on for a moment around the lump in her throat.

187

Kate pushed aside the pain in her skull, stroked the blonde head, whispered nonsense and let Jay cry herself out. She knew Jay needed to release all of the pent-up emotion. It was the only way for them to get past this.

"Hey, what happened could've happened with anyone. It was an accident, honey. An accident, that's all. I'm here and alive thanks to you. Your quick thinking and skill are what saved me. I'm so impressed with what you did, Jay. The guys couldn't stop talking about it all the way back here."

"I thought I was ready. I thought I could handle it. I was having so much fun."

"And you were doing a great job. You just need a little more experience and you'll be a great skipper."

"I'm never going out there again."

"Nonsense. It's like riding a horse...you have to get right back on. Love, I don't even want to tell you all the mistakes I made when I was first learning. Let's just say that there was a stretch there when the boat spent more time upside down than it did right side up."

"Maybe, but I bet nobody drowned as a result of your screwups."

"No, they didn't, but that was just by dumb luck. And, thanks to you, nobody drowned today, either." Kate chuckled, reminiscing, "I did get us trapped under the hull on more than one occasion."

"You're just saying that to make me feel better."

"Jamison, look at me." She picked Jay's head up with her fingertips. "I will never, ever, tell you something just because I think you want to hear it. There will never be anything but the truth between us, remember?" The intensity of her gaze, even with eyes clouded with pain, bespoke how seriously Kate meant what she said. "I have made plenty of mistakes in my life, and yes, some of them have been pretty costly, but I know I can't do anything to change that. I can only live with the knowledge and move on, using those experiences to make me a better person."

"God, I love you so much, Kate. I don't think I could've have gone on if I'd lost you."

"But you didn't lose me, love, you saved me. Your refusal to give up on me is the reason I'm alive. Jay, accidents happen to everyone. Did you mean for the boom to hit me in the head?"

"Of course not!"

"Did you mean for me to get knocked unconscious and fall overboard?"

"No!"

"Right, that's exactly my point. Sometimes things are beyond our control. I never should have put you in a position where something like that could happen, I should have known better."

"How could you know what was going to happen? Don't be ridiculous."

Kate smiled, having led her partner right where she wanted her. "Mmm-hmm."

Jay looked up sheepishly. "That was sneaky."

"Well, you know I'm like that."

"Yep, I do."

❧

They spent the next day resting and relaxing in a secluded spot in the shadow of their villa and in view of the water. Jay was tired, having awakened several times during the night with nightmares and every two hours to check on Kate as instructed. She could tell that Kate's skull was pounding and her body was sore. Jay fell asleep in her arms.

When she awoke, Kate asked, "Could you tell me a story? My head hurts too much to read."

"A story?"

"Yeah, you know, make something up, or pick one that you know. Didn't you write your own fiction in college?"

Jay laughed. "Yep, most of it was about you."

"Me?"

"Uh-huh. Remember how I told you about Sarah reading my journal and accusing me of having an affair with you in my heart?"

"Oh yeah," Kate said unenthusiastically. "I think I was trying to forget the part where you had a previous lover in your life."

"Sweetheart, that wasn't love, that was comfort and companionship. This, now, this is love." Jay pulled herself up and kissed Kate in a way that clearly reinforced her point.

"Mmm." Kate licked her lips. "Okay, so tell me one of those. Please," she pleaded, batting her eyelashes.

"You asked for it..." For the rest of the afternoon Jay regaled Kate with the stories that she created about the mysterious, remarkable dark-haired siren who had captured her heart.

❧

Saturday morning Kate awoke far more clear headed, the pounding in her skull reduced to little more than a dull ache. It was their last full day of vacation, and she had plans to set in motion. She kissed Jay's fair head and ran her fingers through the silky strands. When that didn't rouse the sleeping beauty, she took more drastic measures, nibbling Jay's exposed neck and along her jawline and brushing her fingers ever so lightly over her rib cage.

Jay groaned and snuggled more closely. "It can't be time to get up already," she mumbled into a breast.

Kate chuckled. "Well, I guess that depends." She nipped an earlobe.

"On what?"

"On whether you want to stay in bed alone all day or spend it with me."

"Urgh. That is so unfair. You know that, right?"

"Uh-huh."

"But you don't care, right?"

"Uh-huh."

"Wench. I bet I could find a way to put you back to sleep." Jay waggled her eyebrows suggestively. She bit down on a convenient nipple.

"Oh, no you don't, princess." Kate shook her head as she captured Jay's hands and pulled away from her questing mouth.

"Hey, I was enjoying my breakfast."

"Ayup, and so was I, but it will have to wait for later, doll. We've got things to do."

"We do?"

"Yes."

"Like what?"

"What do you say, since it's our last full day of vacation..."

"Don't remind me."

"That I get to choose how we spend the morning, and you get to pick the afternoon activity."

"Sounds fair enough. You go first."

"Okay, we're going sailing." She felt Jay go stiff as a board against her and tremble slightly. "Hey, we won't go far, and I promise to stay right by you."

"Oh, no you don't. We only go if you take the tiller." Jay was terrified and it showed.

"No can do, love," Kate said gently. "You need to get past this, and I need for you to. Sailing is something I really enjoy, and I know you do too. I've always wanted to own a sailboat," she admitted. "I want to keep it docked on a lake not far away from my house, and I want us to be able to spend time together on it. More than that, I want to be able to sit and enjoy the ride sometimes while you play skipper, which I know you're going to love. Please, this is important to me."

"Okay, but you stay right by my side."

"Every second."

"And then we get to go over to St. Thomas and go shopping this afternoon."

Kate rolled her eyes and sighed, thrilled that her plan was working out perfectly. "Deal."

The day was calm, with not much wind and no chop to the water. Still, they did not venture out of the shelter of the bay, and Kate stayed by Jay's side the entire time. At first, Jay was so petrified that she could barely function, but Kate kept talking to her, instructing her and encouraging her, until at last she began to relax a little.

Gradually, Jay learned how to tack, when to let the sail out, when to pull it in and how much, how to read the wind, and how to prepare to drop anchor. By the end of the morning when they returned the boat, she was actually laughing and having a good time.

She looked at Kate, who sat beside her the entire time, patiently teaching, cajoling, and correcting. "Thank you," she said with as much feeling as she could convey.

"Hmm?"

"I said thank you. Thank you for making me do this, thank you for showing me that I could, thank you for being patient with me, and thank you for trusting me."

Kate beamed. "Thank you for humoring me and being brave. Going out there today took a lot of courage, and I want you to know how much it means to me that you would do that, despite your misgivings."

"If it's important to you, it's important to me, love. And besides, you were right...I did enjoy that."

"I have to tell you that you're the fastest learner I've ever taught. You understand the concepts intuitively, and your reactions are quite good. I'm really impressed."

"You're just..." The rest of the phrase died on her lips at the raised eyebrow she received—message understood. "Thanks," she murmured instead. "Now can we go shopping?"

"You, young lady, are incorrigible. Yes"—she sighed dramatically—"we can go shopping."

"You're the best." Jay kissed Kate on the lips, then led her into the villa to change for an afternoon of shopping and dinner on St. Thomas.

&ev&

"I can't believe we have to leave here today. It's not fair." Jay, whose hair had bleached to an even lighter shade of blonde after nearly a week in the Caribbean sun, was snuggled securely in Kate's arms as they watched the Sunday morning sunrise from their balcony. Surprisingly, she was first to waken and suggest they throw on some clothes and step outside. She turned to see the face she knew so well and to look into eyes that held her soul, eyes that now gazed at her indulgently.

"I agree, sweetheart, and there's nothing I'd rather do than stay here with you forever. Unfortunately, reality has a way of intruding, and since neither one of us is independently wealthy, there is the small matter of having to get back to work tomorrow." As she told Jay before they left for St. John, when Kate bullied the news director into giving her the time off, he grumpily gave in, but only on the condition that she be back on the air Monday night, the day the *Time* cover story was to hit the newsstands. After all, it was sweeps month, the time of year when ratings are calculated and advertising rates set accordingly. Good ratings meant big bucks, and every station pulled out all the stops to draw viewers.

"Kate, what are we going to do when we get back? I mean, you're in Albany, and I'm in New York City." She had waited all week for Kate to say something about their future together, and, now that they were about to leave, she was getting anxious about it.

Kate rose quickly from the lounge chair. "Take a walk on the beach with me, love?"

Jay was puzzled and not a little concerned about the abrupt change in subject but, as she was already being propelled back inside the villa, she had few options except to go along.

&ev&

The two women had the stretch of brilliant white sand all to themselves in the moments just after dawn, and they strolled hand in hand, their feet in the surf and their hearts beating in synchrony. Reaching an old piece of driftwood down the beach just out of view of the resort, Kate motioned for Jay to sit, which she did, surprised when Kate didn't immediately join her.

The newly risen sun shone on Jay's face, making her emerald eyes dance and glitter. The sight took Kate's breath away, and she had to pause for a moment to gather herself before speaking. She knelt before Jay and fidgeted in the sand.

"This vacation has been like a dream come true to me, spending five uninterrupted days with you. I never imagined that I was capable of feeling for anyone what I feel for you, nor did I think anyone could ever love me as I know you do." Kate swallowed audibly. This was even harder than she thought it would be. "I know that as long as you're by my side, my heart will always be full of love and joy and my soul will always be complete." She peeked up at Jay through dark bangs. Jay's eyes were focused intently on hers.

Kate looked down at her hands and pushed ahead. "I've been doing a lot of thinking these past few days, and a lot of soul searching. I know with absolute certainty what I want, and I can only hope that it's what you want too." She looked directly into Jay's eyes with a gaze as honest, open, direct, and full of love as she could muster. She reached out and took Jay's hands.

"Love, I can't imagine a day—no, a minute of my life without you in it. I want us to be together always, not a hundred fifty miles apart, not fifteen miles apart. I will go anywhere and do anything I have to do to make that happen. Believe it or not, I've always been an old-fashioned sort of gal, so I'm going to do this the old-fashioned way. Jay, will you marry me and live with me as my wife?" Kate let go of one hand, reached into her pocket, brought out a small velvet box, placed it in Jay's palm and closed her fingers around it. Jay looked down at her hand, and said nothing.

Nervous beyond measure that she had read Jay wrong and moved too far too fast, Kate began to babble into the silence. "I know it hasn't been that long, and I know we can't legally get married, and I know there's a lot of logistics to work out, but I don't care about any of that, all that matters is that I want to be with you for the rest of my life, and I want that to start right away, today, right now..."

"Yes," Jay whispered so quietly that Kate wasn't sure she heard her. "Yes," Jay said more strongly. She lunged forward, wrapped

Kate in a huge hug and knocked her over backward onto the sand, where she landed on top of her. "Yes I will marry you, yes I will live with you, yes it can't happen soon enough, yes I love you more than life itself. Yes!" She punctuated her exclamation with a kiss that left no doubt as to how she felt about the proposal.

After several heart-stopping moments, Kate managed to say, "As much as I'm enjoying myself, and believe me I am, perhaps we should take this somewhere more private, love."

Jay, who seemed to have lost any sense of time or place, looked around her sheepishly. "Yeah, maybe that would be a good idea, Stretch." She got up, dusted herself off, and helped Kate to her feet.

"Aren't you going to look at what's in the box?"

"Oh, my God, yes." Jay unclenched her fist to reveal the small box still in her grasp. She opened the lid and gasped. Tears sprang to her eyes and rolled down her cheeks when she saw the sight before her.

"May I?" Kate asked, lifting from its velvet nest the platinum band with diamonds around most of its circumference.

Jay nodded mutely as Kate slipped the ring onto her left ring finger. "Sweetheart, it's the most beautiful ring I've ever seen." She turned it in the sunlight, watching as the rays reflected off it, creating rainbows. "And it fits perfectly…how did you do that?"

Kate blushed. "I cheated a little and borrowed the emerald ring you wore to the LCA Show and had it sized by a jeweler friend of mine while you were squeezing the produce that Sunday in Albany when you made me go to the grocery store." She had made a quick call to her jeweler, asking him to meet her at the store with his circle full of ring sizes in hand.

She met him in the frozen foods department, gave him the ring, and he sized it before handing it back to her. When they got home, she slipped the emerald ring back onto the nightstand where Jay left it the night before. The next day, after she dropped Jay off at the train station, Kate met the jeweler at his store and explained exactly what she wanted. He didn't have it in stock, or anything like it, but he located it for her—handily enough, in St. Thomas at a store called Diamonds International with whom he had an ongoing relationship. Kate predicted accurately that before going home Jay would want to browse the stores on the island that was famous for its jewelry. She picked up the ring when they were window-shopping, using the excuse of finding a restroom to leave Jay several blocks away in another store.

Jay was silent for a moment. "But, Kate, the LCA Show was more than a week ago and we had only spent one or two nights together." She looked up, shocked recognition on her face. "You had this all decided and planned out that soon?"

"Um, I knew how I felt, and I knew what I wanted, and I usually go after the things I want, Jay, especially when they mean everything to me. I didn't have any doubt what I was going to do, only the timing of it and how you would react."

"You had no need to worry there, love."

When they reached the villa, Jay fitted the key into the lock and let them into the air-conditioned comfort. She walked deliberately to the dining table, placed the key on it, turned back around and took a running leap into Kate's surprised arms, wrapping her legs tightly around her and kissing her with unbridled passion. *I can't believe she wants to marry me. How can she be so sure, so soon? Get real, Parker, you're more than sure yourself, why shouldn't she be?*

Kate returned the embrace, her hands cupping Jay's backside as she maneuvered them into the bedroom.

Before they even crossed the threshold, Jay managed to divest Kate of her top, and she was busy licking and biting her way down to taut nipples that begged for her attention.

Kate gasped as Jay found a particularly sensitive spot. She barely managed to deposit Jay safely on the bed. Within seconds she was shorn of the remainder of her clothing, and Jay, who somehow managed to strip herself as well, was in complete command, straddling her and taking her in a haze of pure lust.

Two hours later Kate and Jay ordered room service and sat at the dining room table, feeding each other a breakfast of scrambled eggs, bacon, toast, and home fries. "I'm really glad we decided to take the later flight, honey, even if it means we're dragging our asses tomorrow," Jay said.

"Yeah, that was good planning on our part. Now we can spend a couple of hours on the beach before we head out. Speaking of which, you about ready to hit the sand and surf?"

"Mmm-hmm, just need a little lotion on my back and I'll be all set."

"I think that can be arranged." Kate winked at her and began massaging the sunblock onto her lightly tanned back. When she finished, she placed a small kiss on one shoulder and gently shoved Jay ahead of her out the door.

They found that they still had the beach to themselves with most of the tourists preferring the pool or the shopping on St. Thomas to the heat of the sun and the beach. They sat on their towels side by side for a while, holding hands and watching the surf roll in and out.

"Want to go in the water?" Jay asked.

"Sure, why not."

Jay got up and moved to the water's edge, her back to the beach and a stand of nearby trees and brush. Kate ran past her into the surf up to her knees and splashed her on the way by. Jay splashed a little return spray in Kate's direction and started a small water fight. The two played with each other, having fun like children.

Finally Kate got to within arm's reach of Jay, faced her, and wrapped her arms around her, effectively pinning Jay's arms to her side and preventing her from further splashing. Just as Jay was about to protest, Kate leaned down and kissed her gently on the mouth, silencing her.

At that exact moment, hidden in the brush about one hundred feet away, a man in a camouflage vest and shorts was busy taking photos of the women with a Nikon camera and a lengthy zoom lens. He couldn't see anything of the shorter woman except her blonde head, her back, and a tiny bit of her profile, along with a nice view of her bikini-clad backside, but he had a clear shot of the dark-haired woman, who was his main concern. He snapped off a few shots in quick succession of the two women, clearly lovers, frolicking in the surf and kissing. Oh, he was going to get paid well for this.

This is my kind of assignment. Follow a beautiful woman to an exotic island and take pictures of her without her knowing it. And to make it even better, it turns out she's a lezzy and I've got the snaps to prove it. Yeah, it just doesn't get any better than this, although I wish I could get a click of the blonde's face—that might make it worth even more.

He briefly entertained the notion of staying around for a few more minutes to see if he could get a clearer shot, but thought better of it when the tall one paused and began looking around. After creeping quietly away, he headed directly for the airport and a flight back to Miami. *Heh, the press photo didn't do that bitch justice, she's much better looking in person and in less clothing.* He laughed as he considered that the images he just captured of her would be splashed all over country in the gossip rag by Tuesday morning.

He had been distracted with other things when the editor from the *National Enquirer* called and told him he had a job for him, but his ears quickly perked up when he heard what the assignment was. He showed up in the man's office less than an hour later. The editor handed him a release from *Time* promoting the upcoming cover story on a new breed of journalist and naming Katherine Kyle as the subject. It was the kind of advance publicity major magazines put out all the time to increase the buzz about the next issue to hit newsstands. The magazine helpfully supplied a publicity photo of Kate and a little background about her.

The editor fixed the photographer with a meaningful stare. "Find this woman. No one knows anything about her except what they saw on CNN. *Time* is only interested in her professionally. I want to know the more...personal side to her." He turned up his lips in what amounted to more of a snarl than a smile. "I don't care what it costs, but I want the goods to go to print Monday and to hit the newsstands on Tuesday, got me?"

The freelance photographer agreed, getting to work right away. He was surprised at how easy it was to track his quarry to the Virgin Islands. He merely posed as a friend looking for her, and the helpful receptionist at WCAP-TV was only too glad to tell him that she was on vacation in St. John. She even told him that it was the first vacation the anchorwoman had taken in the five years she was at the station. The fact that she was taking time off was the talk of the newsroom. He was most grateful for her help, and hightailed it out of there and onto the next plane so that he could meet his deadline.

Kate paused for a second after the first gentle kiss at the water's edge, and looked around, a troubled expression on her face.

"What's the matter?"

"I don't know, I just..." The hair on the back of her neck was standing on end. "Nah, it's silly."

"No, go ahead, what is it?"

Kate didn't want to alarm Jay. "I feel like we're being watched... it's nothing, I'm sure."

And, as quickly as the sensation came, it passed. "We better get back, though, if we're going to have time for a shower before the flight." Kate leaned down once again and brushed her lips against Jay's, and the two women picked up their towels and headed off down the beach arm in arm toward the resort, home, and a new life together.

CHAPTER NINETEEN

Having just taken off on the second leg of their journey from Miami to New York, they were buckled into their seats, Jay in the window seat and Kate, with her longer legs, comfortably sprawled in the aisle.

"Kate?"

"Hmm?"

"Can we talk about the logistics now?" Jay asked.

"Sure. I meant what I said, Jay. I will go anywhere and do anything to make this work."

"I know you did, love, and I can't tell you how much that means to me. I've already been giving this considerable thought."

"Oh you have, have you?"

"Mmm-hmm."

"And?"

"Okay, here's the deal." Jay turned to face Kate fully, her breath momentarily stilled by the sight of piercing blue eyes in a face more relaxed, deeply tanned, and beautiful than she'd ever seen it. "Really, I can do what I do from anywhere, as long as I show up in the office for assignments and to meet with my editor when I'm supposed to, which is usually on Monday mornings. Other than that, I can write my stories anywhere I can take my word processor or a pad of paper and pen, if necessary, and do the interviews as I always do, wherever the story takes me, as long as I have access either to my car or major transportation like an airport or a train station. Given that Albany has all of those things, there's no reason I couldn't move in with you in your house." Jay paused and looked Kate. "Assuming that's what you would want."

Kate was speechless. She never expected Jay to make that kind of offer. "You want to live in Albany? But what about your place?"

"Well, I've thought about that too. I think we should hold on to my place for now. It will be convenient to have a place in the city for those times when I absolutely have to be near the office or am doing a New York-based story, and the rent is reasonable, for New York anyway, and the location is good. As to whether or not I want to live in Albany, darling, wherever you are is home to me and where I want to be. Your house is gorgeous and far more of a home than my apartment could ever be, Fred will be much happier there, there's plenty of space, I love what I've seen of the area so far, and besides, you need to be there every day." Jay shrugged. "It makes all the sense in the world."

"Huh. Seems to me like you've thought this out pretty thoroughly, Scoop."

"Yep," Jay said smugly.

More seriously Kate asked, "Are you sure? It's a lot to ask...giving up your comfortable home and everyday life to fit into mine."

"I've never been more certain of anything in my life, love. What do you think?"

Kate's smile was brilliant. "I think I love you more than anything in the world and nothing would make me happier than to share my home and my life with you. When do you want to move in?"

Jay laughed. "Tonight would be great. But since that doesn't seem realistic, how about this—you stay with me tonight at my place, since we'll already be getting in fairly late, and tomorrow I'll drive you and the first load of my stuff to Albany before you have to get to work. I'll stay with you tomorrow night, leave my car at your house since I don't need it in New York, and take the train back to the city Tuesday morning to be in the office at ten a.m., which was when Trish said I needed to be there."

Kate shook her head in wonder. "Is there anything you *haven't* thought of?"

"I'm sure there is, but I've got another"—she looked at her watch—"three and a half hours to figure it out."

Kate entwined her fingers with Jay's, thrilled once again to note the ring on her finger as it sparkled back at her. "You're amazing, have I told you that?"

"Probably, but feel free to tell me again anytime."

"We could turn the third bedroom into an office for you, unless you'd prefer your office downstairs, in which case I could either give you mine or convert the library."

"No, I love the library, and so do you. The third bedroom would be fine, it has a nice view of the backyard."

"I'll have a second phone line installed for you, and we can even forward your phone in the city to that so the move will be transparent to anyone calling you, unless you want them to know you've relocated. What do you think?"

"I think that's a stroke of genius."

"And the guest bedroom can be your room."

Jay looked at her oddly.

"For your clothes and when you need space, goofy. I meant that there would be our room, and then you could have an additional room, okay?"

"Aha. I see. That's more than generous, Kate."

"What else would make you feel at home, love? Do you want to bring some of your furniture or anything?"

"No, I don't think so. Can we shop together to outfit the office?"

"I'd love to. Anything you want, you shall have."

"I want to be clear." Jay fixed her with a stern look. "I intend to pay my equal share, nothing less."

Kate scowled.

"I mean it, Stretch. Otherwise, no deal."

Kate was taken aback. "You can't be serious."

"Oh, yes I can. Ours is a partnership, fifty-fifty. I am more than capable of pulling my own weight. Anything less will make me uncomfortable."

"Okay, but *fair* share, not necessarily *equal* share. We pay as a percentage in proportion to our income and assets."

Jay started to protest.

"Ah, ah, that's more than reasonable and as far as I'm willing to go. Love, my living expenses are a lot higher than yours, and I won't have you taking on the burden of paying for my lifestyle. I've got more than I need to cover my tab and more on my salary alone, and on top of that my parents made sure that I was well provided for. Please, you don't know what it's taking for me even to agree to let you do that."

Jay chewed her lip. "It's a start, I guess, but I get the right to re-open the discussion at some point after we've had a chance to settle down and see how things are working."

"You drive a hard bargain." Kate squeezed the hand she was holding.

"Mmm. And all this negotiating is making me sleepy. Mind if I take a nap and use you as a pillow?"

Kate smiled indulgently, flipped up the armrest that separated the seats, and opened her arms, not caring what any of the neighboring passengers might think.

Jay took another sip of strong coffee and stretched. It was amazing how motivated she could be in the morning when the objective was important enough to her. After they returned to her place the night before, she spent several hours organizing her things and deciding what to bring home in her first carload. *Home.* She liked the sound of that. It was barely seven a.m. and she was in the middle of packing two suitcases full of clothes and sundries, having already packed several boxes worth of stuff. She decided to leave some work clothes and some play clothes in the apartment just in case, but she was taking the bulk of her wardrobe with her.

Kate was in the living room. An advance copy of that week's edition of *Time* was waiting when they got home, and Jay gave it to Kate to read. She fretted about having her lover read the story in her presence, but in the end, Jay bit the bullet and gave it to her without comment. And then she went to busy herself packing since she was so nervous she didn't know what to do with herself.

Kate looked at her own image staring back from the cover. Her soot-stained face, bloody hands, and torn suit were testaments to her efforts following the detonation of the second bomb. It was a gritty picture, one that bespoke dignity, professionalism, and humanity, all without a single word. The title on the cover, in big, bold print, was *A New Breed of Journalist.* In slightly smaller print below were the words, *Katherine Ann Kyle of WCAP-TV in Albany, New York.*

Inside was a three-page spread including Jay's story and four pictures—three of her and one of the capitol building following the explosion. The snapshots of her included one of her anchoring taken on the set, one of her interviewing one of the victims, and one of her working with Gene in an editing room. There was also a sidebar story by another writer debating whether or not journalists should ever take an active role in a story they are covering.

Kate read it all in silence, re-reading portions and staring hard at the pictures. When she was finished, she nodded to herself and smiled a private smile of pride for her partner. Then she went into Jay's office and placed a phone call.

❧

Jay was deep in her walk-in closet when Kate's long arms wrapped around her from behind. She tensed, not sure what to expect. A low, sultry voice whispered against her ear, "You are the most talented writer I have ever read. I am so humbled by you, love. You wrote an incredibly insightful, lively, interesting piece under incomparably difficult circumstances. It was balanced, and fair, and remarkably objective. You didn't let your own personal feelings or knowledge color the content, your approach was fresh and unique, and I am impressed beyond words. Thank you."

Not knowing what to say to that, Jay turned in the circle of Kate's arms, her eyes bright with pleasure at the unexpected praise and her smile big enough to light the city without electricity. She rose up on tiptoes and kissed the waiting lips, murmuring, "I'm so glad you thought it was okay, sweetheart. I think that was the hardest thing I've ever done. Maintaining professional distance and detachment from you was a virtual impossibility. It took me quite a while to decide how to avoid letting my personal feelings for you bleed through."

"Well, I think you succeeded masterfully, and you should be very proud of the job you did. Now about these pictures..."

❧

They pulled into Kate's driveway at a little after eleven a.m. and opened the front door to be greeted by a mass of flying fur.

"Hi buddy. Easy, guy, easy, Fred. Yeah, I'm happy to see you too, baby," Kate cooed as the excited golden threaded his way back and forth between her legs, talking the entire time even though he had a stuffed animal firmly held between his jaws. When he was finished with her, he gave Jay the same treatment as she scratched him behind his ears and on his haunches.

"How did he get here? I thought you said Peter had him."

"He did. I called him this morning and asked him to drop him off for us."

"Wow, now that's service."

"Yep, it sure is. I told you, he's a great friend to have."

They made their way inside.

"Shouldn't we get the stuff out of the car?" Jay asked.

"In a minute. First, there's something I want to show you in here." She disappeared into her office and smiled when she saw that her instructions had been followed precisely. She owed Peter big time now. She walked back out into the entryway. "Close your eyes."

"Why?"

Kate sighed in mock exasperation. "Do we have to go through this every time about you following instructions, woman? Close your eyes." She poked Jay.

"Okay, but last time I did that I ended up in paradise, and you have to be at work in a few hours."

"Don't remind me. Come with me." Kate took Jay by the arm and guided her carefully into her office. "You can open your eyes now."

Jay obediently cracked first one eyelid and then the other. When she opened her mouth to speak, nothing came out. She pivoted and looked at Kate in wonder. "There's a word processor on your desk, and it's identical to the one in my apartment."

"Mmm-hmm."

"That wasn't here before, I would have noticed it."

"Very observant, Watson."

"But sweetheart..."

"Listen," Kate argued, holding up her hands, "it only makes sense for you to be able to do your work in either place and not have to cart a word processor back and forth. I thought we could set you up in here just until we have time to shop for office furniture for your office. You don't mind, do you?"

"Mind? Are you kidding me?" Jay looked from Kate to the brand-new word processor, the two reams of typing paper lying neatly next to it, and the three pads of legal paper and pens resting nearby. Tears sprang to her eyes. She turned into Kate's arms and buried her head in her chest. "I don't know if I will ever get used to being this spoiled, love."

"You'd better start, sweetheart, because I intend to spoil you for the rest of your life." Kate wiped the tears from Jay's cheeks and replaced them with tender kisses. Before long the caresses turned more ardent, and hands began to wander. Kate backed them out of the office and over to the stairs, managing to lead them to the bedroom without losing contact with Jay's increasingly naked body.

"You have to go to work, love," Jay panted in between kisses.

"Not for a few hours," came the muffled reply.

Strolling into the newsroom at exactly 2 p.m., Kate found her desk just as she left it six days ago. She smiled to herself as she revisited the intervening time. So much happened and so much changed in her life in such a short period of time, it was hard to believe. Before settling down to business she picked up the phone and dialed a familiar number.

"Hello."

"Hey, Technowiz."

"Hey, Anchorbabe. What's happening? Did I get everything right?"

"You are a prince, and don't let anyone tell you otherwise."

"So, does this mean that something is officially going on between you and Jay?"

"Um," she lowered her voice so that no one else could hear, "I've asked her to marry me and she's moved into the house."

"You're kidding me?" Peter sounded stunned. "Way to go, Kate! I'm assuming she said yes, then?"

"Yep, she did," Kate said with a note of wonder in her voice. "In fact, she's there now and I thought maybe, if you weren't doing anything, you could drop by and take her to dinner. She doesn't know anyplace around here and there's nothing in the refrigerator. I'd tell you to call her, but I'm not sure she'd answer the phone yet, since nobody knows she's here except for you now."

"Hmm. Am I available to take a beautiful woman to dinner? I'll have to think about that and get back to you." He paused for a second. "Kate, I'd love to take Jay to dinner. I can fill her head with all sorts of stuff about you and then..."

"Peter?"

"Yes?"

"Stick to the truth, okay? And don't scare her too much."

"Geez, you take away all my fun."

"Yeah, I'm like that."

"I've got you covered, Anchorbabe, don't sweat it."

"Thanks, buddy, I knew I could count on you. And thanks again for getting the word processor and supplies. I owe you."

"Ooh, I like the sound of that. Bye, Kate."

"Bye, Peter."

As she was hanging up the receiver, her producer walked by.

"Hey, you look great. You should go on vacation more often...it obviously agrees with you."

"Thanks, Phil. Anything big happen while I was gone?"

"You mean locally? Nah, no one's saying anything much about the bombing except that it appears to have been done by professionals. Other than that, it's been the usual quotient of fires, murders, robberies, and political shenanigans. You know how it goes. Glad to have you back, kid, we missed you."

"It's good to be back." Kate turned her attention to her inbox and a stack of telephone messages, immediately re-immersing herself in the job.

∽∾

At the house, Jay was busy unpacking boxes and suitcases, filling the huge walk-in closet in her room and the dresser drawers, as well. So engrossed in the task was she that she was shocked when she glanced over at the digital clock to find that it was 5:58 p.m. She ran downstairs into the family room and turned on the television just in time to catch Kate teasing the upcoming stories for the 6:00 newscast.

"My God," she mooned. "She is the most gorgeous creature alive. And she's mine." She shook her head in wonder at her incredible good fortune. "Parker, you dreamed about her for years, and now you're going to be married to her. Never in a million years..." She shut up as the news came on and she turned her complete attention to the chiseled features that she now knew as well as her own.

At 6:30 p.m., the doorbell rang. Jay wasn't sure what to do. She knew it wasn't Kate, because she was just getting off the air and wouldn't have rung the doorbell anyway. Should she answer it? It rang again. Fred was barking and whining. Whining? Why would the dog be whining? She decided to investigate. Cautiously approaching the peephole, she peered through to see someone familiar on the other side of the door.

"Um, hi, Jay, it's Peter. Can I come in?"

She unlocked the door immediately and stepped aside to let him in. Fred danced around him until he petted him and said a proper hello. "Is there something I can do for you, Peter?"

"Actually," the tall man shifted from foot to foot, "I was wondering if you've had dinner yet?"

"No, I haven't gotten that far. How did you know I was here?" She was starting to smell a plot.

"Um, a little birdie told me."

"Hmm, I'm thinking it was more of a big birdie, say, oh, about six feet tall with fabulous blue eyes?"

"Well, I guess I'd better come clean. Kate called me this afternoon and told me you were here and that there was nothing in the house for dinner and suggested that you might want to go out to dinner with me, since you don't really know the area yet. She wasn't sure if you would pick up the phone if I called, so she told me to stop by."

"That's so sweet," she sighed. "She is the most thoughtful person I've ever met."

Peter looked down at Jay's hand. "Hey, that's a really nice ring you've got there. I don't remember you wearing that the last time I saw you. Is it new?"

"Um, yeah, it is." Jay's eyes were shifting everywhere around the room.

"Huh, you must have found yourself a great guy. That sure looks like a wedding ring to me."

She didn't know what to say. She didn't like to lie, but she wasn't sure what Kate would have told him or wanted him to know. She knew they were close, but...

Peter started to laugh, and Jay's head whipped up. "It's okay, small stuff, Kate told me she proposed and that you're living here now." He gave her a huge bear hug. "I think it's great. I couldn't be happier for the two of you. And it is a beautiful ring, by the way. Now, are you hungry, or what?"

"Yes, and I have another job for you too. Lead on, Technowiz."

"Ugh, not you too."

"Oh yeah."

లుపా

At 6:35 p.m. Kate, Gene and Phil were heading out the back door to grab something to eat. Kate exited first and froze in her tracks as flashbulbs exploded and she was surrounded by fans seeking her autograph on the cover of the *Time* magazines they waved in front of her face. Both men stepped quickly in front of her to protect her from the crowd as they made their way to Phil's car. Kate stopped them with a hand on their arms, then turned and graciously and patiently began signing autographs until every one of the two dozen or so fans had been satisfied.

The guys continued to give her grief all through dinner about her newfound goddess status, and she took it good-naturedly, although inwardly she was a bit discomfited by all the attention. Even their normal waitress wanted an autograph. She got the same treatment after the 11:00 news when she exited the station for her car in the parking lot, but this time the powers that be had taken precautions and hired security guards to escort her and keep her safe.

Nothing felt better to her, though, than arriving home and being greeted at the door by an irresistible blonde wearing nothing more than a lacy negligee and a smile. God, she was going to love coming home to that every night! Within seconds she had been relieved of her suit jacket, with her skirt and pantyhose not far behind. By the time she made it upstairs, she was wearing only her panties and bra, and those quickly became history too.

A while later, she remarked, "Now that's something to come home to." She stroked the blonde head resting on her chest. "How was the rest of your day?"

"Come see for yourself," Jay said as she jumped up off the bed, pulling Kate with her.

"Where are you getting all this energy, Scoop?"

"Dunno, must be just being here with you."

They arrived in Jay's room, which had been transformed from a generic guest suite into a true living space.

"Wow, this is amazing. You did all this after I left?"

"Yep."

"Incredible." Kate looked around the room. "You got everything unpacked?"

"Yep. And I had time to play ball with Fred too, and watch both newscasts and have dinner with Peter in between."

"I'm impressed."

"Yeah, me too," Jay laughed, wrinkling up her nose. "How was your day?"

Kate told her about the overzealous fans, Phil and Gene coming to her rescue, and the security people assuring her safety after the late newscast. "You know, I've had people approach me before in the mall or at a restaurant occasionally, but never anything like this frenzy. It was disconcerting."

"Mmm, I bet. Are you okay?"

"Yeah, I'm fine, it just caught me a little off balance, that's all. It turned out all right, though, everybody was nice enough."

"Well," Jay said as she wrapped her arms around Kate, "if anybody so much as lays a finger on you, they'll have me to answer to."

"Ooh, that ought to keep them away."

Jay swatted her on the behind.

"Come on, shorty, we've got to get you to bed. You've got to be on the six a.m. train, and I don't want you to be cranky."

"I'm going to be cranky in any event because I don't know what the next assignment is or whether I'm going to be able to come back home tomorrow night."

"Let's just wait and see, huh? No sense getting our knickers in a knot until we know, right?"

"Yeah, I guess," Jay sighed. "You're far too practical and pragmatic, love, you know that?"

"Mmm, I do now."

CHAPTER TWENTY

Having delivered Jay to the train on time, Kate was just completing her workout and run, albeit earlier than usual, when she noticed the message light on her answering machine blinking. She glanced at her watch—8:32 a.m. That was odd. She depressed the play button and was surprised to hear her news director's voice.

"Kate, this is Les. I need you to come in as soon as possible to meet with me. It's eight fifteen a.m. now. I'll be waiting for you in my office."

It was the first time in memory that Les had called her at home, and certainly the first time in the five years that she'd been working at WCAP that he had been in the office before 9:00. He sounded gruff, but that was nothing unusual—he always sounded gruff. Well, there was no sense speculating, she would just get showered and get to the office.

When Kate arrived at the station forty-five minutes later, the same two security officers from the night before greeted her at her car. "Hi, guys. It's okay, I don't see any unruly fans this morning." She smiled at them.

Neither one of them smiled back. In fact, neither would even look at her. "Boss's orders, Kate. We're to escort you to his office."

"Okay." She drew out the word. The uneasy feeling she'd had since hearing the phone message was blossoming into a full-fledged knot in her stomach.

The security guards waited with her as she knocked on Les's door. "Come," he bellowed.

Kate poked her head in. "You looking for me, boss?"

"Yes, Kate, come in." To the guards he said, "It's okay, fellas, you can wait outside."

Stepping across the threshold, Kate closed the door behind her. She was beyond shocked to find the station's general manager, the owner, and Phil all seated around the room. "Wow, this is quite a welcoming committee. Randy, it's good to see you," she acknowledged the owner. "How's your daughter doing with tennis?" The little girl had an aptitude for the sport, and the station owner, knowing Kate was an excellent player, had asked her one day to talk to his daughter about training and the finer points of the game. She did and, from that moment on, the girl sought her advice on any number of topics.

"She's doing fine," he mumbled, not shifting his gaze from a spot on his trousers.

None of them would meet her eyes, which was making her angry, although she was careful not to let it show.

"Have a seat."

"No thanks, Les, I'm fine." She smiled, but it didn't reach her eyes. This felt suspiciously like an ambush, and she intended to use every advantage—towering over the four men in the room was certainly one of them. "What can I do for all of you fine gentlemen?" Whatever this was, she had no intention of making it easy for them.

The news director fidgeted in his seat, picking up and then dropping his pencil. "Um, our switchboard started lighting up kind of early this morning with some rather ridiculous nonsense, but it raised a flag, so the receptionist called me." He still hadn't looked up. Kate remained silent, in an effort to make him feel even more uncomfortable.

"We know it's just garbage, Kate, but still we have to take it seriously." John Isaac, the station manager, picked up the ball. When she said nothing but continued to regard each of them steadily in turn, he stumbled on, "There were some pretty irate callers, you see, and they were insistent that we do something."

Kate merely raised an eyebrow.

"We know it's a hoax, I mean, we know you, right?" Randy chimed in. "I mean my kid idolizes you, for God's sake."

"Anyway," Les picked up the thread, "I had Phil here go out and get a copy of the thing so we could see for ourselves how trumped up it was. But when the receptionist started babbling at me as soon as she saw me about how sorry she was and how she thought the guy was really a friend of yours and she only told him where you were because she was trying to be helpful, well..."

Kate was truly perplexed. What the hell were they talking about? She was tempted to tell them just to spit it out, but she had a sinking feeling she wasn't going to like where all this was going, so she decided to play it cool and wait them out. Outwardly she maintained a relaxed posture, seeming as though she hadn't a care in the world, even as her insides were churning.

"Oh heck. Here." The station manager threw something down on the desk.

Glancing down, she saw that it was that week's edition of the *National Enquirer*, with the headline in huge bold print, *A New Breed of Journalist? Indeed!* There were two large, grainy pictures side by side underneath the headline. One of the pictures showed two women kissing on a beach. The second snapshot showed the women playing in the surf. In each picture the tall woman was clearly visible and identifiable. The other woman's back was to the camera and her face was almost completely obscured with the exception of a tiny bit of her profile. The caption underneath the photos read, *What Time magazine didn't tell you about stunning journalist/heroine Katherine Kyle, seen here getting up close and personal with an unidentified blonde in celebration of her cover-girl status.*

"We know they probably just took a picture of you and pasted the other woman in there, I mean, geez. Right, Kate?" Randy looked at her hopefully.

Kate knew she could probably get away with agreeing. After all, it's what they wanted to hear. But she wouldn't do that. She loved Jay too much to cheapen their relationship by hiding or lying about it. In the past she chose to remain silent because there wasn't anyone worth fighting for, but to deny that the kiss with Jay that was captured on film was anything other than what it was, was to deny her own heart, and Jay's importance in her life. Kate wouldn't do that, no matter the cost or the consequences.

Her silence seemed to make the men in the room exceedingly uncomfortable. "Hell, you don't even know who that other woman is, right? You've probably never even seen her, never mind—well, you know."

Kate shifted her gaze discreetly to Les, and then to Phil, realizing that even they, who had met Jay and spent time with her, didn't know who the blonde was. Good. She straightened to her full height, looking each man in the eye before responding.

"No, you're wrong, John. As you gentlemen can see, that is clearly me, and the woman you see with me is my fiancée." She lifted her chin and stared at each man defiantly.

"Your *what?*" Les exploded.

"I believe you heard me, Les."

"Who the hell is she? What the hell is going on? What are we supposed to do now? You're a lesbian? You've got to be kidding me! Why didn't you tell us? You're going to ruin us."

With a calmness belying the anger seething in her veins, Kate said, "To answer your questions in order, Randy... None of your business. I'm in love and getting married, and I was on vacation on a remote Caribbean island with my soon-to-be wife when some lowlife obviously hunted us down and invaded our privacy. I have no idea. Yes. No. I think it's obvious given your reaction why I didn't tell you, apart from the fact that it has no bearing on the job I do. And finally, I'd like to think that the job I have done, the consistent number-one ratings we've gotten since I've been anchoring, and the recent positive nationwide publicity for WCAP that resulted from my coverage of the bombings speak for themselves."

John had his head in his hands, Randy's mouth was opening and closing but nothing was coming out, the veins were popping out of Les's neck, and Phil simply stared at his shoes, unable to look Kate in the eye. Finally, Les spoke up. "You know there's a morals clause in your contract, Kate."

"Yes, I'm aware of it. I believe the clause states that I must maintain dignity and the upstanding reputation of the station and myself."

"Right."

"Are you saying I haven't done that?"

"Well, um, ah, Kate, you've done a great job for us and we all know it," John said. "It's just that this is going to create a landslide of negative publicity. Already there are people threatening to boycott the station and advertisers are talking about pulling spots."

"We just can't afford to lose that kind of money, Kate. Nothing personal," Randy added. "Listen, we're going to honor the remainder of your contract, which is another two years, and pay it out to you in a lump sum. In fact, here's the check." He handed her an envelope that he pulled from an inside pocket of his suit jacket.

She glanced down at it and up into his eyes, cobalt blue burning into him. "Are you firing me, Randy?" Her voice was low and measured, without a hint of the anger, incredulity, or disappointment she felt.

He looked to the others for support. "Um, I'd rather not call it that, Kate. I'd rather just say that you have decided to pursue other opportunities and leave it at that. In fact, we have prepared a statement to that effect that we're ready to release as soon as you agree." He handed her a piece of paper.

With a shock she realized that this was all rehearsed and choreographed—they were just going through the motions. "In fact," she emphasized, using Randy's terminology as she took a step forward, "I'm guessing it doesn't really matter one way or the other what I want or how I want to play this. You seem to have everything figured out." There was no rancor in her statement, just a frank assessment.

"I'm sorry whom I love or how I love offends some of your viewers. That's most unfortunate for them. I have always had the utmost respect for all of you and this news operation. I wish you all the best." She started to leave. With her hand on the knob, she turned back and said, "As for what you say in the press release, you do what you feel you must, but I will not be quoted in it, is that clear? You may lie or put a pretty face on it if you choose, but I will not demean my credibility for the sake of expedience. Good luck, gentlemen, I will always be grateful for the opportunity you gave me. Thanks."

With that, she was gone.

The men waited until the door clicked closed, then slumped back in their respective chairs. "Whew. Glad that's over with," Randy said, running two fingers under his shirt collar.

"Yeah, you got that right," John agreed. "That was easier than I thought it would be. I thought she would put up a fight. Well, you can't say we weren't prepared for anything. Sitting down with the lawyers in that conference call before she got here was a stroke of genius, boss. I'm sure they're right and paying off her contract will keep her from suing or making a public fuss. Heck, we treated her better than most places would've."

"I've got to admit," Les threw in with a note of grudging respect, "I thought she was pretty classy and pretty gutsy about the whole thing. She never once lost her cool."

"Like an ice princess," John agreed.

"I can't believe she's really a lesbian. She's so hot, she could have any guy she wanted. What a waste," Randy intoned. "I don't know what I'm going to tell my kid when she asks why she can't talk to her anymore."

Phil just sat there glumly, knowing that the station had just lost the finest anchorwoman and one of the best reporters it had ever had and that he had lost a good friend. He didn't know how he could ever face her again, or if he would ever get the chance, but he hoped he would, someday.

৵৹

At 9:34 a.m. Jay was riding the subway on her way to the office. She was standing in one of the middle cars, as was her custom, thinking about what she wanted to outfit her home office with when her stomach suddenly clenched. Caught off guard, she nearly doubled over. *What the hell?* Just as she was regaining her equilibrium a surge of adrenaline pumped through her, as if she were responding to some sort of threatening situation. She looked around her for the source of her discomfort, but could find nothing.

After getting off at her stop, she made her way into the building and onto the elevator. She was alone in the car when she was bombarded with a rush of anger so strong it scared her. What was going on? She shook her head to clear her mind. What could she possibly be angry about? She was completely puzzled. Nothing like this had ever happened to her before.

Once at her floor, she went directly to the ladies' room, where she splashed her face with cold water in an attempt to alleviate the pressure in her head. When she reached her desk she relegated the odd sensations to the back of her mind. She focused instead on organizing her workspace and seeking out Trish to find out what her next assignment might be.

"Hiya, kid. Hey, that's some tan you got there. You look great. And it's a good thing you're well rested, 'cause I got a doozy for you. How do you feel about being a globetrotter?"

"Okay, Trish, now you've really lost me."

"I know you were hiding away somewhere and probably didn't pay too much attention to the news, but did you hear about the *Stark*?"

"The what?"

"The USS *Stark*. Got blown up on Sunday, killed thirty-seven and another five or more were injured. They've been taken to the military hospital at Wiesbaden, near Frankfurt, Germany. I want you to go over there and interview some of the injured."

"Okay. Now I remember seeing something last night about it. The USS *Stark*, hit by two Iraqi Exocet missiles in the Persian Gulf while out protecting the oil shipping lanes."

"Right. I want you to do a little research and then fly over there tonight. We've got you clearance to be on the base tomorrow for the interviews. Then I need you to be flexible, 'cause we're thinking there might be a memorial service somewhere. If there is, you're going to cover it."

"Okay. I'll get right on it." Making her way back to her desk to plan her next steps, Jay tried to order her thoughts. She needed to get the newspapers for the last several days, as well as the Associated Press wire reports, and talk to sources at the Pentagon to see what she could find out about the injured sailors ahead of time. And she'd need to make plane reservations for later that day.

But first, she wanted to call Kate and tell her that she wouldn't be home that night, and probably not the next night either. She might not be able to get home for the rest of the week, which was a depressing thought. Dialing the now-familiar number, she was surprised when the answering machine picked up. She looked at her watch: 10:22 a.m. That was odd, Kate should have been home. One thing Jay quickly discovered about Kate was that she was a creature of habit. By 10:00 a.m. she would have worked out and run, played ball with Fred, and been inside reading the newspaper or a book in the library, or out on the deck.

"This is Kate. I'm not home right now to take your call, so please leave a message after the beep and I'll get back to you as soon as possible. Thanks."

Beep.

"Hi, sweetheart, it's me. I can't imagine where you are, but I'll try you again in a little while. Seems like I'm heading to Germany to interview injured sailors from the USS *Stark*, which was attacked in the Persian Gulf over the weekend. Unfortunately, that means I won't be home tonight, and probably not tomorrow night, either. I'm bummed." She thought about mentioning the unsettling emotions she'd been experiencing all morning, but decided to wait to tell her in person. "Anyway, I'll try you again, or you can try me at the office. I've got some background research to do, so I may be away from my desk for a while, but you can leave a message if you want." Lowering her voice, she added, "I love you, Kate. Bye."

∾⋅∾

At 12:30 p.m. Jay was just getting back to her desk from the research room. She couldn't shake the roiling feeling of misery and despair that seeped into her consciousness, replacing the anger that preceded it. Was she just upset at having to go out of the country and not being able to see Kate? It seemed to her as though the reaction was out of proportion to the situation, if that was the case. But she didn't think it was. Something else was going on, although she couldn't imagine what, and it was really disconcerting.

Trish appearing at her elbow interrupted her ruminations. "Hey, kiddo. Have you seen this yet?" She pointed to something she held in her hand.

Jay glanced at the newspaper and shook her head.

"Well, it seems there's a little something we didn't tell our readers," she said glibly as she offered Jay the newspaper.

Jay unfolded it and realized that it was the *National Enquirer*, hardly something she would have taken notice of. Then she saw the big, bold headline, caught a glimpse of the pictures, and read the caption. Her face drained of color.

"Are you okay, kid? You look like you saw a ghost or something."

Jay took a moment to compose herself. A thousand thoughts ran through her head at the same time, but they were superseded by one overwhelming desire—she had to find Kate. God, what if she had seen it? What if her bosses had? Did that explain the strange emotions Jay had been experiencing all day? She looked again at the pictures with a sinking feeling in the pit of her stomach. Kate was clearly identifiable, though anyone would have been hard-pressed to know that it was Jay with her. She refocused on Trish. No, she didn't seem to have figured it out.

Trying to control the quaver in her voice and the angry sparks in her eyes, Jay pointed at the pictures and said, "I didn't think that was something the reading public needed to know. It wasn't germane to the story. Does it matter to you?"

"What, that the woman is gay? Nah. Love is love. I told you we were only interested in her professional life, and I meant it. This kind of crap isn't anybody's business but hers and her lover's."

Relieved beyond measure by her boss's attitude, Jay considered telling Trish that she was the other woman in the photo, but she didn't want to take anything away from the story she had done about Kate. It was a fair piece, a good piece, and she didn't want to taint it, or Kate, by raising questions of objectivity in her editor's mind. All she could think about was getting to Kate as soon as possible. Then she remembered that she needed to be on a plane in five hours. *Damn.* She needed to get moving.

"Thanks, Trish. You know, I've got to hustle if I'm going to catch that plane. I've got to go home and pack. I've done all the preliminary research I can from here. I've got three or four interviews lined up for tomorrow at the hospital in Wiesbaden and I hope to catch up with some of the family members of the injured as well. I'll call you when I'm done with that to find out if you want me to cover the memorial service, if there is one, okay?" She was already gathering her things and putting them in her briefcase.

"Sounds good. You have a safe flight, you hear? Be careful over there."

"I will. Thanks, Trish."

As Trish moved away, Jay immediately picked up the phone and looked at her watch. It was just after 1:00 p.m. Surely Kate would be at home. She dialed the number and was greeted by the answering machine. She hung up and tried Kate's work number.

The receptionist picked up. "WCAP-TV, may I help you?"

That had never happened before. Jay knew that she had dialed Kate's personal extension. "Is Katherine Kyle there, please?"

"I'm sorry, Ms. Kyle is not available at the moment."

"Is she in? When will she be available?"

"I'm sorry, Ms. Kyle is not in today. Would you like to talk to the news director?"

The news director? Not in today? What is going on? "No, thank you," Jay said distractedly, hanging up the phone and hustling out the door.

ംൟൟ

After leaving the station, Kate went directly home. She put on her favorite pair of ripped jeans and a black t-shirt, then went into the yard to play ball with Fred. She was furious, but not surprised, at the spinelessness of the station management. When she had taken over the anchoring chair, the station was number three of the three major networks in the market. Within a month she took them to number one, where they remained the entire time she was in the hot seat.

Even so, they were unwilling to stick with her and ride out a little adverse publicity that probably would have increased their ratings anyway. She had no doubt that people would have tuned in just for the curiosity factor. But viewers didn't account for profits, advertisers did, and a threat to pull ads was the kiss of death. The thing that stung the most was not even that they fired her—it was the machinations and the premeditation of it all. It was clear to her that the station lawyers had been consulted and had called the shots. Did those idiots honestly think she was going to sue them? Fools. The job was never about the money to her.

Well, this wasn't getting her anywhere. Her biggest concern at the moment was Jay. It was clear that Les and Phil hadn't put two and two together and figured out who the other woman was, but what about Jay's boss? Would she see it and would she know? Kate couldn't bear the thought that this could jeopardize Jay's career. She needed to get to her as soon as possible and make sure she was okay.

Within a half-hour she was on a train bound for New York City. She would be at the apartment by 1:30 p.m. The question was what would she do once she got there? As she sat looking out the window at the river passing by, she considered her options. Some things she knew with absolute certainty. The first was that her face had just become one of the most recognizable in the country. And the second was that she would protect Jay no matter what, which meant that she had to stay away from her. It was the only way to guarantee that no one could connect them.

She knew that making this decision unilaterally without getting Jay's input would likely destroy any trust she had earned—after all, walking away without explanation would no doubt make Jay question Kate's true feelings for her. And hadn't she promised that whenever trust issues came up they would discuss them until there were no doubts? Tears formed in her eyes and leaked out as she thought about the idea of leaving Jay and breaking that vow, even if it was the right thing to do to preserve Jay's privacy and career. Kate replayed every conversation in which she had assured Jay that she could always trust her, never foreseeing a circumstance where she would break that solemn promise for any reason. *God, I never envisioned something like this happening.*

Leaving this open to discussion would be impossible. Loyal to a fault, Jay would never agree to Kate's plan and she knew it. *I love*

you, Jamison Parker, and nothing and no one is going to change that.
But I don't see any good alternatives here. I have to do this.
As a writer, Jay had the advantage of anonymity, something Kate
would never have again. So far, no one knew who her lover was. Kate
intended to make sure it stayed that way, which meant that she
couldn't take a chance on their being spotted together. It would be
hard for both of them, but at least Jay could move on and continue to
advance professionally.

Kate's heart ached. How could she say goodbye to the other half
of her soul so soon after she'd found her again? She closed her eyes
against the pain, wondering how she would survive without Jay, and
hoping against hope that Jay's road would be easier. After all, she
would still have her career, and as gorgeous and outgoing as she was,
Kate had no doubt that Jay could have any woman she wanted.

Wiping her eyes, she exited the train and took the subway
downtown to the Village. She knew what she had to do. *I hope
someday you'll understand and forgive me, Jay.*

CHAPTER TWENTY-ONE

Jay waited for the elevator doors in her apartment building to close.

"Hi, sweetheart. Fancy meeting you here."

Preoccupied with trying to figure out how she was going to find Kate before she had to board a plane for Europe, Jay hadn't noticed the tall shadow that slipped in after her, but there was no question that she knew that low, sultry voice that made her heart race every time. She turned and threw her arms around Kate. "My God, I've been trying and trying to get you on the phone. What are you doing here?" Noting the ripped jeans, t-shirt and sunglasses, Jay swallowed her dread and added, "I even called you at the station. The receptionist answered your personal line and wanted to transfer me to the news director. What's going on?"

"Let's get upstairs and I'll explain, okay?"

"Sure."

As soon as they stepped inside the apartment, Jay turned, dropped her briefcase on the floor, and wrapped her arms around Kate. When Kate removed her sunglasses, Jay could see that she had been crying. Jay reached up and brushed her fingers along the chiseled planes of the face that she wanted to wake up to every day of her life. She grabbed Kate's hand and led her to the couch.

"What is it, sweetheart?" Jay asked, even as she was afraid she already knew the answer.

"Why are you home so early?" Kate answered the question with one of her own.

"For one thing, my assignment has me going out of town, so I need to pack and, more importantly, I was worried sick about you and needed to get out of there so I could track you down."

"Why were you worried about me?"

"Trish showed me the *National Enquirer* at lunchtime. Oh, love, I'm so sorry." Tears formed in her eyes.

"Did she recognize you as the other woman?" Kate's jaw was tight.

"No."

"Did you tell her?"

"No, I didn't want to detract from the story, or you, by making her wonder whether I had been objective or not."

"Good."

"Now will you tell me why you're here and why my guts have been in knots since nine thirty this morning?" Jay climbed into Kate's lap.

"Your guts have been in knots?"

"Yeah, it was the weirdest thing. First it was as if someone was twisting my insides, then it turned to a burning anger, and finally, just this overwhelming feeling of despair. I can't explain it, but I have a sneaking suspicion that it has something to do with what was going on with you. Am I right?"

Kate was flabbergasted. She knew that twins shared bonds like that, where they could feel each other's distress, but lovers? "Yeah, the timing sounds about right."

"Please, love, let me in." Jay patted Kate's chest.

Kate took a deep breath and recounted the events of the morning. By the time she finished, Jay's eyes were brimming with tears.

"I can't believe they did that. That is so wrong. Why didn't you take the out they gave you and just let them think it was fabricated? You could've and they would've believed it."

Kate tipped Jay's chin up and locked eyes with her. "Because, love, I will never deny what we have and what you are to me. You are my love and my life, the other half of my soul. Don't ever doubt that, no matter what happens." Kate uncharacteristically broke eye contact.

"Oh, Kate, this is all my fault."

"What?"

"If I hadn't written that story, they wouldn't have been gunning for you."

"Jay, look at me. Did you assign yourself to write the piece? Did you determine that it was going to be the cover? Did you take us on vacation to St. John? Heck, did you initiate that kiss the slimeball caught on film?"

"No," she answered quietly.

"Right. Sweetheart, first of all, you wrote a beautiful story, one that you should be proud of...I know I am. Secondly, I'm not sorry about us, and I never will be. You're the best thing that's ever happened to me, and I will always believe that. Always," Kate said with feeling. "We can't change what is, so there's no sense playing the what-if game. It won't serve us well. My main objective now is seeing that folks don't put two and two together and figure out that you're the other woman."

"I don't care what they think."

Kate smiled at Jay's natural feistiness. "Well, I do. You have a great career in front of you and your whole life before you, and I will not sit by and watch that be jeopardized by some sleazebag with a camera trying to make a little money."

Jay's eyes opened wide. "What are you saying?" When Kate didn't answer right away, Jay captured her face between her hands. "What are you suggesting here?" The note of rising panic was clear in her voice.

Kate chewed on her lower lip, something Jay had never seen her do before. Jay attributed the gesture to stress.

"You said you were packing to go out of town on assignment. What's the assignment and where are you going?"

"I've got the sidebars to the main story this week. I'm going to Wiesbaden, Germany to interview some of the sailors injured Sunday when two Iraqi missiles hit the USS *Stark* in the Persian Gulf. Then, depending on whether they have one or where it is, I may have to cover a memorial service for the thirty-seven who were killed in the attack."

Kate nodded. "Okay, that's good."

"It is? You want me to go away? That's the last thing I want to do right now."

"Frankly, sweetheart, I want to spend every minute of my life with you. But right now, your being out of the country is a positive for us. They can't put us together if we're not anywhere near each other, now can they?"

"Right. Kate, I'm only going to be gone a couple of days, the rest of the week maximum. Do you think the story will die down by then?"

"It's hard to say. Maybe, maybe not."

"If it doesn't, what are we going to do when I get back and we're living together?"

Kate wouldn't look at her. "We'll cross that bridge when we get to it."

Jay felt a wave of uneasiness settle in her guts. "What, exactly, does that mean?"

❧

Kate was feeling exceedingly guilty. She knew she should come clean and tell Jay the whole truth. The problem was that if she did, then their parting words would no doubt be angry ones, because no matter what Jay said, Kate knew she would stick to the plan and leave anyway. She didn't think she could stand it if their last moments together became an angry confrontation. No, that wasn't what she had in mind at all.

"It means first things first. Let's just get through one day at a time, okay?" Kate couldn't talk about it anymore. All she wanted was to spend the remaining time they had together holding the love of her life in her arms and making love to her. "What time is your flight?"

Jay looked at her watch. "Three and half hours from now."

"Good, we have time," Kate said huskily as she leaned down to kiss waiting lips.

Their lovemaking was slow, deliberate, and poignant. Kate wanted to savor every touch, every taste, every sensation, every sound, knowing it could be the last time. *My God, love, how will I ever live without this? Without you? I need you more than I need air to breathe.*

"Uhh, Kate. Oh, love, right there!"

When they were satiated, Jay lay spent in her arms and Kate was content just to hold her, stroking her hair and back, breathing in her scent and memorizing the way their bodies fit together. She made sure that Jay couldn't see the tears in her eyes.

"Kate, what are you going to do now?"

"You mean professionally? I don't know. I think it unlikely that I could get another job in television. I really haven't thought about it. The fact that they paid me the remainder of what would have been due on my contract means I don't have to figure it out for a while yet."

"Mmm. I'm going to miss you so much while I'm gone. I'll call you every day, though."

"Um, I may not be home, love."

"Why, where will you be?"

Kate sighed. "I'm going to go away for a little while, get out of sight and out of range of the vultures." *And besides, phone records could be traced.*

Jay stiffened in Kate's arms. "How long and where are you going?"

"I'm not sure." Technically that was accurate, since Kate hadn't picked up the tickets and finalized her itinerary yet. In truth, she thought it best for Jay if she didn't know too much, and she was afraid Jay would try to find her.

"How will I find you? How will we keep in touch?" The note of panic was back, and it made Kate miserable.

"If anything comes up and you need something, call Peter. Do you have his numbers?"

"Yes, he gave them to me last night when we had dinner. But surely you're not suggesting that—"

Kate cut her off before she could finish the question she didn't want to answer. "Peter will be the point person. If we need to talk, we can do it through him."

"We're going to pass messages through a go-between?"

"Possibly. Also, he has conferencing capabilities and we could set up a conference call via his phone line if need be."

"If need be? Love, I don't want to talk to you only in case of an emergency. I love you, I need you, and I want to talk to you all the time."

"I know, sweetheart. Me too, but for now, at least, this is the most practical solution."

"Maybe the most practical solution is for me to quit my job and disappear with you."

That was exactly the reaction Kate was afraid of, and why she rejected the notion of talking her decision out with Jay. No matter what, she couldn't let Jay ruin the rest of her life, not for her. "No, Jay. No. Everything will be fine, you'll see." Kate kissed her on the top of the head. "Right now, though, we'd better get you packed or you'll be late."

Jay rose from the bed and set about her task, while Kate lay in bed, soaking up every opportunity to watch her and memorize everything about her.

When Jay finished packing and they both were dressed, Kate said, "You'd better get going or you're going to miss the plane."

"Aren't you coming to the airport with me?"

"I can't, love. That would be way too obvious," she said regretfully.

"I'll be home Friday night at the latest. Will you be there when I get there?"

"I don't know, Jay. Are you sure you want to be in Albany?"

"Yes," Jay said vehemently. "It's our home."

"Okay, I just wanted to be sure." Kate didn't see any harm in Jay being in the house—her phone number and address were unlisted and it was unlikely that anyone would find her there, especially if it was clear that Kate was out of town. At the very least, they would try to follow Kate wherever she went, leaving Jay in peace.

"I don't like not knowing where you're going to be or when I'll be able to talk to you or see you next."

"I know, sweetheart, but the truth is that wherever you are, that's where I'll be. I'll always be thinking of you, love, and carrying you in my heart. Remember how much I love you." Kate worked hard to keep her voice from breaking.

They were at the door to the apartment. "Aren't you going to walk out with me?"

"No. I'll give you a few minutes and then head out."

Jay's head was down. "I hate this."

"Me too, sweetheart, but it won't be forever."

Jay dropped her suitcase and threw herself into Kate's arms. She reached up and pulled Kate down into a scorching kiss. "That's just to remind you what you'll be missing until we see each other again."

"Mmm," Kate hummed. "As if I could forget." She returned the favor, saying, "That's to remind you how very much I love you. Be careful over there, sweetheart."

"I will. You too, Stretch. I miss you already."

"Me too."

"Bye."

"Be safe, love." Kate waited until she saw Jay catch a taxi from the living room window. Only then did she go to the door of the apartment, looking back one last time. "Never forget how much I love you, sweetheart. You will forever own my soul, and in my heart we will always be together. Goodbye, Jay."

She couldn't stop the tears then. She didn't want to.

※

A while later Kate was on a train headed back home. She had just taken a window seat from which she could watch the river when she felt a presence standing over her.

"If it isn't my very favorite celebrity. I just knew there had to be some advantage to coming to this conference in the city. Is this seat taken?"

Kate looked up into the smiling countenance of Dr. Barbara Jones. Although she wasn't sure she was really up to company, Kate was grateful for the appearance of one of her best friends.

"Depends on who's asking."

"Ooh, you sound rough, there, kiddo. Having a tough day?" the doctor asked sympathetically, pointing to the sunglasses Kate wore, despite the fact that they were inside the train.

"I suppose you could say that."

"Well, I got my copy of *Time* magazine yesterday, and I happened to catch the cover of that filthy gossip rag a little while ago at a newsstand as I was passing the time in the train station, so I think I can imagine a little bit of what might be going on in that brilliant head of yours." Reaching out, she put her hand on Kate's arm. "Want to talk about it? I'm a great listener, as you know."

Kate stared out the window, not sure how much to share, even with her good friend.

"Let me start, then," Barbara said. "It's nearly four thirty in the afternoon, and you're sitting on a train in ripped jeans and a t-shirt. That tells me that you're not going to work today. You don't have any luggage with you, or even a briefcase, so that tells me that this is a day trip, and that you probably didn't pre-plan it, but came to the city to do something specific. Like maybe talk to the other person in that picture, who I do believe, if I'm not mistaken, is someone you introduced me to not that long ago in the middle of a very long night."

Kate's head snapped around.

"How am I doing so far?" The doctor gave Kate a wry smile. "It is Jay, isn't it?"

Kate nodded minutely. "How did you know?"

"Well, I didn't need to be Sherlock Holmes to see the way you looked at each other that night. I figured if something wasn't already going on between you two, it would be soon." She lowered her voice. "I'm glad for you, Kate, she seems like a wonderful person, and you deserve nothing less."

"Thanks. That picture was taken on the day I proposed to her. We were on a beach in St. John."

"You're getting married? That's fantastic! Congratulations."

Kate sighed. "We were getting married."

"What do you mean?"

"Barbara, no one else has figured out that she's the other woman, and I intend to keep it that way. She has a great career ahead of her, and her whole life, and I'm not going to screw that up for her."

"You're leaving her? Have you told her that? Is that why you were in the city?"

"Not exactly. I needed to make sure she was all right and that she knew what happened. I also needed to tell her that I got fired this morning."

"What?"

"They invoked the morals clause in my contract. It seems they were getting some threats from advertisers who were going to pull spots, and it was going to cost them money that they didn't want to lose more than they didn't want to lose me."

"Those ungrateful sons of bitches. Who the hell do they think got them those advertising contracts in the first place! They were in the cellar until you came along and gave them some class. You made them number one, and this is how they repay you?"

Kate had to smile at Barbara's righteous indignation. "All's fair in love, war, and television news, I guess," she said resignedly.

"That's a load of bull and you know it. Tell me the whole story."

And Kate did.

When she was finished, Barbara whistled. "That took guts, woman, to tell them it was your fiancée and that who she was wasn't any of their business. You were right, of course."

"When I saw that even Les and Phil, who met her and spent time with her, didn't know who it was, I knew she could be okay in all this. That was the one bright spot."

"What's your plan?"

Kate explained about Jay's assignment and her intention to get away for a while.

"Where are you going?"

"I don't want to say. The less people know, the better," she said bluntly.

"This is me we're talking about, Kate, not some fly-by-night acquaintance," Barbara said, clearly a little bit annoyed. "Does Jay know where you're headed?"

"No, and that's the way I want it. I've set it up so we'll both be talking to Peter at some point every day. If there's an emergency, he can be the point person for a two-way conference call. If she knew where I was she might try to find me."

"Might? I don't think there's any question that she'd move heaven and earth to locate you. Why are you doing this?"

"I told you," Kate sighed exasperatedly, "if we're not seen together, she'll be safe and she'll be able to maintain her anonymity. If she shows up anywhere near me, someone will make the connection and she'll be exposed. It could ruin her career."

"Instead, you're going to ruin her life."

"What?"

"Kate, that woman loves you with all her heart. Do you think she's just going to be able to forget about you, put you in the past? Your disappearing is going to kill her. My guess is she'd rather lose her job than lose you, and if you were thinking straight, you'd know that too. Did you even give her a choice?"

"No," Kate answered quietly. "She doesn't know I'm planning an extended absence."

"Well, that's a fine euphemism. She's a big girl. Don't you think she should have some say in what happens here? What gives you the right to make decisions for both of you?"

Kate ran a hand through her hair. She couldn't listen to this, not after spending the morning asking herself the very same questions. God, she felt so impotent. "Look. All I know is that I'm the juicy story of the day, and every idiot and his brother is going to try to dig up more dirt. The most obvious piece of gossip would be the identity of my lover, and if they figure that out it will raise questions about the reliability of the story she wrote. That woman bent over backwards to make that piece objective and fair. She has more integrity in her little finger than most people have in their entire bodies. I won't have anyone call that into question. It would kill her personally and professionally. I will do anything it takes to make sure the vultures don't find her, and that includes disappearing out of her life so that she can have the future and career she deserves."

Barbara reached out a soothing hand. "Kate, they're not going to be out there gunning for you forever. Don't give up your chance at happiness because some money-grubbing opportunists are making you the meal of the day. Two days from now or a week from now they'll move on to someone else and all of this will be forgotten."

"And what if you're wrong and it isn't? I can't take a chance on that. You can never put the genie back in the bottle, Barbara. I'll never be able to go anywhere without someone pointing and saying, 'Look, there goes that famous lesbian. What's her name again?' Jay doesn't deserve that, and she doesn't have to live with it."

"All I'm saying is that it should be her choice whether she wants to stay with you and face the consequences or not. It doesn't matter where you go, Kate, she's going to try to follow you. I know that I would if it were me, and she seems like a pretty determined young woman. Do you love her?"

"With all that I am."

"Does she love you?"

"Yes."

"Then don't give up and let those fools win. Because that's what you're doing."

"Do me a favor?"

"Anything."

"Watch out for her? She says that she wants to be in Albany because that's where our home is, and I think that's where she'll go when she comes back from her assignment later this week. Will you check up on her, make sure she's okay? Try," Kate's voice broke, "try to help her through this? She's going to need some friends who know and understand. I can't think of anyone I'd trust to help her more than I trust you and Peter."

"Thanks for the vote of confidence. You know I will do anything I can, but I do wish you'd reconsider. I think you're making the mistake of a lifetime, or maybe it's just that you don't think you deserve happiness and love in your life."

Kate glared at Barbara. "Since when did you start specializing in psychology?" she snapped.

"My friend, I've been watching you for a lot of years now, and I've seen enough to know that what I say is true, although I still don't understand why. Well, let me tell you something—you *do* deserve to be loved and to be happy, despite what you think. This woman is the best thing that ever came into your life. Don't let her go...I'm not sure either one of you could survive it."

Kate knew it was true. Jay *was* the best thing that ever happened to her, and she wasn't at all sure she could make it without her. She only knew that she had to protect her, and this was the only way she knew how. "Jay's a survivor, she'll adapt and find her way. She's tougher than she looks." Kate hoped it was true.

Barbara just shook her head.

They were silent for the rest of the ride to Albany.

CHAPTER TWENTY-TWO

Jay arrived in Germany just in time to see the sun come up on Wednesday. She tried her hardest to sleep on the flight but found it virtually impossible, as thoughts and emotions kept running rampant through her mind. She couldn't shake the feeling of dread gripping her heart and was finding it difficult to focus on her assignment when all she could think about was where Kate might be and when she could see her next. *Parker, you owe it to these men and their crewmates to do a good job here. Stick to the issue at hand and the faster you complete the assignment properly, the sooner you can go home and concentrate on Kate.*

Jay found a driver willing to take her from Frankfurt to the US military hospital at Wiesbaden, and spent the ride going through her notes. When she arrived, she was forced to waste an hour slogging through mountains of red tape and "helpful" public affairs officers, despite earlier assurances from her sources at the Pentagon that she would have no problems on site. Once she convinced the watchdogs that her interest lay in the sailors' personal stories and not in vilifying the navy or condemning the military's readiness for an attack, she was allowed to visit with three of the injured.

The interviews went well, with the men responding instantly to Jay's naturally sunny personality. They seemed to be happy to open up to her and talk about their lives, their choice to join the military, how they viewed that decision after the attack, what they'd felt and thought during the attack, and how they thought the incident on the *Stark* might have changed them.

By early afternoon Jay had everything she needed to write a great human-interest story, and she had a choice to make. Rightfully, she could do some sightseeing, check into a hotel in Frankfurt, and sleep until the next day before catching a plane back to the States. Or, if she were so inclined, she could leave right away. Unbidden, the thought came to her that if Kate were there, they would have a great time seeing the sights. But, alas, that wasn't the case. Jay looked at her watch. It was 8:00 a.m. New York time. She smiled at the vision of Kate working out to *Charlie's Angels* in the basement gym. Her smile faded, however, when she considered that Kate probably already left for parts unknown. Jay sighed. The first thing she needed to do was to call Trish to find out if there was a second leg to her journey to cover a service for those who died in the attack. Since Trish was usually in early, Jay figured she wouldn't have any trouble finding her at her desk.

"Hiya, kiddo. How's tricks?"

"Hi, Trish. Everything's great. I think I've got some really good stuff that'll make a great sidebar. These guys have been through a lot and, as you might expect, it's had a pretty profound impact on them. It's a very human story."

"Terrific. Listen, I got a line on the memorial service. It's going to be Friday morning at the Naval Station Mayport near Jacksonville, Florida. That's the *Stark's* home base. Looks like the president is going be there. And guess what? So are you, what a coincidence!"

"You're in a good mood."

"Eh, doesn't pay to complain, you know what I mean?"

"Yeah, I do. Okay. Well, I'll come home now so I can write this story tomorrow in the office and then get on a plane for Florida tomorrow night."

"Sorry about that, kid, doesn't look like you'll be getting a lot of sleep this week."

"That's okay, Trish, I know you'll make it up to me." Jay smiled into the phone. Her editor really did take pretty good care of her.

Jay was exhausted, and her stomach was in knots. She thought about trying to call Kate, but knew in her heart it would be fruitless. She would call Peter when she got to New York later. While it would be near 10:00 or 11:00 Wednesday night in Germany when she touched down, it was six hours earlier at home, putting it closer to 4:00 or 5:00 in the afternoon in New York.

⋘⋙

By 8:00 Wednesday morning Kate was somewhere over the Midwest on her way to Chicago and then Denver, the jumping-off point for her journey. It had been a long evening and a longer night after she returned from Jay's. She went from the train station to her travel agent, then to her florist, then to the house to feed Fred, play with him, get his things together, and take him over to Peter's, where she had dinner and more discussion than she bargained for.

Like Barbara, Peter was convinced that Jay would try to follow her and not at all certain that Kate's solution was best for either one of them. Kate was tired, emotionally drained, and grumpy. "What do you suggest, then, smart man? Let them feast on us and have Jay lose her career in the process? Never. I won't do it."

"You don't know that Jay will lose her career...you're making an assumption. And that should be her choice, not yours."

It was the first time they ever raised their voices to each other. They faced off across Peter's kitchen table, where Kate's meal sat untouched. "Jay is too kind and too compassionate, she would never choose her career over me, even if it was what she really wanted. I will not be pitied. I am not some charity case."

"Then stop feeling sorry for yourself and playing the martyr," he boomed. More quietly he pleaded, "Go away for a few days and get your head together if you need to, Kate, but for God's sake, don't disappear from Jay's life. That girl is head over heels in love with you and can't wait to be your wife. The two of you are strong enough to face whatever challenges come your way. Your friends will be here to support you. If you want, I'll arrange it so that no media can get within a mile of either one of you."

"I know you would, my friend, but even you can't hold them off forever," Kate said quietly. "I'll ask you the same thing I asked Barbara—please, please look out for Jay and help her through this. I will take you up on your offer to make sure that no media go anywhere near her. I don't think anyone who would be looking for a story can figure out where I live, but I can't guarantee that. I'm hoping that by making my departure from the capital district painfully obvious, they'll trail me instead." Kate hadn't made any secret of the fact that she was leaving the area and had, in fact, called the station earlier in the day, deliberately telling the receptionist that she was leaving the next morning at 7:00 for an extended period of time to visit relatives in Chicago if anyone called looking for her. She might as well put the idiot's helpful nature to good use.

She sighed heavily. "Jay will be calling you. I trust you not to tell her where I am. You're the only person who will know. I'll be moving around, so I'll check in with you once a day, most likely in the evening after you would have talked to her. You're my eyes and ears, my friend, so if there's something I need to know I expect you to tell me."

She stood and Fred rose from under the table where he was lying on her feet. She knelt down before him and gave him a big hug. "As for you, big guy, I expect you to be a good boy. When your other mother comes home, I expect you to keep her company and give her lots of love, okay? You take extra special care of her for me and make sure she's not lonely." Kate kept her head down to hide the tears that spilled from her eyes. "I love you, buddy." She kissed him on the top of his head and he licked her chin.

After she composed herself, she stood and faced Peter. "You know I can never thank you enough for everything you do for me, right?"

"Yeah, I know, but I'll think of something."

"So you keep threatening. I'm scared." She made a mock-frightened face. "I'll be in touch."

At home again late that night, Kate spent a couple of hours doing laundry and packing, walking around the house making sure that everything was in order, and admiring the dozens of red and yellow roses that she placed in strategic locations for Jay to find.

Each had a card standing against its vase, all with different sentiments but expressing the same love and devotion. *Eternally yours. Jay, you are my light and my joy, always. I love you with all my heart and soul. Yours forever and beyond. Thank you for the gift of your love, I shall cherish it always. My heart belongs to you for all time. I love you, Jay, always remember that.* She knew she shouldn't have done that. After all, if she was leaving her, why not make a clean break? But Kate couldn't do it—the ache in her heart was excruciating and she needed to let Jay know how she felt about her.

She couldn't live with the idea that Jay might think she was using this as an excuse to walk away, and she wasn't willing to let Jay's insecurities get the better of her without making an effort to set the record straight. She hated hurting her, even if it was for a good reason.

Up in the attic, Kate found her boxes of old comic books, separated out all of the Green Lanterns, and set them aside. Then, for good measure, she made piles of the Aquaman, Flash, and Captain America comics too, then took them all to the bedroom. She wrote a note to accompany them and put a flashlight and a fresh set of batteries nearby.

Finally, at 3:30 Wednesday morning, Kate tried to lie down and sleep for a couple of hours. It was 9:30 in the morning in Wiesbaden, and she wondered what Jay was doing. She pictured her interviewing injured sailors, listening intently to their stories, her sparkling green eyes alight with sympathy and curiosity. It made Kate's heart ache painfully. God, she missed Jay already.

At 5:00 a.m. Kate gave up any pretense of sleep and went downstairs to work out and then to run before showering and leaving for the airport, where she made her presence well known. Standing in line waiting to check in for a flight to Chicago, Kate removed her sunglasses and talked with the other passengers and signed some autographs for those who approached her timidly with issues of *Time*. She made a special point of making eye contact and saying hello to those few who gave her disgusted looks and pretended not to notice her. She even took the time before departure to browse through the newsstand near the gate, where she signed some more autographs. She made sure that her one-way boarding pass to Chicago was visible to anyone who cared to take notice before she boarded the flight.

She spied two still photographers and one reporter lurking nearby. It was nice to know the WCAP receptionist was good at her job. None of the journalists got on the plane with her. She knew she would have to put on a show in Chicago on the other end in case they had other colleagues waiting there, but she already made provisions for that.

For the moment, she sat in the air, her heart thousands of miles away and her soul feeling as if it had been ripped to shreds.

The first thing Jay did when she arrived at her apartment shortly after 5:00 p.m. on Wednesday was to pick up the phone and call Peter, who answered on the third ring.

"Peter Enright."

"Hi, Peter, it's Jay."

"Ah, the world traveler. Where are you now?"

"I just got off a plane from Frankfurt, Germany. I'm at my apartment in New York."

"You sound exhausted."

"Well, I tried to sleep a little on the plane, but I haven't been having much luck in that department the past twenty-four hours or so."

"I bet," he said sympathetically.

"Do you know where Kate is?"

"Not exactly."

"What does that mean, have you heard from her?"

"Not yet today. I saw her last night. She left Fred with me before leaving town."

"She's gone?"

"Yes, she left early this morning."

"Driving or flying? I guess that's a stupid question…if she was driving she probably would have taken Fred, right?"

"Right. Are you done with your assignment?"

"Part of it. I have to go into the office tomorrow morning and finish writing the story from Wiesbaden. I started writing it on the plane, but I've got a lot more to do. Then I have to fly to Jacksonville, Florida, tomorrow afternoon to be at the Mayport Naval Station on Friday morning in time for a memorial service for the sailors killed on the *Stark*. I'm planning to fly directly back to Albany from there. I can write the story at home over the weekend and take the train to the city to turn it in Monday morning."

"Sounds like they're running you ragged."

"A little bit. I can't decide whether that's a good thing or not. I guess being distracted right now can't hurt." She sounded dejected. "Do you think she's okay, wherever she is?"

"I'm sure she's fine, honey. Kate is a very strong woman, she'll be all right."

"She was hurting so badly yesterday. She was trying hard to be tough, but I know that whole thing with her bosses really threw her. I'd like to wring their scrawny little necks."

Peter laughed. "Get in line, you're not the only one who feels that way."

"Do you really think the story's not dead?"

"Well, I know your fiancée thinks it's not, and I can't really disagree with her there. She's got amazing instincts when it comes to that kind of stuff. She's taken some measures to handle it though."

"I'm not sure what that means, but whatever it is, I'm sure she's cooked up something good." Jay chuckled, thinking about Kate scheming and devising ways to play with the media. "Well, I'd better get going." She hesitated for a moment. "Peter?"

"Yeah?"

"She is going to call you sometime today, right?"

"Yes, Jay, she promised to call in every day at some point."

"Would you...would you tell her I love her? And that I miss her terribly?"

"Of course, honey, you know I will." He paused. "Jay?"

"Yeah?"

"She loves you too, you know. Very much. That's why she's doing this. She just wants to keep you safe and out of the spotlight."

"I know, but I don't have to like it or agree with it, do I?"

"No, I suppose you don't."

"Can I call you again tomorrow, Peter?"

"Honey, you can call me anytime you want. I'll always be here for you, Jay...for one thing, Kate made me promise that I would, and for another, I would have done it anyway."

"You're such a sweetheart."

"Don't let that get around, you'll ruin my tough reputation."

"Your secret's safe with me, Technowiz. And Peter?"

"Mmm-hmm."

"Would it be okay if I took Fred home Friday when I get to Albany? I have a feeling I'm going to need his company."

"Of course. Tell you what—why don't I plan on picking up dinner and bringing it, and Fred, over to the house Friday night. Okay?"

"Yeah, that would be great. I can't promise that I'll be wonderful company, but..."

"It will be good to see you, Jay."

"Yeah, you too. Bye, Peter, thanks for everything. You won't forget to give Kate my messages, will you?"

"Never. Bye, Jay, try and get some sleep, okay?"

"Sure."

৵৩৶

Stepping off the plane in Chicago late Wednesday morning, Kate spotted them—two more photographers and one reporter. *Good,* she thought, *they're taking the bait. That ought to keep Jay in the clear.* Just thinking Jay's name gave her a pang, and she sighed as she made her way unhurriedly to the baggage claim area. She wanted to be sure to give her tails plenty of time to follow her. It wouldn't do to lose them yet.

Once her suitcase arrived she exited the terminal, noting that her shadows followed. She waited at the curb for a few moments until a big Crown Victoria pulled up and an older, matronly woman stepped out. Kate approached the woman and gave her a big smile and a warm hug, saying loud enough for anyone nearby to hear, "Aunt Marie, it's so good to see you. It feels like it's been forever. Thanks so much for letting me stay with you for a while, I really appreciate it. I just need some time to get away for a couple of months, and it will be so good to spend time with you and Uncle Nick."

In an unsteady voice, the old woman replied, "Oh now, Kate, you know you're always welcome in our home. You're like a second daughter to us and we're honored to have you around. Besides, you can reach all those things Nick puts up in the tall cupboards that I can never find. Come along now, let's get you settled in and unpacked."

The two women got in the car and drove off. Once they were a safe distance away, Kate reached over and squeezed the woman's hand. "Marie, you never cease to amaze me. Where in the world did you come up with that costume on such short notice? It's brilliant. You almost had me fooled."

"Hey, sweetie, that's what you pay me for, remember?" The voice belonged to a woman no older than Kate.

"Yeah, boxes and boxes of Freihofer's chocolate chip cookies, as I recall. You were addicted."

"Yes, and you fed my habit quite nicely, thank you."

"Well, you were my roommate and the only theatre major I knew. Who else was I supposed to enlist to play practical jokes on unsuspecting fools?"

"Mmm-hmm. It would be nice if you just said that I was the most talented actress you knew and that's why you hung around with me."

"Yeah, that too, I guess." Kate paused and looked seriously at her old college friend. She and Marie were paired together randomly freshman year and hit it off right away. She loved the fact that Marie accepted her just as she was and gave her space, while at the same time offering her unconditional friendship. They roomed together until Kate got a single junior year. Marie was one of the few people whom Kate let get close, and one of the very few in college who knew that she was a lesbian.

"I can't thank you enough for putting yourself on the line like this for me, Marie. It's an awful lot to ask."

"For you, Kate, anything, you know that. I was glad you called. I just about burst a button when I saw the cover of *Time*. I couldn't think of anyone who deserved the recognition more. And then when I saw the *Enquirer* yesterday I was mad enough to spit nails. It'd make me only too happy to screw them up." After a moment's silence, Marie asked, "Are you all right? I know I haven't been the best about keeping in touch, what with doing the show at the Improv and all, but I'm still here for you, you know?"

"I know you are, friend, that's why I felt comfortable making the call. I knew you would come through for me."

"You haven't answered the question."

"Oh, haven't I?"

"No, smart ass, you haven't."

Kate sighed, trying to figure out how to answer. She never lied to Marie before and found her to be a good listener on those few occasions when she wanted to talk. "No, I'm not okay," she said quietly. "I got fired yesterday, I have no idea what my future holds, I had to leave my fiancée behind so she wouldn't lose her career and get caught up in all this, and my heart is sick over it."

"Oh sweetie." Marie squeezed her hand that rested on the seat. "I'm so sorry for you. I'm assuming your fiancée was the one in the picture, right?"

Kate poked Marie. "No, I'm sleeping around, but don't tell her, okay? Of course it was her. In fact, that was taken on the day I proposed to her. We were on a beach in St. John. I had taken her there to get away from everything." She sighed wistfully.

Marie noted the ironic tone in Kate's voice. "It will be all right, you'll see. This will blow over and the two of you can ride off into the sunset."

"I wish I could believe that."

"Who is she? All I could see from the pictures was the back of her head. Nice kissing technique, by the way."

"God, you are such a brat."

"Just part of my charm, remember? And, my dear, once again you haven't answered my question. Am I going to have to beat it out of you?"

"Huh? You and what army?"

"Just remember my husband is bigger than you are."

"Yes, but he'd probably be on my side."

"Not if he wants me to put out anytime in this century."

"Ooh, now there's a threat."

"We're getting off the subject, missy. Are you going to tell me who the lucky woman is?"

Kate sighed heavily. "Her name is Jamison Parker. You might remember her...she was two years behind us...an Am lit major. And, Marie—I'm the lucky one."

"Wow. You've got it bad. Jamison Parker, Jamison Parker. Where have I seen that name recently?" Marie drummed the steering wheel. "You can't mean the same Jamison Parker whose byline graces the *Time* magazine story about you, can you?"

"Mmm-hmm."

"My, what a tangled web we weave. Yikes. No wonder you're trying to keep the hounds off the scent. That could look really bad for her."

"Right. Marie, she's an incredibly talented writer, she's got a brilliant future in front of her. I can't take a chance on her credibility being called into question."

"I see your dilemma here. Why didn't she just recuse herself from the story in the first place?"

"It's all my fault. We weren't involved sexually when she was given the assignment. In fact, we had only kissed a couple of times and had really just found each other again the week before."

At Marie's inquiring look, she explained, "She was in Albany doing a story on the governor when the bombing happened. She saw me on television and came to find me. That's how we got reacquainted. We met briefly a couple of times in college and she really made an impression on me and, I guess, me on her. So we began talking on the telephone. When her editor gave her the piece to do on me, she made it clear up front she needed to maintain professional distance from me. I was the one who pushed her. And even then, we didn't sleep together until she had done all of the interviews and research for the story. By the time she actually wrote it, we were head over heels in love, and just after she turned it in, I whisked her off to a remote Caribbean island and asked her to marry me."

"That's quite a tale. And they said romance was dead...apparently it's alive and well and living in Albany, New York. Who knew? I have to say, Kate, I never would have known the depth of your relationship from the story. She did an amazing job of staying objective, there's no hint of anything too personal in there."

"I know, I was so proud of her. Now you see why I have to let her go."

"No. Now I see why you want to keep her out of the spotlight, but not why you need to ditch her."

"I'm not ditching her!" Why couldn't they see? First Barbara, then Peter, now Marie. She had to do this for Jay's sake, that was all there was to it.

"What would you call disappearing and not telling her where you're going?"

"Look, the less she knows, the less she's likely to try and follow me, and the less likely she is to lose her job and her future."

"Seems to me if she loses you, she is losing her future. But that's just me," Marie said. "A job is a job and love is everything. Katherine Kyle, you are one of the most desirable women on the face of the planet. Why, if I weren't straight and happily married to Nick, I'd chase your skirt myself. I can't imagine this woman is just going to let you go and be okay with that."

They arrived at their destination, a nice, solid brick home in a respectably middle-class neighborhood. Getting out of the passenger side, Kate watched with awe as Marie transformed herself back into an elderly aunt in the blink of an eye. She had always loved watching Marie work—it fascinated her. Anyone watching would assume Kate was visiting with a beloved relative, which was just what she wanted people to think.

Once they were inside the house, Marie turned to Kate. "How much time have you got before your next flight?"

"A little over two hours."

"Okay, that means you have to leave here within a half-hour to get back to the airport in time."

"Fine. There is a back way out of here, right?"

"Yep, through the backyard where there's a small path over to the next neighborhood. I'll call Nick and tell him to meet you over there."

"You don't need to do that, I can call a cab."

"Don't be ridiculous, I won't hear of it. You might want to be careful, though, in case your friends are still hanging out waiting at the airport for a flight or something."

"I will, but I'm guessing they're based here in Chicago or on the West Coast somewhere and will either be watching your house or be gone by the time I get there."

"I hope you're right. Just in case, do you want a disguise?"

"Mmm. That could be fun."

"We'll make it something easy to take off, so you can be yourself by the time you get on the plane if you want."

"Okay, and if they're still lurking about I'll just stay in character."

Within twenty minutes Kate was transformed into a stooped old lady, warts and all, with the help of baggy clothes, a large bra stuffed with feathers, and some fake wrinkles that looked so real even she had to do a double take in the mirror. A wig of finely woven salt-and-pepper hair completed the look, with her real hair swept up underneath.

"My, my, Katherine, you really should take better care of yourself. Why, you're positively going to seed!"

Kate leaned over and kissed Marie on the cheek. "Thanks, doll, you're the best."

"Watch your voice there, Grandma Kate, and I know. Just you take care of yourself. And don't give up on your lady either, my friend. I can't wait to meet her. It sounds like she's a keeper, and so are you."

They hugged and Marie, still in costume, checked the backyard. "All clear. And don't worry, Kate, if I see any sign of anyone sniffing around, I'll just get back into costume and yell from the porch into the house for you to 'come out and get some fresh air, young lady, you stay cooped up too much for your own good.'"

Kate laughed at Marie's old-lady voice. "That ought to work. I'll be in touch sometime, I promise," Kate said as she stooped over and made her way slowly across the backyard and over into the next neighborhood. Her suitcase had already been transferred to Nick's car in the enclosed garage away from any potential prying eyes fifteen minutes ago, before he headed back out to wait for her.

The remainder of the trip was uneventful, with no sightings of any reporters or photographers. Still, Kate chose to stay in costume until she reached Denver, where she disappeared into a ladies' room and removed the makeup and costume, paid cash for a rental car, picked up a large container of coffee to fight off her exhaustion, and headed off in the direction of her first destination, the Great Sand Dunes in the Sangre de Cristo Mountains.

By 9:00 p.m. Wednesday, after nearly seven hours of driving, Kate arrived in tiny Mosca, Colorado, the town closest to the dunes, where she stopped for the night at a small bed and breakfast called the Inn at Zapata Ranch. She was grateful just to be able to get out and stretch her cramped legs.

After checking in, she put her suitcase in the homespun room, noting that there was no telephone. She frowned and headed back out to the main lobby. "Excuse me," she said to the elderly night clerk, "I'm looking for a telephone."

The white-haired gentleman smiled a smile that was missing two prominent teeth and pointed to a lounge chair in the corner of the lobby closest to the communal fireplace. "That's the only phone available to the guests, miss. Just dial 9 to get an operator."

Great, thought Kate, looking around and seeing several people milling about the lobby. *Just what I need—no privacy.* She sighed heavily and sat down in the lounge chair. she dialed Peter's number from memory. According to her watch, it was a little after 11:00 p.m. back home.

"Yello."

"Hey, Technowiz."

"Hey Anc—er, woman. How's things?"

"Peachy. I'm so far beyond exhausted...hey, what comes after exhausted, anyway?"

"Um, dead?"

She chuckled. "Well, that's helpful. Let's just say I'm halfway there and leave it at that."

"How'd the trip out go?"

"Like clockwork. Two photographers and a reporter at the airport in Albany, two different photographers and a different reporter in Chicago. My friend met me and put on a great show, which I think they bought, and no one followed me to Denver that I could tell. Certainly no one followed me here. I'm in the middle of nowhere and I didn't see another set of headlights in either direction for the last hundred twenty-five miles."

"Sounds good. Where exactly is the middle of nowhere?"

"Are you sure you want to know? If you don't know, you can't lie about it." She was only half joking, and they both knew it.

"Kate, someone ought to know where to find you in case of emergency, don't you think?"

"Is everything all right? Have you heard from Jay?"

"Everything's okay, and yes, I heard from Jay seven hours ago."

"How is she?"

"Lonely and depressed, from the sound of it, but otherwise okay. She sounds about the same as you, come to think of it. Imagine that."

"Okay, I get your point, that's enough. Where is she?"

"She's back in New York at the apartment. You could probably get her there now if you wanted."

"No, it's too late…I'm hoping she's sleeping. It sounds like she had a whirlwind trip. She wasn't even there twenty-four hours. And besides," she added softly, "it will only make things harder."

"She's going into the office tomorrow morning to write the story on the injured sailors, then she flies off to Jacksonville, Florida, tomorrow afternoon or evening for the memorial service for the dead, which takes place the following morning. The president is going to be there. She says she's, and I quote, 'coming home to write the story over the weekend and then take the train to the city Monday morning to turn it in.' She's flying directly from Jacksonville to Albany on Friday after the service. I told her I'd pick up dinner and bring it, and Fred, to the house Friday night."

"Thanks, Peter, you're a prince, as always."

"Yeah, yeah, tell it to somebody who believes you. Oh, and she had two messages for you. She said to tell you she loves you and she misses you."

Kate's heart clenched. "Tell her I said the same, okay?" she asked huskily.

"Of course. Now are you going to tell me where in the world you are?"

"Right now I'm sitting in a lounge chair in the lobby of a bed and breakfast fifteen minutes away from the Great Sand Dunes, one of the great wonders in this country. Unfortunately, this is the only phone they have for the guests to use, so it's not the most private place in the world. I'll probably spend the day tomorrow at the dunes and I may stop at the Zapata Falls, which are nearby. Then I'll move on before nightfall. I'll call you again tomorrow night from the road."

"Good. Oh, and Fred says good night and to tell you he misses you too."

"Give him a kiss on the nose for me. I'll talk to you tomorrow, bud. See ya."

"Bye, Kate. Be careful out there."

She held the dead receiver in her hand a moment longer. God, she so wanted to talk to Jay. But she meant what she said to Peter—it would only make things harder for both of them, and she knew Jay would want to know exactly where she was and when she was coming home. She could picture the conversation now.

"Kate, where are you?"

"It's better if you don't know, love."

"How can that be better? Don't you trust me with the information?"

"It isn't a matter of trust, Jay, it's just a matter of practicality."

"Oh, so now I'm on a need-to-know basis and I don't need to know, is that it?"

"No, sweetheart, of course not."

"Well, can you at least tell me when you're coming home?"

No, talking to Jay would only make things worse. With a heavy heart, Kate went to her room, where she lay down and cried herself to sleep.

CHAPTER TWENTY-THREE

Jay spent Wednesday night in the apartment, surrounded by Kate's scent and the lingering fragrance of her perfume on the pillows and sheets. While Jay found that somewhat comforting, it also made the longing for her more acute.

She turned in the first sidebar, then left for Jacksonville Thursday afternoon. When she checked into the hotel, she called Peter. He told her only that Kate was in touch late the night before, that she was followed in two places by the media, and that she managed to lose them, then went on her way. When Jay asked him if he thought Kate would be home soon, Peter simply indicated that he told Kate of her impending trip to Florida and her plans to be at the house in Albany over the weekend. He never answered the question one way or the other.

Friday night, true to his word, Peter met Jay at the house with Fred and dinner in tow. She had already been there for a couple of hours and found six dozen roses in various locations throughout the house—three dozen red and three dozen yellow, each with a card containing some expression of love and devotion that made her ache for Kate's presence. She also found the stash of comic books, with a note indicating that they "ought to keep you busy and out of trouble for a while," and that Kate expected that, if Jay gave it a chance, she'd understand the draw of Aquaman, Captain America, and the Flash too. Jay smiled wistfully, thinking to herself that she'd much rather be personally persuaded by a certain someone than discover an affinity for them on her own.

The dinner with Peter was a nice diversion, although he seemed somewhat uncomfortable. She imagined that was because he could not tell her what she really wanted to know, which was when she might see Kate again or where she might be at that particular moment.

"Where is she?"

"I don't really know. She hasn't told me."

"When do you think she'll be back?"

"I can't say, Jay, because I really don't know."

For yet another night, she cried herself to sleep, this time in Kate's bed with Fred lying nearby. He seemed to sense her distress and followed her everywhere. He stayed close by her side, put his head on her lap as she sobbed, and gave her his favorite stuffed toys to comfort her.

On Saturday she sat down to write the story of the memorial service, but was too distracted. She called Peter to find that Kate had, indeed, called in late the night before after he returned home from dinner. She said that she was fine and to tell Jay that she loved her and missed her. Jay felt the walls closing in on her after that and set out for Kaaterskill Falls with Fred and a little lunch. The two hiked the same route they had taken with Kate and stopped to have lunch by the waterfall, where Jay cried, thinking back to the sweetness of that first real date they shared. She closed her eyes and could feel the moment all over again as if Kate were there with her.

Jay sighed heavily and shook herself to clear the memory, since it only increased the agony of being apart from Kate.

❧

Saturday night Barbara stopped by to see how Jay was doing. She related that she had bumped into Kate on her way back to Albany Tuesday, the day all hell broke loose, and that Kate asked her to check in on her. Jay got to know Barbara a bit better and discovered that the two of them shared some common interests and philosophies.

After Barbara left, Jay dialed Peter to discover that she just missed Kate, who again sent her love. "Did she say she was coming home?" she asked hopefully. She missed her so much it was making her sick to her stomach.

"No, honey, she didn't. She just said she'd call again tomorrow sometime. I'm sorry."

"That's okay, Peter, I appreciate everything you're doing."

"You're welcome, Jay. You know I'll do everything I can for both of you, right?"

❧

After he hung up the phone, Peter spent a moment longer thinking about his newest friend. Her appearance worried him the night before and he told Kate so on the phone. Jay looked tired and drawn, with no sparkle in her eyes, she hardly touched her dinner, and she was clearly getting more depressed with each passing day. He would feel better, he thought, if she at least was angry. Somehow he expected her to react differently. After all, she was spunky and seemed an equal match for Kate in terms of determination and will. Then again, he was smart enough to realize that there was probably a lot about her he didn't know.

For Jay, Sunday was set aside for writing the memorial service sidebar, which she did, sitting down in Kate's office for the first time at her new word processor. There was a note on it. *"Jay, I know that the next great American novel will be penned on this machine some day in the not-too-distant future. I can't wait to read it. I'm so proud of you. All my love, K."* Reading the loving words, Jay cried for what seemed like the tenth time that day.

She talked to Peter again that night just to check in and let him know she was going to the city via train in the morning to turn in the story. She planned to leave her car at the train station, but Peter offered to come by and get her instead. By that time, Jay was so depressed she even stopped asking him for any details of Kate's whereabouts or actions. She only asked Peter to pass along the usual message—that she loved Kate and missed her and wished she were coming home. At her core, Jay was afraid that she had been right—nothing as wonderful as Kate could really be meant to happen to her.

Kate, meanwhile, was in no better shape than Jay. On Thursday morning she got up early and took a run, then climbed to the top of one of the tallest sand dunes in North America and watched the sun rise over the spectacular snow-covered peaks of the Sangre de Cristo mountains. It was breathtaking. She selected that spot, as she had the others she would visit, because it was among the most spiritual, most peaceful places in the country. She hoped the vistas would be a balm to her tattered soul. She was all alone up there, not another soul in sight at that early hour, and Kate sobbed until she had no tears left.

She cried for the happiness she was forced to sacrifice, and the love that was so far away. She cried for the pain the separation was causing Jay. She cried for a future she had just begun to consider, but given recent events, knew she would never have. Kate sat like that for hours, knees pulled up tight to her chin, rocking back and forth in a vain effort to comfort herself. There was only one thing, one person, who could bring her solace, and she wasn't selfish enough to put her own needs above Jay's. No, she would have to work through the pain on her own.

Eventually, Kate descended the dunes and detoured to the Zapata Falls on her way out of the area, but the water was running so high she wasn't able to get too far and turned back to the car to continue on her journey. It took her nearly five hours on US 160 west, climbing over the treacherous Wolf Creek Pass, to make it to Mesa Verde. On the way through the pass, she got out at a scenic overlook to peek over at a breathtaking valley below and to stretch her aching body. By the time she stopped for the night at the Far View Lodge in the Mesa Verde National Park, Kate was so tired she could barely see straight and wanted simply to be able to close her eyes and shut out the emotional pain that had been buffeting her continuously for two days. God, was it only that long since she last held Jay and made love to her?

She called Peter to let him know she was at her next destination.

"Hey, Kate."

"Hi, Technowiz. What's up?"

"Not much. Jay has landed safely in Jacksonville. I'll be having dinner with her at the house tomorrow night after she gets back home."

Around the lump in her throat Kate choked out, "Give her a hug for me, will you? Good night, Peter."

Unable to get her mind to stop spinning, Kate was once again up and dressed in running clothes before dawn on Friday, her long legs eating up the winding curves of the pavement as she wended her way up and down the inclines, occasionally catching glimpses of Shiprock, New Mexico, and Four Corners, where Utah, Colorado, Arizona and New Mexico intersect.

Kate spent the rest of the day hiking the trails in the park and touring the ruins of cliff dwellings. The history and architecture fascinated her, and the engineering skill of the long-ago peoples astounded her. Beyond all that, there was something inherently spiritual about the place that beckoned to her, and Kate felt the pull of that at her core. She decided to spend a second night at the lodge before heading out in the morning.

Once she made the arrangements, she settled in for the evening and tried to read for a while. Her mind kept drifting to Jay though, and she found herself reading the same paragraph over and over again. Finally, she gave up, set the book aside and turned on CNN instead. That, however, made her even more melancholy than she already was, so she turned it off and closed her eyes, allowing her mind to wander.

She felt so off balance, so rudderless. What was she going to do with her life when things settled down and she didn't need to be out of sight anymore? By then, surely Jay would have gotten over her. In truth, at that moment she didn't care about her professional future, but she knew that sooner or later she would have to do something. She was pretty sure her days as a broadcast journalist were finished—the business had very little use for out lesbians.

So then what? A degree in American history made her well rounded, but not specifically qualified for anything. She could go to law school, something she considered when she graduated from college. It wasn't as if she couldn't handle the coursework. But she didn't think she really wanted to go back to school at this point in her life, not to mention the financial resources it would take to do so. Frankly, she was too tired to think clearly about what she wanted to be when she grew up.

She checked her watch. It was close to 11:00 p.m. Friday night in Albany. *Peter should be back from his dinner with Jay by now.* She called him and got him on the second ring.

"Hey, Technowiz."

"Hi yourself."

"How was your dinner with the most lovely woman in the world?" She couldn't help the smile the mere thought of Jay brought to her lips.

"Well, I enjoyed it. She, on the other hand, barely ate a bite."

"Why, did you cook it?"

"Very funny, string bean. No, I brought takeout Chinese, which she said she loved, then managed to push around her plate for the better part of an hour."

"Hmm. That doesn't sound like the Jay I know. That woman can eat more than most NFL linemen. I never understood where she put it all."

"It's not good, my friend. She looks drawn and tired and emotionally distressed. It's odd, really, I would have expected her to be more angry and insistent on getting answers from me. All she wants to know is when you're coming home."

Tears tracked silently down Kate's face. Peter knew nothing of Jay's background, and therefore couldn't understand what Kate knew—Jay wouldn't push this because, deep down inside, she expected the worst and thought she deserved it. It was what she had always gotten. There hadn't really been enough time for Kate to establish a trustworthy track record. By disappearing, she unleashed all of Jay's doubts and insecurities.

Kate knew a moment of uncertainty. *Was* she doing the right thing by staying away? There was silence on the line for several moments. "Did she make out okay in Jacksonville?"

"Yeah, said she got some great human-interest stuff and a few minutes with President Reagan. Said he was very charismatic."

"Mmm. I know. I've met him too. Lousy politics, but an engaging man."

"That's pretty much what she said."

"Did she, um, say anything about finding anything in the house?"

"No, but I did notice a profusion of roses in vases everywhere I turned. You wouldn't have had anything to do with that, now would you?"

"Me? Nah, not a romantic bone in my body." She knew Jay was a very private person and probably wouldn't have shared the information about the flowers and the comic books, but it was worth asking. Anything that told Kate that Jay knew how she felt would have helped soothe the pain a bit.

Peter snorted. "Where are you and where are you heading next?"

"I'm still at Mesa Verde. I'll head out first thing in the morning and point myself in the direction of Sedona. I'll probably make some side trips along the way, so I'm not really sure how long it will take me or where I'll detour to, but I'll call you when I settle for the night."

"Okay. Kate, I called Barbara when I got home tonight and asked her to stop by and see Jay tomorrow night."

"Why?" There was a note of alarm in her voice. "Is she sick?"

"Heartsick, to be sure. And if she keeps going the way she is, she'll be physically sick soon enough." He was silent for a moment. "I just thought maybe Barbara could get her to talk a little. Right now she's trying hard to bottle everything up inside, and I'm afraid what will happen when she lets it all go."

"You're a good man and a better friend, Peter. Thank you for taking such good care of her. You have no idea how much I appreciate it."

"I know she means the world to you, Kate. And that means she means the world to me too, and I know Barbara feels the same way."

"Thanks, friend, I'll talk to you tomorrow. Will you talk to Barbara after she sees Jay?"

"Yes, we made arrangements to talk. I figured you'd want a second opinion tomorrow night."

"Yeah. Thanks, buddy." Kate would wait and see what Barbara had to say before deciding whether or not she needed to change strategy.

"You're welcome, Kate. Hey, take care of yourself now, you hear?"

"Bye, Peter."

"See ya, babe."

Kate spent Saturday driving through parts of the Navajo and Hopi reservations, stopping often to talk to the Native American craftsmen who were selling their wares along the side of the road. Unable to resist, she purchased a beautifully woven Navajo blanket for Jay, as well as an intricately carved silver bracelet from a Hopi woman who engaged her in conversation. *I don't know if I'll ever have a chance to give these to you, love, but it makes me feel better to be doing something for you, so...*

She drove through Shiprock, New Mexico, and Monument Valley in Arizona; her mind easily conjured up all those old westerns which used that exact scenery as the backdrop to countless hours of melodrama. She stopped briefly as the shadows grew long on Saturday at the South Rim of the Grand Canyon. She didn't want to linger long there—it was too populated with tourists and she didn't want to take a chance at being recognized; although, as rough as she knew she looked, she doubted anyone would know who she was.

She found a small motel on US 89 south of the canyon, where she stopped for the night. After waiting until she was sure Barbara and Peter would have talked already, she made her nightly phone call, this time getting Peter on the first ring.

"Well, what's the word?"

"Hello to you too, sunshine."

"Have you talked to Barbara?"

"Yes."

"And?"

"And she agrees with me that Jay is seriously depressed and misses you like crazy. She's not eating, not sleeping, and even Fred knows something is wrong. He follows her everywhere, tries to give her his favorite stuffed toys to cheer her up, and puts his head on her lap when she sits down."

"I'm glad he's there for her." *Damn, should I go back?*

"Me too. She told me she tried to sit down and write the memorial service story today but couldn't focus. So she took Fred and went to Kaaterskill Falls for a hike."

Kate's breathing caught as she envisioned Jay sitting alone in the spot where they shared their first picnic and their budding romance. There was a sharp pain in her chest. *Oh, love, it must have been so hard for you, being there by yourself.*

Peter continued, "She said she's going to write the story tomorrow, stay at the house tomorrow night, and then travel to the city Monday morning."

"Have you seen anything?" Kate asked Peter each night whether or not he'd spotted any stories about her or seen anyone anywhere near Jay.

"Still not a word since the TV coverage the day the news release came out."

No, I won't go back now. This way at least I know she's still safe from scrutiny, if not happy. Her future is what's important. She can get over me.

Kate thought about that first bit of news coverage. That had been hard; each of the local news stations reported that Kate had departed abruptly following some "adverse" publicity. To their credit, the competition showed some class and didn't trash her. She was grateful for their respect.

"I think the reporter and photographers who hounded me must have been from the tabloids, probably the *Globe* and the *Enquirer*. Can you figure out when they publish? I guess we know the *Enquirer* comes out on Tuesday. How about the *Globe*?"

"I'll have an answer for you tomorrow when I talk to you."

"Okay. Night, Peter."

"Bye, Kate."

On Sunday she stopped at the Wupatki National Monument to hike the area and investigate some well-preserved and diverse ruins before moving on to Flagstaff and the Kaibab National Forest, where she explored a number of hiking trails. She thought about stopping there for the night, but decided it was too early and ventured instead on a side trip to the Walnut Canyon National Monument. There she found a beautiful canyon with more unique ruins and a clear stream at the base. Finally drained of her manic energy, she returned to Flagstaff to find yet another small motel for the night.

Her conversation with Peter was brief. He relayed that he was taking Jay to the train station early in the morning, and that she told him to tell Kate that she loved her and missed her and wished she were coming home. He also told Kate that the upcoming week's edition of the *Globe* was due to hit newsstands the next morning.

Kate told him that she was in a town big enough to have a newsstand, and that she would check out the story first thing and call him right away to discuss it. They rang off.

Peter dropped Jay at the train station Monday morning in plenty of time for her to make the 6:00 a.m. express to New York. She smiled sadly when she thought, *Ah, Kate, it's easy to be on time when there are no distractions in the house.* Since she had some extra time to kill, Jay wandered into the newsstand. She browsed the magazines briefly before her eyes fell on the front page of the *Globe*. She snatched up a copy and threw some change on the counter just as her train was being called.

Once onboard she picked her usual window seat in an isolated car and pulled the tabloid out of her briefcase. There were two pictures of Kate, the large one on the front apparently taken in Chicago the previous Wednesday, according to the caption. An old woman, identified only as "Aunt Marie, a mother figure to the deposed anchorwoman," was greeting her. They were loading her suitcase into the trunk of a large sedan. The second picture, which was on the inside cover along with an accompanying story, was of Kate at the airport in Albany awaiting her flight to Chicago. As always, she looked calm and regal. Jay touched the pictures, as if the gesture would bring her closer to Kate.

Then her eyes fell on the story with the banner headline that read, *"Gorgeous Lesbian Anchorwoman Leaves a String of Broken Hearts Across the Country."* Jay groaned as she read.

"Sensational beauty and now ex-anchorwoman Katherine Kyle abruptly disappeared from the airwaves on Tuesday, the day photographs were published of her and a mysterious blonde woman cavorting on a beach in the tiny tropical paradise of St. John. The Globe caught up to Ms. Kyle as she fled her hometown to lick her wounds with relatives in Chicago; she was quite alone, the blonde nowhere in sight. Apparently, that is not unusual for Kyle, as the Globe's investigative journalists have uncovered a bevy of broken hearts the statuesque siren has left behind all over the country.

"'I was head over heels in love with her, but she was only interested in a casual relationship, something superficial. I broke up with her because I thought she was in love with someone else.' So says a Vermont forest ranger with whom Kyle had a two-year affair in the early 1980s. Other women have told the Globe similar stories, painting the model-pretty ex-anchorwoman as a love 'em and leave 'em female Lothario who has never settled down, preferring instead to 'use 'em and lose 'em,' as one poor victim of her considerable charms told the Globe. For now, she remains secluded with elderly relatives in a Chicago suburb, no doubt planning her next conquest.'"

Jay read the story over several times, her insecurities multiplying by the minute. She knew the forest ranger quoted had to be Jen, the EMT who treated her the night of the attack that Kate interrupted. She had no idea who the other women the story quoted could be, nor could she figure out who the woman was in Chicago who obviously picked Kate up at the airport.

Peter said that Kate had seen the photographers and reporters and had managed to deceive them and lose them. What exactly did that mean? Who was this mysterious relative? Hadn't Kate told her she didn't have any living relatives, that Jay was her family now? Had she meant that, or was she just another in a long line of jilted lovers? Had she been played for a sucker?

Kate seemed so sincere, so in love with her. Was she really, or was she just a great actress? *Parker, it's the story of your life—if it seems to be too good to be true, it probably is.* Jay started to get agitated. Why hadn't Kate gotten in touch with her? She knew, according to Peter, that Jay was staying at the house. She could have called any time. And why wouldn't she say where she was? Was she already off wooing some other unsuspecting potential lover? Jay's overtired mind leapt to all kinds of conclusions.

By the time the train pulled into the station and she made her way to the apartment before heading to the office, Jay was in a full-blown rage. She was exhausted and emotionally wrecked, and beyond feeling anything but pain and betrayal.

ૡૹ

Kate ran to the nearest newsstand as soon as it opened at 5:00 a.m. local time, knowing that it was two hours later at home and Peter would already have the story in his hands. She looked at the photographs and read the story quickly, then again more thoroughly, raising her eyebrows at the fact that they had managed to unearth Jen. And then built a pack of lies around a truth her ex-lover told to make it more plausible. Typical tabloid bullshit.

She sighed and chewed her lip. Either Jay would see the story on her own or Trish or some other helpful person would call it to her attention. What would she think? Kate's face was grim as she added up the likely conclusions that her sometimes-insecure lover might draw if left to her own devices. She'd better talk to her.

Peter answered his office phone on the first ring. "Peter Enright."

"Yeah, I know who you are."

"Good morning. I take it you've seen this morning's trash."

"Yeah. They took one tiny shred of truth, that Jen and I had a relationship and that she broke up with me because she thought, ironically enough, that I was in love with Jay all those years ago, and blew it up into me being the cold-hearted bitch-slut of the century. Yippee."

"Don't sweat it, babe, you know how ridiculous the whole thing is."

"Yeah, I do, but does Jay? She has a tendency to let her imagination get carried away with her, Peter. She's had a lot of really bad stuff happen to her and she doesn't think she's worthy of being loved. She simply doesn't trust that that kind of love exists for her, and I can't be there to reassure her." She paused, sighing heavily. "I think I need to talk to her now, buddy. I'm sure she'll see this and her brain will start working overtime."

261

Kate looked at her watch. It was nearly 9:10 a.m. in New York. "I bet she'll go to the apartment before she heads to the office. Can you call her there now and conference me with her?"

"Yep. I'll put you on hold, dial her, then bring you back in and take myself out, okay? It will just be you two, I promise."

"Thanks Peter. You're a prince."

"Don't thank me yet."

CHAPTER TWENTY-FOUR

J ay, are you there?"

"Yes."

"Kate, how 'bout you?"

"Right here, Technowiz."

"Okay. Well, I'll leave you two to it then. See ya."

There was silence on the line for half a beat as Kate just enjoyed the sound of Jay breathing at the other end.

"Hi, sweetheart, how are you?"

"Great," Jay answered sarcastically. "You? Are you having fun on your vacation?"

Kate was taken aback by the biting tone. "Is that what you think, that I'm just off having a good time?" she asked softly. "I miss you so much it's tearing me up inside. There isn't a second that goes by that I don't think about you and wish I could be with you."

"I bet that's what you say to all the girls, isn't it?" Jay shot back.

"Don't believe everything you read, love. I take it you've seen the *Globe* this morning."

"Oh yeah, I saw it. So I guess I shouldn't be surprised that you haven't told me where you are or that you haven't wanted to talk to me, even though you knew full well where I was. You've probably already moved on to the next sucker, haven't you? How stupid could I be to think someone as perfect as you really could be interested in me as anything other than the flavor of the month? Jesus, Jamison, just take out an ad that says, 'My name is Jay and I'm naïve, please step on me and then kick me when I'm down.'"

Kate was reeling. She expected Jay to be confused, perhaps even upset about the article, but this—everything she'd done, she'd done because she loved Jay heart and soul. And all Jay could think was that once again someone she loved had betrayed her trust and given her what she thought she deserved. Kate's heart shattered in pieces right there in the hotel room.

"I'm sorry you feel that way, Jay," she said stiffly.

"*That's what you have to say?*"

"Yes." *Go ahead, Kyle, let her get good and mad. She's been conditioned to expect the worst for twenty-five years. That's not going to change in the month that you had together. From where she's sitting, it looks to her like you've just been using her. Let her think that—maybe it will help her get over you faster. This is best for her. Anger always supersedes pain. She'll be fine. Let her go.* This Kate thought even as she was dying inside.

"Fine then. I hope you and...whoever your next conquest is...are having a wonderful time. Don't bother sending me a postcard. Goodbye, Kate."

"Goodbye, my love," Kate said to the dial tone on the other end. "I will be yours 'til the end of time and beyond. I hope someday you'll know that." She dissolved into tears—huge, wracking sobs that echoed off the walls as she lay face down in the pillow.

∼✥✥∼

After slamming down the receiver, Jay picked it up to dial once again with shaking hands. "Peter?"

"Hi, Half-pint, how did it go? It must have been great to be able to talk to her, huh?"

"Oh yeah, a real pleasure," Jay ground out.

"What happened, Jay?"

"Never mind, I just think it would be better if you went over and took Fred, okay? I'll come by later or tomorrow sometime to get my things, give you the key, and have you undo whatever it was you did that allowed me to set and deactivate the security system."

"Whoa, whoa. What are you talking about?"

Jay proceeded to relate in detail everything she said to Kate and Kate's responses.

When she was done, he screamed into the phone, "You said what? You did what? Oh my God, oh my God. Shit, I've got to find her before she really does disappear."

The decibel level of Peter's voice shocked Jay. She never heard him lose his cool before. Testily, she said, "It figures. I'm the one who gets screwed, and you're worried about her. Guess she's got you wrapped around her little finger too, huh?"

"You listen to me, Jamison Parker," he said in a low, barely controlled growl. "I know that you've been hurting over all this. Kate told me that she was worried how you would react to the article. She didn't tell me why, just that you had a lot of bad stuff happen to you and that she was concerned that your imagination would run away with you." He paused a second. "Boy, I guess she got that right, now didn't she?

"Now let me tell you a thing or two about our friend Ms. Kyle. In all the years I have known that woman I have never, ever known her to be anything but painfully honest. I personally have watched her shun gorgeous women who literally have thrown themselves at her feet because she didn't want to hurt or mislead them. She has avoided relationships, yes, even casual sex, for years because, as she always put it, 'The right one is out there for me, and until she comes along, I'll just wait on the sidelines, thank you very much.' Hell, I didn't think people like that still existed! So many people misunderstood and labeled her cold and aloof. The ice princess. She never showed how much that hurt her...she just let them think what they would and went about her life with style and class. Katherine Kyle has more integrity than anyone I've ever known, and that's going a ways.

"When she fell so hard for you, I was flabbergasted and overjoyed. I never thought I'd see the day that my best friend would find true love and happiness. But she found it with you. When she told me she proposed to you, well, you could have knocked me over with a feather. And when all this bullshit happened, I was sick for her that she felt so strongly that she would do anything in the world to protect you. Yes, she went away to protect you, Jay, because she thought your future and your career were worth more than her happiness and her future, despite my arguments and Barbara's arguments to the contrary. She was adamant that she would never do anything to jeopardize you, no matter what it cost her. Being away from you is killing her and, frankly, I don't know what she'll do now."

Jay felt any remaining color drain from her face.

Peter was still on a roll. "Today, this morning, when she didn't refute anything you said, that was her way of letting you get on with your life because she knew that if you were truly angry at her, that would override the hurt you were feeling and you could move on and stay anonymous and have the life and career she thought you deserved. Bully for her, she's a better person than I. I don't think I could have done what she did."

By this time Jay was beside herself. The tears rolled down her cheeks unimpeded and she felt so sick to her stomach she thought she might have to make a run to the bathroom. "God, I'm such an idiot. What have I done? Now she thinks I don't believe in her and she has nothing to come back to. She's hurting and alone and I just threw grease on the fire. Peter, I'm so, so sorry. Oh God, this is all my fault."

"It's not me you need to apologize to, Jay," he said quietly. After a few seconds he asked, "Do you love her?"

"More than life itself."

"You'd better mean that, young lady."

"You have no idea," she answered.

"Okay."

"Can you get her on the phone for me again? If she'll take my call, I mean?"

Peter sighed heavily. "I don't know where she is, Jay. I don't know where she called me from."

"You don't?"

"No, she never gave me the names of the places she was staying, only a rough idea of where in the world she was. She wanted to be so careful. She didn't want there to be any way anyone could trace her. Heck, she's been paying for everything with cash and even took a detour to Chicago with the help of an old theater friend of hers to fool those tabloid jerks into thinking she was going to be staying with a matronly aunt for a few months. All to keep them away from you. She made me promise I would keep an eye out and wouldn't let the media anywhere near you. I've never seen her this crazed about anything. She gave up everything that she was, everything that she had…for you.

"And Jay, despite the things you said to her this morning, she'll continue to protect you and keep you safe. Kate loves you with all her being. Knowing her, no matter what you did…or do…to her, that will always be the case. She never does things in half measures."

"I have to make this right. Somehow, I have to make this right." Jay's head was about to explode. After a minute she said, "I know what I have to do." It was as if she were talking to herself and she'd forgotten that Peter was even there. "I'm going to the office now. I need to talk to Trish."

"Wait a minute, Jay. Wait. Don't do anything rash, now. Kate has gone to a lot of trouble to keep you out of harm's way. If you fly in the face of that, she'll murder me."

Jay smiled for the first time in what seemed like years. "Don't worry, baby, I'll protect you," she teased. "Listen, I have to turn in my story and see what, if anything, my next assignment is. By the time I'm done with that, can you try to pinpoint where you think she might be so that I can go find her?"

"I don't know, Jay..."

"Peter, please. I know you probably don't like me very much right now. Heck, I don't much like myself. But I do love Kate with all my heart and soul, and I'm not giving us up without a fight. I just made the biggest mistake of my life, but I'm going to do everything in my power to fix it. Will you help me? For Kate's sake?"

"God, you are incorrigible, you know that?"

"So I've been told."

"Okay, call me back when you've done what you need to do."

❧

As he hung up the phone, Peter nodded to himself. That was more like what he expected from Jay in the first place. He felt better already. Maybe this could work out in the end. In spite of the fact that she had just trampled all over his best friend and likely broken her heart, he did know that Kate and Jay loved each other more than any couple he'd ever seen, and any fool could see that they belonged together. Beyond that, he liked the little imp. She'd been under a lot of strain and was exhausted and depressed. Clearly she just wasn't thinking straight before she jumped in with both feet. He shook his head. *You're turning into an old sentimental mushball, Enright. Disgusting.*

❧

Jay showed up in the office just before 10:00 a.m. and found Trish buried behind stacks of paper.

"Hiya, kiddo. Got a story for me?"

"Here it is," Jay said.

"Geez, you look terrible, kid. What the hell happened to you? Come on, come with me." Without waiting for an answer Trish led Jay out of the office and downstairs to the coffee shop. "What's up, Jay? This isn't like you. What's the matter?"

Jay couldn't look her in the eye. "I need to tell you something, Trish, and I'll understand, whatever you decide to do about it."

"Sounds ominous. What is it?"

"You remember you showed me those pictures last week in the *Enquirer* of Katherine Kyle?"

"Yeah," Trish drew the word out. "The ones that made her lose her job."

"Yeah."

"So?"

Jay looked up and pinned Trish with a piercing stare, her chin held high. "I'm the other woman in those pictures."

"What are you saying?"

"I'm saying that the woman Kate was kissing was me. We'd gone to St. John to get away from everything. That picture was taken the day she proposed to me." She smiled wistfully.

"Holy Mother...you mean you're getting married...to her? Wow, Jay. Wow."

Jay plowed on, "And now she's disappeared in order to protect my career and my future and to keep the tabloid vultures away from me. When she realized that no one could see my face and even you didn't know who the blonde was, she devised a plan to keep anyone from figuring it out."

Trish whistled. "Now *that's* love."

"Yeah, the only problem is that I saw the item in the *Globe* this morning and I let some ugly stuff from my past get in the way. It was the first time I'd talked to her since she went away, and I said some very nasty things and now she thinks I don't believe in her and there's nothing to come home to, and I have no way to get in touch with her. I don't even know where she is. No one does, exactly." Jay raked her fingers through her hair.

"Huh."

"I'm sorry, Trish, I never meant to mislead you. We weren't involved when you assigned me the story and we didn't get involved until after I'd finished all the research and all the interviews—"

"Jay, stop it, hon. Listen to me. You're the best damn reporter I got. You wrote a fabulous story. I sure couldn't figure out that you were involved with her, so I know it must have been objective. I know you would never do something like that on purpose. It's okay. Really. I don't care. You've got so much potential, Jay, it just doesn't matter to me. You can love anyone you want. Hell, who wouldn't want to be married to that woman!"

Jay smiled shyly. "Yeah, she's pretty amazing, isn't she?"

"Yep, honey, she's a real looker. So this is what we're going to do—I'm going to put you on floater status." She winked. "No firm assignment, just an 'in case' kind of deal. You call in once a day this week to see if I've got anything for you, okay?"

"Are you sure?"

"Positive. You love her, right?"

"Oh God, do I."

"Then go get her and bring her back here. I don't give a damn what they say about you, you're mine and I'm not going to let anyone mess with you. Don't worry. Now, you better get going, and don't forget to invite me to the wedding."

"You're the best, Trish." Jay hugged Trish hard.

"Careful, you'll bruise me. I'll talk to you tomorrow, kid. Let me know how it's going."

Jay nodded and ran out of the coffee shop and out the front door of the building, not stopping until she was on the subway headed to her apartment.

When she arrived, the first thing she did was call Peter. "What do you have? Anything?"

"Nothing solid, but I have a pretty good guess."

"Okay, I'm listening." For the first time that day, Jay felt hopeful.

"I think she was in Flagstaff this morning when you talked to her. She said she was someplace big enough that they had a newsstand, which knocks out everyplace else in the area. I think she was on her way to Sedona."

"That would make sense. She told me once that it was one of her favorite places and she'd been there many times."

"I can't guarantee that she'll follow through with that now, though."

Jay closed her eyes and thought for a minute. "I think she will. It's a very important place to her, and I would think she'd want to seek solace in the familiar." Jay's chest ached at the thought. *Oh, love, I'm so, so sorry. I'm going to find you, whatever it takes, and get you back here with me, where you belong.*

"You may be right about that. If not, there's not much I can do to find her under the radar screen without alerting people we don't want to alert."

"I hope you're right, Peter, and my heart tells me you are."

"Good, 'cause I've taken the liberty of booking you on the next plane leaving from New York for Phoenix in...oh, two hours. And I've got you on a private plane from Phoenix to the Sedona airport."

"You're amazing!"

"Don't mention it. There's a car waiting for you downstairs to take you to the airport when you're ready. Don't worry, the driver won't ask any questions."

"Peter, do you think you'll hear from her again before I see her?"

"I don't know. I don't think so. Kate tends to pull completely into herself when she's wounded."

The thought of that made a tear slide down Jay's face. "Okay, but if she does..."

"Don't worry, I'll handle it. Call me when you land in Phoenix and I'll give you an update."

"Thanks, Peter, you're a prince."

"Now you sound like someone else I know."

"Bye, Peter."

"Bye, Jay. Good luck."

✑

Kate wasn't sure how long she'd lain there crying. Eventually she fell asleep for a short period of time, her body reacting to the extreme emotional release. When she awoke, all she wanted to do was run away and never stop. The pain was unbearable. She had hoped the combination of her love and time would be enough to help Jay over her insecurities. Instead, it seemed that it was something Jay was going to have to work out for herself. Kate had failed. She gambled on the strength of Jay's faith in her and lost. Her lover was gone for good.

Kate thought about her options. There was nothing she needed to be doing, no responsibilities to be taken care of, and no place she needed to be. She literally could drop off the face of the earth and no one would care, except for maybe Fred, Peter, and Barbara. She'd go back briefly and pick up Fred. The other two would get over it.

As she lay there on her back thinking, a wave of nearly nauseating fear struck her. She opened her eyes wide. Odd. It was as if it wasn't coming from her, but from somewhere else. She quieted her mind and concentrated on the feeling. After a few minutes the fear was replaced by self-loathing, resignation, and despair. Huh. Kate remembered her conversation with Jay the day she was fired, when Jay told her she could feel Kate's anger and distress. Could these be Jay's feelings and not hers?

Kate thought about it for a minute. The sensations certainly weren't consistent with her own normal range of reactions, but then, these weren't normal circumstances. It wasn't every day your heart stopped beating while you were still alive and breathing. As she was debating this, the emotion shifted to a sense of determination. Definitely Jay, she thought. It sure as hell wasn't her right now. She wondered what it meant. Then, just as quickly, she tried to put it out of her mind. *No, Kyle, Jay made it clear where you stand. You'd do well to try to train yourself to let go.*

Nonetheless, the fact that she had some connection to the love of her life gave her cause to be grateful. She decided to get up, shower, and move on to Sedona as she planned. It was, after all, one of the most spiritual places in the world, and God knew she needed the help just then.

Jay twirled the ring on her finger for the thousandth time, watching it sparkle, then took it off and looked at the small, neat script Kate had engraved on the inside of the band. *Forever.* Jay could only hope it was still true. She was almost there. If she could have flapped her wings herself, she would have. The flights seemed to drag on for an eternity. There was plenty of time to think, and it made Jay miserable. Once Peter knocked some sense into her, it was all so clear. Kate gave up everything for love, everything for her—her career, her future, her life, and her happiness. *Wow.* For her, Jamison Parker.

And she repaid Kate by doubting her and damning her, judging her not by her actions and words, but by those of a sleazy tabloid reporter. Jay was ashamed of herself. She wished she could somehow turn back the clock and do that morning's conversation over again, but she knew real life didn't work that way. She just had to make it right somehow.

Jay flashed back to the conversations between her and Kate about trust. *She asked me to trust in her, trust in us, and I failed abysmally. Great, Jamison, this time it may have cost you your one chance at love and happiness. Worse yet, you managed to devastate this incredible woman who sacrificed everything for you.* Jay knew she was going to have to work harder to overcome her trust issues. No one else could do that for her, not even Kate. She just hoped she wasn't too late.

As soon as the small plane touched the runway in Sedona, Jay was out of her seat. Now that she was there, she wasn't sure what to do. There were more than sixty trails in the area, and that was assuming that Kate had gone hiking. *If* she was there, which was yet another assumption. Jay chewed her lip.

Peter reconstructed the places he thought Kate had been. He knew she went to the Great Sand Dunes and to Mesa Verde—he also knew she stopped briefly at the Grand Canyon. He'd looked at maps and routes and was fairly sure she went through Navajo and Hopi reservations. He thought she was in Flagstaff the previous night or that morning. He told Jay all of that when she called him from Phoenix. And he told her that he'd had no word from Kate since Jay had talked with her.

Closing her eyes, Jay tried to focus. She knew Kate favored quiet, peaceful places, mountains and water. She also knew Kate loved to hike. She would have gone hiking someplace quiet where she could be alone. Jay looked at her watch. Sunset was a little more than an hour away. She thought about everything she knew about Sedona. Growing up only two hours away, she had spent much time in the land of extraordinary red rock. There were so many beautiful, peaceful places to hike. And then it came to her. All of the places Peter thought Kate had been were spiritually significant. *She would have gone to Bell Rock.* One of seven vortexes in the world, Bell Rock was a fantastic place to watch the sun set, and perhaps the most spiritual place in the area.

In front of the tiny airport, Jay hailed a waiting cab that delivered her to the trailhead for the Bell Rock Pathway. She would have to hustle—it was a three-and-a-half-mile hike each way. Fortunately, she had brought only a light backpack with a single change of clothes and her hiking boots. She put the boots on, settled the pack on her back, and set off up the trail. Although there were several ways to get up Bell Rock, she was fairly confident that this would be the one Kate would take—it had the nicest views from the top.

As Jay jogged up the trail, she tried not to think too much. *What if I'm wrong. What if Kate didn't come to Bell Rock? Heck, what if she's not even in Sedona?* She couldn't entertain such notions. Kate had to be there. There wasn't a soul in sight as Jay made her way up the red rock. Red dust coated her boots and a light sheen of sweat broke out on her brow.

Within half an hour, as the trail turned sharply steeper and more difficult to follow, Jay caught a glimpse of a single figure sitting near the very top of the rock formation. She couldn't make out the features or even determine if it was a man or a woman from that distance, but in her heart Jay knew it was Kate. She redoubled her efforts and poured all her energy into getting to that lone figure. Jay fought for footholds and handholds in the rock. She didn't care about anything but her ultimate destination.

Twenty minutes later, she was close enough to see clearly that the solitary hiker was, indeed, Kate, and that she had her eyes closed. Jay approached cautiously, quietly, unsure of exactly what to say or do. She got to within seven feet, and her heart broke. She could feel waves of despair and hopelessness that she knew belonged to the proud figure seated before her. Silent tears tracked unhindered down Kate's face. She looked so lost, so forlorn and alone. She was gaunt despite her tan, and too thin, and it was obvious that she didn't know she was being watched.

Looking at that immense pain, Jay began to cry herself. *Oh my God, what have I done to you, my love? I destroyed you. What have I done?* She stood there, rooted to the spot, unable to move forward or back.

Sitting there, deep within her own world of pain and anguish, Kate fought with herself and prayed for wisdom. She had been so sure of herself, so positive that walking away would be the right thing. And on one level it was. But on the other hand...she replayed, for the millionth time, that morning's phone conversation.

Can I live with Jay thinking I've betrayed her? That I'm just like everyone from her past?

Kate knew she could survive Jay's believing she was a cold-hearted, scheming bitch who had played her for a sucker. But could she survive Jay's being convinced yet again that she didn't deserve anything better? There was no way Kate could allow the woman she loved more than anything in the world to spend the rest of her life believing that. She had to go back.

Just as she reached that conclusion, she was suddenly bombarded by feelings of deep self-loathing and self-recrimination and a stabbing ache in her heart. Her eyes snapped open as she recognized instinctively the cause of the emotions. There was Jay, standing mere feet away, tears rolling down her cheeks, pain etched in every aspect of her manner. Red-rimmed and bloodshot blue eyes locked on green for a timeless moment before Kate simply stood and opened her arms. Jay dropped the pack off her shoulders, and covered the distance between them in three steps. She fell into Kate's arms and choked on her own sobs. "Oh, Kate, I love you so much. I would give anything to have this morning to do all over again. I'm so, so sorry. I was overtired and stressed, and I missed you so much. I wasn't thinking straight and I was way off base. You didn't deserve that. I...I don't even know where to start or how to begin to apologize to you or ask for your forgiveness. I know I have no right to ask it—"

"Shh," Kate interrupted her. "That you're here is enough, love." Kate felt her heart slide back into place. "I wish that we could have been together longer before this happened. If I had only had more time to earn your trust—"

Jay cut her off. "No, Kate, you're wrong. You *have* earned my trust, with every word and every gesture. If I hadn't been half out of my mind with fear, I would have known that. You can't take responsibility for my mistakes, love...I have to do that, and I will. That's why I'm here." Jay paused. "Well, that and the fact that I love you more than life itself and I can't live without you. Oh, and Fred told me I couldn't come home without his mama."

Kate smiled for the first time in days. "How did you find me?"

"After I hung up on you, I talked to Peter again. It's a long story, but suffice it to say that he helped set me straight."

"I'll kill him."

"Don't, Kate, don't get mad at him. He was right—there was so much I didn't know, wasn't seeing, and didn't understand. I begged him to help me locate you. I just had to make this right. I had to. What I did to you this morning was like cutting out my own heart."

A lone tear slid down Kate's face at hearing her own feelings expressed so succinctly.

The lovers stood there for a time, simply enjoying the feeling of being in each other's arms.

"Kate?"

"Hmm?"

"What were you doing when I walked up?"

"I was asking for guidance."

"Did you get any?"

"Mmm-hmm. In fact"—she squeezed a little tighter—"when you showed up, I had just decided that I needed to come home to you right away and beg you to take me back."

∻

Jay looked deeply into the eyes of the woman she loved more than anything in the world, trying to convey with her expression all that she couldn't say. She nudged Kate back into a sitting position and knelt between her legs. "You know, I was so focused on how bad it felt to be without you after spending every minute together when we were away, all I could think about was how unfair it was and how mad I was at the uncertainty of it all. I felt cheated, Kate. I didn't stop to consider how you must have been feeling and what you were going through and why. My God, love, you gave up so much for me." Jay shook her head in wonder. "I will learn to get past these trust issues, I swear to you with all that I am. I will," she said determinedly, her voice breaking. "And I need you to know, by the way, that my career means nothing without you in my life."

"It's okay, love, your career should mean a lot to you—" Jay stopped Kate by putting a hand on her knee.

"You are everything to me, Katherine Kyle...everything. I told Trish this morning that I was the other woman in the pictures. I told her I was madly in love with you and that we were going to be married..." Jay paused and looked up hopefully into the face she knew so well, seeking reassurance. What she got was a brilliant smile. "She said she would stand behind me no matter what, and that our relationship and any resulting publicity didn't matter to her in the least. She encouraged me to follow my life and my love." More quietly Jay added, "And I have."

"Oh, Jay, you shouldn't have put everything on the line like that..."

Jay's eyes flashed. "Oh I shouldn't, but you should? No double standards here, sweetheart. I won't have it. This is a partnership, remember?"

"Yes, but you could've lost your career, your future."

"You don't get it, love, do you? Losing my job wouldn't matter to me as long as I have you by my side. You're all I care about, Kate...everything else pales in comparison." Tears coursed down Jay's cheeks. "Please, please come home and marry me."

Jay reached into her backpack, pulled out a small velvet box, and held it out in front of her in supplication. "This signifies my commitment to you. I will always love you, Kate, always, and I can't wait to start our life together."

Kate looked down at the box nestled in her hand and opened the lid. Inside was a gorgeous diamond and sapphire ring. The inscription on the inside said one word. *Eternity.*

Kate swallowed hard. "Jay, this is magnificent. I've never seen anything so beautiful."

"I have—you. I want everyone," Jay's eyes glistened as she gazed lovingly at Kate, "especially you, to know that you're mine for now and eternity."

"That I am, love, and I always will be...I give you my word." Kate leaned forward and gave Jay a gentle, tentative kiss. "I love you, Jay, with all my heart and soul. There is no one else in my life, and there never will be. You're all I want and all I'll ever need. I can't wait to be married to you."

Jay wiped a tear from Kate's eye. "I believe you," she said, tracing the chiseled cheekbones with loving fingers, and she meant it. "Just promise me you'll never leave me again."

"I promise, love."

"May I?" Jay asked, indicating the ring.

"Please."

The ring fit perfectly, which was a good thing, since Kate's jeweler had promised Jay it would the night that Jay dragged Peter there before they went to dinner. She leaned forward and kissed Kate with deliberate slowness and smoldering passion. The contact felt so, so sweet. When they parted after breathless moments, Jay murmured, "Perhaps we should head down now and continue this somewhere more comfortable?"

"Mmm," Kate hummed against her lips. "Lead on."

Jay knew there were deep wounds that needed mending and that only time and togetherness would take care of that, but for the moment they had each other, and that was a balm to both of their wounded souls.

Kate and Jay decided to stay the night in Sedona and fly home the next day. Neither one of them was ready to share the other with the public just yet. They needed some time together, alone, before either of them could face that.

The first time they made love that night they both cried, overcome with emotion and the renewed realization of just how precious their love was, and how close they'd come to losing it.

Jay kissed Kate reverently, running her hands gently over the skin and muscles she loved so well. "I'm so, so sorry, love. Your forgiveness is a gift so far beyond any that I deserve."

"Shh, baby. That's all behind us now. From now on, we face every challenge together. We both made mistakes. And it's likely that we'll make more in the future, but if we do, we'll make them together, okay? I promise you."

They continued to make love well into the morning hours, each feeling the enormous strength of their shared connection, and both feeling whole for the first time since everything began.

They slept like babies on the plane to Albany, and by the time they arrived at the house, the dark circles under their eyes started to fade and their hearts began to heal, nourished by the comfort of each other's presence. They didn't talk about the future any further just yet, both knowing that they needed some time to get reacquainted and settled before dealing with anything that weighty. For the time being it was enough to know that they had each other and that they would face whatever challenges lay ahead together, as one.

Kate set the mail aside and scratched Fred lovingly. He was waiting for them thanks to Peter, who dropped him off a couple of hours earlier. Peter was ecstatic when she called him to tell him that she and Jay were coming home...together.

In a hotel suite in downtown Albany, three men in expensive business suits were meeting in secret.

"You're too hot, we've got to move you out for a little bit."

"Yeah, it's causing too much of a stir. We'll create a new position in another agency, get you away from the media, and put you there for six months until this all dies down. Then we'll bring you back."

"What are you going to do with my position? It's not as if you can leave it vacant."

"I have the perfect solution for that, and the big guy will love it— Katherine Kyle."

"Ooh, good thinking. He loves her, and she just got fired. She's probably desperate for a job, since she got canned for being a dyke, and she's expendable in six months. Nobody will care what happens to her after that."

"Perfect. She's got the credentials to do the job, and it shouldn't be any problem getting her to screw up in six months and having to bring me back to fix the mess. I like it."

"Okay, I'll pitch it to him tonight and have him call her personally to offer her the job. He'll be none the wiser, and she'll no doubt accept. That should seal the deal."

"Right, gentlemen. We'll keep in touch only when absolutely necessary, and I'll expect to be updated in three months. Talk to you then. I've got a plane to catch."

❧

Jay ran into the house ahead of Kate. "I win!"

"Never would've happened if I hadn't tripped over Fred's toy."

"Uh huh. Excuses, excuses." Jay swatted Kate on the butt and trotted into the kitchen.

"Sweetheart, there's a message on the answering machine."

"Okay, I'll be right there." Kate jogged in and pushed the play button.

"Hello, Kate, this is Governor Hyland calling. I'm sorry I missed you and I understand you've had a bit of a rough time of it lately, but I think I may have the answer. I'd like to offer you a position in my administration serving as chief spokesperson for the Department of Correctional Services. Next to my press secretary, no public relations person gets more exposure or is more important to me. It's the third-largest prison system in the country, so I imagine we can find a way to challenge you. What do you say? I'd love to have you on board. Please give me a call as soon as possible and let me know. I hope to talk to you soon. Bye, Kate."

"Wow." That was all Jay could think to say. "Wow, that's fantastic! I knew I liked that man." She went to Kate, who was standing in the middle of the room with her mouth open, and squeezed her tightly.

"Um, huh. What do you know?" was all Kate could manage.

"I know I love you and you'll do a great job, and so does the governor. Smart guy." Jay slipped her hands under Kate's shirt, where she found warm skin. She ran her palms over the taut abdomen, hooked her fingers into the waistband, and popped open the button to Kate's jeans in one fluid motion.

Within moments they were naked and lost in each other once more. Despite all the upheaval and against all odds, the future brimmed with promise.

THE END

About the Author

An award-winning former broadcast journalist, press secretary to the New York state senate minority leader, spokesperson for the nation's third largest prison system, and editor of a national art magazine, Lynn Ames is a nationally recognized speaker and CEO of a public relations firm with a particular expertise in image, crisis communications planning, and crisis management.

Ms. Ames resides in the southwestern U.S. with her favorite guy (relax, it's a dog), a golden retriever named Parker.

More about the author, including contact information, other writings, news about sequels and other original upcoming works, pictures of locations mentioned in this novel, links to resources related to issues raised in this book, author and character interviews, and purchasing assistance can be found at www.lynnames.com.

You can purchase other Phoenix Rising Press books online at www.phoenixrisingpress.com or at your local bookstore.

Published by
Phoenix Rising Press
Phoenix, AZ

Visit us on the Web: **www.phoenixrisingpress.com**

CPSIA information can be obtained at www.ICGtesting.com
Printed in the USA
BVOW012324060213

312543BV00010B/728/P